PASSION'S SURRENDER

Leon went down on his knees and draped Emily's arms around his neck. "Look at me," he commanded. Slowly, her head lifted. She tried to focus on him. "Violet eyes," he said, smiling, and let out a long breath. "Are you saying yes to me, Emily?"

She didn't want to talk. She wanted to kiss him. Before he could bring her lips to his, he repeated his question, this time more forcefully.

"Yes," she whispered.

"Then you had better make up your mind to what this means, Emily. There will be no going back. You will become a true wife to me. We shall share the same bed. When I wish to make love to you, I shall, and nothing will stop me."

There was a moment of indecision. Then Emily smiled and said, "Yes."

His lips fastened on hers, and in the space of a single heartbeat, his kisses became frenzied, frantic, and demanding as his fingers worked furiously to free her of her gown.

ANOTHER TIME . . . ANOTHER PLACE . . . ANOTHER LOVE—
Let Pinnacle Historical Romances take you there!

LOVE'S STOLEN PROMISES (631, $5.99/$6.99)
by Sylvie F. Sommerfield
Mitchell Flannery and Whitney Clayborn are two star-crossed lovers, who defy social conventions. He's a dirt-poor farm boy, and she's a South Carolina society belle. On the eve of the Civil War, they come together joyously, and are quickly and cruelly wrenched apart. After making a suitable marriage, Whitney imagines that she will never feel the soaring heights of passion again. Then, Mitchell returns home seven years after marching away. . . .

VELVET IS THE NIGHT (598, $4.99/$5.99)
by Elizabeth Thornton
To save her family from the guillotine, Claire Devereux agrees to become the mistress of the evil, corrupt commissioner, Phillipe Duhet. She agrees to give her body to him, but she swears that her spirit will remain untouched. To her astonishment, Claire finds herself responding body and soul to Duhet's expert caresses. Little does Claire know but Duhet has been abducted and she has been falling under the spell of his American twin brother, Adam Dillon!

ALWAYS AND FOREVER (647, $4.99/$5.99)
by Gina Robins
Shipwrecked when she was a child, Candeliera Caron is unaware of her wealthy family in New Orleans. She is content with her life on the tropical island, surrounded by lush vegetation and natives who call her their princess. Suddenly, sea captain Nick Tiger sails into her life, and she blooms beneath his bold caresses. Adrift in a sea of rapture, this passionate couple longs to spend eternity under the blazing Caribbean sky.

PIRATE'S KISS (612, $4.99/$5.99)
by Diana Haviland
When Sybilla Thornton arrives at her brother's Jamaican sugar plantation, she immediately falls under the spell of Gavin Broderick. Broderick is an American pirate who is determined to claim Sybilla as forcefully as the ships he has conquered. Sybilla finds herself floating upside down in a strange land of passion, lust, and power. She willingly drowns in the heat of this pirate's kiss.

SWEET FOREVER (604, $4.99/$5.99)
by Becky Lee Weyrich
At fifteen, Julianna Doran plays with a Ouija board and catches the glimpse of a handsome sea captain Brom Vanderzee. This ghostly vision haunts her dreams for years. About to be wed, she returns to the Hudson River mansion where she first encountered this apparition. She experiences one night of actual ecstasy with her spectral swain. Afterwards, he vanishes. Julianna crosses the boundaries of her world to join him in a love that knows no end.

Available wherever paperbacks are sold, or order direct from the Publisher. Send cover price plus 50¢ per copy for mailing and handling to Pinnacle Books, Dept. 748, 475 Park Avenue South, New York, N.Y. 10016. Residents of New York and Tennessee must include sales tax. DO NOT SEND CASH. For a free Zebra/ Pinnacle catalog please write to the above address.

ELIZABETH THORNTON

PINNACLE BOOKS
WINDSOR PUBLISHING CORP.

PINNACLE BOOKS are published by

Windsor Publishing Corp.
475 Park Avenue South
New York, NY 10016

First Printing: September, 1993

Printed in the United States of America

This one is for all my American friends
And especially for Orysia Earhart and Linda Hill

ACKNOWLEDGMENT

To Ron Clay, who always has just the right book
to help me with my research,
whether battles, uniforms, regiments, fur trade,
Ron knows it all.

Prologue

As ever, the orchards and flower gardens in Kent that summer were among the first to bloom in the whole of England. Emily walked the ancient cloisters and flagstoned paths of Rivard Abbey, absorbing far more than the profusion of sights and sounds around her. She felt awakened, as if the color and scent of that particular summer pulsed with her own heartbeat, promising she knew not what.

She was lost in contemplation when he came upon her at the water fountain, a young girl poised on the threshold of womanhood. Her looks were as patrician as her lineage, pristine pure and as fair as his were dark. He said her name softly and she lifted her head, shading her eyes with one hand against the glare.

For a moment, she did not recognize him. She saw only a young gentleman in his mid-twenties who seemed out of place in her flower garden. He was too arrogantly male, too arrogantly uncultivated.

"Your guardian told me that I would find you here," he said.

The smile on her face froze.

To give herself a moment to recover from the shock

of seeing him again, she plucked a crimson blossom from one of the rhododendron bushes that screened the fountain from the house. "Leon," she said, and had the presence of mind to offer him her hand.

Unexpectedly, he pressed a kiss to her wrist and the heat of his lips seared a path along her arm, clear through her chest to her throat, choking off her next breath.

The man's charm was potent. Emily had never doubted it. What was mystifying was why he should be turning that charm upon her. She and Leon Devereux had been at daggers drawn since he was a leggy school-boy and she was a grubby hoyden in pinafores. They disliked each other intensely. The last time they had been alone together, he had dunked her in the pond.

Striving for a natural tone, and remembering both her manners and the fact that she was now a young lady of fashion, she said, "When did you arrive in England, Leon? Aunt Zoë said nothing to me. Was she expecting you?"

He answered her cordially, as though there had never been anything between them but amity and goodwill. He had wanted to surprise everyone, he told her. No, he had not told his sister that he was coming. He wouldn't have missed Emily's birthday ball for the world.

"Don't gape, brat," he said, touching one finger to her open mouth. "It's not becoming in a young lady of your advanced years." His eyes made a slow sweep, taking inventory, and he grinned. "Your figure has filled out quite nicely, though I am not sure that I approve the way you have dressed your hair. It suited you long."

She checked the impulse to grind her teeth together

and smiled tightly. Now this was more like the Leon Devereux she knew. From beneath her brows, she slanted him a sidelong glance. "You haven't changed a bit," she told him.

He laughed, and patted her consolingly on the cheek. "Do you know, your eyes change color when you are in a temper? They are glowing like amethysts now."

The words to put him in his place were slow in coming. She was out of practice — two years out of practice to be exact, two years since Leon Devereux had relieved her of his hateful presence to make his way in the world under the wing of a married sister and her husband who lived in New York. She huffed and puffed and made do for the present by throwing him a glare shot with invective.

Leon didn't catch it. His eyes were wandering over the fields and orchards, taking in the setting. There were no acres of manicured lawns as graced other great English houses. Rivard was formerly a monastery. The gardens and farm were very much as they had been in the monks' day. Only the interior of the main building had been substantially altered, and that was not evident from the outside.

"When I thought of you," he said, "I pictured you here. An English rose in an English country garden. Safe. Cloistered. Inviolate."

His odd changes of mood were confusing her. If Leon had given her a passing thought in the last two years, she would be astonished. Without lowering her guard, she said carefully, "How long do you plan to stay, Leon?"

His eyes narrowed to slits but he responded pleasantly enough. "Not very long. New York is my home now. There is some unfinished business I must attend to here in England, then I shall be on my way."

With perfect sincerity, she was able to say, "I hope your business is concluded satisfactorily before long."

"I'll just wager you do," he said, and dazzled her with a slow, lazy grin.

She was still blinking rapidly to dispel the effects of it when Leon made another lightning shift in mood. "Tell me what you have been doing since I was last here," he said.

As they conversed, he had been directing her steps along the flagstoned paths, halting from time to time to admire a bank of honeysuckle or a particularly fine bed of early roses. When they came to a stone bench, he indicated that he wished her to be seated. He remained standing.

"You have been away at school, I believe."

Slowly at first, then with growing confidence when it became obvious that he wasn't going to pounce on her and hold her up to ridicule, she began to relate some of the events of the previous two years. There was very little to tell. She had made a few friends at school and had been granted a fair number of awards on graduation day. What she did not tell him was that she would have traded all her prizes for one-tenth of her sister's popularity. Sara did not have an academic bent but she was the most sought-after girl in school. Emily told him nothing of this because Leon had once accused her of being jealous of her younger sister.

She ended by saying, "Sara will be so disappointed that she is not here to welcome you. When school was over, she went off to visit some friends, but she will be

10

here by the end of the week in time for my birthday ball."

He had no comment to make on this, and after a long silence, he said, "And what of the future, Emily? What does that hold for you?"

She shrugged faintly. "A season in London. Balls. Parties. That sort of thing."

She did not elaborate because she could not believe that Leon Devereux was interested in such things. His life was far more exciting than hers. He was a fur trader, and in little over two years, with only a modest investment of capital, he had made himself a rich man.

"Tell me about America and Canada," she said. "I hear from Aunt Zoë that you have done remarkably well for yourself. Are you still with your sister Claire and her family?"

"Do you mean remarkably well for a French refugee who arrived in England as a boy with little more than the clothes on his back?"

With those fierce words, the mood was shattered and Emily would have started to her feet if Leon had not pressed her back.

"No, no, I don't mean to quarrel with you. That slipped out before I was aware of it." When she stopped struggling, he released her. "Yes, you might say I have done remarkably well for myself. I had help, of course, from two very generous brothers-in-law. I am no longer the poor relation, depending on the charity of others. I don't have to answer to anyone, Emily."

"No one ever thought of you as the poor relation," she said, but very quietly so as not to provoke that unpredictable temper.

"Perhaps not. Perhaps I was too sensitive. Your

uncle paid for my schooling, the clothes on my back, the roof over my head. He made me an allowance. I had no money of my own. How else should I feel? Do you wonder that I was forever getting into scrapes? I was wild. I admit it. But perhaps I had reason to be."

He stopped abruptly and walked a few paces away from her before retracing his steps. He was unsmiling. "Sometimes I forget that your experience is limited. You are only a girl of sixteen. I was just about your age when I first came to England, and my life has been vastly different from yours."

She was well aware of it. Ten years before, Leon had arrived in England in the aftermath of the French Revolution. Though she was not clear on some of the details, she knew that her guardian, Uncle Rolfe, had practically rescued his wife's brother from the jaws of the guillotine.

"I don't think I have ever heard you speak of France," she said, voicing the stray thought that had crossed her mind.

"And you never shall," he answered brusquely. "That chapter of my life is closed."

The man was impossible. He didn't know how to conduct a polite conversation. Half the time she was on tenterhooks, not knowing what was expected of her. Rising gracefully, she offered an inane excuse about having promised Nurse that she would lend a hand in the nursery. She was sure that he would be as relieved as she to bring their conversation to a close. Duty was served and they were now free to follow their own inclinations.

He surprised her by taking her firmly by the elbow.

"Lead on. It's time I became reacquainted with my English nephews."

But when they reached the nursery, Emily's embarrassment was acute when it was revealed that Nurse and her young charges had gone off on a picnic for the day.

Leon's dark eyes danced merrily and for the first time ever in Emily's memory, they laughed together without rancor.

Over the next few days, Emily found that Leon occupied her thoughts. She didn't know what to make of him. It seemed that she could not turn around but she was falling over him. There was a time when he would have turned on his heel and made off in the opposite direction if he had seen her coming. In two years, he had changed radically, and all for the better. The man really did possess a few redeeming virtues—when he wanted to. Sometimes it was hard to remember that he was once that horrid boy who had been the bane of her existence.

Emily acknowledged that she had been a difficult child, not shy, really, but quiet and, in some respects, withdrawn. These characteristics might have been overcome in time if a series of catastrophic events had not overtaken her. Before she was seven, in quick succession, she and her younger sister Sara had lost their father, their mother, and a stepfather who doted on his stepdaughters.

Their father's brother, Uncle Rolfe, was their guardian, and though affectionate in a casual way, he was a bachelor and away a good deal of the time, leaving them in the care of others. When their guardian married Zoë Devereux and brought her to Rivard, a salutary influence was introduced.

By and large, before the advent of Aunt Zoë, the adults who had charge of Ladies Emily and Sara treated them with kid gloves. They were sorry for the two gray-eyed angelic looking infants who had been left orphans at so tender an age. They rarely corrected them. They meant well, but this proved a disastrous course. The girls were spoiled, willful, incorrigible. Aunt Zoë did her best. By this time, however they were used to going their own way. On the surface, they were all demure obedience. Behind Aunt Zoë's back, little had changed, except that now they knew the difference between right and wrong.

In the summer of 1796, Leon Devereux had breezed into their young lives and nothing was the same ever again . . .

Emily was in the nursery, amusing her young cousin, Nurse having slipped away for a moment or two to fetch the laundry. The infant, who was named for her father, Edward, was enthralled with Emily's long hair which, in those days, was practically pure platinum.

"Lee!" said Edward, grabbing for her hair. "Lee!"

Laughing, Emily removed her ribbons. She knew what came next. She and Edward had played this game time out of mind. She shook out her waist-length hair and dropped her head forward so that the infant could reach it. "Gently," she said as Lord Edward grabbed a fistful of hair. "If you hurt me, we won't do this again."

"Lee? Is that your name?"

The voice from the threshold had Emily's head whipping round. The darkly handsome youth who filled the

14

doorway had the look of a Gypsy. He was a stranger to her. Fear leaped in her throat and her eyes dilated, darkening to amethyst. When the stranger advanced a step, Lord Edward gave a little cry and hid his face in Emily's skirts. At fifteen months, Edward had a fear of strangers.

"Don't be alarmed," said the youth. "I'm Leon Devereux, Zoë's brother. You must be Lady Emily," and in an undertone, grinning, he added, *"Et comme je souhaite que tu aies dix ans de plus,"* and he advanced into the room.

There was an interval when neither of them said anything. Then Emily said, "What do you mean, you wish I was ten years older?"

The youth flushed scarlet and scowled at the same instant. Before he could frame a reply, Sara's voice came piping from the corridor. "Emily! Emily! What do you think? Leon is here. Aunt Zoë's brother." She burst into the room like a whirlwind and came to a sudden halt. "Oh!" she said.

From that moment on, Emily was forgotten, as was Edward. Sara's tongue was never still. A spate of questions spilled from her lips. And she insisted upon being taken up in her "cousin's" arms to give him a kiss of welcome. She told him there were a score of things she wished to show him, and they had to be shown at once.

Leon seemed to be captivated by Sara and he allowed the child to drag him from the room. At the door, he halted and turned back to Emily. "Why don't we all go together?" he said.

Emily had been given a task to do. She wasn't going to disappoint Nurse. "Thank you, no," she said simply.

Shrugging, Leon left her to it.

Within a week, Sara simply adored her cousin Leon. Emily was more cautious. She was prepared to like the boy, but while he lavished attention on Sara, for Emily he scarcely spared a glance. Soon, she told herself that she was completely indifferent to him. Before long, however, her indifference had changed to hearty dislike.

It started from such small beginnings. Sara carried tales. She did not mean to be malicious or hurtful. If anything, she was piqued because Emily was not as bowled over by Leon as she herself was.

It would always begin with the inevitable "Leon says." Emily was becoming heartily sick of hearing those predictable words.

"Leon says that you are too retiring by half. What does that mean, Emily?"

Emily stiffened. "Did he say those words to you?"

"No. To Aunt Zoë."

"What else did he say?"

"Oh, that you are full of your own conceit. What did he mean by it?"

"I wish you would tell me how I may be retiring and full of my own conceit at the same time. It's impossible!"

"It's what Leon says. Leon says that you give yourself airs."

"What does Aunt Zoë say?"

"She says he's wrong. She says that you're a dreamer. But what does it mean, Emily?"

"How should I know? Why don't you ask your precious Leon? And while you are at it, you may tell him that Emily says Leon Devereux is a snake in the grass."

In her child's way, she had tried to get back at him,

playing tricks on him, calling him names, mimicking his far from perfect command of the English language. She came off the worse in every battle.

Emily was never so glad as when the day arrived for Leon to go away to university. For a day or two, Sara was inconsolable. Before a week was out, however, their days followed the familiar pattern. Sara took to dogging Emily's heels. They were the best of friends again.

Leon returned for the holidays. It was as if he had never been away. The old antagonism flared to life.

Emily's aversion to Leon and vice versa became so much a commonplace as to be unremarkable. All members of the same family did not always get along, Aunt Zoë carefully pointed out when her husband would have meddled. Leon and Emily were civil to each other. It was wiser to let sleeping dogs lie.

If Emily's manner toward Leon was tepid at best, Sara's was proprietary to a degree. Leon was her personal property. She brooked no rivals, not even her young cousin, Edward. When she surprised Leon kissing and fondling one of the downstairs maids in the pantry, her ire could not be contained. The girl must be dismissed at once.

Leon was as much annoyed as he was embarrassed. He protested that it was a great to-do about nothing. Sara was practically in hysterics, Aunt Zoë was visibly upset, and Uncle Rolfe tried to make light of the whole affair. No harm was done, he said. Leon was a young man, and in spring—Well, never mind that now. The maids at Rivard, however, were a different matter. They were under his protection, Leon was sternly given to understand, and completely out-of-bounds.

Emily clapped a hand over her mouth and, with a telling look at Leon's flushed face, gloating, walked off in a fit of the giggles. Leon's flush intensified.

Later, after due consideration, Emily confessed herself stymied. Leon Devereux, she supposed, was a taking creature, if one had a fancy for tall, darkly handsome boys with the wild look of a Gypsy about them. She preferred something quite different. Uncle Rolfe's blond good looks were more to her taste. Uncle Rolfe was refined.

Sara, Emily decided then, needed her head examined. She was sweet on Leon. "When I grow up," Sara had declared, "I'm going to marry Leon," and all the grown-ups had laughed. Emily had decided that it was all beyond her ken and not worth troubling her head about.

"What are you thinking?"

Leon's voice brought her back to the present with a start. His broad shoulders blocked out the light from the candle on the mantelpiece.

Emily delayed answering, giving herself time to come to herself by the simple expedient of bringing her cup to her lips and sipping at her lukewarm tea. A quick glance over Leon's shoulder revealed Aunt Zoë ostensibly busy at her embroidery but with one ear surreptitiously cocked to catch the conversation.

Uncle Rolfe was more direct. Laying aside the newspaper he had been perusing, he said, "You've been lost in a brown study these last several minutes. What on earth have you been thinking about, Emily?"

"I've been thinking that tomorrow is a big day for me, and I ought to have an early night."

She was smiling when she left them, but at the top of

the stairs, her smile faded. What she was really thinking was that Sara would be home on the morrow and it would be interesting to see if they would fall into the old familiar pattern. Leon and Sara would be inseparable, and she would be the odd man out.

Within five minutes of Sara's arrival, Emily had her answer. Sara came tearing into the breakfast room shrieking like a banshee. "Leon? Leon? Where . . . ?" Leon had risen from the table and had just time to fling down his napkin before Sara catapulted herself into his arms. "I can't believe it!" she cried out, laughing and crying on the same breath. "When the footman told me, I couldn't believe it! You devil! Why didn't you let us know that you were coming? Have you seen my new hunter? He's in the stable. Uncle Rolfe gave him to me for Christmas and on my next birthday . . ." The torrent came to a temporary halt as a new thought struck her. "Many happy returns, Emily," she called out over her shoulder. "You'll adore the present I've picked out for you." She linked her arm through Leon's and made to lead him away. "Come along, Leon. Don't dawdle! I've got so much to tell you."

He didn't disengage himself but he did manage to halt her momentum. "Sara!" he admonished, amused, exasperated. "You are still an incorrigible tearaway!"

"Oh, Emily and Aunt Zoë don't mind, do you, dears?"

"Well . . ." Aunt Zoë began uncertainly.

"Not in the least," said Emily. Her expression was one of amused tolerance. "Run along, both of you. As you may understand, Aunt Zoë and I have a million things to occupy our time before our guests begin to arrive."

"You don't mind?" Leon resisted the tug of Sara's hand on his arm, but not very forcefully. He took a step toward the door and then another.

"I shall be glad not to be falling over you at every turn," said Emily, forcing a smile and inwardly congratulating herself on the way she was carrying the whole thing off. It was just as she had anticipated. She was the odd man out.

As it turned out, Emily had a million and *one* things which required her attention. She was everywhere at once and nowhere to be found. Guests were arriving in droves and though everyone was sure they had seen her, no one could quite catch up to her. Emily made sure of it.

She did not see Leon again until just before the ball got under way, when the family gathered for the present giving. Emily was hardly aware of what she received or what was said to her. She had only one object in mind—to get through the evening without disgracing herself.

"I think she is all grown up now," Leon said, kissing her on the cheek, flashing some unspoken message to her guardian.

She didn't feel grown up. She felt like a child again, and Leon Devereux was the horrid boy who knew every trick ever invented to humiliate her. She would fall on her face and he would walk away laughing—with Sara. She was bound and determined that it wasn't going to happen this time around.

"It would not surprise me," said Rolfe, "if I were to find myself fending off scores of marriage proposals before your ball is halfway over."

Emily smiled brilliantly. "Don't be a goose, Uncle Rolfe. You know perfectly well how much I am looking forward to my come-out in London."

Rolfe's eyebrows rose. "Indeed?"

That brilliant smile on Emily's face was to endure until it came time for her dance with Leon. She knew that she could not face him. Her wits were too dull to engage in the rapier-sharp thrust and parry their verbal contests brought. Before he could find her, she slipped away to her uncle's book room where she could lick her wounds in private.

But she was there for no more than a minute or two when Leon walked in. At the click of the latch, she jerked.

"This is our dance, I believe," he said, and there was a wariness about him.

The words spilled heedlessly from her lips. "I'd as soon dance with a snake as dance with you."

Shaking her head, putting one hand out to fend him off, she backed away. She had seen that murderous look in his eyes once before, when she was a child and had played a wicked trick on him, and he had thrashed her for it.

"Words don't work with you," he said. "Perhaps this will teach you a lesson."

There was no point in trying to evade him. He stood between her and the door. Like a mesmerized little rabbit cornered by a cobra, she waited for him to strike.

When he moved, pure instinct took over. She lashed out with nails curved like talons. He deflected her movements effortlessly, forcing her arms behind her back. She opened her mouth to cry out. In an instant,

21

his mouth was pressed fiercely against hers, smothering her scream. His arms were clamped so tightly around her body that she thought her ribs would crack.

Though Emily knew nothing of love, she knew that this could not be a lover's embrace. It was too rough, too smothering, too wild. He released her so suddenly that she stumbled back. Tears of mortification slipped from beneath her lashes. "I hate you," she said brokenly, and scrubbed the taste of him from her bruised lips.

Leon's eyes were not on her, but on a point beyond her shoulder. "Rolfe," he said, and grinned crookedly.

Keeping her head well down, Emily picked up her skirts and made her escape.

"I warned you," she heard her guardian say before he closed the door, shutting her out.

Not a long time was to pass before Rolfe and Leon entered the great hall together. She went as cold as marble when Leon's eyes found her. Without hesitation, he crossed to her.

"Lady Emily," he said, "I owe you an apology."

His eyes weren't apologizing. They were mocking her. Conscious that her guardian was watching them from across the room, she managed some polite commonplace.

Leon made as if to say something more, then, with a coarse obscenity, he turned on his heel and left her.

The party was over. Rivard's guests had long since retired for the night. Emily was too keyed up to sleep and had yet to undress when Sara burst into her chamber. Dismissing her maid, Emily waited for the predictable torrent of words.

Sara was in a passion. Leon had humiliated her in the worst possible way. He had defected to another lady. Emily was well aware of it. Her eyes had trailed Leon all evening. He had made quite a spectacle of himself, with his frequent trips to the punch bowl, and outrageous flirting with anything in skirts. His interest had finally settled on Lady Judith Riddley.

"They made an assignation right in front of my nose," wailed Sara. "Oh, not in so many words. But anyone who knows anything would have divined what was going on. Can you believe it? They have arranged to meet at the dower house when everyone at Rivard is snug in his bed."

"But Lady Riddley is a married lady," Emily objected. "And her husband is a connection of Uncle Rolfe's."

Through her tears, Sara made a grimace of disbelief. "What has that to say to anything? She is a veritable trollop! And Lord Riddley, the doddering old fool, is three sheets to the wind. He wanted two footmen to carry him upstairs. Sometimes, Emily, I despair of you. You're such a child!"

As Sara swept from the room, Emily ran after her. "What do you intend to do?" she cried out.

"Do?" sobbed Sara. "What *should* I do? I think I shall take a whip and go after them, or perhaps fetch Uncle Rolfe's pistol. Leon Devereux is a knave! It would serve him his just desserts if I put a bullet in his brain." Her voice cracked. "Or perhaps I shall put a bullet in my heart. I might as well. And then think how sorry he will be."

It would all blow over, Emily assured herself. She'd

seen Sara in these takings before. Her temper was like a flash fire. Once ignited, it was soon spent. Still, she did not care for the reference to Uncle Rolfe's pistol. There was no saying what mischief Sara might get up to. It was safer to remove the pistol from Sara's reach.

This was soon done. The pistol, a toy really, was kept in the bottom drawer of Uncle Rolfe's desk. The drawer was locked, but Emily and Sara, unbeknownst to their guardian, both knew where the key was hidden.

Emily was never sure afterward why she chose the course she followed that night. Her emotions were in a turmoil and had been thus since Leon had humiliated her with his hateful kiss. She knew she wasn't thinking straight. And one thought seemed to have taken possession of her mind. Leon Devereux must not be allowed to desecrate the house where her grandmother had once lived.

The dower house had stood empty for years. The doors were locked and the furniture was under Holland covers. Leon would know all this. Without reflecting too deeply on the wisdom of what she was doing, Emily slipped out a side door.

The house was shrouded in darkness. An owl hooted, and Emily jumped, bringing the pistol up. She let out a shaky laugh. Thankfully, she had come on a fool's errand. She must be more like Sara than she suspected. Her anger had quite dissipated. Even if she were to find Leon Devereux making free with her grandmother's house, she knew perfectly well that she would creep away with her tail between her legs before anyone was the wiser.

The locked doors of Rivard, like the locked drawers,

had never been known to keep Ladies Emily and Sara out if they had a mind to enter. At the back of the house was an old laburnum tree. Climbing it was child's play. One branch gave onto a small landing window, the neck of which had been broken for years. Within minutes, Emily had gained the interior. When she entered her grandmother's bedchamber, she was overcome with nostalgia. Moonlight streamed through the window, casting ghostly shadows. She sat down on the edge of the bed and tried to recall her sixth birthday. She had spent it here, with Grandmama. In those days, she and Sara were the best of friends. That was not the case now. Her last thought was of Leon Devereux.

"Leon?"

Had she said his name out loud? Blinking the sleep from her eyes, Emily pulled to her elbows. She must have dozed. The pistol was clutched to her bosom in a death grip and she was chilled to the marrow.

"Leon! Please!"

Emily froze. The husky feminine voice belonged unmistakably to Lady Riddley. She was in the bedchamber across the hall, directly opposite. The door was open, as was the door to the chamber Emily occupied. From her bed, Emily could see straight into the room. A candle was burning, casting grotesque shadows on the wall. A man with his back to her was peeling out of his garments. The woman on the bed was naked. Hair like black silk spilled over her milky-white shoulders and breasts.

"Hurry," said Lady Riddley. "I burn for you."

Low, masculine laughter answered her. "You're like an animal in heat, do you know?"

Leon's voice. His speech was slurred, but Emily had no difficulty recognizing it. She felt sick to her stomach. Not in her wildest fancies had she imagined anything so ugly. An "assignation" Sara had called it, and in her ignorance Emily had thought of the time Leon had been kissing the downstairs maid in the pantry. She didn't want to be a witness to *this*. She had to get away.

Clamping down on her chattering teeth, she swung her legs over the edge of the bed and rose unsteadily to her feet. Inch by slow inch, she approached the open door, keeping to the shadows.

"If I'm an animal in heat, what does that make you?" asked the woman coyly.

More masculine laughter. "A stallion who has caught the scent of a mare?"

Emily's hand flew to her mouth, catching back her gasp of horror. She had never seen an aroused male before. Her eyes swept over Leon's powerful naked torso, irresistibly drawn to his swollen, jutting sex. "Stallion," he had called himself. It was the truth. Once, when she was where she was not supposed to be, she had watched as a stallion had cornered a mare and forcibly mounted her. It was brutal. The poor creature had wailed her terror. The men observing from the edge of the paddock had applauded. Emily had been violently sick.

Leon crouched over the woman. She was moaning and panting. His breathing was labored. He groaned and came down on her hard. Muscles clenched and rippled across the breadth of his shoulders. They might have been gladiators locked in mortal combat.

Emily's brain was frozen. She did not know how long she stood there as though rooted to the spot. Finally, like a sleepwalker, she moved her feet. A few steps and she was past the open door and into the corridor.

It was then that the woman screamed. He was hurting her and he did not seem to care. Tears streamed down Emily's face and she sagged against the wall. Something awful was happening in that room. The grunts and groans sickened her. At last, they were silent. She had just about steeled herself to move away when the woman's voice, drowsy with spent passion, arrested her.

"I've had my eye on you since the moment I caught sight of you."

"I know." Leon's tone was amused.

Throaty feminine laughter. "Why this sudden turnaround, Leon? What finally decided you to notice me?"

"No particular reason."

"I think I know the answer. Rivard's niece . . ."

Leon's voice was curt. "We shall leave her out of this conversation, if you please. She is a mere child."

More feminine laughter. "*Make* me forget about her."

"You are insatiable, do you know?"

There was a rustling sound. The bed ropes creaked and the woman moaned. When Leon laughed softly, the bile rose in Emily's throat and she began to retch in great shuddering gasps that left her weak at the knees.

"Who is there?"

Leon's strident tones steadied Emily's nerves as nothing else could. With one hand over her mouth and the other clutching her pistol, she began to back toward the landing window. Leon, naked as the day he was born, appeared in the open doorway.

27

His eyes closed upon seeing her. "Emily!" he groaned. "Oh, God, Emily!"

He took one step toward her and she bolted. She practically threw herself out the landing window. Hands and knees were scraped raw in her blind haste to descend the gnarled laburnum. Her gown and hair caught on branches and the pistol fell from her hand. Crying, sobbing, she dragged herself clear, oblivious of pain, uncaring of the rents to her garments or the splinters in her fingers, unheeding of Leon's cries. Once her feet touched the ground, she retrieved her pistol and was off and running.

The Abbey was a good half-mile away. There were no sounds of pursuit, and before long, her strides slackened to a stumbling gait. From time to time she rested, then forced herself to go on.

When she entered the great hall, she took a minute or two to come to herself. She was distraught, on the point of hysteria. Breathing was painful. Mounting the stairs in a daze, without thought she made for the little turret room, her sanctuary, the place to which she always retreated, even as a child.

At once she turned the key in the lock. Here, in the confines of this small space, she felt as safe as a babe in the womb.

Sobbing, she groped her way to the small table by one of the windows. After a few false starts, she managed to control the trembling in her fingers to get a candle lit. She was wheezing like an old woman.

"Emily!"

The softly spoken word acted on her like melted wax on a raw burn. She flinched away, then slowly turned to face him. It was Leon. She could not believe her eyes. How had he had the time to get dressed and get here before her? How had he known she would come to the turret room?

His voice was taut with suppressed violence. "How long were you there, Emily? What did you see?"

She stared at him with huge, frightened eyes.

His profane exclamation loosened her tongue. "I was there before you. I fell asleep. When I awakened, you were there with that woman."

"*Where* did you fall asleep?"

"In the room across the hall. My grandmother's room."

She was terrified at what she read in his expression. He'd looked just so when he had kissed her earlier that evening. Only now she knew of other ways, more degrading ways, that a man could use against a woman if he really wanted to debase her.

"I'm almost twenty-seven years old," he said viciously. "What did you think? What did you expect?" Striving to restrain himself, he said more gently, "Emily, what you saw, what you heard — it won't be like that for you. When you marry, your husband will love you. He will cherish you. In that room — that wasn't love." He wasn't aware that he had raised his hand in a gesture of appeal.

Inching away from him, leveling her pistol, she said tremulously, "Don't touch me. I don't want you *ever* to touch me. Please, just leave me alone. I know how to use this, so don't think I'm bluffing. If you go away, I won't tell a soul. I promise you I won't say a word to Sara. Please, just go away."

"What in hell does Sara have to do with anything?" he asked savagely, and lunged for her.

29

Her reaction was reflex. She pulled the trigger. The sound of the explosion was deafening. When the smoke cleared, Leon was propped against the door; blood was seeping from a wound in his shoulder. His response was not what she expected.

Shaking his head, laughing softly, he said, "Can you hear them? You've roused the whole house. There's going to be the devil to pay. No. You can't see it because you can't see yourself. Emily of the violet eyes, you have the look of a virgin who has been well and truly ravished. There's no getting round it. We'll be forced to wed at once."

"No," she said. "I hate you. I shall hate you to my dying day," and she meant it.

Three days later, they were married by special license in Rivard's private chapel. Almost at once, Leon departed for the United States to attend to his business interests.

Chapter One

The London Season was in full swing. The gaiety, in that year of our Lord, 1811, was surpassing any previous time. It was as though all thoughts of the war with France were consigned to oblivion. Even the dashing young officers in their redcoats seemed unaffected, though it was tacitly understood that, at any moment, they might receive marching orders which would send them to far-flung military outposts. Their conversation, at least in polite society, gave no indication that a new Colossus straddled Europe or that the British and their allies aimed to topple him. His name was Bonaparte, more widely known as the Emperor Napoleon.

Emily was decked out in her finest gown. The high-waisted, transparent gauze with its square, low-cut bodice was a vogue which had long since ceased to shock the modesty of the more straitlaced dowagers. Every lady had adopted the latest mode from France. Where fashion was concerned, patriotism, it seemed, counted for nothing.

As her eyes skimmed over the glowing scene under the blaze of chandeliers in Lady Spencer's ballroom, Emily was thinking that the young men in their scarlet tunics were not the only ones in uniform. Those gentlemen not attached to the military followed Brummel's preference for dark coats and elaborately arranged neckcloths, while the ladies' pale muslins were almost indistinguishable one from the other. Even so, the scene was glittering.

"Penny for your thoughts."

Emily's eyes warmed the instant before she raised them to her escort. William Addison, at something over thirty, returned her unaffected smile. His impeccable dark coat was snugly tailored to the breadth of his shoulders.

"I was speculating," said Emily, "where all these handsome young men in their scarlet uniforms will be posted in another month or so." Her gaze rested briefly on her companion's strongly carved features and short crop of dark hair before dropping away.

She felt a little breathless. More and more of late, William was beginning to have this effect on her. He was doing it on purpose, making her feel self-conscious to a degree. He was a handsome, virile male and he wanted her to know it. Beneath her gloved hand, she could feel the muscles in his arm tense.

"William, please," she said, her eyes downcast. "Don't look at me so."

The gentleman was silent as he maneuvered Emily through the double doors which gave onto the gallery. From the long windows, elegantly draped in primrose silk, could be seen the blaze of lights from Buckingham House just across the park. Several other couples were strolling about the room, or taking in Earl Spencer's extensive picture collection.

"How would you like me to look at you?"

Catching the amusement in his tone, she frowned slightly. "Can't we be natural with each other?" she asked.

"Isn't it natural for a man to admire a beautiful woman?" His eyes made a sweeping assessment of her, from her coronet of variegated dark-blond hair to her lithe womanly contours set off admirably in the almost transparent white gauze.

He lowered his voice to a seductive murmur. "Forgive me. I did you an injustice. You are not merely a beautiful woman. You are the most beautiful woman of my acquaintance."

"A *married* woman." Her answer was terse.

His voice chided her. "Emily, we both know that may be remedied very easily."

Faint color came and went under Emily's translucent complexion. She did not contradict him. In her usual composed manner, she steered the conversation into safer channels. But behind her cool smile and poised air, her thoughts dwelled on what William had said.

She was a wife in name only. In five years, the marriage had never been consummated — would *never* be consummated. Her hatred of Leon Devereux was not so virulent as it once was. The passage of time and his absence had effected a change in her. Nevertheless, their marriage could never be a normal one. She knew it. Leon knew it. They had an understanding. If and when either of them formed an attachment to someone else, their marriage would be annulled and they would each go their separate ways.

In an unguarded moment, she had revealed as much to Sara. It was Sara who had thoughtlessly betrayed the truth about Emily's marriage to William Addison.

From that day to this, William had been pressing her. He was her most constant escort, not that they were ever alone for more than two minutes together. In Leon's absence, Uncle Rolfe and Aunt Zoë guarded her virtue zealously. Having disgraced them once, she would not be permitted to do so again. They hedged her about with chaperones.

A gentleman, however, if he had a mind to, could always circumvent chaperones. On more than one occasion, William had maneuvered things so that they were alone together. He had kissed her. And she had discovered something about herself. She had discovered that she was not a "frigid little virgin," as her husband had flung at her on his last visit to England. She was a grown woman with a deeply passionate nature. She was susceptible to William; she was very susceptible to him.

She darted a lightning glance at her companion. Any woman would be proud to be the object of William Addison's attentions. It was not merely the handsome face that drew Emily. Her own husband had more than his fair share of good looks. But William had a way with her. He made her feel safe, cherished. He was a widower whose young wife had died tragically in a boating accident. This sorrow had touched him deeply. He was a sensitive man. Not only did he like women, but he respected their intelligence. At the War Office, where he worked with her guardian, his abilities were openly recognized. Uncle Rolfe was always singing William's praises.

"Tell me," he said, studying her cameo-pure profile appreciatively, "how many times in the last five years has the elusive Mr. Devereux set foot in England?"

"Very infrequently, as you well know." It was only once, but Emily kept that to herself.

"And never for more than a month at a time?"

Her eyes were twinkling. "With some people, a month can seem like an aeon."

He laughed. "You are quite indifferent to him, aren't you, Emily?"

"Need you ask?" But that wasn't quite true. Indifference denoted an *absence* of emotion. She could never be indifferent to Leon Devereux. He aroused feelings of acute . . . she wasn't quite sure *what* feelings he aroused. She only knew that being with him was an ordeal.

"I look forward to meeting him."

"What?" His observation startled her.

"Forgive me, that was a facetious remark. On the other hand, the sooner I meet him, the sooner things can be settled. Strange that I was never introduced to him when he was last in England."

Thoughts flitted through Emily's head. She could not imagine a meeting between Leon and William. What would they say to each other? Would she be the subject of their conversation? The thought was distasteful. William was pressing her again.

"Why haven't I met him?"

"Leon has not been in England for some time," she said. "Long before I came to know you, William."

As the recollection came back to him, he patted her hand. "I had forgotten."

When William had first met Emily at Rivard Abbey, he had been Sara's suitor. Emily had liked the young man well enough, but she had scarcely spared him a thought.

It was to be some months before they met again. By this time Sara's interest had shifted to another young man. Everyone believed Sara's affections were fickle— Emily knew that they were not. Sara was as deep in love with Leon Devereux as she had ever been.

Her escort moved so quickly, so smoothly, that she was inside the curtained alcove before she was aware of what he was doing. He closed the curtains with a snap. She had to laugh.

"Emily."

The sound of her name was like silk moving over her skin. His arms went around her waist. Her smile faded.

"Put your arms around my neck," he said softly, and Emily obeyed.

She liked the feel of William's strong arms circling her. She liked the ardent look in his eyes. She wanted him to kiss her. She raised her head and her eyelashes swept down.

His lips were soft. The pressure increased so gradually, she scarcely noted it. When his hand closed over her breast, and squeezed gently, the leap of her senses took her unawares. With a little sob of alarm, she pulled away from him. Her breathing was uneven.

The glitter in his eyes told her that her response had gratified him. "Yes," he said, "it could be good between us. And now you know it, too."

His scrutiny took in her fear-bright eyes. "Emily," he said, shaking his head, "you have nothing to fear from me. I respect you. I want you for my wife. I would never force myself upon you. I may steal the odd kiss, and a little something on account," he chuckled softly, "but I promise you, that is as far as I would dare. I swear it on my honor. Do you believe me?"

"Yes," she said, still striving to bring her breathing under control.

He touched a hand to her cheek. "I love you. You already know it. And I think that you love me. When will you be my wife?"

She stared at him with huge, unblinking eyes.

Frowning, he went on more roughly. "It's time to end your farce of a marriage to Devereux. You need a real husband, a man to love you. You need a home of your own, and children. I can give you all those things. But first your marriage to Devereux must be annulled."

His words acted on her powerfully, touching a responsive chord deep inside her. She *did* want a man to love her. She *did* want children and a home of her own. More and more of late, she was possessed of a woman's yearning for fulfillment. And she did not know why she would not give him the answer he wanted.

"Are you afraid of Devereux?" he asked.

Her eyelashes lowered. "No. It's not Leon I'm thinking about. It's my guardian, my uncle. I think he will take a very dim view if I suggest that my marriage be annulled."

"Then *I* shall speak to him."

"No!" she said quickly. "Please, William, don't press me. I need time to think how it may be done."

"But you will think about what I have said?"

"I'll think about it. I promise you."

He returned her to the ballroom, to the safekeeping of her guardian, on the clear understanding that he would be the one to take her into supper.

Anyone seeing the marquess with Emily might have supposed that he was an older brother. The resemblance was remarkable, and Rolfe's healthy head of blond hair gave him the appearance of someone younger than his years. Unhappily for Emily, he took his role of guardian seriously. Very seriously.

His eyes were leaping. Between his teeth he said, "And where did you get to, miss? Your aunt has been in quite a taking. We had no clue to your whereabouts."

"Rolfe!" exclaimed Aunt Zoë, looking daggers at her husband. "I was not in a taking."

Emily flashed her aunt a grateful look. Though Aunt Zoë was Leon's sister and shared his dark good looks, Emily could never think of her in that role. Their friendship had been set long before Leon had come into her life.

The marquess muttered something savage under his breath. Emily's delicate eyebrows arched. With calculated coolness, she surveyed the couples who were forming sets on the dance floor. She noted that Sara was partnered by the Honorable Peter Benson for the third time that evening. That would explain Uncle Rolfe's uncertain temper. Though Peter Benson and William Addison were distant cousins, they were nothing like each other. The one was a bit of a weakling and the other was as steady as the Rock of Gibraltar.

"Well? I'm waiting for an answer. Where did you get to?" demanded her uncle.

She smiled brilliantly at the young Hussar officer who solicited her hand for the dance and, turning to her uncle, for his ears only, murmured, "Probably where you were imagining I was, Uncle Rolfe."

For the most part, Emily enjoyed herself. She never lacked for partners. She was with young people of her own age. But William's words had started something in her that nagged like a dull toothache. She wanted the fulfillment William promised her.

Her worst moment of the evening came when they were sitting down to supper. It took her a moment or two to recognize the lady opposite who was holding forth on her recent sojourn in the United States of America.

"New York is quite cosmopolitan for its size," said the lady in a voice that stirred some memory in Emily.

She had a flash of recall, a picture of a bed with a naked woman upon it, her black hair spilling over her shoulders and breasts. *"I burn for you"* were the words the voice had said then.

The little color in Emily's cheeks washed out of them. Careful not to draw attention to herself, she set down her cutlery and raised her wineglass to her lips. Through the protection of her lashes, she observed Lady Riddley closely.

She could not think why she had not recognized the woman at once. Five years had made very little difference. She was as beautiful as ever. The last time Emily had seen her was on the stairs to the little turret room at Rivard Abbey. Lady Riddley was one of those who had dashed out of her chamber to investigate the report of the pistol shot. She had been clothed in a silk wrapper then, her hair loose about her shoulders, her expression dazed, giving the impression of one dragged rudely from the depths of slumber. Emily had been beside herself. Disregarding Leon's stern admonition to remain in the turret room, on hearing her guardian's voice, she had come tearing down the stairs to push past Leon and fling herself into her uncle's arms.

Emily gave a start as Lady Riddley captured her unwary stare. "Lady Emily . . ." she said. "How delightful to see you again. It's been all of five years, has it not?" Her eyes were neither mocking nor hostile, but surprisingly friendly, and Emily remembered that before the scandalous events of that night, she had once been kindly disposed to the woman.

Though she thought her face would crack from the strain, she curved her lips in as natural a smile as she could manage. "It's been too long," she drawled, and never once blinked at the blatant untruth. If a hundred years had passed in the interim, it would still be too soon for her comfort.

Evidently, Lady Riddley was not aware of the slight chill in the atmosphere. "And Leon, I mean, Mr. Devereux—is he present this evening?"

"No," answered Emily boldly. "To my knowledge, Mr. Devereux is to be found in New York." And her tone indicated that Mr. Devereux might be found at the end of the world for all she cared.

The buzz of conversation in the vicinity became muted. Lady Riddley's glance faltered a little, then rallied. Her smile became fixed. "Lord Riddley and I had the pleasure of renewing Mr. Devereux's acquaintance in New York. I may be mistaken, but I understood that he hoped to be in England before long."

Emily bristled. So her husband and his inamorata were still on the friendliest terms? Her eyes darted to Lord Riddley, a little ways farther down the table. As ever, the gentleman gave every evidence of having drunk himself insensate.

Her voice was tipped with ice. "Mr. Devereux," she said, "comes and goes as he pleases."

"Devereux? Devereux?" The name was taken up by

Lord Riddley. He blinked rapidly as he came to himself. "Isn't that the fellow whose mistress was attacked? Yes, Devereux, that was his name. He had given the poor woman a set of gems worth a king's ransom and some knave tried to take 'em off her. What was her name again? Belle something or other."

If a feather had dropped, Emily would have heard it. She swallowed and wished only that a pit would open at her feet and she would sink into it. She was conscious of William's searching glance. Summoning her formidable poise which seemed to have quite deserted her, she opened her mouth to make some comment. Lady Riddley got there before her.

With a convincing laugh, she turned on her husband. "Arthur," she admonished, "the gentleman who figured in that scandal went by the name of Deveril. Don't you remember, dear? Not Devereux, *Deveril!*"

Lord Riddley's face was purple. It had suddenly struck him that he was in Polite Society, and not in his club as he had at first supposed on awakening. A gentleman did not talk broad in a lady's hearing, unless that lady was his wife.

"The name was Deveril, don't you remember, dear?"

The earl stared at his wife sheepishly. His somnolent gaze traveled the faces of his companions, coming to rest on Emily. "I beg your pardon," he mumbled, looking more annoyed than sorry. "Names always escape me. Deveril, that was the fellow's name. Yes, now I remember. It was definitely Deveril."

No one believed him, though everyone gave the semblance of doing so. The buzz of conversation at the table gradually resumed. Emily was conscious of several commiserating glances. Lady Riddley's face conveyed an agonized apology.

What she said to William as she picked her way through a plateful of mouth-watering delicacies Emily could never remember afterward. She scarcely ate a bite. As soon as she decently could, she asked him to return her to the ballroom. In the gallery, he halted before a portrait which was hung a little way off the beaten track. They both feigned an interest in it.

"I understood that Devereux means nothing to you," he said harshly.

"He means less than nothing to me," she quickly denied.

His eyes roamed her face. "Then why this exaggerated response when you hear that he keeps a mistress?"

"I could not care less if he keeps a score of mistresses," she hissed. She breathed deeply and found her control. "It was vulgar," she said in a lowered tone. "Do you think I like to be an object of pity? Do you think I like to have my name coupled with a rake like Devereux! Those glances! Those snide smiles! I feel unclean."

The harsh lines on his face gradually relaxed. "Devereux is a fool," he said. "He deserves to lose you. You'll think about what I have said? You will press for an annulment?"

She nodded her acquiescence.

On the drive home to the house in St. James Square, the temperature inside the coach on that warm April evening was frigid. It was plain that Uncle Rolfe was out of humor. Emily braced herself to receive the sharp edge of his tongue. But it seemed as if that honor was largely reserved for her sister.

"I should like to know, miss," said the marquess, addressing Sara, "what was in your head when you allowed Peter Benson to partner you for no less than four dances? Let me tell you, the whole world now expects the announcement of your betrothal."

Eyes snapping, Sara tossed her blond ringlets. "Perhaps I *shall* marry Peter. I must marry someone. Why not him? He is handsome. He comes from good stock. Peter will do as well as anyone."

"Over my dead body! The man is a fortune hunter. You are the biggest matrimonial prize on the market, leastways as far as fortune goes. How many times must I remind you? You are an heiress. Your stepfather, not to mention your own father, left you and your sister both so well placed that you can buy and sell your poor guardian ten times over. Peter Benson knows it. He is up to his neck in tick. All he wants is to get his hands on your fortune. When he does, he'll soon go through it. He lost the fortune his father left him. He'll do the same to yours."

"Thank you," said Sara with scathing politeness.

"Now that is going too far, dear," Aunt Zoë remonstrated. "Sara has more than fortune to recommend her. She is the toast of the ton. And it's not only because of her beauty. She is a popular girl, and quite rightly so, in my opinion."

"Thank you, Aunt Zoë," said Sara in a very different tone from the one she had employed with her uncle.

"All I am saying is this . . ." The marquess was visibly striving for reasonableness. "When you marry, your husband will have the management of your affairs. I have no qualms about Emily's husband. Leon understands finance. He has never risked Emily's capital unless he had good reason. On the other hand, Peter Benson thinks that money is to be spent, not invested with an eye to the future."

"Oh, very good," stormed Sara. "I see how it is. All my suitors must pass a test in bookkeeping before they have your blessing. For all you care, they may be as dull as ditchwater."

"No! That is not what I am saying." Seeing that he was making heavy weather of the matter, the marquess tried to inject a little humor into the conversation. "Take William Addison, for example. He's not as dull as ditchwater. And he has money of his own. The worst thing you did was let your sister steal your beau. Why don't you employ all those feminine wiles of yours to get William back? Now there is a gentleman I would be happy to see you wed."

Aunt Zoë interjected, apropos of nothing, "Did I tell you that I had received a letter from young Rolfe? He has found a new friend, Lord Barton's boy. He seems to be quite enjoying school now. Isn't that nice?" Rolfe was Zoë's youngest, and still very much the baby of the family.

No one was deflected by this non sequitur. Huffing, Sara said, "Emily did not steal William away from me. I made her a present of him."

That remark gave the marquess a new direction. "Emily, I wish you would not encourage the attentions of William Addison, or any particular gentleman. You have a husband. Try to remember it."

Emily heard the reproof and ignored it. Her thoughts were occupied with a remark that had been dropped some time before. "Are you saying," she said, frowning, "that Leon has the management of my affairs?"

"Naturally."

"But . . . but . . . the fortune my father left me, and my stepfather? You are my guardian, Uncle Rolfe. Surely *you* have the management of my affairs?"

"My dear child, the day you married Leon was the day I ceased to be your guardian. The law is very precise on this point. Your husband has full control of your fortune. You should be glad of it. Leon put your money to good use. It has made him a rich man ten times over."

Emily could hardly draw breath for spleen. "It has made *him* a rich man?" she said faintly.

"Very rich." Her guardian laughed easily. "I can tell you, for a time there, he had me worried. Leon thinks that nothing is to be gained by money sitting in the bank drawing interest. No, that young man was in a hurry to recoup all that he had lost because of the Revolution. And he has done it! In five short years, by Jove, he has done it!"

Emily strove to hold on to her patience. "I understood his American brother-in-law, Adam Dillon, helped establish Leon in the New World."

"Certainly he did. But we are talking substantial wealth here. The modest loans that Leon received from his relations, together with what he salvaged from his father's financial holdings in France, were very modest, relatively speaking."

"Not to be compared to his wife's fortune?" said Emily, smiling through her teeth.

"You were quite an heiress," agreed her uncle.

Emily was speechless, but only for a moment. "And

now I am a pauper," she burst out.

The heavens chose that moment to open. There was the crack of a thunderbolt and the rains came driving down, bouncing off the roof and sides of the coach like pellets from a shotgun.

Aunt Zoë smiled brightly. "In England it never rains but it pours," she said.

Rolfe's sigh was long and audible. He removed his neckcloth and threw it over the back of a chair. "I'm only in my forties," he said. "I feel like a hundred. Those girls are driving me to an early grave."

Zoë was sitting up in bed braiding her dark, glossy hair. To her way of thinking, her husband had scarcely aged in their sixteen happy years of wedlock. It was the thick pelt of blond hair, she decided, which gave that impression. At Rolfe's age, many gentlemen had silver wings at the temples. If Rolfe had one gray hair in his head, she had yet to find it. He was more than ten years her senior. She hoped she would age as gracefully as her husband.

Another long sigh was exhaled on Rolfe's breath. "Those girls are a handful, and that is putting it mildly."

"I hope our own girls are not going to give us so much trouble," Zoë observed.

Rolfe blinked. "What girls?" he said. "Last I counted, we had five boys, and after tonight, I thank God for it."

"I've been meaning to talk to you about that," said Zoë, her mischievous grin giving her the look of a woodland nymph.

Rolfe's eyebrows lowered. "I don't know if I want any girls, thank you. I don't think I'm up to it."

"Don't be crude, dear."

"What? I wasn't being crude!" He saw that she was mocking him. Chortling, he joined her on the bed. "You have changed, do you know? There was a time when a comment like that would have sent roses to bloom in your cheeks. What makes you so bold?"

"Living with a man will do that to you." She planted a lingering kiss squarely on his lips.

After several minutes of pleasurable activity, Rolfe said, "I can't seem to put a foot right with those girls. What did I do wrong?"

Zoë made a small sound of commiseration.

"No, I mean it," said Rolfe. "Really. You can tell me. I won't bite your head off."

"I think you know yourself," answered Zoë with wifely diplomacy.

"I'm too dictatorial."

"There is that."

"I should talk less and listen more."

"I could not put it better myself."

"I *know* it. I just can't seem to *do* it. That damnable temper of mine keeps getting the better of me."

"Your nieces know it, dear, and they delight in testing it."

"What?"

"It's a game. And you never fail them. You always rise to their bait."

"Well, it's a damn dangerous game, let me tell you." Rolfe rolled from the bed and began to strip out of his garments. "Peter Benson!" he said testily. "A known fortune hunter! And Emily—getting up a flirtation

47

with William Addison! I thought the girl had more sense. I thought William had more sense. Nothing can come of it."

"You don't suppose Emily is serious about William, do you?"

Zoë's words arrested Rolfe as he was reaching for her. His hands dropped away. "How can she be serious about William? She is married to Leon."

"It's not much of a marriage."

"Not yet, it isn't."

He returned to the bed and set his fingers to unplait his wife's hair. Zoë grasped his wrists, stilling his movements. "Something is going on. I wish you would tell me what it is."

"You are imagining things."

"Oh? Then why have you been on edge for months past? There is something troubling you, something to do with Emily. What is it, Rolfe? What scrape is she in now?"

For a moment it seemed that he might shrug off her suspicions. One look at the determined set of his wife's little chin warned him of the futility of evasive tactics.

Propping his back against the pillows, he linked his fingers behind his neck and stared into space. "Emily comes of age in another month," he said.

Zoë was tactfully silent.

Sighing, Rolfe went on. "Before Leon and Emily were wed, your brother made me a solemn promise. Emily was so young. She wasn't ready for marriage. And then, of course, she had developed this childish aversion to Leon."

"I understand," said Zoë. "What was the promise?"

"That he would give her time to come round to the

idea of marriage."

"But she hasn't come round," Zoë pointed out. "And they have been married for almost five years."

"Yes, and that's the damnable thing! You see, Zoë," he turned his head to study his wife's expression, "Emily's time will run out on her birthday."

At Zoë's appalled look, Rolfe's shoulders came away from the pillows. "Darling," he said, "it was inevitable that one day Leon would come and claim his wife. You must have known it."

"I suppose. I just never thought about it. What is more to the point, I'm sure that Emily does not know it." After a considering silence, she observed, "Perhaps we are worrying about nothing. Perhaps Leon won't come for her."

"He will come for her. You may take that as given."

"She needs more time."

"No."

"You can't expect . . ."

"It's not me we have to consider. My hands are tied. Leon is her husband."

"Perhaps if we both talk to him . . . No, that won't do. When Leon makes up his mind to something, he is positively immovable."

"Don't you think I am aware of that?" Rolfe groaned. "She won't accept this without a fight. She will try to get round me. She will use every weapon in her arsenal to wear me down. She knows that I am putty in her hands. Leon is immune to her threats and blandishments. She knows that, too. She will never believe that I must stand aside, if only for her own good."

For a time they were silent as each considered Emily's unhappy plight. At length, Zoë said, "It's strange that she never outgrew this childish antipathy to Leon. It leads me to wonder if there is not something there, something between them that we know nothing about." Her eyes anxiously searched Rolfe's face. "You are sure Leon didn't . . . what I mean to say is—"

"Of course he didn't ravish her," he interrupted. "How could you think such a thing about a man of Leon's character?"

"Ravish? That was not what I was thinking! I hope I know my own brother better than that! No. What I was thinking was that Leon might have made love to her a little. Well, you know Leon. He always had an eye for the girls, and it seemed to me that his youthful aversion to Emily was too exaggerated to be credible."

"He didn't lay a finger on her. He gave me his word on it and I believe him."

Zoë studied Rolfe's expression. "Do you know, it has always struck me as something wonderful that you accepted my brother as though he were an ordinary boy?" To Rolfe's questioning look, she answered, "You knew the kind of life he led during the Revolution. Yet it did not seem to affect your opinion of Leon's character. Most people would have shunned him."

There was a grimness to the set of Rolfe's mouth when he replied. "As they would no doubt shun me if they knew the half of what I had been forced to do as an agent behind enemy lines."

Zoë's eyebrows winged upward and Rolfe shook his head. "No, kitten. There are some secrets I could never share, not even with you."

Her look was very tender. "Stupid man," she said lovingly. "My opinion of your character could never alter." After a moment, she went on. "Are you saying that

50

your experiences and Leon's experiences create a bond between you?"

"That's exactly what I am saying."

She smiled. "I am glad. But to get back to Emily—"

"Leon has been more than patient with her," he cut in brusquely.

She eyed him curiously. "I'm right, aren't I? There *is* something between them, something that has given Emily a thorough disgust of Leon?"

Rolfe's expression was unrevealing. "Shall we say that Emily's disgust is natural to any chaste young girl who discovers that the male of the species has a carnal appetite which need not involve the finer feelings."

Zoë's brow puckered. "Carnal appetite? Are you suggesting that Emily discovered that Leon kept a mistress?"

There was an imperceptible hesitation before Rolfe replied, "In a manner of speaking, yes."

Zoë made a moue of distaste. "Men!" she said with patent loathing.

"Quite."

She shook her head. "Poor Emily. Still, I suppose if that is all it was, there is hope for them yet." Her dark eyes danced. "Well, look at us."

Rolfe chuckled. "Yes, let's look at us, shall we? Now where were we? Oh, yes, you were upbraiding me for our lack of daughters, and I was itching to run my fingers through your glorious mane of hair. Mother Nature has worked things out wondrously well, has she not? We shall both of us get what we want."

"Yes," Zoë agreed breathlessly. She could not breathe when his hands possessed her so intimately.

Rolfe pulled back as a thought struck him. "What if

51

we have another boy? It's possible, you know."

"Will you be disappointed?"

"Lord, no! Boys are no trouble at all."

"Give them time," murmured Zoë, pulling Rolfe's head down to renew the embrace.

Chapter Two

The following morning everyone slept late, everyone, that is, except Emily. She was too keyed up, having spent a restless night working out in her mind exactly how she would word her letter to her husband. The time for prevarication was long past, she told herself. The humiliation she had suffered last night was only a portent of things to come. Leon Devereux would soon be notorious on both sides of the Atlantic. She would not put up with it.

There were a million things she wanted to say to him. She wanted to unbraid him for the lecher he was. She wanted to tell him of her mortification the night before when he had been the subject of the most salacious gossip. But more than anything, she wanted to hurl abuse at him for using *her* funds to lavish jewels and the Lord knew what else on his string of women. That was what galled her the most. She was supporting not only *him*, but his bits of muslin. The very thought made her gnash her teeth together. The man was a parasite!

She wrote none of those things for the simple reason that Leon held the upper hand. She was the one who was pressing for the annulment. If it killed her, she had to be diplomatic. Leon was a dangerous man to cross swords with, as she had learned to her cost over the years.

Dawn had hardly begun to chase the shadows from her chamber when she was up and at her escritoire, sharpening her pen. It took her the better part of two hours and a score of balled sheets of paper before she was satisfied with the letter she had composed. She wrote simply:

Dear Leon (and how she agonized over that *Dear*),

> *The time has come for us to seek an annulment. I am holding you to your promise. There is someone else. May I leave everything in your hands? Naturally, I shall expect the return of my fortune.*

> *Emily*

After due consideration to the last sentence, she added two words, *with interest*. Leon Devereux was not the only one who understood high finance!

The most logical thing would be to seek out Aunt Zoë and put the letter into her hand. There would be no eyebrows raised. Aunt Zoë was religious in writing to her brother at regular intervals. For appearance's sake and as a sop to Aunt Zoë's sense of what was fitting, Emily would obligingly contribute a one-page missive. There was never anything personal in her letters. She wrote about the one thing that she and Leon had in common: Zoë's children. She left it to Sara to keep him informed of the trivialities of their daily round. When Leon bothered to write, which was not

54

often, he wrote only to Aunt Zoë, but there were messages for all of them included in his letters to his sister.

Without thinking about the matter too deeply, she set the letter aside, and wandered down to the breakfast room. Sara was sitting right there at the table. Their conversation was vague until the servants had withdrawn.

"You have an ink stain on your finger," observed Sara.

"I've been writing to Leon."

A silence was maintained until Emily had made a selection from the covered silver servers on the sideboard. Though there had been a marked reserve between the two sisters since Emily's marriage to Leon, Emily was conscious that in the last number of days, Sara's attitude was faintly hostile. She swallowed a sigh, thinking that what she was about to say to Sara could only improve their deteriorating relationship.

Seating herself at the table, she smoothed her white linen napkin over her knees and said quietly, "I am asking Leon to proceed with an annulment, Sara."

Sara's face registered not a flicker of interest. Her attention was all on the piece of dry toast on her side plate.

Emily sat back in her chair. "Did you hear me, Sara? I said . . ."

"I know what you said." The eyes that lifted to meet Emily's were flashing like lightning. "It makes no difference to me."

Emily leaned forward slightly to give her words due emphasis. "Leon will be free, Sara, as I shall be. We may each go our own way. It's what you have always wanted."

"Leon and I can never wed."

The words broke the silence like hammer blows on a blacksmith's anvil. Emily's ears were ringing. When she could find her voice she said, "But . . . but surely this is what you both have been waiting for? Are you saying that you no longer love Leon? Are you in love with Peter Benson?"

Sara shot to her feet, and her face crumpled. "I have loved Leon forever," she cried out. "I shall love him to my dying day. Don't you understand anything? Everything is spoiled! Oh, God, there is no hope for me!"

She left the room so swiftly that Emily had not gathered her wits sufficiently to call her back. She looked down at her plate. The congealing grilled kipper and kidney turned her stomach. Pushing back her chair, she went after Sara

Her heart was pounding. She did not know what she was thinking. She only knew that she must get to the bottom of this. She had always accepted that one day Leon and Sara would be together. From the time they were children, Sara had come first with Leon. It was always for Sara that he reserved all his smiles and soft words. Leon loved Sara. Emily had never doubted it.

When she pushed into Sara's bedchamber, her breath was not quite steady. Sara was prostrate on top of the bed, sobbing her heart out.

Emily lost no time in crossing the distance between them. Seizing Sara by the shoulders, she administered a rough shake. Later, she would be appalled at her own lack of restraint.

"What do you know that I don't know?" she demanded.

The vibrancy, the vague threat in Emily's tone acted

on Sara predictably. Emily was the elder sister. Somehow, that gave her an advantage. She used it rarely, but when she did, she made the most of it.

"I wrote to him," Sara got out between sobs. "I told him everything. I told him you loved William. I told him you would want the marriage annulled. I told him I would wait for him until that day arrived."

Emily's breath came out in a rush. "You told him? But how could you tell him when I did not know myself?"

"Oh, I knew! I just knew! William has been crazy for you since the moment he clapped eyes on you! And after I told him that he had a chance, that your marriage wasn't a normal one, he started courting you. And you . . . you . . . well, you seemed to like him well enough."

"You wanted me to fall in love with William?"

"Of course I did! Haven't I dangled a dozen suitors and more in front of your nose these last years? William was the only one you showed any interest in. And lately, it seemed to me that you were smitten with him, too."

Tears began to get the better of her, but Sara forced herself to continue. "But you would never do anything about it! You kept delaying and delaying till I thought I should die of impatience. I asked you to write to Leon, about William. You know I did."

"This still doesn't explain . . ."

"I received Leon's reply to my letter a week ago. It's here, under my pillow."

A single sheet of paper was thrust into Emily's hand. "Read it for yourself. He will never marry me, not because he does not love me, but because . . ." Her voice broke and she burrowed her head in the pillows as a fresh fit of weeping overcame her.

Emily moved to the long window. The hand which held Leon's letter up to the light was trembling. She began to read his bold scrawl. The letter was brief and to the point. He could never marry Sara, he said, even in the event of an annulment. She would always be Emily's sister. If he were to do such a thing, the family would be split apart. She had to see that. He would do nothing to incur her guardian's displeasure. He valued Uncle Rolfe's friendship. He would always love her as a brother loves a sister.

Whatever it was Emily had hoped to read, it was not these words. The curious anticipation, the strange excitement that had been building inside her gradually evaporated. In its place, anger rushed in, not at Sara, but at Leon. He was too fainthearted to reach for the woman he wanted. He had led Sara on for years only to dash her hopes like this.

Moving to stand beside the bed, Emily said, "Perhaps he will change his mind."

Sara's answer was muffled. "You know that he will not."

Emily did know it. Tentatively, she stretched out a hand and touched Sara's trembling shoulders. The younger girl shook her off and rounded on her in a fury.

"It's all your fault! You knew I loved him. You didn't have to marry him. You could have refused. Uncle Rolfe would have listened to you. You can make Uncle Rolfe do anything you want. You always could. Why oh why did it have to be *you?* Why couldn't it have been *me?*"

To this there was no real answer. Why indeed? Except that Emily had happened to be at the wrong place at the wrong time.

"Do you know what I think, Emily?"

Emily looked at her sister's pale face, still beautiful in spite of the ravages of her bout of weeping. "What do you think?"

"I think you wanted Leon for yourself. I think you planned the whole thing. Why else would he go to the turret room in the middle of the night?"

"You know why." Emily's tone was curt. She hated to be reminded of that night. No one knew about the dower house. What had happened there was so ugly, she had never brought herself to mention it to anyone. "I told you what happened."

"You fell asleep with Uncle Rolfe's pistol in your hand, and when Leon came to investigate the light under the door, you thought he was an intruder?"

"I explained it all years ago."

"It sounds plausible. But I don't believe you."

Injecting amusement into her voice, Emily said, "Then what do you *think* happened? Do you really suppose that I lured Leon to the turret room in order to seduce him?"

"Why not?" said Sara plaintively. "You knew what manner of man he was. You knew he had a roving eye. What happened, Emily? Did Leon refuse to marry you? Is that why you shot at him? Or was it always in your mind to use the pistol to wake the whole house? What I think is that you loved Leon and you knew that trick was the only way you could have him. You were jealous of me. You have always been jealous of me. And I can't think why."

Her words were the result of hysteria. She did not really mean them. When Sara came to herself, she would be bitterly ashamed. Emily knew all that, but even knowing it, the words scourged her. Her face was ashen as she ran from the room.

The Beaver Club in Montreal was unique among gentlemen's clubs the world over. Its members were fur traders, gentlemen fur traders, that is, hardheaded businessmen, every last one of them. They had one other thing in common. A condition of membership in this select club was that a gentleman must have survived a winter in the wilds of the Canadian interior, more commonly known as the Northwest.

Leon exited through the front doors and inhaled a great gust of fresh air. "I can't believe what the lot of us get up to in those rooms," he told the massive granite column to which he had attached himself. He hiccuped and tried for sobriety. "Without a canoe, we managed to paddle our way clear through to the Great Lakes, and some of us went even farther." And his arms were aching from his labors. He had also managed to consume his fair share of rum.

The doors swung open and yet another gentleman fur trader stumbled down the front steps.

"Is that you, MacGilvary?"

"Aye." MacGilvary evidently had no head for strong drink. He clung to Leon like a limpet. "Och, mon, just point my feet in the right direction and they'll find their own way home."

"That won't be necessary, gentlemen." The doorman appeared at their elbow. His temporary absence from his post was occasioned by a slight altercation between two other gentlemen fur traders who had left the premises ahead of them. A piercing whistle was all it took to procure the services of a hackney. The directions were given and MacGilvary and Leon climbed into the cab.

"Your sword dance was superb," Leon told his companion with heartfelt admiration.

MacGilvary beamed his pleasure. "It *was* pretty fair, if I do say so myself. But, och, mon, wasna the piping simply divine? I thought my heart would burst clear through my breast when the piper played our national anthem."

"National anthem?"

"*Scots Wha Hae.*"

"Quite." Leon didn't wish to involve himself in a discussion on the merits of the piping. Just thinking about it made his head split.

"Are you going west with the fur brigades, Mr. MacGilvary?" he queried, deftly changing the subject.

"Sadly, no. No this year. Some of us maun bide in Montreal to tally the profits." This was evidently a huge joke, for MacGilvary convulsed in laughter for the remainder of the drive.

He was the first to reach his destination. Before the door of the cab could be closed on him, he turned to Leon and said, "Ye're no a Scot like the rest o' us?"

"Eh . . . no."

"Och, it's a great pity." Faint suspicion crept into his voice. "Ye wouldn'a be English, would ye?"

"Certainly not!"

The voice warmed perceptibly. "Is it Mr. Devereux the American, come tae gie us Nor'westers a wee bit o' competition?"

"You have it, Mr. MacGilvary."

Faint laughter. "Och, well, there's room for everybody in the fur trade, that's what I say. Ye dinna mind my saying that a man needs his wits aboot him tae steal a march on us Nor'westers?"

"I don't mind in the least," laughed Leon, "and the warning is well taken."

He stopped laughing when he arrived at his destination to find that he owed the driver for not one fare but two.

The house where Leon was putting up, just off the Place d'Armes, belonged to a good friend and associate who had left with the fur brigades earlier that week. In the foyer, he found a candle burning to light his way to his bed.

He stood staring at that candle for a long moment before he picked it up. He was thinking that for a young man in his prime, a married man, there were too many nights such as this one, too many cheerless, comfortless nights where he had nothing for company but his own cheerless thoughts.

There slipped into his mind a picture of his mother as she had greeted his father when he returned home late, as he often did, from some dreary meeting or other. They would linger in the foyer, and their voices would be low and intimate. Leon did not know why, of all his childhood memories, that one should particularly stick in his mind. It was a very ordinary, domestic scene. And it filled him with nostalgia.

Halfway up the stairs, he caught a whiff of her perfume. It sobered him as nothing else could. Mrs. Barbara Royston was a very determined lady.

"Paterson?" he roared. "Paterson? Where the devil are you, man?"

This was a bachelor establishment and Paterson was used to making himself scarce when there were ladies on the premises. His master, Mr. Fraser, had trained him well. He appeared at the bottom of the stairs with catlike stealth, a not unexpected trait for a gentleman who had formerly been an actor. He played the part of butler with consummate skill.

"Sir?"

Leon's tone was clipped. "Find a hackney. The lady is leaving. At once, Paterson."

The lady appeared at the top of the stairs, and Leon breathed a little more easily when he saw that she was still wearing her outdoor garments.

"Barbara, what on earth brings you here?"

She descended the stairs slowly, with practiced grace. Her voice was husky and equally practiced. "I have a parting gift for you," she said and held out a small velvet box. Her eyes promised far more than the trinket in the box.

Leon rarely succumbed to his need for sexual gratification. He had not been raised to be an unfaithful husband. Given his circumstances, however, there were times when celibacy became an impossible goal, an intolerable burden. Whenever that happened, he chose his bed partners with care.

Barbara Royston had seemed like the ideal choice. In the first place, their affair must be short-lived, for his business took him to Montreal only one month out of every year. And in the second place, she was a woman who knew the score.

Though Barbara had a husband, Leon's conscience was scarcely troubled. Charles Royston was indifferent to his wife's comings and goings, having established another hearth and home, one more to his liking, a thousand miles away in Fort William. Royston had formed a connection with an Indian woman there, by whom he had fathered a brood of children. This was no secret in fur-trading circles, nor was it uncommon, though such things were never mentioned in polite society.

Knowing all this about the Roystons, Leon had embarked on an affair with Barbara and had come to regret it almost at once. The lady, he had soon discovered, lacked discretion. All Montreal knew of their affair and it was Barbara who had broadcast it. This was something Leon would not tolerate. It was over, and he had told her so. Recently, he had assiduously avoided any gathering where they were likely to run into each other. This had only encouraged her to send him notes and make an infernal nuisance of herself.

He curled her fingers around the box. "I'm touched," he said, "but you know I can't accept it."

"It's only a small memento, something to remember me by until you are next in Montreal. Please, Leon?"

She wasn't ready to give up. He had tried to let her down gently and had failed. Sighing, he said, very softly, "Barbara, I am expecting someone." He paused. "A lady."

It took her a moment or two to grasp his meaning. When she did, her beautiful face became mottled, and with a choked cry of rage and a whish of her skirts, she went clattering down the stairs.

Paterson, who had returned just in time to catch the end of the little scene, obligingly held the door open as she swept past.

"See that she gets home safely," said Leon, and

rubbed the tips of his fingers over his throbbing temples. He hadn't been raised to be ungallant to ladies, either, whatever the provocation. It went against the grain. But so did a million other things in his life, and he had done them anyway.

He was maudlin. It must be the rum. He was thinking of his mother and of his misspent life.

A faint cough arrested his attention.

"What is it Paterson"?"

"Mrs. Royston had her own carriage waiting, sir, and was gone before I could catch up with her."

"Thank you."

Another small cough.

"Yes?"

"About the other lady, Mr. Devereux, the one you are expecting?"

"You must have misunderstood. I'm not expecting anyone. Lock up and get off to bed. And . . . Paterson? Thank you for waiting up for me."

Once in his bedchamber, Leon set about packing. He wasn't going home to New York this time around. He had booked passage on a ship sailing for England. There was very little to pack anyway, for most of his trunks had been sent on ahead. The last thing he put into his handgrip was the packet of letters that had caught up with him some days before. He paused and leafed through them.

William Addison. It was a name that was burned into his brain, a name that had cropped up more and more of late in the correspondence from England. Sara's last letter had made everything crystal clear. Only one person avoided all mention of the gentleman's name. Emily.

She was going to fight him every inch of the way, nothing was more certain. He grinned in satisfaction, that notion pleasing him inordinately. There were old scores between his wife and himself that he was itching to settle. For five long years, she had held him off, making him pay for that sordid episode in the dower house a hundred times over. The tables were about to be turned.

He almost reached for the brandy bottle to pour himself a small celebratory drink. Knowing that he would suffer for it in the morning, he resisted the impulse and settled back in a wing armchair which flanked the grate. Paterson, he noted idly, had banked up the fire and the glowing coals diffused a welcoming warmth.

His welcome in England would not be a warm one, not if his last visit was anything to go by. He had returned, so he had thought, like a conquering hero, like a knight returning from a crusade to lay his spoils at the feet of his lady. He'd done well for himself. Hell, he had excelled even his own wildest expectations. And he had done it all for Emily. He had told her he would, right after their marriage in Rivard's chapel. She must be won over. He must erase from her mind that frightful scene in the dower house. He must prove himself worthy of her. He had understood that. Emily was a romantic, a dreamer. This was the sort of gesture that would mean something to his wife.

His optimism had been misplaced. In his absence that childish antipathy to him had, if anything, strengthened. Emily did not want Leon Devereux within a mile of her. If her guardian had been anyone else but the man to whom he owed his very life, he would have soon put a stop to her foolishness. But Rolfe *was* her guardian, and he had promised Rolfe to stay his hand until Emily came of age. That day was almost upon them.

It was inevitable that Rolfe would try to protect her. His two nieces had been orphaned at a tender age and he was used to shielding them from any unpleasantness. For years Emily and Sara had made a study of how to get round their guardian. They knew every trick that had ever been invented. In their different ways, they were both as devious and as wily as foxes. But he, Leon Devereux, was onto them, especially Emily. For more years than he cared to remember, *he* had made a study of *her*, knew every ploy she was likely to come up with. Her wiles would not work on him.

Annulment. He allowed the thought to sink into his mind. He had promised her an annulment and his stratagem had worked, up to a point. She had consented to their marriage. It wasn't the kind of marriage he wanted, but it was a marriage of sorts. With her coming of age, all constraints, all promises, would be removed. The thought made him smile. Very soon, the battle would be joined and Lady Emily Devereux would find herself outflanked, outmaneuvered, and outmatched. He didn't feel sorry for her. In victory, he knew how to be generous.

It was three years since he had last seen her. A lot could have happened in three years. According to Sara, Emily had a serious suitor. It seemed that his little wife was beginning to thaw. No doubt William Addison had been permitted more liberties than her own husband.

He expelled a long breath. It was now or never. He knew one thing. If their positions were reversed, if he were the suitor and Addison were the absent husband, he would have made his move long before now. She was his wife. Suitor or no suitor, she belonged to him. And soon, she would know it.

Chapter Three

The Season was winding to a close. One of the last events scheduled to take place was a masquerade at Fonthill House, Sir Geoffrey Coombe's place on the Thames. Emily and Sara had never been allowed to attend a masked ball before. To Uncle Rolfe's way of thinking, such affairs were not quite genteel. Anything might happen, and usually did, as he well remembered from his salad days. He never said this without emitting a little chuckle, and his wards rightly supposed that what was sauce for the goose was most definitely not to be considered sauce for the gander.

When, therefore, he gave his womenfolk permission to accept Lady Coombe's gilt-edged invitation, speculation in the house in St. James was rife. Emily and Sara knew they had done nothing to merit this show of confidence — quite the reverse. They debated, rather anxiously, whether or not they had gone too far, if perhaps Uncle Rolfe had not taken it into his head to wash his hands of his incorrigible nieces. Aunt Zoë laid their fears to rest. The Coombes were "good ton." The ball promised to be a very select affair. Fonthill House was far enough distant from town to preclude, one hoped, interlopers of unsavory reputation.

Aunt Zoë wasn't to know it, but her words had robbed Emily and Sara of some of their anticipation for the event. It seemed that the Coombes do was to be just another boring affair. Further confirmation came when they learned that Sara's beau, Peter Benson, had not received an invitation, and William Addison found it necessary to refuse owing to government business that would take him out of town.

Sara was laying forth her consternation to Emily on this intolerable turn of events as they were conveyed in the carriage to Madame Germaine's in Bond Street. Madame Germaine was a new experience for the girls. She was a modiste who had made a name for herself by appealing to those ladies of fashion who aimed to turn heads. In short, her creations were always a little daring, and sometimes downright scandalous.

Their guardian knew nothing of Madame Germaine or her dubious reputation. If he had, he would have put his foot down. Emily and Sara were too wise to reveal the names, some of them truly notorious, of Madame's clientele, and Uncle Rolfe was too bored by the subject of ladies' fashions to pursue the matter.

It was all so tedious. From various sources, the girls had gathered that their uncle, in his younger days, was a very gay blade. With old age creeping up on him, he had turned positively puritan. To their great regret, it forced them to be less than scrupulously honest in their dealings with him.

They might be able to pull the wool over Uncle Rolfe's eyes, but Aunt Zoë was wise to her nieces' ways. It was she who oversaw their wardrobes. In matters of taste, everything must be referred to Aunt Zoë.

When they had broached the subject of new gowns for the Coombes's masquerade and mentioned Madame Germaine's name in as offhand a manner as possible, Aunt Zoë had pursed her lips and given them a penetrating look from under her dark eyebrows.

"Madame Germaine?" she said simply. There was a muted twinkle in her eye.

Once, when they were infants, the girls were under the misapprehension that their aunt was something of a witch. She could read their minds as easily as they could read a book. Although they had long since grown out of this childish fancy, there were occasions, such as the present moment, when they almost felt like children again.

Much to their surprise, Aunt Zoë had given way. "But only this once, mind you," she warned them.

In Madame Germaine's fitting rooms they were to discover that Aunt Zoë was not as simpleminded as they had hoped. The gowns Madame had created for them were gratifyingly shocking, but the whole effect was ruined, in Sara's opinion, by the white taffeta domino that covered the whole of both creations.

Emily left Sara in the fitting room arguing it out with the modiste. It seemed that their aunt had been there before them. The white taffeta dominoes were de rigueur. Emily was not sorry. Her reflection in the mirror had both fascinated her and repelled her. There was purity there, but at the same time, there was knowledge as old as Eve. Fanciful notion!

In the anteroom, she accepted the chair indicated by Madame's assistant and composed herself to wait for Sara. She was thinking that their quarrel might never have taken place. To all appearances, things went on as before.

But appearances could be deceptive. Oh, not with Sara, Emily allowed. Sara was transparent. She had said that she was sorry and that meant that the whole thing would be forgotten. To Sara's way of thinking, a good quarrel cleared the air.

Emily wished she could be more like her sister. She was well aware her composed facade was a sham. Inwardly, she was still churning with hurt feelings. Sara had spoken in anger. Nevertheless, she had meant what she had said. *You were jealous of me. You always have been.* Emily didn't want to think about it.

Quickly rising to her feet, she indicated to Madame's assistant that she was going outside for a breath of fresh air. As she stepped onto the pavement, who should step down from her carriage but Lady Riddley. Emily composed features betrayed nothing of her frustration. Lady Riddley's expression was easier to read. She seemed to be steeling herself to perform an unpleasant though necessary duty.

"Lady Emily," she said, "this is more than I dared hope for. Please!" She laid a restraining hand on Emily's sleeve as the girl half turned away. "This will only take a moment."

Nodding her encouragement, she led Emily to her waiting carriage. Once inside, they sat on opposite banquettes.

Lady Riddley moistened her lips and her eyes dropped away. "You hate me, and I don't blame you," she began.

Emily wasn't ready for this. She would never be ready for this. Starting to her feet, she said, "I have no wish to hear about your love affair with my husband."

"It wasn't love," Lady Riddley interjected quickly. She

72

breathed deeply and went on. "Leon never loved me. Even then, he loved you. He has always loved you. But you must know this."

Emily sank back on the cushions. It was as though her heart had stopped beating.

Lady Riddley's face betrayed her embarrassment. It was livid with color. "You were too young. You were an innocent. Leon wanted to protect you. You were never meant to know. We were . . . careless." Her eyes dropped to her clasped hands. "You are still very young, but perhaps old enough to understand that men and women sometimes have needs . . . That is, we were hurting no one that night. My husband's twice my age. The earl could not . . . we were not on intimate terms." Her eyes anxiously searched Emily's face. "Afterward, I was never with Leon again. And everything worked out for the best."

Though Emily had been following everything that her companion had said, she had not heard what she most wanted to hear. "How do you know that Leon loves me?"

"It was no secret," said Lady Riddley, smiling for the first time since they had entered the carriage. "Leon told me that he was waiting for Rivard's niece to grow up before he claimed her."

Emily had heard enough. Leon was waiting for Rivard's niece to grow up before he claimed her. The marquess had two nieces. It was *Sara* whom Leon had always loved, *Sara* whom he had hoped to claim. He had paid dearly for his *affaire* with Lady Riddley.

Her eyes lifted to the older woman. At the Spencers' ball, Lady Riddley's beauty had seemed as vibrant as ever. Candlelight was kinder than daylight, thought Emily, for she saw now what she had missed then. The woman was on the wrong side of forty and showing it. This aging belle bore no resemblance to the voluptuous seductress she had created in her imagination.

"You do understand how it was?"

"I understand," said Emily. The response was mechanical. She didn't understand, not really. She supposed that she was naive. She must be, for what she wanted seemed to be unattainable. She wanted people to be good and kind and honorable. She wanted people to be trustworthy. They shouldn't do things they were ashamed of. They shouldn't do things in stealth. They shouldn't lie and cheat and deceive each other. They should be the best they could be. Leon had loved Sara. Lady Riddley had a husband. Their illicit affair seemed tawdry. To say that they had hurt no one wasn't true.

She wasn't a complete simpleton. She knew that no one could be perfect. But that wasn't what she meant. She was groping for something and could not seem to grasp it entirely.

Conscious of Lady Riddley's half-hopeful, half-anxious look, she said, "Why have you told me all this?"

"At the Spencers' ball, you gave me a look of such loathing! You see, it had never crossed my mind that you knew I was the woman with Leon that night. I want to assure you that I deeply regret any pain I may have caused you. I mean that sincerely. I am not an ogre. I never meant to steal Leon away from you. As I said, you were never meant to know."

Emily relaxed against the cushions. The woman *was* sincere. She wasn't without scruples. In all likelihood, she was a better person than she herself was. It would be mean-spirited to refuse the olive branch she was offering.

"I promise you," said Emily, "you shall never surprise

74

that look on my face again."

The letter to Leon remained hidden away in her escritoire. Emily reasoned that there was not much point in sending it when Sara had got there before her. Leon knew everything there was to know. That her own letter would add weight to Sara's persuasions seemed reasonable but by no means certain. She was prevaricating again and reluctant to examine her motives.

Then something happened that hastened her decision. It was a freak accident that could have happened to anyone. She was out riding. Sara, who normally would have accompanied her, was indisposed. Hyde Park was deserted; both girls were accomplished riders and preferred to exercise their horses in the early hours of the morning before other riders were about, when it was possible to put their mounts through their paces. At Sara's request, Emily was exercising Sara's bay, Hoyden, as spirited an animal as her name suggested. Suddenly, without warning and at the worst possible moment, when Emily was riding hell-bent-for-leather across the turf, the saddle slipped. Emily went flying through the air. The last thing she heard was her groom's cry of alarm before she hit the ground with a sickening thud.

William Addison, who frequently made it a point to meet Emily "by accident" during these early-morning rides, saw the whole thing. Horror-struck, he came thundering up on his huge roan and practically threw himself down beside the stunned girl.

"W-William?" Emily looked up at him in a daze.

Relief shivered through him. He'd thought for one awful moment that she had broken her neck. That first rush of relief was quickly superseded by a different emotion. He wanted to shake her in anger.

"God, Emily, how many times must I warn you not to ride like a hoyden? Are you all right? No broken bones?"

She managed a shaky laugh. "Only my dignity is wounded. William, please help me up?"

He gathered her to him and held her comfortingly. She liked the feel of his strong arms about her and rested her head on his broad chest.

He gave her a moment to come to herself, then set her at arm's length. "If I were your guardian, I would forbid you to ride for the next several months."

His anger touched her, for she saw in it an expression of his devotion. She stood there meekly, accepting his vituperation, knowing that it was merited. He went on at some length. One might have thought that they were already married.

In some things, she recognized that William was a little stodgy. She doubted that he had ever done anything reckless in his life, with the exception of falling in love with a woman who already had a husband. It was a disloyal thought and she quickly suppressed it. Decorum was important to William's family. He had laughingly told her that their unspoken motto was noblesse oblige. He was too aware of their failings to accept their unspoken codes as his own.

She spent the remainder of the day quietly in her room, nursing her aches and bruises. There was plenty of time for soul-searching and reflection. Life was too short, too transitory, to waste it. She did not want second best. She did not want to become a pathetic figure like Lady Riddley, or to regret "what might have been" like Sara and Leon. She wanted to embrace life, to experience the best it had to offer, not in empty riches and pleasures, but in the more meaningful ways that made every day worthwhile. She did not know if those things were to be found with William Addison; she only knew that they were not to be found with her husband.

That evening, she gave the letter she had written to Leon to her aunt.

Leon Devereux scanned the letter in his hand with careless interest before flinging it aside. "She is demanding an annulment," he told his companion.

Rolfe choked on a mouthful of brandy and quickly set his glass down. It was he who had put Emily's letter into Leon's hand only a few moments before. "God, Zoë was right! She must be sweet on William Addison. I should have seen it coming. I should have taken steps to put a stop to it before now. Damnation! I thought it was merely a harmless flirtation."

The two gentlemen were in an upstairs parlor in the distinguished Clarendon Hotel, where Leon Devereux had taken up lodgings since his arrival in London a few days before.

"It *is* only a harmless flirtation," said the younger man. He stretched out his long, booted legs to rest them against the fireplace fender, and slowly brought his glass to his lips.

"Beg pardon?"

"Emily is my wife."

"Quite. I see what you mean."

The silence which ensued was a comfortable one, springing from long-standing friendship and a tacit understanding of the problem which Lady Emily Devereux presented to the two most significant men in her life.

The problem was not a new one. Leon Devereux happened to be married to a girl who did not want him. Rolfe thought his niece was daft. Leon was everything he would choose for a husband for one of his wards. He was of sound character. He was a hard worker. By and large, he had made his own way in the world. True, at one time, the boy had tended to wildness. But his marriage had knocked that trait out of him. There had been not a whisper of scandal attaching to his name in the last five years. If there had been, Rolfe would have got wind of it. It went without saying that there would have been women. Evidently, Leon had learned the value of discretion. He would do nothing to jeopardize his chances with Emily. In point of fact, he had done as much as any man to win the confidence of the woman of his choice. Much good it had done him.

Emily was still very much a child, in her uncle's opinion. Other women were not slow to throw out lures to the handsome man, as Rolfe had witnessed earlier that evening in the hotel's lobby. And why shouldn't they? Leon was a fine-looking specimen.

Rolfe's eyes made a slow appraisal of the man sitting opposite him. The handsomely chiseled profile did not even register. What he admired was Leon's physique—his broad shoulders tapering to a trim waist; his iron-tight stomach, not to mention his muscular thighs and legs beneath the skin-hugging, black pantaloons. The man was in the peak of physical condition, and a welcome relief from the hordes of painted fops with their effeminate gestures who thronged the salons of Mayfair.

Suddenly conscious of Leon's questioning stare, Rolfe said, "I was admiring your tailoring. English, I presume?"

"Is there any other kind?"

Rolfe snorted. "For a Frenchman, that's saying something."

"I'm not French. I'm an American. You forget that I have spent almost half my life outside the borders of France."

"If you really worked at it," said Rolfe, tongue in cheek, "you might eventually be able to pass yourself off as an Englishman." Rolfe was thinking that to hear Leon now, one would never have known that he was not English born and bred. He never lapsed into French as Zoë did when she was agitated. Rolfe suddenly remembered something else: Emily, as a child, mimicking Leon's French accent, much to the boy's chagrin. He supposed that there were others who had sunk to his niece's level, taunting the youth because he was different, perhaps boys he had met at university. Knowing Leon, he would want to make them eat their words.

Leon laughed, showing a flash of white teeth against the tanned skin. "Thank you, no. America suits me very well."

They went on in a similar vein until a chance remark brought them back to the reason for Leon's presence in England.

Rolfe studied Leon's lean face, gauging his reaction to his next words. He made a steeple with his fingers. "If you were agreeable," he said cautiously, "an annulment could be arranged quite easily."

Leon's dark eyes lowered to veil his expression. "I have not waited five years to hear this. I have been more than patient, Rolfe, and you know it. With or without your consent, I mean to claim my wife."

Some perverse impulse goaded Rolfe to say, "If I

wanted to, I could stop you."

"You could try."

"And if I did?"

Silence as gray and flashing black eyes fought for mastery.

Rolfe let out a shaky laugh, half amused, half affronted by the impudence of his young adversary. "I almost relish the thought of the fight you are going to have on your hands. Emily is not about to submit gracefully, let me tell you."

Leon grinned. "Well I know it. What have you told Zoë?"

"I've told her that you are bound to come for Emily. I'm not looking forward to telling her that you have spirited the girl away."

"I'm not abducting her," said Leon in an amused tone. "I merely want some time alone with my wife. You may tell my sister that I intend to bring her back before we set sail for America. There will be plenty of time for farewells."

"That will vastly relieve her mind," said Rolfe dryly.

Ignoring this comment, Leon went on. "Tell me about William Addison."

A twinkle crept into Rolfe's eyes. "What do you wish to know?"

There was a pause before Leon said, "If Emily were not married to me, would you encourage Addison's suit?"

"Most certainly. His background is impeccable. His grandfather was a duke. William has some money that came to him on the death of his wife. We are colleagues at the War Office, but you already know that. He is a steady, dependable fellow. What more can I say? If she were not married to you, Emily could not do better. Is that what you wished to know?"

Leon shrugged carelessly. "He sounds very English, very boring."

This startled a laugh out of Rolfe. "Didn't you know? Guardians, by and large, prefer their wards to marry boring, dependable types. Now, don't get your hackles up. I didn't mean that the way it came out."

Leon's mood changed abruptly. "How are things at the War Office? What am I to make of the reports that have been carried in all the newspapers these last few days?"

"Ah." Rolfe carefully eased himself back in his chair. "I wondered how soon it would be before we got to that."

"Is it true? Was there an assassination attempt on the life of Bonaparte?"

"There was."

"And La Compagnie is claiming responsibility for it?"

"Let us say, shall we, that there is a group of hotheads in France who have resurrected the old name, a name, as you well know, that is like to strike terror into the hearts of men who are highly placed on both sides of the English Channel."

"So." Leon gave his companion a searching look. La Compagnie is on the rise again?"

"I didn't say that. But even if it were true, you have nothing to fear. It's all of fifteen years since you were involved with the sect. Who is there to connect you to it? When La Compagnie was smashed, very few escaped our net."

Leon felt as though someone had just walked over his grave. He took a long swallow from the glass in his hand, then another. "Who are its leaders? What are its aims?"

"It's too soon to say. Assassination—that goes without saying. If I knew, I would tell you. As it is, I only know what I have read in the papers."

"But the War Office is taking these reports seriously?"

"Very seriously, and you know why. We are not forgetting that La Compagnie's tendrils once stretched as far as England."

What both men were thinking was that Rolfe's elder brother had been one of La Compagnie's first victims.

"And Emily?" said Leon. "I presume she has read all the reports? What does she have to say about it? What does she have to say about Le Cache-Cache?"

"Just what one would expect her to say," Rolfe expelled a long sigh. "Leon, most people in England have lived a sheltered existence. Emily is no exception. What do they know about the Terror in France and the straits that ordinary people were put to just to survive? You were only a boy at the time. You did what you had to do. It's the brutes who took advantage of your youthful idealism that deserved everything they got. You have made a new life for yourself. Forget the past. Think of the future. That's my advice."

"You are . . . quite something, Rolfe, do you know that?" said Leon and grinned, but there was no amusement in his eyes.

Long after he had taken his leave of Leon, that conversation continued to revolve in Rolfe's mind. His thoughts slipped back in time to the year he had gone to France to find his wife and her young brother. In those days, Leon was a member of La Compagnie, and one of its most ruthless assassins. Le Cache-Cache, Hide-and-Seek, was the name the popular press had given him. To the populace at large, he was a glamorous figure, a folk hero not unlike Robin Hood. The reality was far different. The boy had wanted out of the society. With La Compagnie, however, the only former members were dead ones.

Rolfe was thinking that it was no bad thing that Leon would soon be on his way back to America. Though he believed every word he had told his young brother-in-law, he saw no point in taking chances. Until he was sure that there was no threat to Leon, it was better to play a safe hand.

That thought led to another. He was thinking of the threat of exposure. There were files at the War Office with Leon's name on them. Though there was nothing there to connect him to Le Cache-Cache, there was a highly confidential report crediting the boy, Leon Devereux, with helping to bring about the society's demise. A clever person could put two and two together. It was a report which Rolfe intended to misplace at the earliest opportunity.

He fought himself free of the nightmare, forcing himself to awaken. When he dragged himself to a sitting position, he was panting as though his lungs would burst. He groaned, hoping that the scream which had been torn from his throat was part of the dream and not reality.

But the dream *was* reality. He was a boy again, and he had just been told that his gentle mother had died of a fever in the dread prison of La Conciergerie and that his father had been executed. His rage knew no bounds. Every man on the Tribunal which had condemned his parents must be hounded down and pay the penalty with their very lives. He would find a way to exact retribution.

Though he was only a boy, he became Le Cache-Cache, a ruthless assassin. Pleas could not move him. He showed no remorse, not until the day he executed the wrong man, an innocent man whose only crime was that he had the same name as one of the judges.

After a while, he sank back against the pillows, conscious that he was soaked with perspiration. As his breathing gradually returned to normal, he made an effort to recall Rolfe's words. *You were only a boy at the time. You did what you had to do. You have made a new life for yourself. Forget the past. Think of the future.*

With his whole heart he wanted to believe Rolfe's words. All of that had happened half a lifetime ago. He was not the hotheaded youth he was then. He had helped Rolfe smash La Compagnie, and he had never looked back.

La Compagnie. It was on the rise again. None knew better than he that the society always paid off old scores.

Chapter Four

Fonthill House was a Palladian showplace, a red-brick Georgian mansion in a jewel of a setting. The park and gardens, Zoë noted with interest, followed the English tradition, with everything appearing as though Nature herself had designed the landscape. This was a far cry from the formally laid-out gardens of her native France. At Versailles, there were terraces with symmetrical box hedges and a plethora of magnificent marble fountains, each one a work of art. At Fonthill, towering avenues of old oaks and cedars, judiciously set out by former generations of Coombes, drew the eye to the house itself and beyond, to the River Thames.

The grounds were brilliant with lights. It was evident that Sir Geoffrey was eager for his guests to take in the park as much as the house. There were interesting-looking walks which disappeared into clumps of flowering bushes, or around corners of buildings.

"You won't get lost," their host told them. "Each path has a destination. You'll find refreshment waiting for you when you get there. Later, on the front lawn, there will be a fireworks display. After that, the dancing will start."

"Not unlike Vauxhall Gardens," murmured Sara to her sister, referring to the public gardens across the river from Chelsea, where the walks and entertainments were justly famous.

Her guardian caught the remark. "No," he contradicted. "Not like Vauxhall. At this do, the guests are here by invitation. There will be no frolics of the sort that would raise a single eyebrow."

The two girls exchanged a meaningful look. It was Sara who mouthed the words, "How boring!" Emily smiled and nodded.

But she wasn't really bored. From the moment the carriage had swept through the stone gates of Fonthill House, Emily had been captivated. It was like stepping into a fairy tale, a world of enchantment. Lights winked at her from the branches of trees, casting unearthly shadows. When she inhaled, the sultry night-scents of honeysuckle, tuberose, and heliotrope seemed to be absorbed into her bloodstream. Her senses had sharpened. She was acutely conscious of a pervasive stillness in the midst of laughter and revelry. The night seemed to be holding its breath. Something momentous, something wonderful, was about to happen. Her heart and soul were thrilling, and she could not understand it.

The Thames had never looked more lovely or more mysterious. A flotilla of small boats, their lights bobbing, were at the water's edge, disembarking their passengers. Everyone was in masks and dominoes.

"How romantic," said Aunt Zoë. "Now, why didn't we think to come by boat?"

Romantic. The word leaped out at Emily. It was a night for romance. On just such a night as this . . .

Lifting her head, her expression rapt, she gazed into the canopy of trees overhead, and beyond, where the moon reigned in solitary majesty. After an interval, she sighed and turned away.

Sara gave her a strange look. "Whatever has got into you?"

"Nothing . . . Everything." Emily shrugged helplessly. She could not explain herself.

One corner of the walk skirted the man-made lake. There was a small clearing, and they stopped to admire the view. Weeping willows and cedars interspersed with stands of plane trees framed the still expanse of water. Lanterns hanging from branches were reflected in ghostly profusion around the perimeter of the lake.

Uncle Rolfe made some comment about the army of gardeners required to keep up the place. Emily wasn't listening. On the far side of the lake, she could just make out the figure of a man in a scarlet domino.

"Emily!"

Sara's voice brought her head round and she hastened her steps to catch up with the others.

At the Orangery, she had her first taste of champagne. The bubbles went to her head. She decided she rather liked it.

"You have an admirer."

"Mmm?" Emily's eyes focused on Sara.

"The man in the scarlet domino." Sara sucked in her breath. "I think it's William. I thought you said he would not be here tonight?"

"So I understood," said Emily. Her eyes found the figure of the man in the scarlet domino. Could it be William? Black mask and scarlet domino lent him an air of glamour and mystery and danger. At that moment, his eyes captured hers and held them. He raised his glass in a silent tribute before bringing it to his lips. The gesture was just the sort of thing William would do to put a dent in her composure. Emily bit down on a grin.

The next lap of their walk took them to a Doric temple, a small stone edifice, complete with Grecian columns, with a view of the river.

Though Fonthill and its grounds were impressive, Uncle Rolfe infinitely preferred his own domain at Rivard. The Abbey was stolidly English and unpretentious. This neoclassical nonsense, so he confided to his ladies, came too close to affectation for comfort.

Aunt Zoë did not agree with him. "It's delightful," she exclaimed. "It must be a summer dining room. What do you think, Emily?"

Emily looked about her with interest. The walls were decorated with stucco medallions of female Greek deities. "I think it's a shrine to Venus," she said unthinkingly, startling her companions. To cover her confusion, she accepted another glass of champagne from one of the gold-liveried footmen who hovered in the background.

People were coming and going as they pleased. Uncle Rolfe struck up a conversation with someone he had recognized in spite of the dominoes and masks. Aunt Zoë and Sara were closely examining the medallions on the walls. Sipping her champagne, Emily wandered out in to the night.

There was a crush of people on the lawns. The man in the scarlet domino was there, at the edge of the crowd, in conversation with another masked gentleman. His eyes, so dark and fathomless, held Emily's in a curiously familiar stare. The fine hairs on the back of her neck began to rise, not in fear, but in anticipation.

It must be William. He was the only man who had ever had this effect on her. She stood there like one of the marble statues in the temple as his eyes wandered over her at will, devouring her. Across the distance that separated them, she could almost taste his hunger. Her own senses leapt in response. She was shaken.

There was something new here, something that was completely outside the realms of her experience. It was as though she had conjured the man out of her imagination. He was part of the fairy tale, part of the enchanted world she had woven around herself all evening. But it was wishful thinking on her part. The man in the scarlet domino represented something that did not exist outside her imagination.

As the hours slipped away, she diligently rebuked herself for her flights of fancy. She was moon-bewitched. She was a love-starved spinster whose lonely heart cried out for love. If the man in the scarlet domino was William, and it seemed he must be, he would laugh himself silly if he could read her mind. William was no dream lover.

He was keeping his distance to pique her interest. And he was succeeding. Oh, God, how he was succeeding! She was noticing things about William she had never noticed before. She liked the way he moved, with unselfconscious masculine grace. She liked his smile. His mouth was beautifully shaped, with a faintly ironic slant. His thick dark hair had a curl to it, and fell past his collar in back. How was it, she asked herself, that she had never noticed these things before? She knew why. Tonight, William wanted her to be aware of him.

He was telling her that he was a potently virile male with just a hint of the predator about him, and she was his quarry. In the interests of self-preservation, she had better keep her eye on him.

It was all a game. She could play it and no harm would come to her. William was a man of honor. Hadn't he promised that he would dare no more than steal the odd kiss? The conviction that she could play his game with impunity lent a recklessness that was foreign to her. Her smiles held a hint of promise, her eyes returned stare for stare. She wasn't acting. It was William's doing. He was deliberately exercising a power over her that she would not have believed he possessed. It was almost a tangible thing.

In his own good time he would come for her. He would spirit her away and in some quiet corner, he would kiss her. She wouldn't try to stop him. This kiss would be different from all the other kisses he had ever given her. This kiss would burn away all her uncertainties. She could feel it in her bones.

"Emily!"

It was Aunt Zoë's voice this time that brought her out of her reveries. Flashing her admirer one last lingering look, she turned on her heel and went to answer the summons.

Leon Devereux absorbed his wife's smile with a considering look in his eye. It was clear to him that his wife did not have the faintest suspicion that the man who stalked her was her very own husband. Why should she? She believed him to be conveniently located thousands of miles away in New York. She had no way of knowing that he was in England, or that her letter demanding an annulment of their marriage was, at that very moment, burning a hole in his pocket. She had no way of knowing that, with her uncle's connivance, the scene had been set to allow him his chance with her.

The ironic slant to his mouth softened and became a grin. Everything was working out just as he had hoped it would. The current, that indefinable something that leapt to life between them, was as strong as it had ever been. Not that Emily would ever admit to it. She clung to her childish aversion to him, using it as a means of keeping him at arm's length. Tonight, however, things were different. Tonight, she did not recognize him, and not recognizing him, she did not scent her danger. For once, she had not armed herself against him. He would never be given a better chance to storm the citadel.

His fingers tightened around the stem of the glass he was holding. Becoming aware of the betraying movement, he set it down. He was annoyed because he was forced to use subterfuge to approach his own wife. He was annoyed because circumstances made it imperative for him to act without delay. This wasn't what he wanted. But William Addison was a threat he would be a fool to overlook.

God, she was playing with fire! Those sidelong looks she slanted him! Those smiles! In his absence, his little wife had turned into a flirt. On one level, he experienced a surge of pure masculine elation. She was responding to him. On another level, he was furious with her. She was a married woman. She thought he was a stranger. Those smiles and glances belonged to her husband. It set his mind to wondering about William Addison, and how far her flirtation with Addison had progressed.

He had to consciously uncurl the fists he had made

of his hands. Jealousy, he was coming to see, was a powerful emotion. He knew Emily better than that. Emily had integrity. She would never betray her marriage vows, no, not even if she hated the man to whom she was bound. If he had not believed that, he could never have allowed her free rein while he established himself in another part of the world. But there was a change in her. A blind man would have been aware of it, and where Emily was concerned, he had a sixth sense.

He chose his moment with care, approaching her in the circular greenhouse. Rolfe flashed him a wink before leading Zoë and Sara away to view Sir Geoffrey's prize pineapples in another part of the building. Emily's eyes were trained on a vine that was heavy with blossom. Leon recognized the absorbed look on her face. She was lost in a dream world. The thought brought an ineffably tender light to his eyes.

She took a step back, straight into his arms. "I beg your . . ." Her words dwindled into silence.

He smiled down at her. Deliberately lowering his voice so that she would not recognize it, he said, "Your uncle asked me to conduct you to him."

His words made no impression on her. She gazed at him in rapt attention, unaware that his arms were still holding her.

"The fireworks display," he prompted. "We are to assemble on the front lawns."

Her breath came out in a rush. "Fireworks display?" She smiled shyly. "Of course. How stupid of me." She looked down at the toes of her white satin slippers. "I presume my uncle thinks that I am lost?"

He did not answer, but merely held out his arm, inviting her to lay her fingers on the back of his sleeve. She obeyed the unspoken command. The air between them crackled with awareness.

It was some time before she realized that he wasn't making for the house. He was making for the river. Her hand dropped away and her steps slowed, then faltered. He turned to face her and for the first time she felt a shiver of unease.

"Where are you taking me?"

"Somewhere where we can be alone together."

It was what she wanted, of course. William would carry her off to some quiet corner where he would kiss her, and all her uncertainties would be resolved. The quiver of alarm that danced along her skin was merely a wariness that was natural to the female of the species. He was a male and so much more powerful than she.

He was also William and a guest of Sir Geoffrey's. William was as safe and as dependable as the Bank of England, else he would not be here. Hadn't Uncle Rolfe said as much?

"Do you come with me?" he asked.

He was making an attempt to disguise his voice. It seemed that William was a bit of a romantic, too. The thought gratified her. "Yes," she said simply, and smiled.

Almost as though her acquiescence had not pleased him, he grabbed her wrist none too gently and swung on his heel. She had to run to keep up with him. Her ankle twisted and she stumbled. He was on his knees instantly, gathering her into his arms. She heard the rasp of his breath, she saw the glitter in his eyes, and then his head descended and his mouth took hers.

She had been right. This kiss was like nothing she

had ever known before. He wasn't wooing her, he was *claiming* her. And she was responding. It was as though every cell in her body possessed a knowledge that went beyond logic. While her mind warned her to be cautious, every feminine instinct urged her to yield to him.

When he pulled back, she stared at him with huge, bemused eyes. His teeth flashed white in the moonlight. As he swung her into his arms, breast to breast, their two hearts beating wildly in tempo, she made an involuntary protest, which he ignored. She was confused, but one thing was becoming clear to her. This man could not possibly be William. William was squarer, more solid. This man was as lithe as an athlete. His scent was different. And his kisses were too confident by half.

"I don't understand," she whispered, turning her lips to his cheek.

He brushed his lips over hers. "I've come for you. You always knew that I would."

Her head was buzzing. She felt as though she were floating. The three glasses of champagne she had consumed were having an effect on her. They must be. The man in the scarlet domino even spoke like a dream lover. But this was reality. This man was a stranger. Why then did she feel as though she had known him all her life? Even though she did not know him, she trusted him.

Her head lifted and she gazed up at him. His jaw was square, giving him an air of resolution. This man was not one to be trifled with. "Who are you?" she asked, not knowing why she was whispering, why she was trembling.

From behind his mask, his eyes glinted down at her.

His lips curved in an intimate smile. "You know who I am. I'm your fate. Better get used to it."

The words took her breath away. So it was true. These things really did happen. Her ardent heart had sent a silent message into the void, summoning her true lover, and he had come for her. Just like that. It was . . . absurd!

When they came to the last turn in the path, the river was before them. There was a dock, and a yacht ablaze with lights moored beside it. In a few swift strides, the man in the scarlet domino carried her across the gangplank, shouting out instructions to one of the crew who was standing by.

"Whose boat is this?"

"A friend's."

"I shouldn't be here. My uncle . . ."

"He knows you are with me."

She assimilated this in silence as he carried her below deck. The cabin in which he set her down was sumptuous. A huge feather bed seemed to fill the small space. Quickly averting her eyes, she encountered a small table set with two places. The scene was intimate. Seduction in capital letters was written all over it.

It was the act of removing his domino which loosened her tongue. "You must return me to my uncle at once." There was a catch in her voice. "This is . . . this is insane."

"Don't be frightened," he replied. The domino was thrown carelessly over the back of a chair. "First we eat. Then we talk. Everything will become clear to you in a little while. No, really! There is no cause for alarm. Your uncle knows that you are with me."

His eyes were hot on hers. When he came to tower

over her, she could not swallow, could not draw air into her lungs.

"You'll be more comfortable if you remove your domino," he said gently.

"No."

"Yes."

She didn't want to quarrel with him. Already she was more than halfway in love with him. But dream lover or no, he was going too fast for her. She simply shook her head and looked up at him miserably.

He laughed softly, mockingly, and bent to her. Emily clutched the folds of her domino more closely about her, but he only kissed her. Gentle and sweet it was, and more heady by far than champagne. She shivered with excitement. Casually, with one hand, he slipped the domino from her shoulders.

His harsh intake of breath brought her out of her languor. The tender light in his eyes had faded. He was staring at her as though he had been struck by lightning.

Chapter Five

Her gown was no more than a wisp of gauze. It clung to her lissome contours and hollows like a second skin. The neckline plunged to her nipples, barely concealing them. His eyes moved slowly over her length, absorbing the tantalizing glimpse of rose-tinted skin beneath the sheerness of the material.

She was every man's fantasy. She was his wife. Leon could not remember a time when he had been more furious. Suspicion burned into his brain. Only a woman of easy virtue would tart herself up like this. Only a woman of easy virtue would allow a stranger to take her on board his yacht without a murmur of protest.

The silence was charged with violence. Emily understood that it was her gown that had angered him. Madame Germaine had excelled herself. The garment gave the illusion that she was wearing nothing beneath it. She reached for her domino.

He was there before her. The domino was yanked out of her hands and flung into a corner. She inched away from him and fell against the bed. He crouched over her, his dark eyes glinting through the slits of his demi-mask. When his hands went to her hair, pulling the pins out, she gave a little gasp of fright.

His voice was low and frighteningly cordial, frighteningly familiar. "When I think I held off because you were not ready for this! When I think I was made to promise, even now, not to go too fast for you! God, you have made fools of us all."

Her mind was too paralyzed with fright to make sense of his words. Her eyes were fixed on his powerful hands. When they moved to untie the strings of her mask, she flinched away.

"Tears, sweetheart?" The calloused pads of his thumbs brushed over her cheeks. Her eyes went huge in her face when he brought one tear to his lips, moistening them in a gesture that was blatantly erotic. He shook his head. "Tears won't work with me. But you already know that."

"This is all a misunderstanding," she got out feebly. "I am not the sort of woman you think I am."

This was turning into a nightmare. It was her own fault. She had misread the man, imbuing him with heroic qualities that were only to be found in the imagination of a green girl. Her woman's intuition had failed her. This man was of a breed she had never encountered until tonight. He was a dangerous, untamed specimen.

Drawing on remnants of her dignity, she said, "My husband will k-kill you for this."

Her words shocked him into immobility. There was a moment of indecision. "Emily," he said, "you must have guessed who I am?"

Emily. That one word penetrated the fog in her head like a shaft of radiant sunshine. Her brain made instant connections and she went weak with relief. Laughing and sobbing at the same time, she said, "Oh, God, Leon, I've never been so glad to see anyone in my whole life. Where have you come from? How did you get here?" The next thought touched a spark to her temper. "What the devil do you mean by terrifying me half out of my wits? If this was meant to be a joke, I'm not laughing."

"It's no joke," he said, "and you'll observe I'm not laughing, either. I did not mean for it to be like this, but hell, who has a better right to take what you are offering than I?"

Without haste he removed his mask and then his coat. His long fingers quickly undid his neckcloth.

Emily was not panicked, but she was far from easy in her mind. With any other man, she would have recognized the sexual threat. But this was Leon. He had never wanted her in this way before. "Leon?" she said uncertainly.

His eyes were moving over her. "My God," he said, "my imagination did not do you justice. You are exquisite. But how many men have told you that?" The mockery turned into a more vicious emotion. "Take off the gown. I want to see you naked."

The words were so shocking that she was sure she must have misheard him. But when he pulled his shirt out of his waistband, every sense to her peril came alive. She could not believe it. And then it came to her. It was the gown. The gown made him think that she was any man's for the taking, and like any man, he was not too particular about which woman he chose to ease his carnal appetite. She could be anyone for all he cared.

She was too afraid to be angry. "This gown means nothing," she told him quickly, earnestly. "Don't you see, Leon, it was a prank, a lark? Sara's gown is almost identical. Aunt Zoë insisted that we were to wear our dominoes at all times. Look," she lifted the hem. "It's quite decent. It has a pink underskirt. Oh, God, Leon, why won't you believe me? It means nothing at all. I swear it."

He believed her. He grasped at once that this was a familiar pattern for Ladies Emily and Sara. From the time they were little more than infants, they were used to going their own way. And this little act of defiance had Sara's stamp upon it. Emily would never think to make herself more alluring for any male. She was too unaware. Oh, yes, he believed her. But he did not *wish* to believe her. His insane jealousy had shaken his control. There could be no turning back now.

He believed her. She could see it in his eyes, and in the release of tension across the breadth of his powerful shoulders as he shrugged out of his shirt and threw it aside. What she saw, she did not like. His masculinity was too stark, too intimidating. It made her aware of her own vulnerability in a way that she had never been aware of it before. She had always known that Leon Devereux was barely civilized. As each second passed, that thought became firmly fixed in her mind.

"Leon?" She was pleading with him now.

His tone was one she barely recognized. It was tender, and one he might have employed to calm a frightened child. "I've shown my hand before I meant to. There is no going back now. Try to understand, Emily, I've waited for this moment a long, long time. Give in to me and everything will be all right. Please, don't

100

make me hurt you." Turning his back on her, he doused the lantern.

From two small windows, moonlight bathed the interior, casting an unholy glow. Emily fought its strange power. Then suddenly, as though a cloud had covered the moon, everything in that small cabin was veiled in darkness. With quick stealth, she slipped from the bed. Though she had not made a sound, he was aware of her every movement. Fingers like the jaws of a steel trap curled around her shoulders. She twisted from him and fell backward onto the bed. Scathing words, annihilating words, gathered on her tongue. They were smothered on her lips as his mouth took hers in a fury of possession.

He held her effortlessly, passively absorbing her wild blows, using his weight to still her frantic movements. When she began to tire, he pulled back slightly.

"Emily," he said, and kissed her deeply, following her relentlessly as she tried to evade him. "This was inevitable. I am your husband. I have the right."

"No," she moaned against his mouth. She didn't want this, couldn't want this, not with him. She had hated him for years.

But she *did* want it. Her senses were flaming. It had nothing to do with Leon Devereux. It was a combination of circumstances. She'd been susceptible from the moment she'd alighted from her uncle's carriage and had sensed something magical in the air. And months before that, she had been possessed of a strange restlessness. She had wanted a man to love her, had craved a woman's fulfillment. But not with *him*. Never with *him*. Leon Devereux was reaping a harvest he had not sown.

He kissed her softly, then with rising hunger as he felt her responding. "Yes," he said. "Yes," and one hand curved around her breast in an intimate caress. The hardening of her nipple under his sensitive fingers brought a harsh sound of pleasure from his mouth. His dark head descended and Emily felt the moistness of his tongue and lips as they clamped down on her distended flesh. The intensity of her response stunned her. She was gasping, moaning, twisting restlessly, arching herself into him.

By the time he pulled back and stripped her of her garments, Emily was in a sensual daze. A moment later, light flooded the cabin. He had lit the lantern. As he stretched out beside her, naked now, too, he nuzzled her throat. "I had intended to spare your blushes, I can't help myself. I want to see you, Emily." He laughed deep in his throat. "Otherwise, I may think this is just another dream."

He didn't wait for her reply. His hands began a slow exploration, sweeping boldly from shoulder to breast, breast to thigh. "Emily!" he said. "My dear Emily!" and the rush of his breath was warm on her lips. "My imagination isn't a shadow on the reality!" He began to punctuate his words with small kisses. "Kiss me back. Touch me! Show me that you are a woman now."

He didn't wait for her to take the initiative. Bringing one hand to his chest, he splayed out her fingers, letting her feel the thundering of his heart beneath the warm skin and hard muscle. He studied her shadowed expression. When he heard the little catch of breath at the back of her throat, his eyes closed momentarily. Catching her close to him, he pressed his face into her hair and draped her arms around his neck. "Do you know how long I've waited to see you like this?"

"Leon." She could barely breathe. She was burning with fever. Her skin was so sensitive that each brush of his hands, each caress of his lips scorched her like flame. Her fingers curled in the hair at his nape, bringing his head up. "Leon . . ." she pleaded.

His mouth opened wide on hers, feeding on her passionate response to him. She was beyond resistance when he eased her legs apart. When his fingers found her and invaded the secret core of her femininity, the breath froze in her lungs.

Unbidden, horrible in its graphic intensity, a picture flashed into her brain. Leon and another woman, Lady Riddley, both naked on a bed, and his hand between the woman's thighs.

She moved so quickly, so adroitly, that he was taken completely off guard. Lashing out at him, sobbing, rolling, she scrambled off the bed.

"Emily!"

She was at the door, fumbling for the latch, before he came to his senses. One leap and he was off the bed and on her, swinging her round to face him. His fingers bit into the tender flesh of her arms. "Emily," he said softly. "What happened?" His hands kneaded the taut muscles of her shoulders. "My darling, did I do something to frighten you? Am I going too fast for you? It's all right. Come back to bed. I swear, I won't do anything you don't want me to do." There was a smile in his eyes.

The tears spilled over. "The dower house!" she said scathingly. "How could I have forgotten the dower house? You, and that woman, Lady . . . Lady . . ." The words died on her tongue as his strong fingers moved threateningly to the life pulse at her throat. She quailed before the violence that blazed out at her from his eyes.

"You cold, unfeeling little jade! You must spoil the moment! You must dredge up ancient history!" As she opened her mouth to vilify him, the pressure on his fingers closed alarmingly around her throat. "Don't! Don't dare breathe another woman's name at a time like this! Don't dare degrade this by bringing a third person into what concerns only the two of us. You and I, Emily. Your day of reckoning has been a long time in coming." He was breathing hard as if he had just run a race.

"My uncle will see you dead if you lay a finger on me," she spat at him.

"Your uncle's wishes don't come into it. I am your husband. Oh, what's the use! When have you ever listened to reason?"

She wasn't given time to think. Bending, he slipped an arm under her knees and swung her high against his chest. His kiss was savage, and devoid of the tenderness he had lavished on her only a short while before. She cried out when he flung her on the bed. He stood above her, infinitely masculine, infinitely menacing. As he came down beside her, blind panic seized her. She fought him like a cornered wild thing.

He subdued her struggles as easily as if she had been a child. Seduction was no longer his object. He was claiming her, conquering, demanding her abject submission. Before long, she was held down by cruel, uncaring hands, her body heaving in helpless defiance. Closing her eyes, she resigned herself for the final humiliating violation.

He sensed the exact moment she had brought herself to accept him. His lips moved over her face. "Emily?" he murmured, her name no more than a breath of a sound. "Emily?" and there was an age-old masculine plea in his voice.

She wasn't going to give in to him. He didn't deserve it. And then his mouth found the peak of one sensitive breast and an unwilling moan of pleasure slipped from her throat. Leon's head lifted. His nostrils flared. He absorbed the flush mantling her face and breasts, the quivering lips, the pleasure-dazed eyes.

"Yes," he said fiercely, exultantly, and, pressing her shoulders into the mattress, he imposed his body upon hers.

The pain of his possession was intolerable. Emily could not cry out. Just to breathe was agony. Fresh tears started to her eyes. She wasn't to know that, for her sake, he had forced himself to a control he could barely maintain. Convulsively, her hands clenched and unclenched on the bunched muscles on his shoulders. "Leon . . . Leon," she breathed brokenly, trying to convey her torment, trying to shame him into releasing her.

His mouth captured hers, swallowing her small moans of distress. "Soon, my love, soon the pain will pass," he soothed.

He was right. The searing pain was suddenly gone, as if it had never existed. She sighed, and her hands unclenched, slipping from his shoulders to his waist. Beneath his tender ministration, her muscles went lax. Sudden fury engulfed her. The eyes she raised to his flashed with violet fire.

"Later," he said, laughing softly. "Chastise me later."

He eased deeper into her body, sheathing himself to the hilt, submerging her in a storm of sensation. She caught her breath. She could no more hold back her response to him than she could turn back the tide. Nor would he have permitted it. He was unrelenting in his determined assault on her every feminine defense. Clamping her body tightly to his, he took her plunging into a world of passion where nothing existed but the demanding clamor of their senses and the hurtling ride toward rapture. His hoarse cry was only a breath behind her own surprised cry of ecstasy. Holding her to him, kissing her feverishly, with hard, violent thrusts, he emptied himself deep in her body.

She awakened with a start. Though there was no lantern burning, she knew exactly where she was and who was bending over her.

His lips brushed her ear then he bit gently into the soft flesh of one earlobe. "You slept through the fireworks," he whispered in that lazily teasing tone which never failed to annoy her. "I'm glad you are not going to sleep through this."

His hand curved around one sleep-warmed breast, kneading it gently. The pulse at her throat beat so rapidly, so strongly, that she could not draw her next breath. She sensed the sudden leap of his passion as he became aware of her arousal. She tried to draw away.

"Leon . . ." she said weakly, meaning to say something of grave import. Her mind could not seem to form one sensible thought.

He turned her on her side, facing him, and drew her left leg to lie across his flanks. She murmured something incoherent which he ignored. His teeth nipped the sensitive swell of her underlip, and her lips parted of their own volition. The invitation was instantly accepted. His tongue slipped inside, learning her intimately. Tentatively, she touched her tongue to his. He went perfectly still, then emitted a soft sound before driving deeper into her mouth. The embrace seemed to melt her very bones. The blood was pounding through her veins. When he pressed his hand to the secret place between her legs and slipped a finger inside, her shoulder jerked up from the pillows.

"Easy," he said, in that same amused drawl. "Easy," and he gently pushed her back into the depths of the feather mattress.

Her hands were on his shoulders. He brought first one then the other to his lips and kissed each passionately on the open palm before drawing them down the length of his body. He smoothed her fingers around his swollen sex. When he removed his hand, so did she. Laughing softly, he recaptured it.

"Touch me," he said in a strangely pleading tone, and he moved her fingers in a voluptuous caress, showing her what he wanted.

There was a moment when her mind resisted, leaping back in time to another scene: Leon Devereux in the dower house, stripping out of his clothes. Before the picture could form in her brain, as though her thoughts were transparent, he caught her to him, pressing his face into the hollow of her throat.

"I won't let you think of that other time," he said fiercely. "This is different. I told you it would be." She was turning her head away, trying to set him at a distance. She gasped when his fingers bit into her shoulders, dragging her round. "Once and for all, we are going to exorcise the past. When you think of me like this," he forced her hand between their bodies, compelling her to accept the hard, silky length of him, "you will remember only the pleasure we shared and you will relive every second of it in your mind."

He rolled from the bed. Emily pulled herself to her elbows, her ears and eyes straining through the darkness to make out what he was doing. A moment later, a light flared as he lit the lantern. He moved to the small windows and closed the curtains. Her heart jarred against her ribs when he spun to face her.

Now that she had time to observe him, she saw that Leon Devereux was all male. His skin was tanned. From throat to groin, silky black hair grew in profusion. He was as sleek as a panther and twice as lethal.

Clutching the bedsheet under her chin, swallowing, she said, "Wh-what are you going to do?"

There wasn't a shred of modesty in him as he came to stand at the foot of the bed. "Listen," he said. "What do you hear?"

She did not know what game he was playing and she shook her head nervously.

In a voice that was charged with tension, he said, "Tell me what you hear."

This time, Emily really listened. When he rested one knee against the mattress, she said quickly, "I hear the water, the river, as it laps against the sides of the boat."

"What else do you hear?"

"I hear . . . you . . . breathing, as though . . ."

"As though what, Emily?"

"As though you were angry."

"I'm not angry. I hear you breathing, too. Are *you* angry?"

108

"No."

Her quick denial brought a flashing smile to his lips. "When I am near you, my breathing always quickens. It's been like this for years. Didn't you know that?"

She shook her head.

"And when you are near me, it's the same for you. I've known that for years, too."

All this talk of breathing was having a peculiar effect on her. She wasn't breathing. She was panting. With restless fingers, she combed long tendrils of fine hair back from her face.

"Now tell me what you see," he said.

It was a relief not to have to look at him. Quickly averting her eyes, she glanced around the cabin. She noted the table set with fine crystal and silverware for the late supper which had never materialized. The walls and windows were draped in gold silk; the bed cover and upholstery on the chairs and sofa were white velvet. A handsome rosewood dresser inlaid with ivory stood between the two small windows. The interior was luxurious. The yacht was a pleasure craft and obviously the property of some rich man.

"Well?"

Obedient to the command in his tone, she described the cabin.

"You will remember this cabin. In fact, it will be indelibly impressed on your mind, as it will be on mine also."

The remark was obscure and Emily let it pass without comment.

"What else do you see?" He straightened, and stood with hands on lean flanks, a grin on his face.

Emily moistened her lips. "That's all there is."

"If I'm not mistaken," he said, enjoying her discomfort immensely, "there is a man in this cabin, Emily."

There was no way she was going to describe Leon Devereux without his clothes. Setting her jaw, she looked at him with reproachful eyes.

"Shy, Emily? Then I shall take the initiative, shall I, and tell you what *I* see?" He leaned against the bedpost with unconcerned animal grace. "I see a woman men would kill for to have in their possession." The words were electrifying. Emily's eyes widened even further. His smile was ironic. "Don't you believe me?" he asked whimsically.

"Don't be absurd," she said. "I'm just an ordinary girl."

Laughter glinted in his eyes. "I've sometimes wondered if that's what Helen of Troy said when her husband besieged Troy with his Greek armies. She mistook her husband's character, you see, and so did her suitor. They learned a hard lesson."

Though his manner was pleasant, the words held an underlying threat. Emily absorbed it in wide-eyed silence. Helen of Troy, as far as she knew, had never had an understanding with her husband, whereas Leon had promised that their marriage would he annulled at an appropriate time.

"But I am digressing," he went on when it was obvious that Emily meant to preserve her silence. "I see a woman who is the embodiment of everything I admire in a woman. I've wanted to possess you for a long, long time. Now it's your turn. Tell me what you see."

Her eyes traveled over his naked length. His virility was potent and completely unnerved her. Her eyes fell away. "Leon," she said weakly, not understanding why

110

he should be so cruel to her.

He came to her at once. Cradling her in his arms, he said, "Emily, don't look at me like that. I'm only a man—your husband. You must never be afraid of me."

One hand tipped her head back, forcing her to look into his eyes. "It's not me you fear, Emily. Don't you know that yet? What you fear, what you are fighting, is in your own mind. If you were to give yourself to me without reservation, you would come to see the truth of my words."

His gaze moved down to her mouth, then to her breasts, which quivered with her quickened breathing. The nipples were dark and engorged.

His eyes flew to hers. Holding her gaze, he took one hand and pressed it against his chest. Slowly, deliberately, he lowered it. Beneath the sensitive pads of her fingers, she felt the warm, smooth flesh, the graze of coarse hair, powerful masculine muscles, tensed and straining.

Her hands lifted as she sensed the tightly leashed control. If he wanted to, this man could really hurt her.

"No," he groaned, intuitively grasping her thought. "Feel how much power you have over me."

He guided her hand to his jutting sex, refusing to allow her to draw back. His eyes closed. His head was thrown back. With a dawning awareness of her own power, she watched the rise and fall of his chest as he dragged air into his lungs. His nostrils were quivering. His mouth was open. When he released her hand, she did not draw it away as she had done before.

He opened his eyes. "Now kiss me," he said, "the way I kissed you," and he brought his lips to within an inch of hers.

Hesitantly, she slipped her tongue between his teeth. He deepened the embrace, kissing her avidly, his hands urging her closer, positioning her till she was half sprawled over him. His mouth descended, lingering at the hollow of her throat, the slope of her shoulder, closing hotly over the peak of one breast. Her breathing became labored, and her body began to shake.

Suddenly, he rolled with her, and the soft mattress was at her back. His kisses were fervid, demanding a response from her. Moaning with need, she pressed herself against him.

"Open your legs for me," he breathed thickly.

When she obeyed, he pulled back, disengaging himself from her arms. She cried out in protest, reaching for him.

He knelt between her thighs, desire blazing from him as he looked down at her. "When you think of me with a woman, this is what I want you to remember." Her eyes were closed. "Look at me," he said harshly, then more gently, *"Look* at me."

Her eyes were bewildered with passion as she tried to focus on him.

"Look at me," he repeated, unrelenting in his determination to wipe the ugly memory of the dower house from her mind. When he saw that he had her attention, he kissed one knee, then the other. "Look at me, crazy with wanting you. Look at you, open to me, inviting me to enter your body. Think of this cabin. Think of the sounds, the scents, of our lovemaking. You and me, Emily. That is what I wish you to remember."

For a long moment, his eyes held hers in a heated, passionate caress. Then he arched his body, taking her

112

mouth with his as he slowly filled her with the pulsating heat of his masculinity.

As he moved above her, the sound of their breathing became harsher; their movements became rhythmic. He whispered love words. She emitted soft cries of surrender, arching her throat, giving herself up to the demands of his body. As the shattering release engulfed her, tears came from nowhere and spilled over, drenching his neck. Afterward, when she was still quivering in his arms trying to get her breath back, he turned her into him, removing each heedless tear with the tip of his tongue. His gentleness, his tenderness, was her undoing. She fell asleep weeping into his throat.

Chapter Six

She awakened to a rush of unfamiliar sensations and scents. Whimpering, she fought herself free of a tangle of bedclothes and dragged herself into a sitting position. The curtains at the windows were pulled back, admitting an unwelcome radiance. Soft footfalls sounded overhead and the muffled cries of rivermen echoed over the Thames. The boat was in motion. She had been abducted!

With a little cry of alarm, she swung her legs over the edge of the bed, then quickly pulled the covers up to her chin as the door opened to admit her husband. He stood on the threshold, smiling, holding a mug in one hand. He wore no jacket, and the white lawn shirt was open at the throat, showing a column of tanned skin. His black pantaloons clung to his long, muscular legs. One comprehensive glance conveyed a multitude of impressions. A panther, she thought, and one who had gorged himself on his kill. Leon Devereux was inordinately pleased with himself. She missed the trace of wariness in his eyes.

"I would like to know where you are taking me," she said, trying for dignity, wincing inwardly at the betraying wobble in her voice.

"You'll feel better after you have bathed and have had something to eat," he replied.

For some reason she took exception to his cordial tone. "And you should know, I suppose?"

"Meaning?"

"Meaning . . ." She caught the look of amused comprehension, and concluded crossly, "Oh, never mind."

"No, I am not in the habit of abducting virgins and having my way with them," he said cheerfully, and deposited the mug on the small table. Ignoring her sullen look, he crossed to one of the draped walls and pulled back the curtain to reveal a door. "Milady's bath awaits," he said. "You'll find everything you need to be comfortable on the other side of this door."

She was combing the long tangles of wayward hair back from her face in a characteristic gesture that hit him in the stomach with all the impact of a kick from a horse. He had noticed that when Emily was confused, her hands invariably went to her hair, rearranging it whether or not it was necessary. This morning, it definitely needed to be rearranged. His doing. He had to bite down on a smile. His wife was in no mood to appreciate a show of unabashed masculine gloating.

She was unsure, off balance. Good. At long last, Lady Emily Devereux was looking at her husband with feminine awareness, and not as though he were a maggot she had discovered in an apple from which she had just taken a bite.

He didn't give her time to think. Crossing to the bed, he pressed a long, possessive kiss on her surprised lips. "Drink your coffee," he said. "Bathe and dress. You'll find your clothes in the dresser. We shall talk over breakfast."

Everything about him annoyed her. She didn't like the way he whistled as he left the cabin. She didn't like his cheery air. She didn't like the way he looked at her, as though he owned her. And she most particularly did not like the way he had remembered that she always started the day with a cup of freshly brewed coffee.

In a flurry of motion, with only a sheet to cover her, she dragged herself to the door he had indicated. The aroma of coffee was irresistible. Swiping the mug from the table, she stomped into the bathing room.

The room was almost half as large as the cabin she had shared with Leon. Against one wall was the ubiquitous commode, but one so ornate, so opulent that it might have been the throne of some Arabian sheik. Two doors gave entrance into the room, one from her cabin and the other from the gangway. The tub had already been filled with water. The fragrance was unmistakable. Gardenia, *her* fragrance.

She stayed submerged in the bathwater for a long time, sipping her coffee, putting her thoughts in order. Men, she decided, were perverse, vexing creatures. They were no better than animals. Leon loved Sara. That did not stop him from taking any other passable female who happened to be available. She gritted her teeth, remembering how she had contributed to her own downfall. She had longed for a woman's fulfillment, but what she had wanted was *love,* not this storm of the senses that did not involve the finer feelings. And love did not come into it. She had hated Leon Devereux for years. That could not alter. Then why had she accepted him as her lover last night?

The answer came to her almost as soon as her

thoughts had formed the question. It seemed that men and women, at least *some* women, were not so very different after all. Lady Riddley had said as much. *Men and women have needs,* Lady Riddley had said. It was the truth. It must be. But there was one major difference between the sexes. Females had more gumption, more willpower. She might lust after Leon Devereux, but that did not mean that she would give in to her baser nature. Now that she knew she was capable of experiencing the most rapturous pleasure, she would be on her guard to prevent a repetition of last night.

For a full half minute, she tried to console herself with that thought. She was vigorously soaping her knees when a picture flashed into her brain. Leon, pressing kisses to those knees, his face flushed with passion and his husky words blatantly arousing her.

"Look at me, crazy with wanting you. Look at you, open to me, inviting me to enter your body."

She bolted from the bath as if she had discovered a snake in it. Shivering, shaking, she wrapped herself in a towel and sat on the lid of the commode, trying to compose herself. This would never do. She must forget about last night. She must remember that Leon Devereux looked upon all women as fair game.

Closing her eyes, she cast her mind back in time to the night she had surprised Leon in the dower house with Lady Riddley. Her recall was vivid, as it should be. The picture had been one that had haunted her for years.

Leon was crouched over the woman. She was moaning and panting. His breathing was labored. Muscles clenched and rippled across the breadth of his shoulders. His hand was between the woman's thighs. The woman was . . . Emily shot to her feet. *She* was the woman on the bed. *She* was the woman moaning and panting, urging him to take her, just as she had done last night. Damn Leon Devereux! What had he done to her?

A sharp rap on the door brought her back to the present with a start. "Emily? What's keeping you? Come and eat. Your breakfast is getting cold."

What was he up to? What game was he playing? She squared her shoulders. There was only one way to find out.

She was every inch the daughter of a marquess when she swept into the small cabin. Her dignity suffered a small setback, however, when her husband plucked the damp towel from her and wrapped her in her own brocade dressing gown as if she were a child. Quickly belting it, she obediently accepted the chair he indicated. Grilled kippers and kidney. Her favorite. It seemed that there was no end to the man's gall.

"Your favorites," he said, seating himself on the other side of the table, his eyes alight with suppressed laughter.

If she had not been at starvation's door, she told herself, she would have politely declined his offer of breakfast. But having forgone supper the night before, she could not resist the aromas which tickled her nostrils. For some few minutes, no words were spoken as she ate with relish. Leon, as was his habit, partook sparingly of breakfast.

"More coffee?"

She nodded, glancing into his eyes, then quickly looking away as he refilled her cup from a silver coffeepot. Leon Devereux was as smug as a cat who had

118

swallowed the canary. He was gloating and she could not bear it.

When the pangs of hunger were satisfied, she delicately touched her napkin to her lips and placed it carefully on the table. Only then did she speak. "I should like to know," she said, icily calm, "why I am being abducted."

"Abducted?" His eyebrows shot up. "There are no locks on the doors. In any event, you were willing enough last night when I brought you here."

In the cold light of day, the girl she had been last night was an enigma to her. She couldn't begin to explain about the odd mood that had overtaken her, or her even more bewildering attraction to the stranger in the scarlet domino. She made do with a half-truth. "I didn't know it was you," she said. "I thought you were someone else."

His compelling gaze held hers when she would have looked away. Leon wasn't gloating now, and the thought wasn't as gratifying as she had expected it to be.

"William Addison," he said.

In spite of his lazy pose, every instinct warned her to proceed with extreme caution. "I take it you received Sara's letter."

"I did."

"Then you must know about William and me."

"What is there to know?" He regarded her quizzically over the rim of his coffee cup.

She took a deep, shaky breath. "William has asked me to marry him."

His lashes drooped to half-mast. "It may have escaped your notice," he said, his voice very dry, "that you already have a husband."

She stared at him in amazement. "Husband? You are not my husband. We have never lived together. The marriage has never been . . ." Her eyes went wide as comprehension dawned.

"Precisely," he said, nodding. "Last night changes everything."

Her mouth opened and closed, and her bosom began to heave. Anger was an emotion that rarely troubled Emily. Only Leon Devereux had the uncanny knack of testing a temper she would have sworn she did not possess. Eyes flashing, she said, "You promised me an annulment. You know you did, and I am holding you to that promise."

"A promise that was made under duress."

His reasonable tone only exacerbated Emily's sense of ill-usage. "Duress?" she demanded incredulously. "What does that mean? No one forced you to make that promise."

"You did. Don't you remember? You refused to marry me until you had my assurance that the marriage would be in name only, and that it would be dissolved at some date in the distant future. You wouldn't listen to reason. What else could I do? I had to make that promise, if only for your own good. You were too young to understand it then. But now that you are a grown woman, you must see that I had no choice."

She pressed a hand to her throbbing temples as the recollection of that night and its aftermath came back to her. Whatever the truth of the matter, her uncle had told her, there were witnesses who would swear that she had been dishonored. There was only one way to set things to rights and that was for Leon and her to marry at once.

She had been distraught that night, but not too distraught to realize that marriage to Leon Devereux was the last thing she wanted. Leon Devereux would make her life wretched. Social ruin, so she had passionately averred to her guardian, was infinitely to be preferred. It was then that Leon had begged some time alone with her and, over her protests, Uncle Rolfe had acquiesced.

Leon had said many things to her, even going so far as to touch upon the sordid episode in the dower house. Judith Riddley meant nothing to him, he had sworn. The woman had thrown herself at his head and, in a weak moment, he had taken what she was offering. Emily need never fear that he would use her as he had used Judith Riddley.

Even that promise had not the power to persuade her. It was then that he had gone one step further. Their marriage would be in name only. One day, she would meet someone who was worthy of her love. When that day arrived, the marriage would be annulled. In the meantime, Leon must return to New York to take up his life there. It was that more than anything which had calmed her. Husband or no, Leon Devereux would be thousands of miles away. There was no reason not to accept his assurances. Leon wanted the marriage no more than she herself.

In an anguished whisper, she said, "Why have you done this? Why have you gone back on your promise?"

He regarded her for a long moment and then said calmly, "Emily, you are not a green girl now. You must see that an annulment was never a possibility. Your name would be bandied about in every salon in Mayfair. Your reputation would be in tatters. No one would believe your innocence. To have our marriage annulled would hardly be a kindness to you."

"I should be the judge of that," she snapped.

With an exaggerated sigh, he reached for the coffee-pot and replenished his own empty cup. Emily strove to hold on to her tongue. Leon Devereux was not a man to be pushed. If there was any way out of their present difficulties, it behooved her not to antagonize him.

She tried a different tack. "Leon," she said appealingly, managing a small smile, "I love William. He loves me. What do we care for what the world thinks? I promise you, an annulment will make no difference to him."

Though he made no overt movement, she could sense the violence in Leon. She moistened her dry lips.

Finally, he said, "You love William Addison?"

She nodded, but not very vigorously.

"Then how do you explain last night?"

"Last night?" She said the words carefully.

"Yes, last night." He waited for her to say something, to give him a clue to what she was feeling. When she remained wide-eyed and silent, he went on. "How will you explain last night to William Addison? How do you explain it to yourself?"

Her color heightened. Her eyes slid away from his. In a stifled tone, she said, "You are a man. You must understand these things better than I do."

He arched one brow. "Must I?"

"Uncle Rolfe explained it all to me when we married, after you went away. Something to do with a carnal appetite. I did not understand it then. I do now."

"Carnal appetite? That's all it was? Emily, there are none so blind as those who will not see. I know you better than you know yourself. No, I won't quarrel with you. But I wish you would tell me how you are going to explain last night to William Addison."

At her look of shocked mortification, he chuckled. "On second thought, don't bother to tell me. The question has become academic. Our marriage was consummated. From now on, I don't want you anywhere near Addison."

In spite of her uneasiness, her temper flared. "This has gone far enough! Why are you toying with me like this? What is it you really want, Leon?"

The gravity of his tone underscored the quiet words. "I'm thirty-one years old. It's time I settled down. I want a wife, a real home, and children. Is that so very hard to understand?"

"You are not the marrying kind," she said, not taunting, not sneering, merely stating the obvious. "You would never have married me if you had not been forced into it. I just can't see you tying yourself down to one woman. But you wouldn't, would you? No, your kind likes to have his cake and eat it, too."

At the scathing words, his expression hardened. "Thank you," he said. "But your opinion of my character can hardly matter to me. You don't know me, Emily. In the last five years, we have rarely been in each other's company, and on those few occasions when we were together, you could hardly bring yourself to be civil to me."

For a moment, she thought that she might have hurt him, but almost immediately she discarded that impression. Her good opinion had never mattered to

Leon. Even so, she was guilty of rank impertinence. It was worse than impertinence. Her thoughtless words carried a sting that was meant to wound.

Squirming in her place, in as contrite a tone as she could manage, she said, "I beg your pardon, Leon. That was inexcusable. You are right. I really don't know you very well. Please say that you forgive me."

His lips curved. "I like to see you humble," he said. "No, don't spoil it by flying into a temper. It's a new experience for me. You are usually such a spitfire."

"I wasn't a spitfire last night," she contradicted, then colored hotly from throat to hairline when she realized that she had spoken her thoughts aloud. "Forget about last night," she said hurriedly. "We both know it means nothing. Think about the future. *Your* future. Leon, if we pretend that last night never happened, we could still procure an annulment. Then you would be free to marry . . ." She almost said Sara but quickly amended it to ". . . the lady of your choice."

"You are my choice, Emily. And that's an end of it."

He was so icily matter-of-fact that Emily drew her dressing gown more tightly about her as though his words had chilled her. Her eyes searched his face. "Leon . . ." she began with deliberate patience, "listen to me . . ."

"No, *you* listen to *me*. We are married. The sooner you get used to the idea, the better it will be for you. I am not your uncle, so don't think to try and get round me. Perhaps it's not the kind of marriage that either of us would have wanted. But it is a marriage of sorts. If you would give it half a chance, I think we could make something of it. Last night proved that. Emily, why won't you admit that you are not so indifferent to me as

124

you pretend? Meet me halfway. Let's agree to bury the past and start fresh. What do you say?"

There was a strange wistfulness in her eyes, and Leon found that he was waiting for her answer with bated breath. As suddenly as the look had come upon her, it was gone.

"I'm not interested in the sort of marriage you describe," she said. "I believe in love, Leon. *Love*. I want the kind of marriage that Uncle Rolfe and Aunt Zoë have. If I can't have that, I don't want anything. I don't want second best."

He shrugged. "So, I'm to be cast in the role of autocrat? Though it's not a role I relish, so be it. Your choice, Emily, not mine. Remember that." Slowly, he rose to his feet and crossed to the door. "Better get dressed," he said. "You'll find a selection of your gowns in the dresser. We'll be docking at Westminster Pier before long."

She called his name before he had made his exit. "What are my gowns doing here? I don't understand. Where were you taking me? Why did you abduct me? For heaven's sake, tell me what is going on."

"If things had been different, we would have been cruising the Thames on a belated honeymoon. Somehow, the idea has lost its appeal."

He made for the bow of the boat and stood with his hands gripping the rails wishing that he was gripping William Addison's throat and throttling the life out of him. Anger was an emotion Leon thoroughly detested. It served no useful purpose. More often than not, it clouded a man's judgment. And the last thing he could afford in his dealings with Emily was for anger to get the better of him.

Until Addison's name came into the conversation, he had felt on top of the world, convinced that winning Emily was going to be so much easier than he had anticipated. He was halfway persuaded that the battle was already won. How could he help gloating a little? Then she had said those three little words, and had deflated him like a burst balloon.

I love William, she had calmly told him. It couldn't be true. Emily could not have surrendered so sweetly to *him* if she were in love with another man. He let that thought revolve in his mind, coming at it from all sides. By degrees, he got his anger under control. There were women who could give their bodies for the pleasuring, but Emily wasn't one of them. She was a romantic. She had too much respect for herself. She *must* feel something for him. It wasn't a shade compared to what he felt for her, but it was a beginning. He could build on it if only she would let her guard down, let him get close to her.

As he stood absently looking out over the river he reflected that this time yesterday, he would not have believed that he could have come so far with her. They were lovers. She had given *him* the gift of her innocence, not Addison. That gave him an advantage over all challengers, including Addison.

He stayed by the rail lost in reverie for some few minutes. Coming to himself, smiling whimsically at some private joke, he went below to his own cabin.

Emily heard his footfalls as he passed her door, and her heart beat a little faster. She didn't know what to make of her rioting emotions. She knew one thing, though. She was seeing Leon Devereux in a new light. He wasn't merely Aunt Zoë's hateful younger brother

126

and the bane of her life. He was a virile male. He was a passionate, tender lover. He was . . .

The sudden throb at her nipples froze her train of thought. Gingerly, she touched her fingers to them. They were as hard as little pebbles and as sensitive as a patch of sunburn. Groaning, she palmed her breasts, intending to ease the ache. Without volition her mind made electrifying connections: Leon, the night before, his dark head against her white breast, her fingers tangled in his crisp hair, holding him to her as he . . .

She felt as weak as a kitten. Leaning against the bedpost for support, she strove to subdue the sensations which threatened to overwhelm her. Think. She must think.

Leon had consummated the marriage. He wanted to ruin their chances of an annulment. Why?

She was prepared to believe him when he said that he wanted a more settled life. Most men, even the roués, seemed to set great store by having heirs to follow in their footsteps. Men wanted sons. What she could not believe was Leon's reasons for choosing *her* for his consort. She did not believe him when he said that an annulment would tarnish her reputation, and even if it were true, such things meant little to her — or to Leon for that matter. She didn't know why she knew this, she just did. Leon Devereux did not give a fig for the good opinion of any man. No. There was another reason, a more devious one, for his decision to hold his wife to a marriage that neither of them wanted. For the moment, none came to mind, and she soon gave up that fruitless avenue of thought to concentrate on how she might extricate herself from her predicament.

Her best course, she decided, was to appeal to her

Uncle Rolfe. He would help her if she played her cards right. And if that route failed, she would appeal to William.

At the thought of William, another groan escaped her lips. She didn't know how she was going to explain last night to William. And she must explain it. She couldn't hide it from him. She didn't *want* to hide it from him. Between true lovers, there must be no deceit. Their hearts, their minds, must always be open to each other. William would be hurt. He would be angry, and rightly so. Oh, God, how could she possibly find the words to explain something she herself did not understand? If only she could say that Leon had forced himself upon her. But it hadn't been like that. Not really. There was a language that went beyond words, and Leon had read her correctly. And later, during that long night, she had not tried to deny him, no, not once. If only it had been William who had taken her and not Leon!

That thought led to another. William as her lover. Closing her eyes, she tried to imagine William kissing her, caressing her intimately, as Leon had done.

Look at me, crazy with wanting you. Look at you . . . .

With a little cry of anguish, she flung herself to one of the open windows. Images of Leon making love to her were burned into her brain, burned into her body. She would never be rid of them. She would never be rid of him.

When the door to her cabin opened, she spun round to face the intruder. Leon was framed in the doorway, as though he had answered her silent summons.

"Charming," he said, his first glance taking in the high-waisted, spotted muslin morning dress she was wearing. "It occurred to me that you might require some assistance with the buttons at the back of your gown." He slanted her a long, sardonic look. "I'll act as lady's maid for you, if you like."

She stared at him as though she were seeing a ghost. Her fist was pressed to her mouth, her breathing was shallow. Catlike, his gaze narrowing on her, searchingly, assessingly. Awareness flared in his eyes the instant before he pounced.

"No," she moaned, struggling with him.

His lips captured hers in a searing kiss. Her head fell back, arched over his arm. He deepened the embrace, opening her mouth wide to the intimate intrusion of his tongue. His hands were moving over her back, molding her to his hard length, lifting her into the masculine arousal. Her body began to shake. His kisses became hotter, wetter, more demanding as he sensed the excitement building in her. Sobbing his name, she twined her arms around his neck and returned his kisses with equal ardor.

Leon's heart was thundering painfully in his chest as he backed her to the bed. His breathing was thick and strident. He had never experienced such a sudden storm of passion for any woman.

There wasn't time for preliminaries. She was ready for him, and he was in a fever of need. He swept aside her skirts and deftly disposed of her drawers. Releasing himself from his trousers, he pressed into her. Holding her to him, showing her the rhythm he wanted, he rode her to a fast and furious finish.

They lay for long minutes, panting in the aftermath of spent passion. Under his smothering weight, Emily grew restless. He eased away slightly to adjust their clothing, then pulled back to gauge her expression. She could hardly bear to look him in the eye.

"Emily?" he said, bringing her head up, anxiously scanning her face. She looked adorably guilty.

"I . . . I don't know what came over me," she said faintly.

He laughed softly, sinking his lips into hers in a long, lingering kiss. "Don't you? I've awakened you to passion. Your body craves mine, as mine craves yours."

"You make it sound like a sickness."

"That's exactly what it is—a chronic sickness."

"Oh, God!" she groaned. "I wish there were a cure for it."

There was a moment of silence before he threw out carelessly. "There is a cure for it."

Her eyebrows lifted. "There is?"

Rolling to his back, he stared at the ceiling overhead. "Like all cures, it's almost as bad as the disease."

She raised to one elbow and gazed down at him. "Well?"

"Well what?"

"Well, what's the cure? Aren't you going to tell me?"

"Oh . . . you wouldn't care for it."

"Leon?" she said threateningly.

He looked at her through the spikes of his long lashes. His fingertips traced a lazy path up one bare arm to her shoulder. "We sate ourselves on each other," he said quietly. "That is the only way to burn out a passion such as ours."

Whimpering, twisting away from him, she pulled herself up, hugging her knees to her chest.

"Emily?" He rose at her back, cupping her shoulders, his open mouth slowly brushing her nape. "What

130

is it? What have I said?"

She shrugged off his hands. "I may be stupid, Leon, but I'm not *that* stupid."

"One day. Give me one more day in this setting," he said urgently. "That's all I ask."

He was pleading with her, and she found herself yielding, as though it was the most natural thing in the world to want to please him. "Then what?" she said, not knowing what she was saying.

"Then we return to your uncle's house. Emily, what difference can one more day make? What difference can it make if we are here or there? Darling, just one more day. This was supposed to be our honeymoon. I want to love you. You want me to. You know you want me to. You are ready for love. You've already surrendered to me, not once, but many times. Emily, you are my wife. Lie with me. Come lie with me."

His voice could have charmed the birds from the trees. Soft, soothing, mesmerizing, the sound of it flowed over her, flooding her with a mindless, sensuous inertia. When his hands brushed her shoulders, easing the gown off, she made no move to prevent him. He turned her to him, pressing her into the depths of the mattress. Only when he was satisfied that she was accepting him did he begin to divest himself of his own garments.

Chapter Seven

When Emily came face-to-face with her sister on the stairs of their uncle's townhouse, the enormity of what she had done struck her with nerve-shattering remorse. Sara loved Leon. Emily had never made any bones about her dislike for the man. Sara trusted her and she had betrayed that trust. Conscience-stricken, she quickened her steps as she made for her chamber. Sara was hard at her heels.

"Where are Aunt Zoë and Uncle Rolfe?" asked Emily for something to say.

She stationed herself in front of her cheval mirror, her attention riveted on her reflection as she removed the pins from her bonnet.

"Uncle Rolfe is out and Aunt Zoë is entertaining some ladies in the drawing room. I was on my way downstairs when you came in. Emily, where is Leon?"

Emily chanced a quick look at her sister. Sara's expression was unclouded. She seemed almost exuberant. The weight of Emily's transgressions pressed more heavily on her heart.

"He will be along directly," she said, not liking the little catch in her breath. "He has gone round to the

132

stables, something to do with a mare he purchased for his stud in America."

"I told Uncle Rolfe and Aunt Zoë that it wouldn't work," said Sara, and she did a little pirouette in the center of the floor, then fell against the bed in a fit of the giggles. "You've only been gone two days."

"What wouldn't work?"

"A honeymoon between you and Leon." Sara smiled commiseratingly. "You two are like cat and dog together. You always were. I tried to tell Uncle Rolfe, but he wouldn't listen. But I was right, wasn't I, Emily? Otherwise you would not be here now. You would be with Leon on your honeymoon." She rolled to her stomach and looked up at Emily with a mock-sorrowful expression. "Oh, my dear, was it so very bad? I've been in fear and trembling, wondering which of you would first give in and stoop to murdering the other." The thought set off a gale of laughter which she did nothing to suppress.

"It didn't quite come to that," said Emily in a constricted tone. She had moved to her wardrobe and was hunting for a hatbox in which to place her bonnet. "Though I have a few choice words I would like to say to our guardian when I see him."

"I don't blame you. What a trick to play on you! Aunt Zoë was fit to be tied when you could not be found. You would have laughed yourself silly if you had been there. I have never seen her in such a taking. She was raging. I was weeping. Uncle Rolfe was properly chastened by the time we returned home from Sir Geoffrey's, I can tell you."

"I'm glad Aunt Zoë was not part of the deception," said Emily. She felt miserable. She wanted to throw herself at Sara's feet and beg her forgiveness. With great concentration, she positioned her bonnet in its hatbox, then became involved in rearranging various articles of clothing in her wardrobe. She removed a gown and held it up to the light.

"Well?" Sara slipped from the bed and moved to one of the chairs beside the empty grate.

"Well what?"

"Tell me what happened. Where did you go? What did you do? What did you find to talk about?"

Emily laid the gown on the bed. "My gown is travel-stained," she said by way of explanation. "I should wash up and then change it."

Sara did not take the hint. "No need to send for Perkins," she said, referring to the abigail they shared with their aunt. "That would ruin our privacy. I'll act as lady's maid."

In a matter of minutes, Emily was down to her underthings. She moved to the washstand and poured cold water from a china pitcher into its matching basin and wondered desperately how many more tasks she could invent to delay the dreadful moment when she must look her sister in the eye and confess the awful truth.

She was patting herself dry with a linen towel when, without warning, Leon walked in. He paused for a moment, taking in the shocked expressions of both girls. Then he let out a laugh and crossed the room to Emily. She stared at him in frozen alarm, as though he were a footman who had suddenly taken leave of his senses. The next moment, she was in his arms.

He was putting on a show for Sara's benefit. There was nothing loverlike in his embrace. His arms were like iron shackles, the fierce pressure of his mouth on hers was suffocating, allowing no evasions. Everything she had hoped to conceal from Sara was cruelly and blatantly revealed in that possessive, masculine embrace. When the kiss ended, she did not know where to look.

Leon did not suffer from a like confusion. Tweaking her on the nose, he said loud enough for Sara to hear, "You brazen hussy! Cover yourself, else you'll embarrass your sister."

Suddenly conscious that she was down to her drawers and chemise, Emily reached for a towel and quickly wrapped it around herself. Anxiously, her eyes darted to Sara.

Sara's bosom was heaving. She was shaking her head. Her heart was in her eyes.

Ignoring that hurt look, Leon closed the distance between them. "Sara," he said calmly, "how is my little sister? It's good to see you again," and he brushed her cheek with his lips in a brotherly caress.

With a little cry, Sara pulled away from him. "I cannot believe this," she said passionately, then in an anguished whisper, "Leon, tell me it isn't true! You hate Emily. You know you do. It's me you love. It was always you and I. You must remember how it was. At the Abbey, Emily was *always* the odd one out."

Emily covered her mouth with one hand to catch back a moan. She felt as though she were living through a nightmare. She wasn't aware that Leon had come to stand beside her until she felt his arm slipping around her waist.

"It was always Emily," he said simply. "I've loved her since I was a boy. I was waiting for her to grow up." His

135

laugh was very convincing, very natural. "Shall we say merely that Emily finally relented and rewarded my patience when I abducted her from Fonthill House two nights ago? She has made me the happiest man in the world."

The silence was so profound it was almost unbearable. Then, in a tortured voice, Sara said, "Emily, tell me it isn't true."

Emily would have gone to her sister then, if Leon's arm had not tightened about her waist with crushing pressure. Her guilt was written clearly on her face for anyone to read.

Sobbing, moaning, Sara moved to the door. Before she could slip away, Leon's strident tones arrested her in midstep. "Sara, I would be obliged if you would refrain from making free with my wife's bedchamber. She has a husband now. My only wish, you understand, is to spare you embarrassment."

When the door crashed closed, Emily sagged against her husband. In the next instant, she tore herself out of his arms and spun to face him. "Why were you so brutal to her?" she demanded hoarsely. "My God, Sara didn't deserve that."

"Deserve *what?*" he asked, his face every bit as white as hers.

"That faradiddle about loving me since you were a boy. When we were children, Sara adored you. The sun rose and set on Leon Devereux. And you encouraged her."

"She is not a child now. I don't want her adoration. I never did. Do you imagine I wanted to tell her that lie about waiting for you to grow up? I don't want to hurt Sara any more than you do. What would you have had me say to her?"

"I don't know, but whatever it was, you should have spoken to her in private. You should have let her down gently. You should not have shamed her in my presence."

"Sara isn't like you, Emily. She is not easily put off. I should know. Believe me, I've tried. It *is* a hard way for her to learn that she has no hope with me, but in the end, it's the best way. She wouldn't listen to me, not after you had told her that there was a chance that our marriage could be annulled." He inhaled sharply. "Perhaps I should not blame you for that, though. I should have set my house in order long before this. At all events, she knows now that there is no hope of an annulment. It was your expression that convinced her, not anything *I* said or did."

He was as upset as Emily was. She did not see it. To her, it seemed that Leon's conduct was motivated by practical considerations. As was the way of men, personal happiness must be subordinated to their dynastic ambitions. Leon had persuaded himself that Sara was beyond his reach. In that event, she, Emily, would do for a wife as well as the next woman, better, in fact, because she was the possessor of a handsome fortune. If the marriage were annulled, he must return every penny he had taken from her. And having chosen his goal, he was prepared to pursue it with a callous disregard for anything or anyone who stood in his way.

Like a furious, impotent kitten, she flounced away from him. Finally, she said, "It's all very well for you to take that attitude. You will be in New York for a good part of the time. I am the one who has to live with Sara. She will never forgive me and I don't blame her."

There was a silence, then Leon said, "Your thinking is quite beyond me. In the first place, you are my wife. There is nothing to forgive. In the second place, what makes you think that you will be here when I am in New York?"

"You're . . . you're not considering settling in England, are you?"

"No. Not a bit of it," he answered easily. "My home, my interests, are in New York."

Her sigh of relief was almost audible.

"Naturally," he went on, "where my home is, your home will be also. You are my wife, Emily. How many times must I remind you of that fact?"

Emily felt as though all the breath had been knocked out of her. Her eyes squeezed tight, then opened wide. When she could trust herself to speak, she said, "You can't be serious."

"I assure you, I have never been more serious in my life."

"But why? Why won't you listen to reason? Why are you so determined to make my life miserable? What have I ever done to you? Do you hate me so much?"

A muscle jerked at the corner of his mouth. "I've already given you my reasons. There is no point in repeating myself. As soon as it may be arranged, we sail for New York." And with those crushing words, he turned on his heel and left her.

Emily was down, but she was not beaten — or so she sternly tried to tell herself during the following few days. Her moods swung to extremes, veering from black despair to determined optimism. She never doubted that Leon Devereux was a formidable opponent. But she was not some cringing, defenseless female who did not know how to take care of herself. She was Lady Emily, the daughter of a marquess. She had a will as strong as Leon's. In her fight against him, she had weapons she had yet to employ. Her husband had won the first battle. It was a major victory. That did not mean to say he had won the war.

If there was a war going on between husband and wife, no one would have known it, for the simple reason that Leon was hardly ever at home. His time was taken up in various occupations, not least his interest in acquiring prize stock for his stud in New York. This necessitated frequent absences, a circumstance his wife looked upon with unmitigated favor. Nor did he come to her bed when the rest of the house had retired for the night. This was more than Emily had hoped for. It never once occurred to her that it was for her sake that her husband displayed this forbearance, that it was to spare her scruples that he forced himself to forgo his conjugal rights. On puzzling it out, Emily decided that she owed her good fortune to Leon's remorse over the callous way he had betrayed his love for her sister, Sara. For all his talk, Leon did not wish to hurt Sara. It was Sara's presence that acted as a restraint to Leon's ambitions. Once Sara and England were left behind, the restraints would no longer be there.

Emily had thought out a vague strategy in her fight against Leon. She meant to gain her uncle's support. Failing that, she would appeal to William Addison. Her purposes, however, were doomed to frustration. Something had come up at the War Office, something which necessitated her uncle's undivided attention. Whole days went by when she caught only a glimpse of him. He was preoccupied, and had no time for her. As for William, he was in Dover and wrote to her that he did not know when he would be returning to town.

Emily's spirits were at a low ebb when Zoë walked into the music room to find her at the piano, idly playing what sounded like a dirge, or at the very least, a lament. Unaware that her aunt had entered the room, Emily played on.

Zoë halted just inside the door and absorbed the dejected droop of the girl's shoulders, the pallor of her complexion. When the piece came to an end, Zoë immediately made her presence known.

"You did not go riding with Sara this morning?" she remarked, and came to stand by the piano.

Emily's shoulders straightened. Her lips curved in a smile that did not quite reach her eyes. "Sara has given up our early-morning rides," she said, her voice showing none of her dejection, "in favor of riding with Peter Benson. She is with him now. Poor Peter!" She laughed. "He is besotted with Sara."

"You did not wish to go with them?"

"No," said Emily, not wishing her aunt to know that she had not been invited. In the week since that scene in her chamber, Sara had politely though firmly spurned every overture on Emily's part. There was no quarrel, but their conversation was composed of trivialities. They might as well be strangers. Sighing, Emily absently leafed through the sheet music on the piano.

Zoë's heart went out to the girl. More than anything, she wanted to put her arms around her and tell her that it was all right to show her feelings, that no one would think any the less of her if she put down her head and cried her eyes out, as Sara had done two nights ago and for much the same reasons. Zoë said nothing, knowing that this was not Emily's way. Ever since Zoë could remember, Emily had been a reserved, undemonstrative child, preferring to keep her feelings to herself.

Having briefly known the girl's mother, Zoë understood why this should be so. Emily had her fair share of her mother's reserve. But it went deeper than that. Though Emily was a year older than her sister, it seemed to Zoë that the elder girl had lived very much in Sara's shadow. It was to be expected, she supposed, for where Sara was forward, Emily hung back. Sara's ways were impetuous and winsome, had always been winsome, ever since she, Zoë, had come into the family. Sara was used to being the center of attention. It was in her nature to wear her heart on her sleeve, and people responded to her open, affectionate manners. Emily's reserve begot an equal reserve from those who did not know her well. Very few took the trouble to penetrate the composed facade to discover the sensitive dreamer beneath the surface.

It would have been so much simpler, Zoë was thinking, if it had been Sara and not Emily who had been found in the tower room with Leon.

"No, don't run away," she said, as Emily made a small movement toward the door. "I've been waiting for an opportunity to speak to you in private." She smiled encouragingly as Emily obediently sank back on the piano stool. Zoë seated herself on a straight-back chair which she had maneuvered into position. "With everyone out of the house, I shall never have a better chance," she said.

Without preamble, she went on. "I want you to understand, Emily, that if I were a foot taller and three stone heavier, it would give me great pleasure to, quite literally, hammer some sense into the heads of those two incorrigible gentlemen who happen to be our respective husbands."

Her words won a little laugh out of Emily, as she had hoped they would. "That's better," said Zoë. "No man is worth more than a tear or two, you know."

"Not even Uncle Rolfe?" quizzed Emily.

"Not even Uncle Rolfe, though, of course, I've wept whole oceans in my time over that particular gentleman."

Emily's expression was frankly skeptical.

"I assure you," said Zoë, "all marriages are not made in heaven. There was a time when I believed mine had been conceived in hell." Zoë could not help chuckling at Emily's shocked look.

"But . . . but you and Uncle Rolfe love each other," disclaimed Emily. "Your marriage is sublimely happy."

Zoë chose her words with care, knowing that what she said in the next few minutes could go a long way to helping her niece accept her future role as Leon's wife. "Yes, well, it wasn't easy, but I finally made your uncle fall in love with me, and that was a long time after we were wed. You see, I had made up my mind that my parents' marriage was going to be the model for my own marriage. They loved each other. They were happy together. I wasn't going to settle for anything less. My sister Claire and I were of the same opinion. Sisters confide in each other, as you well know. With brothers, it's different. Female talk embarrasses them. Even so, it would surprise me if Leon were not of the same mind. Our home was a happy one. I am sure he will want the same for himself. Couldn't you try to put your differences behind you and give Leon a chance?"

Emily had never been closer to breaking down and making a complete fool of herself in her whole life. She felt as though her heart were breaking. Unshed tears clogged her throat. The picture that Zoë's words evoked was bittersweet indeed. Emily wanted all those things for herself, but not with a husband who loved another woman. She knew without a doubt that such a marriage would eventually destroy her spirit, if not her very soul. Her aunt was the last person in whom she could confide. Emily could not bring herself to discuss Leon with anyone, least of all with a sister who loved him.

Zoë looked into those huge vulnerable eyes and prayed that her words were having some effect. Patting Emily affectionately on the shoulder, sighing, she made to leave the room.

Emily's tremulous voice halted her as she opened the door. "Aunt Zoë, how did you make Uncle Rolfe fall in love with you?"

Zoë's dark eyes danced wickedly, partly because the question betrayed Emily's turn of mind and gave her hope for the girl's future, and partly because the recollection of ancient history concerning Rolfe tickled her sense of humor. "I divorced him," she stated baldly.

"I'm sorry," said Emily. "I didn't quite catch that."

Zoë bit down on her lip. Neither Rolfe nor Leon, she knew, would thank her for putting ideas into the girl's head. On the other hand, neither Rolfe nor Leon deserved to have an easy time of it. It would be a very long time before she would forget what they had both put her through, not to mention what Emily had been made to suffer. As though a forced abduction with an

143

unwilling female could ever be considered romantic! She did not know where men got such fanciful notions, and so she had stormed at them. In the last little while, both gentlemen had tactfully if not strategically absented themselves from the house on the vaguest pretexts. Men, she had long ago decided, were cowards every one of them when it came to facing the music, at least on the domestic front. Her one consolation was Rolfe's assurances that Leon would never harm a hair on Emily's head. She believed him. Emily seemed to have suffered no ill effects from her abduction. There was no denying, however, that the girl was cast down, and Zoë was just beginning to recognize the symptoms.

The light in Zoë's eyes matched the mischievous smile on her lips. Very slowly and carefully, she enunciated. "I divorced your Uncle Rolfe under French law. That is how I made him fall in love with me. You should ask him about it some time," and she left the astonished girl gaping.

Once on the other side of the music room door, Zoë's expression gradually sobered. She was thinking of Sara and the girl's infatuation for Leon. Shaking her head, ascending the stairs, she resolved to have a lengthy and serious discussion with her husband about his younger ward before something dreadful happened.

Sara was beside herself. She knew that she was responding mechanically to her escort's spate of small talk. She tried to concentrate on what Peter Benson was saying, but her thoughts kept drifting. Even her favorite mount, Hoyden, could not distract her.

Leon. Loving him was as natural to her as breathing. She could not simply stop loving him because another woman had a claim on him, not even if that woman were her sister. Though it had sunk in upon her mind that his marriage to Emily was now a real one, she would not, could not accept that Leon preferred Emily to her. Leon and Emily were like oil and water. They had taken a dislike to each other almost from their first encounter, when they were children. Sara had not exaggerated when she had reminded Leon that Emily was always the odd one out. This was not an unkindness on anyone's part. It was simply that Sara had been drawn to Leon like a needle to a magnet, while his effect on Emily had been exactly the opposite.

For years, Sara had lived on hope. That hope had quickened when, as a young girl of fifteen, she had overheard Leon in conversation with Lady Riddley. He was waiting for Rivard's niece to grow up before he claimed her, Leon had confided. Leon could never convince her now that it was Emily to whom he had referred. In those days, he avoided Emily as though she were a leper. No. It was she, Sara, whom Leon meant to claim. And her heart had been ready to burst with joy. Leon loved her.

It was then that some capricious, malevolent spirit had turned her happy world on its head. It was on Emily's sixteenth birthday that she learned the sad truth that although a man might profess love for one woman, that did not prevent him from taking another to his bed. Leon and Judith Riddley had made an assignation to meet in the dower house later that night. Sara was not the innocent Emily was. She knew perfectly well what *that* signified, and she thought her heart

145

would break. And then it did break, hours later when she rushed out of her chamber to investigate the report of the pistol shot. And over her anguished protests, over Emily's distraught pleading, their guardian had insisted that Leon and Emily marry at once.

After that night, Sara had not wanted to go on living. Thankfully, those days were shrouded in a mist. All she knew was that she had gone into something of a decline, and nothing that Aunt Zoë or Uncle Rolfe could say or do had the power to bring her out of it.

It was Emily who had thrown her a lifeline. Though her sister had promised Leon that she would tell no one about it, she had inadvertently let slip that the marriage was a sham, that it would never be a real one, that it would be annulled when Emily met someone she could love. And everything had become clear to Sara. Leon was a man of honor. He could not, in all conscience, allow Emily to face social ostracism. For the present, he must marry her. Later, at a more propitious moment, the marriage would be dissolved and he would be free to claim the sister he truly loved.

But the marriage *was* a real one. That unpalatable truth had been written indelibly on Emily's guilt-stricken face. Sara was finally convinced that there was no hope for her, and knowing it, she was in desperate straits. She did not care for decorum, or consequences, or the world's good opinion, and she most particularly did not care for the two people who had conspired to wreck her happiness. Leon Devereux and her sister could go to the devil for all she cared. They deserved to be taught a lesson.

Without thinking, she dug in her spurs and sent her mount thundering across the turf. She heard Peter

146

Benson's shout of alarm, but could not have cared less for her own safety. If she was thrown and broke her neck, she thought wildly, it was all the same to her. Then Leon and Emily could never be happy, knowing that they had caused her death.

The tears misting her eyes clouded her vision. She did not see the long arm that reached for Hoyden's reins, but the sudden cessation of movement almost unseated her.

And then she was hauled out of the saddle and across the broad back of Peter Benson's bay.

"What do you think you are playing at?" he demanded roughly, almost as distraught as she. He crushed her to him, and Sara collapsed against his broad chest.

"Peter," she said brokenly. "Peter, I am so unhappy." She knew she was giving him a false impression. He had told her only that morning that his elder brother, the earl, had paid off his debts on the clear understanding that he had to accept a commission in His Majesty's service. Peter's affairs were too desperate to decline the offer. It only wanted to see where he would be posted.

"Sara, Sara," he murmured, his lips brushing over her tear-stained face. "Can it be true? Do you really love me?"

She was in the grip of a strange despair that made her reckless. "I shall die if you leave me here," she declared. "You know that they will never allow us to marry. Peter, if you feel anything for me, if you care for me, marry me now, before it is too late for us."

Chapter Eight

Instructing his groom to see to the horses, Leon jumped down and helped Sara alight from the curricle. It was early afternoon, long before Hyde Park would fill up with the elegant equipages of the aristocracy. There were few riders, and those pedestrians who were about were of the lower orders — soldiers in uniform squiring girls on their arms, apprentices on errands using the park as a shortcut. By five o'clock, as though by tacit consent, only those of rank and fashion would show their faces.

"Let's walk a ways," he said, directing Sara to the grass verge.

Sara's heart was hammering against her sides. Her breathing was quick and audible, and hope was shining in her eyes. "Leon," she said, "you do love me. I know you do."

He might have been deaf for all the notice he paid to her words. "I wish to speak to you about Emily," he said.

Her eyes sought his. The old teasing, affectionate manner was completely absent. In its place was a well-bred mask, not unkind, but at the same time, distancing. His words, his concern, were all for Emily. Emily must not be hurt by Sara's coldness, he told her. It was wrong to blame Emily for what had happened. He blamed him-

148

self. He should have nipped Sara's childhood infatuation in the bud. His only excuse was that he could not have foreseen how tenacious she would be in her loyalties.

He smiled when he said this, and went on. "I was not the only gentleman who caught your fancy. When you were barely out of the schoolroom, grown men were vying for your favors, and you encouraged them. I was sure you would have been wed long before this."

This was not what she expected to hear. This was not why she had agreed to come out driving with him in her uncle's borrowed curricle. She clutched convulsively at his sleeve. "Only tell me that you love me," she said, "and I can bear anything. Yes, even the thought of your marriage to Emily."

She looked into his dark eyes and saw only pity, and then a twinkle kindled in those dark eyes, and he said humorously, "This has all the makings of a Greek comedy, or tragedy. The irony is consummate. So much unrequited love—and I am speaking for myself as much as anyone. How the gods must be laughing!"

That he could laugh in the face of her suffering scraped a raw sore. Rage blotted out every other feeling. Heedless words rose up and spilled over. "Emily *does* love William Addison," she said. "She will never love you. She has always hated you. She always will. In her eyes, you will always be a foreigner."

Suddenly, it was as though she were a child again, and all the old resentments rose up in her, petty resentments, childish grievances that she would not have believed had still the power to hurt her. Because Emily was the elder, she was the favored one. Everything came to Emily first.

Her mind leaped with a confusion of memories. When they were children, Emily was allowed to stay up later.

She was first to go away to school, first to have a grown-up party with a grown-up ballgown. Not that Emily cared. But Sara cared. It was so unfair.

Greater than her sense of injustice was her sense of betrayal. Emily was her sister. For a time, they had been inseparable, but with the arrival of Aunt Zoë's babies, everything had changed. Sara was no longer first with Emily. Emily doted on her little cousins, and the boys looked up to her. Emily was the one they preferred.

But Leon preferred *her*, Sara. She wasn't the elder, like Emily. She wasn't clever like Emily. But she must have something that Emily did not, else she would not have captured Leon. Leon was *hers*. And Leon had made no bones about the fact that he found Emily wanting.

"You can't just suddenly change like that," she said, snapping her gloved fingers. "You were forever trying to take Emily down a peg or two. You once called her a stuck-up scarecrow, don't you remember? And you were right. She doesn't have feelings like the rest of us mortals. She . . ."

"I once said a lot of things I did not mean. Sara, I was only a boy. Can't you see how it was? It was always Emily."

Her humiliation could not have been more complete. It wasn't only that Leon had suddenly become smitten with Emily. It had always been Emily. He really meant it. She could see it in his half-pitying, half-satirical expression. And all the golden moments of her childhood, moments in which Leon had figured prominently, turned to ashes in her mouth. She would never be able to recall a single incident of their shared intimacies without reflecting that, even then, it was Emily whom Leon had wanted.

Burning shame fueled her hurt pride. She willed away the hot sting of tears and listened in smiling, frozen silence as he articulated words of nonsense about some mythical man whom she would one day meet and love.

Leon was helping her into the curricle when the accident occurred. There was the sound of an explosion, like a firecracker going off. The horses reared in their traces. In the same instant as they bolted, Leon threw himself into the curricle. It was all over in a matter of minutes, but those minutes were the most terrifying of Sara's life. She was sure the vehicle would overturn and they would break their necks. Only Leon's quick thinking and powerful, steadying hands on the reins prevented a catastrophe.

When he pulled his team to a plunging, shuddering halt, she could no longer keep a tight leash on her emotions. She was only too glad to have a pretext for the flood of tears and the trembling which engulfed her from head to toe.

"Please," she said brokenly. "Please take me home."

In shivering misery, she crouched in one corner of the coach as Leon jumped down and went to inspect the horses. She heard the low murmur of voices as first the groom came running up and then a group of noisy spectators. She heard their excited chatter, but it made no impression on her. Her heart was broken. Her pride was crushed. Her life was over. She did not care what happened to her. That she had cared very much a few moments before when it seemed that she might break her neck if the curricle overturned was an irony that escaped her. She was desolate and might as well be dead.

"It was no accident," reiterated Leon. "It was a deliberate attempt on my life."

Some hours had passed since he had returned with a distraught Sara and had seen her safely into the care of Zoë and Emily. He had debated with himself whether or not he should track down his brother-in-law in the government offices in Whitehall or wait for his return with as much patience as he could muster. Not wishing to alarm the ladies, he had decided on the latter course.

Rolfe was at his desk, idly playing with a pencil. "Tell me again how it happened," he said.

Leon folded his arms across his chest and edged one hip on the flat of Rolfe's desk. "By all accounts, the shot came from a rider, a man whom no one can describe with any accuracy, but who everyone agrees took off at the speed of lightning toward Piccadilly when your chestnuts bolted."

"Was he young or old? How was he dressed? What about his mount? Someone must have seen something."

"Oh, yes, there are a dozen witnesses, each one of them willing to swear under oath to a different description. I fear that will prove a fruitless line of investigation."

"What makes you think it was a deliberate attempt at murder?"

"You saw where the ball entered the coach."

"It might have been a prank, or someone who took exception to the crest on my curricle. These are desperate times. The streets are teeming with lunatics. Why, only last month, some ruffians got into my stables and very cleverly partially sawed through the girths on Sara's saddle. There might have been a fatal accident. As it was, poor Emily took a tumble. Thankfully, she is an accomplished rider. My nieces know how to take a fall."

Leon straightened with a frown. "Are you saying that

152

someone tried to do Emily an injury?"

"Not Emily in particular, no. It was her misfortune to be the first to go riding that morning. It could just as easily have been Sara. Once my groom examined her saddle, the whole affair came to light."

"Emily said nothing of this to me."

"Well, naturally, I did not wish to alarm the ladies. As far as they know, it was an accident. But you see what I am getting at, Leon? This isn't an isolated incident. There's unrest among the general population, and, I am sorry to say, there is a fanatical element who blame all their troubles on the upper classes. You may believe that the Revolution in France has had an influence here. There are some who would like nothing better than to see our heads roll."

"That may be, but I still say that what happened today was not the work of some stray lunatic who saw an opportunity and seized it, but a deliberate attempt to do away with me in particular."

There was speculation in Rolfe's gray eyes as they absorbed Leon's intent expression. "Go on," he said, "I'm listening."

Slipping off the desk, Leon wandered to the console table positioned against one wall. "May I?" he said, and at Rolfe's quick nod, poured a liberal splash of brandy into a crystal glass. Slowly sipping it, he retraced his steps and deposited himself in a stuffed leather armchair. "I recognize an assassination attempt when I see it," he said simply. When Rolfe made to say something, he continued in the same calm tones. "You might be able to dissuade me from that opinion if La Compagnie had not reared its ugly head. The coincidence is remarkable, wouldn't you say?"

Rolfe eased himself back in his chair. "What about enemies? A man in your position . . ."

"Oh, yes, I have enemies, but not the sort who would wish to put a bullet in me. No, this has all the marks of a fanatical group. I should know." There was an interval of silence, and then Leon said, with emphasis, "This attack has all the marks of La Compagnie."

Rolfe's groan was long and audible. He flung down his pencil. "But look here, Leon, La Compagnie does not even know of your existence. It was a secret society. All the men in your cell were eliminated, not by us, but by your own leader. And all of that took place years ago. They can't possibly be hunting you down after all this time."

Leon held his glass up to the light and examined it before taking a long swallow. "One of the tenets of our creed was that there were no former members of La Compagnie, only active ones or dead ones."

"I am aware of that," said Rolfe testily, angry at both Leon and himself for reasons he could not quite articulate. After a moment, he went on. "Death threats against men in high places reach my desk every day. As I said, there are plenty of disgruntled people in this world, people who are angry about the progress of the war, people who are angry because they are poor. And we take these threats seriously. The Prince Regent, the prime minister—they are hedged about by a host of bodyguards if they only knew it."

"I fail to see what that has to do with La Compagnie or me," Leon said reasonably.

"All I am saying is that La Compagnie is not the only lunatic secret society in existence."

"No, but it's the only one to which I have any connection. Tell me about it. It was my understanding that it was completely smashed fifteen years ago."

"And so it was. Frankly, I know very little. My sources in France have almost completely dried up. I shall promise you this, though—from this moment on, I shall put my agents onto it. It's one thing for La Compagnie to operate within France's borders, it's quite another if it makes forays into *my* territory."

For some few minutes, both gentlemen became lost in private reflection. Leon came to himself first. Observing his brother-in-law's absorbed look, he chuckled and said, "You can put that thought out of your mind."

"What thought?" asked Rolfe, managing to look innocent.

"Rolfe, you are too old for that game. And what would Zoë say? No, if anyone should go to France and infiltrate the society it should be I."

"The thought never crossed my mind," Rolfe protested, and laughed ruefully. "Well, only for a moment. But as for your going to France . . ." He shook his head. "If La Compagnie is behind the attacks, I'm sure they would like nothing better. You would be playing into their hands."

"Then what's to be done? You saw what happened today. The bullet might have hit Sara. If I am a target, so is anyone who is near me."

"Let me handle it."

"While I do—what?"

"Take Emily and go to New York."

Leon pounced on that last remark. "So you are having second thoughts about Emily's riding accident?"

"Lord, I don't know! But after what you have told me, I'd be a fool not to see that there might be a connection.

155

All things considered, until I get to the bottom of it, I'd be happier if she were away from here."

Rolfe pressed one hand to his eyes. "Be a good chap, Leon, and pour me a brandy."

Leon was at the console table when there was a light tap on the door. The door opened, momentarily concealing him, and Emily entered. Shutting the door softly at her back, she stalked toward her uncle.

"Uncle Rolfe," she said appealingly, laying her hands flat on his desk, leaning toward him, "I thought I would never find you alone. If I did not know better, I would say that you had been avoiding me." She smiled and fluttered her lashes to take the sting out of her words.

"Is it Sara?" asked Rolfe, starting to rise. "When I saw her earlier, she seemed to be quite recovered from her fright."

"Sara is fine," she assured him. "It's not the first time she has been in a runaway carriage, though it *is* the first time it was the result of a malicious prank."

"Prank?" murmured Rolfe, sinking back in his chair.

"Rowdy boys and their fireworks! No, what I wish to say to you concerns myself." Drawing a deep breath, she began on what was obviously a rehearsed speech. "Uncle Rolfe, I am the most wretched girl in the whole world. You are my last hope. You *must* help me." Sighing dramatically, she went on. "I can never be happy with Leon. You always knew this. Leon knew it, too, *does* know it is what I mean." She floundered as though she had lost the train of her thought, then went on resolutely. "He promised me that our marriage would be annulled. And now he is going back on his promise. You must agree, that is not very gentlemanly—to give your word and then break it. It's not British, Uncle Rolfe. It puts me in a delicate

156

position, to say the least. You see, I am half promised to someone else."

Rolfe's face was a comical blend of alarm and horror. Taking his silence for acquiescence, Emily concluded triumphantly, "I knew I could count on your support, dearest uncle."

The ensuing silence was broken by a slow, derisory handclap. Emily spun to face her audience. Her mouth opened and closed before she managed a choked, "You!"

"My dear Emily," said her husband pleasantly, coming forward to hand Rolfe his glass, "you are to be congratulated! What a performance! What talent! What drama!" Smiling, he raised his glass to his lips and imbibed slowly. "And what drivel! So—this is how you manage to twist your uncle round your little finger? I'm not your uncle, Emily. I'm immune to all your little feminine tricks."

His stance was easy, careless, and she knew an irresistible urge to say or do something, *anything*, to fracture that cool, contemptuous pose. Rounding on Rolfe, she said desperately, "He only married me for my money. He doesn't care a fig about me. He has a mistress, a Belle something-or-other in New York. Everyone knows about her. He's given her a set of jewels worth a king's ransom, jewels he bought with *my* money. Why, it would not surprise me to learn that he had squandered every last farthing of my fortune."

It was Leon who answered her accusations. "How very well informed you are—up to a point. The lady's name is Belle Courtney. She is not my mistress. The jewels were not bought with your money. And your capital, at my last reckoning, has more than trebled." His dark eyes were laughing at her.

"Thank you," she said between her teeth. "I stand cor-

157

rected. As a banker, you are to be commended. As a husband—"

"This is where I beat a strategic retreat," Rolfe interrupted, abruptly rising to his feet. Coughing harshly into his hand to cover his laughter, he began to edge his way to the door.

"Uncle Rolfe!" she cried out. "I beg you! I am depending on you to find a way out of this muddle."

Rolfe flashed a quizzical look at the younger man.

"There can be no question of an annulment," said Leon blandly, "not unless we perjure ourselves. The marriage was well and truly consummated. Isn't that so, Emily?"

Emily felt as though she had suddenly been stripped of all her clothes in a roomful of people. Since her aborted honeymoon with Leon, not once had anyone put an indelicate question to her, not even Sara. She had been content to leave them to their speculations. Her husband was bound and determined to set them right. If the word "consummated" was written across her forehead in indelible ink, she would not have been surprised. Flushing to her hairline, in utter confusion, she turned away. When she heard the click of the door latch as Rolfe exited, she said hoarsely, "You lose no opportunity to humiliate me."

"You brought it on yourself. And the same might be said of you. Do you think I like my affairs made public knowledge?"

"*Affaires!*" she spat at him, giving the word the French intonation. "An honorable man would have nothing to hide. An honorable man would have kept his promises."

"Which promises? The ones we made together before God or a promise made with the best will in the world to allay the fears of a distraught child?"

Emily's gaze flew to his. "You are a fine one to talk of

sacred vows," she scorned. "What of Belle Courtney?"

He regarded her with an infuriating grin. "Emily, you unman me. Does this mean that you care?"

Seething, she shot at him, "I might have known I would not get a straight answer out of you."

His brows rose. "When have you ever asked me a straight question? You never cared where I was, or what I did, or who I did it with. You never cared whether I lived or died. Now, suddenly, you are flinging accusations in my teeth. I think I am the one who should be asking for explanations. Why do you want to know about Belle Courtney, Emily?"

He was implying that she was jealous! That answer she swiftly rejected. She had been trying to prove something. But he had got her so muddled, so unhinged, that she could not remember what it was. She had never yet won an argument with Leon, but she was a past master at the crushing rejoinder. Her mind leaped about, but all she could find to say was, "There's no arguing with you! There never was."

Her exit was meant to be regal, and so it might have been, if Leon had not reached for her and grabbed her by the shoulders.

"I don't owe you an explanation, but I shall give you one." His cool, detached tone and manner were at odds with the steely strength imprisoning her. "A man has needs that are usually met by his wife. That did not happen in our case. If you had been a wife to me in more than name only, there would have been no other women in my life."

"*Women!*" she exclaimed, scandalized. "In the plural! I might have known it!"

His teeth flashed white in his swarthy complexion.

"Did you think that I would pine away for love of you?"

"Hardly! You forget, I was an unwilling witness to what happened between you and Judith Riddley in the dower house. I should have known that there would be other women, and I thank God for it, if they kept you away from me."

His hands dropped away. Though his smile was still in place, Emily sensed a subtle change in him. "You can say that, after what has happened between us?"

"There is no explaining what happened between us," she said fretfully. "But I know this . . . if you had only kept your distance, if you had refrained from kissing me and . . . and touching me, there would be nothing now to regret."

His spontaneous burst of laughter only added insult to injury. Observing her look of burning indignation, he said softly, taunting her, "What about William Addison?"

"What *about* him?"

"Don't play games with me. You know what I mean. From what I know of the man's character, he is something of a laggard. Even so, he is reputed to be your suitor. Hasn't Addison made so bold as to steal the odd kiss . . . and more besides?"

The color which had gradually receded from her cheeks returned in full force. Leon's eyes narrowed and the smile on his lips died.

"I see," he said.

"William is a gentleman," she said hurriedly. "He is a man of honor. There has been nothing to regret, I swear it."

"And not much to report, either, if I am any judge."

"What does that mean?"

He grinned wickedly. "Emily, you were a complete

novice. Don't you think I know that? You did not even know how to kiss me. I had to teach you everything."

For a fleeting moment, caution kept her tongue still. But no woman worth her salt could permit this last jibe unless she were a complete doormat. "Perhaps you are not the judge you think you are," she said frigidly. "Perhaps you have been consorting with the wrong women. Some of us are immune to flirts and libertines and so on. Some of us are chaste because we choose to be."

"I wasn't finding fault, far from it. I approve of chastity—in a wife." He cupped her chin in one hand, forcing her head up, looking down at her stormy eyes with a faintly amused expression. "Yes, I know. You hate me, and you love William Addison. But you are my wife, Emily. You will obey me in this. For the little time that remains before we sail for New York, I don't want you within a mile of Addison. Understood?"

He took her acquiescence as read. It was he who made the dignified exit, and Emily who was left fuming and staring.

Chapter Nine

It was settled. They were to sail for New York the first week of July. If Leon had had his way, the three weeks remaining to them in England would have been passed at Rivard Abbey. The Abbey was off the beaten track. Strangers would not go undetected. In the interests of safety, Rivard Abbey could hardly be bettered. He had not reckoned on the wishes of the heir to the British throne.

"The Abbey? Are you mad?" This was from Zoë. "My dear Leon, we have our invitations to the Prince Regent's fête. A gentleman or a lady would have to be on his or her deathbed before they declined such an honor. It is a slight Prince George would never forgive."

Rolfe confirmed his wife's words. "We cannot get out of it. The event is the prince's first formal do since he was sworn in as regent. The ladies have been talking about nothing else for weeks past. If you have not heard them, then I am forced to the conclusion that you are a deaf man, Leon.

"I know what you are thinking, and you are wrong. You may take my word for it, security at Carlton House will be as tight as a drum. Why, I had to pull a few strings just to obtain an invitation for you. No one beneath the dignity of an earl has an entrée, and, of course, the upper echelons of government circles."

Sometimes, Leon ruefully acknowledged to himself, it slipped his mind that his wife's family held a position of eminence. By and large, his forgetfulness was Rolfe's doing. Though Rolfe had been born and bred to a life of wealth and privilege, he was no snob. His manners were natural. His views were liberal. He did not suffer fools gladly, whether they were aristocrats or of the lower classes. Rolfe believed that a man should be judged on his merits, that his advancement must not be impeded by an entrenched aristocracy. There was a lesson to be learned from the Revolution in France.

Rolfe's liberal views were not universally held, especially by his peers. They guarded their privilege jealously. Leon was well aware that they admitted him to their ranks for only one reason: his connection to the House of Rivard. As a young man of some pride and ambition, this unpalatable truth rankled. It always had. In America, things were different. A man's birth counted for little. It would not be true to say that there was no elite, no aristocracy. It was, however, based on far more than an accident of birth. It suited him better than the English system. Whether or not it would suit his wife remained to be seen. In England, she was addressed as "Lady Emily." In America, she would be plain "Mrs. Devereux." The thought brought a wicked grin flashing to his lips.

On the night of the Prince Regent's fête when Emily descended the marble staircase flanked by Zoë and Sara, Leon had eyes only for his wife. He was aware of Rolfe going forward to compliment the ladies on their toilettes. For some few minutes, Leon could only stand and stare.

Her gown was in the current mode, high-waisted with low neckline and puff sleeves. It was the color which arrested him. He was used to seeing Emily in pale pastels. This gown, of sheer silk net, was as blue and as dark as midnight, and just as dramatic. Her dark blond ringlets, piled high on her head, were kept in place with a diamond clasp. Diamonds were at her ears and throat — his bridal gift to her. Long white gloves, white feather fan, and matching pochette completed the ensemble. She was as regal as a queen.

He could not know that it was nerves which froze Emily's features into an unsmiling mask — that and the little contretemps which had occurred at the head of the stairs when Sara, in her pale muslins, observed her sister's new ballgown. Fashion decreed that only married ladies could wear intense colors, Sara was incensed.

Leon knew nothing of this. The first rush of awe gave way to annoyance. Emily was too perfect by half. The old, familiar impulse to take her down a peg or two rose up in him. On the tedious carriage drive to the prince's residence on Pall Mall, he hardly said a word.

Over two thousand guests were crammed into the opulent reception rooms of Carlton House. Though the orchestra played almost continuously, there was no space cleared for dancing. There was not a space to be had.

The Prince Regent, in scarlet regimentals, a saber dangling from his waist, graciously presided over his glittering affair. Flanking him were the guests of honor, the remnants of the French royal family. With such a crush, it was impossible for everyone to be properly presented. Leon could not have cared less. He felt no affinity for either the British or the French royals, and since Ladies Emily and

164

Sara were far more interested in the prince's house than they were in its owner, he steered them to where the crush was less severe. Rolfe and Zoë waved them away and with sighs of resignation joined the long queue which snaked its way to the receiving line in the ballroom.

Emily plied her feather fan and made a show of admiring the prince's most recent acquisition, a painting by Rembrandt. From the corner of her eye, she was busily watching other ladies watching *her* husband! From the moment they had swept into the torchlit portico, she had been conscious of the stir Leon created. He was a handsome creature. She had always known it in a sort of indifferent, careless way. Formerly, however, she had been far more involved in cataloging his failings. On this occasion, she was aware of him in a way that she had never been aware of him before. In the space of half an hour, they had been importuned for introductions by a dozen ladies and their escorts, who normally would have been content to acknowledge her presence from a distance. She did not know whether she was flattered or insulted.

In a quiet aside, for her ears only, Leon murmured dryly, "Don't despair, Emily. I promise not to disgrace you."

"What?" She turned startled eyes upon him.

"I may not be a member of the British aristocracy, but I know how to conduct myself at these functions. You forget, many of the gentlemen here are known to me. We were at university together. Besides, I could hardly be married to the daughter of a marquess and not be schooled in all the pitfalls of British protocol."

For all that his tone was edged with amusement, she sensed that he was offended. "*That* is not what I was thinking!" she exclaimed.

"No? Then what *were* you thinking?"

165

She bit down on a smile that refused to be stifled.

"Well?" His eyes narrowed on her face.

From behind her fan, she said, "What I was thinking was that I have never remarked such odd conduct . . ." He stiffened slightly and she quickly concluded, ". . . in the members of my own sex. For a moment there, I thought Lady Rossington would positively eat you whole."

She laughed and he laughed along with her. His smile died suddenly and Emily tilted her head in a silent question.

"You have a beautiful smile," he said, "when you condescend to show it."

Sara chose that moment to make her excuses to fall in with a lively party of acquaintances of her own age. Emily watched her go without comment. Turning to Leon, she touched her gloved hand to the sleeve of his dark coat and instantly withdrew it. "Leon, it never once occurred to me that you could not hold your own in this setting."

"Didn't it?" he asked moodily, directing her steps toward the Great Hall. "Shall we take a turn in the gardens?"

Emily followed his lead blindly, oblivious to the splendors of magnificent marble Greek columns and elaborately gilded ceilings. Conversation was impossible until they entered the two-storied octagonal vestibule. At this point, the crush to pass through the arch leading to the staircase was so dense that their steps halted altogether. Emily took up the conversation where it had left off.

"You must think I have a very high opinion of myself," she said stiffly.

"I do."

She was so taken aback, so stung by the injustice of the remark, that for a moment she was speechless, and when she could find her voice, all she could say was, "I do."

166

"You are Lady Emily, the daughter of a marquess, and woe betide us lesser mortals who refuse to give you your due. Do you know, I never truly understood the meaning of the word 'ladylike' until I made a study of you. A stare, a flick of your long lashes, a smile that isn't quite a smile — I've watched you employ all these devices to cut down any poor, innocent trespasser who has the misfortune to tread on your toes, figuratively speaking."

She was almost tempted to demonstrate just how 'ladylike' she could be. Conscious, however, that the subject she wished to pursue would become lost in the ensuing argument, she said diffidently, "There may be some truth in what you say. But in this instance you do me an injustice."

"This instance?"

"I don't count myself better than you, and if I have given that impression, I apologize for it."

"Come now, Emily. You think of me as a foreigner. Admit it. You are English to the tips of your little fingers. You look down your nose at anything and everything that is not English."

His face was a slate wiped clean of all emotion. Emily could not know that it was Sara's words which were burned into his brain. *In Emily's eyes you will always be a foreigner.* She frowned, trying to recall a conversation when she might have used that barb against him. Though it was entirely possible, no such conversation came to her mind.

"When did I say that you were a foreigner?"

"I believe the first time was when you were a child of eight or nine summers. Since then . . ." He shrugged his shoulders eloquently.

She slanted him a quick glance. His expression was aloof, distancing, as though she had insulted him — or hurt him. She squirmed, knowing full well that she had said some very uncomplimentary things of late in her battle to be free of him. She did not want to hurt him. She hated hurting people. She simply wanted to be free to find her own destiny. Surely he must see that? Evidently not.

Fluttering her fan, in a constricted tone, she said, "Sometimes you provoke me into saying things I don't really mean. I may not want you for a husband, Leon, but that does not mean I think I am better than you. I have no fault to find with you, except in your dealings with me. Since I was a child, we have always been at daggers drawn. That does not auger well for the future."

Laughter flickered in his eyes as he gazed down at her beautifully appealing expression. With the fingers of one hand, he stilled the agitated fluttering of her fan. "You are wrong, you know. In the first place, it's my opinion that it does auger well for our future, and in the second place, we are not always at daggers drawn." To her blank look he elaborated. "May I remind you of the two delightful days you spent aboard my yacht?"

Emily's cheeks bloomed scarlet. They had entered the arch to the famous double staircase. She snapped her fan closed, then angrily flicked it open and looked about her with interest, completely ignoring the man at her side.

In an amused undertone, from behind his hand, Leon drawled, "I do beg your pardon. I believe I just trod on your toes."

At half-past two, in the small hours of the morning, supper was announced and the Prince Regent's two thousand guests sat down en masse under a large marquee which had been erected in the gardens. An army of liveried footmen was on hand to serve the several courses as well as dispense an unending supply of iced champagne. The prince's private table, at two hundred feet long, had been set up in the privacy of the conservatory.

Rolfe, who was summoned to dine with the Prince Regent's party, managed a few words with Leon and Emily before escorting Zoë to their places.

"This is quite something, isn't it?" he said in a tone of voice that left his hearers in no doubt of his distaste for the extravagance of his prince's hospitality. "Who would believe that a war is in progress or that English soldiers are existing on starvation rations on the Peninsula?"

Leon's eyes traveled the glittering array of guests. "It was spectacles such as this which led to the Revolution in France," he observed idly.

"Where is Sara?" asked Zoë.

"She met some friends," Emily interjected. "You know them, Aunt Zoë, the Berkeley girls and their brothers. We are all to meet up here. Sara will be along presently." It was second nature for Emily to make excuses for her sister. Sara would do as much for her.

"Damn the girl!" said Rolfe. "Isn't this just like her? Look, we must go. We can't keep the prince waiting." His flashing smile did not quite mask his uneasiness. He was worried about Sara and it showed.

"I think I know where Sara is," said Leon. "Leave it to me. I shall find her."

When Rolfe and Zoë had melted into the crowd, Leon picked up his soup spoon and calmly began to eat.

Emily's brows winged upward. "Well? Where is Sara?" she demanded.

"Knowing Sara, she could be anywhere."

"But you said . . ."

"I know what I said. What I should have said was that

Sara is playing out one of her little games. For some reason, she is in a sulk, and when Sara is sulking, everyone must be thrown into a tempest. She's not like you. She doesn't withdraw hoping no one will notice her. Quite the reverse. You of all people must be familiar with this pattern. When she was a child, it was an endearing trait. Now . . ." His half-finished sentence spoke volumes.

In considering silence, Emily picked up her spoon and followed Leon's example. There was a constriction in her throat and after a moment, she merely toyed with the liquid in her bowl. She was thinking that Sara's heart must be breaking, and when Sara was overcome with emotion, there was no telling what she might do.

As though he could read her mind, Leon set down his spoon and said softly, "All right. If it will set your mind at rest, I shall go and look for her. But I don't expect to find her."

"Then if she is not here, where can she be?"

"At home, in her bed." He gave a disbelieving laugh. "I am just coming to see that you don't know the first thing about your sister." Rising, he swiftly left her.

Emily ostensibly gave her attention to her dinner, though her thoughts remained on Sara. Before long, her neighbors at the long table began to make polite conversation. Her answers were brief and noncommittal until she recalled her conversation with Leon.

She had a high opinion of herself, he had intimated. She could set down innocent trespassers with a flick of her lashes or with a smile that was not quite a smile.

But it wasn't true. She didn't have a high opinion of herself. It was just her way. Unthinkingly, she frowned, and the young man on her left, who had begun on what he hoped was an amusing description of the prince's table in

170

the conservatory, halted in mid-sentence.

"I beg your pardon," he mumbled, a flush creeping from under his collar. "I daresay you've seen it. I daresay you're bored to tears with the subject."

"But I am not bored!" She gave him her undivided attention and smiled encouragingly. "It sounds like quite a spectacle. Pray, continue."

"You're sure?"

"Oh, quite. I don't know how I came to miss it. An artificial stream, you say, meandering down the middle of the table? How . . . original."

Taking encouragement from Emily's animated expression, the young man started over. "Like the Serpentine in Hyde Park," he said, "with miniature bridges — oh — and rocks and plants of every description." He slanted her a sidelong glance, gauging her interest.

"How . . . amusing." She flashed a brilliant smile and bobbed her head.

"But that's not all."

"No?"

"There are fish in the stream, real ones, gudgeons and roach and dace, swimming about as if they were in the Thames."

Others joined in the conversation. Not everyone endorsed Prince George's taste, though no one criticized it too vehemently. On the morrow, in the gentlemen's clubs and ladies' drawing rooms, they would have more to say.

Leon's words still fresh in her mind, Emily made a determined effort to be gracious. She did not have a high opinion of herself. If she had given that impression, she must correct it.

She was on her second glass of champagne when she became conscious that someone was watching her covertly.

Glancing over her shoulder, she looked straight into the diamond-bright eyes of William Addison. Her heart lurched.

Holding her gaze, slowly rising from the table, he moved off in the direction of the house. The message was unmistakable. He wanted a word with her in private.

Emily swallowed. Her eyes darted about, frantically searching for her husband's tall figure. Leon was nowhere in sight. She did not know whether she was glad or sorry. If Leon were with her, there would be no question of a private tête-à-tête with William. The decision to meet with him would be taken out of her hands.

Making her excuses to her neighbors, she scraped back her chair and followed William from the marquee. He was waiting for her at the doors which gave onto the prince's private apartments. On this special occasion, all the chambers were open to the public. Murmuring a greeting and a few words of apology for his long absence, he led her to the library. With vigilant footmen stationed along the corridors and at every doorway, there could be no real privacy. Emily was relieved. It would not do for her husband to find her alone with another man.

They made a show of admiring the ornate bookcases and gilded columns.

"Devereux is in town, so I've been told."

Emily nodded. This was the moment she had been waiting for. Uncle Rolfe, having failed her, William was now her last resort. She would put the whole sorry story before William, knowing he would take her part against Leon. He would know how to extricate her from her unwanted marriage.

"He must be told about us." He gave her a searching look. "Now is the time to press for an annulment, Emily."

She moistened her dry lips. Her eyes grew misty. William did not deserve this. He loved her. He trusted her as she trusted him. What she had to say was bound to devastate him.

He was smiling at her tenderly, love shining in his eyes. She felt like a murderess.

"Emily, what is it?" he asked softly, his eyes moving over her frozen features.

Hoarsely, she got out, "Leon won't even consider an annulment. He has booked passage for us both on a ship sailing for New York. We leave from Falmouth at the beginning of next month." It was as close to the truth as she could force herself to come. Knowing herself for a coward, she hung her head.

His tone was grim. "We shall soon see about that. Don't worry, my darling. Devereux isn't dealing with a helpless female. I am not afraid to stand up to him."

The words trembled on her tongue, but she could not force them past her lips. "He is adamant," she prevaricated.

"Does your uncle know this?"

She nodded.

He uttered an explosive profanity. "I am amazed! Rivard must have taken leave of his senses! He must know what manner of man Devereux is."

"Uncle Rolfe admires Leon. He . . . he wants the marriage to become a real one."

"That must never happen. I would not trust Devereux as far as I could throw him. I am not only thinking of our happiness. The man is dangerous. I am onto something, something which Devereux, yes, and your uncle, are trying to conceal. Promise me, Emily, you will never be alone with him."

"What are you saying? What have you discovered?"

As they spoke, they had idled their way into the adjoining drawing room. The low basement ceiling, the unrelieved gold of the pillars and walls—all contributed to Emily's sense of overpowering doom. She seated herself on a crimson sofa in one of the alcoves. William remained standing, to one side of a round Boule table.

"What have you discovered?" she repeated softly.

He shook his head. "Frankly, I'm not sure. At the War Office, I have come across records, snippets of this and that which have set me to wondering. The information is confidential. I can't divulge it, but I repeat my warning. Until the annulment is a settled thing, you had best beware of the man."

Emily was not alarmed. Nor did she take her companion's words seriously. Leon was dangerous, but not in the sense William was suggesting.

Hints weren't working, and she had run out of ways to break the news gently. Inhaling a quick breath, forcing herself to look into his eyes, she said achingly, "Oh, William, please forgive me, and tell me what I must do. You see, the marriage . . . the marriage has been consummated."

For a moment, uncertainty flickered in the depths of his eyes. As the full import of her words sank in, the uncertainty vanished and shock stiffened every feature.

Emily sprang to her feet, her hand raised in a placating gesture. "Ah, no!" she cried out. "Don't hate me! I could not bear it if you hate me."

She waited in abject submission for the spate of questions to begin, not knowing how she could answer him. If he had struck her, she would not have been surprised. There was no greater betrayal than the one she had committed.

His control amazed her. His willpower was almost a tangible thing. She could feel it as he forced himself into a calmer frame of mind, forced down the murder that was in his eyes.

"Oh, William, tell me what to do and I shall do it!" she whispered.

Harshly, he answered, "If the marriage has been consummated, there is nothing to be done. You always *knew* this!"

"There must be something . . ."

"I warned you . . . I told you . . ." She could hear his teeth grinding together as he strove to hold onto his patience. "You should have told me that you preferred Devereux."

"But I don't prefer Leon! It's you I love."

"You have a fine way of showing it!"

Her head drooped and she bit down hard on her lip to stop its trembling. Tears dewed her lashes. She could not defend herself, for what she had done was inexcusable. As though from a great distance, she heard him say something to the effect that although he could never be her husband, he hoped she would always regard him as a friend.

At the end, his voice broke. "I shall always love you, Emily," he said.

Swinging on his heel, he made to leave her. His path was blocked by Leon. How long he had been standing there, negligently propped against one of the pillars, was uncertain. The tension was palpable as Leon straightened and both gentlemen faced each other, standing their ground, each carefully taking the other's measure. Though both were of a similar height and build, and both were darkly handsome, Emily would never have mistaken one for the other. Where William made her think of strength and determination, like the British bulldog, Leon brought to mind a sleek jungle cat, unpredictable, sometimes playful, sometimes fatally dangerous.

When a smile edged his lips, she let out a shaky breath. No word was spoken as William brushed past Leon and strode from the room.

"You told him." Leon's voice was oddly without inflection. It told her nothing.

"Of course I told him. What else could I do?"

He shrugged carelessly. "What a thousand other women in your place would have done."

"Which is?"

"Lie in their teeth." He caught her chin and held her face up for his inspection. Her eyes were swimming. "That's what I like in you, Emily. You are as honest as the day. I shall never have to wonder whether or not you are telling me a pack of lies. As a husband, I am to be envied."

She shook off his hand. "I won't return the compliment, since we both know I would be lying."

"Your meaning escapes me."

"What I mean is that you are a master of deception. You lied to Sara when you told her that I was the one you always wanted. You lied about that woman in New York, Belle . . . Belle . . ."

"Courtney," he supplied helpfully.

Goaded, she hissed, "Do you deny that you lied?"

Something came and went in his eyes, but he merely remarked, "I thought I told you I didn't want you within a mile of Addison."

"I never agreed to that! What did you expect me to do? Write him a letter? Simply ignore him? He loves me! I told him I would marry him when I was free. It would have

176

been cowardly not to tell him to his face." A choked sob escaped her. "It was the hardest thing I have ever had to do. I never want to go through anything like that again. And before you hand me my halo, let me tell you that my actions were not completely disinterested. I was counting on William to find a way out of this muddle I am in."

"Ah! And did he?"

She flashed him an angry look. The more patience he displayed, the more her annoyance grew. The panther, it seemed, was in playful mood. "You know very well that he did not."

"What did he have to say?"

"You should know," she retorted. "You were eavesdropping."

His eyes gleamed brightly with laughter. "I came in at the end, you know, when he was swearing his undying love."

"I see nothing to laugh at. He was hurt. Can't you understand that? Have you no heart? It would not have surprised me if he had hit me."

"And it would not have surprised me if he had challenged me to a duel." There was a note in his voice that Emily did not care to hear. She tightened her lips and said nothing.

"I said it would not have surprised me if he had challenged me to a duel!" His tone was low and savage. "Answer me, damn you!"

They were in the lower vestibule. He had crowded her between two Corinthian columns with her back to the wall. A stream of people were coming and going from the gardens to the main staircase. The din was rising, blotting out their own heated exchange.

"Why . . . why should William challenge you to a duel?

He is not like that. He is not like you."

"No, he is not like me, for if our positions had been reversed, if I had loved you, I would have called *him* out." There was a leashed violence about him that made her tremble in her shoes. "Love!" he went on in the same savage tone. "What do you know about love? What does he know? Doesn't the man have red blood in his veins? If he loves you, as you say, how can he permit you to come to me without a fight? Does he suppose that I shall respect your virginal scruples?" He made a derisory sound. "He knows better than that! He doesn't love you, Emily. I knew it when he backed away from my unspoken challenge not five minutes ago. And think on this. If Addison and I were to fight a duel over you and he killed me, your troubles would be over. That is one sure way of extricating yourself from a marriage you say you do not want."

He didn't understand. She didn't want men fighting duels over her. She hated violence of any description. A duel would solve nothing.

He was studying her so queerly. What did he expect to see? Moistening her lips, she said, "I would never forgive myself if such a thing happened."

"On the other hand," he said, "I may yet challenge Addison. I'd be within my rights, if he does not keep his distance from my wife."

"I won't encourage him," she said hurriedly. "I won't see him again, I promise you."

He was standing over her, looking down at her, a slow sardonic smile beginning to tease the corners of his mouth. The anger that had stirred him was gone. "So . . . I have my answer. You don't love Addison any more than he loves you. If you did you would not give up so easily."

He moved aside to let her pass. She wished more than

anything that she could hit him, or spit on him, or do something to wipe the cool mockery from his handsome face. Lady Emily Devereux could do none of those things.

"Violet eyes," he whispered tauntingly, ushering her through the arch to the staircase.

"Where are you taking me?" she asked with what she hoped was icy dignity.

"You may remember that you sent me to find Sara."

She had forgotten about Sara. "Where is she?"

"Well on her way to Gretna Green, I should say."

"What?" Her mouth fell open. She could not believe that she had heard aright. Leon did not seem to be the least bit affected.

"Your sister," he said, "eloped some hours ago with Peter Benson."

Chapter Ten

Within a few hours, Sara was to discover that she had made the biggest miscalculation of her life. It had never seriously occurred to her to tie herself irrevocably to any man who was not Leon, especially not Peter Benson. Her uncle had impressed upon her the unsuitability of the match. She had no doubt that Rolfe would catch up with them long before their carriage reached the Scottish border. There would be a scene. There would be the devil to pay and she would be brought home in disgrace. But the whole episode would be suppressed as though it had never happened. And everyone would be sorry for the slights she had been made to suffer. Especially Leon. And especially Emily. If there was one thing on which Sara was intent, it was to teach Leon and Emily . . . She wasn't quite sure what she was going to teach them. She only knew she wanted them to suffer as much as she had been made to suffer.

But it hadn't worked out as she had foreseen. Everything had gone wrong. Peter had mismanaged the whole affair. From the moment she had entered the chaise, she had smelled the liquor on his breath. To her sharp query, he had uttered something about "Dutch courage." He had not wanted to elope with her. Even then, with her port-manteau sitting on the opposite banquette, he had tried to dissuade her.

"In less than a year, you will come of age," he told her. "This is absurd. When you are one-and-twenty, we can marry without your guardian's consent."

"If you don't love me enough to brave my uncle's wrath, then say so now and we need never see each other again."

Her words had given him an unpleasant jolt. "Sara, you don't mean that."

"Try me, and see if I don't."

He was seeing a side of her that she had been at some pains to conceal. Fearing that she had gone too far, that he would back out of it, she had resorted to tears. She was so unhappy, she told him. He must join his regiment. He could be sent anywhere! There was no telling what might happen. She could not bear it if they did not have this time together.

Finally, he relented, and as the coach rattled over cob-blestoned streets, she settled into a corner and let her thoughts drift. She was using him. She had no desire to marry him. Peter Benson wasn't the man for her. The best she could say about him was that he was an amusing, attentive escort. He was not precisely handsome, but he was pleasant to look upon, if one had a taste for fair-skinned gentlemen with nondescript fair hair. Sara preferred something different. Leon's face flashed into her mind.

Before the night was over, her uncle would catch up with them. She had made sure of it by leaving farewell notes for them all. When her guardian found her, she would never be permitted to see Peter Benson again.

The small twinge of conscience was easily quashed. Though she was quite sure that Peter imagined himself to be in love with her, it was not *she* he loved but a girl who did not exist. He thought she was like all the other delicately nurtured females of his acquaintance, such as his mother and sisters. But she wasn't like that, not one whit. Few women were. It was a pose, a courtesy to convention to permit men to cherish the illusions which were dear to their hearts. In her experience, limited though it was, men did not understand the first thing about women, and knowing this, women were afraid to show their true colors.

It was just as well that she and Peter would be forced to part. They could never be happy together. He was weak. In a battle of wills, her stronger will must naturally prevail. She could never respect a man who allowed her to rule the roost. When she measured him against Leon, Peter fell far short.

He was younger than Leon by a year or two. She judged him to be in his late twenties. His background was impeccable. Peter was the younger son of an earl, and though the title and the estate had gone to his elder brother, Peter, on reaching his majority, had come into a handsome competence — and had soon lost it. Like most young men of his generation and class, he led a life of indolence. He was a gamester. Money slipped through his fingers.

Though Sara would never have countenanced a match with Peter Benson, for her purposes he would do as well as the next man, better, in fact, for at any moment, Peter would have a posting in His Majesty's Service that would take him out of England and her orbit. He would soon forget her. It was for the best.

She had fallen asleep and had a rude awakening. Just outside Islington, their coach ran off the road and into a ditch, almost overturning. Peter had taken a nasty crack on the head and had slipped into unconsciousness. She was forced to take charge.

Ever afterward she was to wonder why she had not told

182

the landlord of the Queen's Head that she and Peter were brother and sister. With no chaperone and no maid in attendance, she was forced to concoct some plausible story. Mr. & Mrs. Smith was the best she could invent. It wasn't exactly that she was panic-stricken, but she *was* alarmed. Peter was unconscious and a physician must be sent for. She must engage a private chamber if only to keep them both out of the public eye. Unfortunately, the Queen's Head appeared to be a popular hostelry. There were more carriages in the inn's courtyard than she would have wished.

From the moment of the physician's arrival, the events of the night took on the aspect of a nightmare. Peter was not injured but was as drunk as a lord. Dr. Mearle was incensed, having been dragged from his bed for no good purpose, and Sara could not blame him. He had hardly taken his irate departure when the door burst open. Three dandies filled the doorframe, three leering, tipsy louts who ogled Sara shamelessly. Only later would she learn that they had recognized the chaise in the inn's courtyard. It bore the crest of the earls of Latham. As was his wont, Peter had borrowed his brother's chaise, and his cronies had known it. Unhappily for Sara, those same cronies moved in her circles. By morning, the story would begin to circulate that Mr. & Mrs. Smith, better known as the Hon. Peter Benson and Lady Sara Brockford, had spent the night together in an inn just outside London.

By the time Rolfe and Leon had tracked them down, Sara had taken refuge with the landlord and his wife. One look at her guardian's stern face and she knew there was no persuading him. This time, she must face the consequences of her folly.

It was noon of the following day before the dread interview with her uncle took place in his bookroom. Peter was sober, but far from well. Rolfe was as grim as Sara had ever seen him. She could not bear to look him in the eye.

"You do realize," said Rolfe, addressing Peter, "that if I were in a mind to stir things up, I could have you court-martialed for this little debacle."

Peter straightened in his chair. His expression was as grim as Rolfe's. "I don't see how, sir."

"This is conduct unbecoming in an officer of the British Army," flashed Rolfe. "You know regulations as well as I do. You are obligated to obtain permission from your commanding officer before you marry. In this case, that did not happen."

"But I wasn't getting married, sir." At the look of surprised indignation which crossed Rolfe's face, the younger man hastily interposed, "I was taking Sara to my mother. I didn't know what else to do with her. She was in one of her strange takings. Well, you know how reckless and impulsive she can be. If I had said no to her, she would have run off with some other gentleman. I could not let that happen. I was going to send word to you as soon as we reached Barnet. Damn! I don't know how everything could have gone so wrong! That's a stupid thing to say! I . . . I'm afraid I made too free with my brandy flask. I became inebriated. It was inexcusable."

"And perfectly understandable!" Suddenly conscious that he had voiced the stray thought, Rolfe shrugged and went on lamely, "My nieces can do that to a man. Ask me. Ask Leon. Ask anyone who tries to order their lives." Both gentlemen exchanged a weak smile.

Sara's bosom was heaving. They were making fun of her. They weren't taking her seriously. Her life was in ruins and they were treating the whole thing as a huge joke. Her voice was scathing when she addressed Peter. "You said you wanted to marry me."

"Well, of course I did. I do. But not in that irregular fashion! You would not listen to reason. I thought, I hoped, that a few days with my mother would calm your temper and no harm done."

Sara was on her feet. Rolfe sank back in his chair and placed his laced fingers on the flat of his desk. He was staring at Peter Benson as though he had never seen the young man before. When Sara stamped her foot, his eyes reluctantly moved to his niece.

"How dare you toy with me!" she cried out, her mouth moving convulsively. "I know my own mind! If you didn't want to elope with me, you should have said so."

"I did say so! I told you that we should wait till you came of age. You didn't want to marry me. Don't you think I knew that? You were using me for your own purposes."

The silence which followed this heated exchange was long and profound. It ended when Sara ran from the room and slammed the door behind her.

"Almost," said Rolfe, eyeing the dejected slump of his companion's shoulders, "almost, I can feel sorry for you both." He reached for the brandy decanter and poured a liberal measure into two glasses, then offered one glass to the younger man.

Though he accepted the glass, Peter made no move to bring it to his lips. "She doesn't want to marry me," he said morosely. "She never did!"

Rolfe had a fleeting impression of déjà vu. As on another occasion, he used the exact same words. "Her wishes are immaterial, as are yours. It's gone too far for that. You must marry at once, and there's an end of it."

Without thinking, Peter bolted half his drink. He groaned, and pressed one hand to his aching temples. "I never meant it to end like this. I hope you believe me."

"What exactly did you intend? If you knew Sara had no

185

thought of marrying you, what did you hope to gain in the long run?"

"But I didn't know she had no thought of marrying me, or if I did, I wouldn't admit it to myself . . . that is . . ." He emitted a long sigh. "Sara is not the girl I thought she was."

The occasion was anything but amusing. Nevertheless, Rolfe had to bite down on a smile. He knew exactly what his young companion was getting at. Sara, like her sister Emily, was not made from the common mold. Gentlemen expected the softer sex to defer to their opinions, to their superior knowledge of the world. Ladies Emily and Sara thought themselves the equal of any male. Few men would have known it. Rolfe's nieces gave every appearance of observing the unwritten codes. It made life easier. It was only when they were challenged or crossed that each girl betrayed a will that was far from becoming in a female—at least in the eyes of gentlemen.

Rolfe frowned, thinking that there was something here with Sara that gave him cause for unease. Self-will was one thing, and easily curbed. Any man worth his salt would soon tame his female to his hand. No woman respected a man who allowed her to ride roughshod over him. And so he would advise Peter Benson. But this escapade went further than that. Sara had used Peter Benson for her own ends, uncaring of the young man's affections. It betrayed a self-regard, an egoism, that he would not have believed of Sara.

So unpalatable was this train of thought that Rolfe immediately began to search his mind for excuses to exonerate Sara's conduct. He fastened on his own culpability in the affair. He had made no attempt to conceal from Sara his contempt for the young man. He had given her the impression that young Benson was a profligate whose only interest in her was her fortune. He should not be surprised if Sara showed herself unscrupulous with a man whom she had been led to believe cared not a fig for her feelings.

Without giving the appearance of doing so, Rolfe studied his companion. Peter Benson, he supposed, was no better or no worse than others of his station. He had made it his business to probe into the boy's background. He had wanted something more for Sara, not merely because young Benson was up to his ears in debt, but because the boy lacked ambition. He was a younger son, and must make his own way in the world. Peter Benson had been content to drift with the tide. It was his brother, the earl, who had purchased his commission.

That thought led to another. "My niece may be an heiress," Rolfe began carefully, "but before this marriage goes forward, I insist that her fortune be tied up in such a way that—"

"I want no part of Sara's fortune!" Peter cut in vehemently. "Tie it up, by all means, so that only her heirs can claim a farthing of it. It was always in my mind that we should manage on my income."

"Income?" echoed Rolfe. "You mean . . . your Army pay?"

"I am not destitute," averred Peter stiffly.

"Well, not precisely, no, but . . ."

"I have an income from a trust that came to me through my grandmother's estate in the sum of a thousand pounds a year."

"Oh? Then why was it necessary for Latham to buy your commission? Why didn't you buy it yourself?"

Dark color ran across the younger man's cheekbones. His eyes dropped away from Rolfe's. In a halting tone, he got out, "I . . . I was a fool. I got into debt. My brother was kind enough to make me a loan." His eyes lifted and he

187

squared his shoulders. "George has generously agreed to cancel the debt on the occasion of my marriage."

To Rolfe's way of thinking, it was little enough for Latham to do. Then again, knowing that his younger brother had snagged an heiress, the earl probably saw no need to dip into his own coffers. As for Benson's income — a thousand pounds a year would scarcely keep Sara in pin money. Rolfe did not have the heart to point this out to the younger man.

In a reflective mood, Rolfe slowly sipped his brandy. Sara was a handful. It was worse than that. She was almost unmanageable. She didn't love this boy. Her heart was still set on Leon. For some obscure reason, she had embroiled herself in a scandal, had embroiled them all in a scandal. Whatever one might say about Peter Benson, one must give him his due. He had tried to avert the very catastrophe which had overtaken them. There was no doubt in Rolfe's mind that Peter Benson was in love with Sara. He did not envy young Benson the lot that had fallen to him. Sara would draw rings around any man who did not have the backbone to stand up to her. Young Benson was his own worst enemy. He was too nice, too malleable. If he were the boy's guardian and not Sara's, he was sure he would advise him to leave the girl in the lurch, yes, and snap his fingers at her considerable fortune. Money wasn't everything. A man must respect himself else . . .

That thought gave Rolfe the glimmer of an idea. "I believe you told me your regiment has been posted to Canada?"

The young man nodded and expelled a long breath. "Yes, the 41st," he answered without enthusiasm.

There was no need to elaborate. Rolfe understood perfectly. There was no glamour attaching to Canada, not when the British were waging war against Napoleon's armies in Spain. Young men hoped to cover themselves with glory serving with Wellington. Canada was a backwater and relatively safe, even supposing the Americans were making a damn nuisance of themselves. Hence Britain's decision to send some of its crack troops to patrol the American-Canadian border. It was all show, of course. Wellington could not spare the men.

"Where will you be stationed?"

"Possibly Montreal, or it could be York."

"York?"

"Sometimes known as Toronto," Peter clarified.

"Ah, *that* York. Mmm, yes . . . York . . . may do very well for our purposes," mused Rolfe.

"Sir?"

Breathing deeply, Rolfe began, "I don't wish to alarm you, Peter, but I do want to forewarn you," and he went on to describe the attacks which had been made against Sara and Emily.

They told her that she was a beautiful bride. She could not have cared less. Her heart was breaking. Only pride kept a smile on her face, pride and the knowledge that the man she loved was one of the select group of intimates invited to Rivard Abbey for the wedding. Though she scarcely spared him a glance, she was aware of Leon's every move, burningly aware of the arm that loosely clasped Emily's waist, as though it was Emily who must be supported through the frightful ordeal.

It didn't seem like a wedding. Everyone was too straight-faced. "Grim" was the word she wanted. Only Rolfe's boys seemed to take pleasure in the proceedings and that was because they were too young to know any better, did not dream that if Sara had her way, she would have been anywhere rather than here. The actions of Peter's mother and sisters didn't improve matters. They were weeping into their lace-edged handkerchiefs as if doomsday had arrived. The harder they cried, the more fixed became Sara's smile.

She scarcely recognized Peter. In his dress regimentals and with everyone referring to him as "Major Benson," he seemed like a stranger to her. The whole experience was an upsetting one — the ceremony, the introduction to Peter's relations in these unhappy circumstances, the sad, commiserating looks, her young cousins' artless, embarrassing questions, and the stilted toasts and conversations during the wedding breakfast. Sara knew what they were all thinking. So did Emily, if her heightened color was anything to go by. Their sympathies were all for poor Rivard whose nieces had both betrayed his trust in their time. Nothing could be worse than this, thought Sara as she sipped champagne and blinked back the hot tears of self-pity.

She was wrong. What followed was infinitely worse. The intimacies of married life were not at all as Aunt Zoë had described. It wasn't thrilling. It wasn't nice. It was downright undignified and distasteful. After the first night, Sara wanted no part of it, and so she had sobbed out to her new husband on the second night he came to her bed. He was gentle. He was forbearing. He was also as deaf as a doornail. Some misguided meddler, his elder brother to be precise, had warned him that a husband must expect tears and entreaties from a new bride.

It came to Sara, then, that a terrible injustice had been perpetrated against her own sex, yes, and married women connived at it! Young girls should be told what awaited them in wedlock. Then there would be no balls, and no flirting, and no babies. If she had only known what was in store for her, she would have resolved to remain unattached for the rest of her life. And, really, there was no necessity for her to marry. She was a woman of independent means.

Marriage to Peter had changed everything. Her fortune was no longer her own. She did not understand the ins and outs of it, but it seemed that there was a trust and settlements, and goodness knows what else that practically reduced her to penury.

"Your income is quite substantial," Rolfe had reassured her.

"Then what's to stop me from spending it?"

"Only your husband. No, it's no good arguing with me, Sara. Your husband has the management of your affairs. You must be guided by Peter."

Sara absorbed this intelligence in smoldering silence. A moment's reflection reassured her. Peter Benson had always been putty in her hands. For the present, Peter had adopted the role of her trustee. He was taking his responsibilities seriously — too seriously. When the novelty had worn off, he would be more approachable. She knew how to get round Peter.

There were compensations to marriage, and Sara was resolved to enjoy every one of them. She wasn't going to be like her sister. She wasn't going to share her guardian's roof while her husband was off in foreign parts carving out a career for himself. That would inhibit her ambitions. She was going to set up her own establishment. She was going to give balls and parties and have her own carriage. She was going to become fashionable and sought after. Lady Sara Benson was going to be a somebody.

Her hopes helped to raise her spirits until Emily and Leon made to depart on the first leg of the journey that would take them to New York. It was an emotional farewell. Emily was loathe to tear herself away from her family. Sara thought she understood her sister's misgivings. New York was on the other side of the world. The society to be found in the colonies was hardly to be compared to the society to be found in England.

But it was so much more than that. Sara and Emily had never been apart for more than a few weeks at a time, and that only when they were away at school. There had been many upheavals in their young lives, but they had always faced them together. Now, suddenly, they could no longer be confidantes, not because of the distance that was fated to separate them, but because two specimens of the male gender had cut them out of the herd. A wife must naturally turn to her husband. It was enjoined on her not only by custom, but also by law and church dogma.

In that moment of leave-taking, old hurts and rivalries were forgotten.

"It won't be for long," said Emily, clinging to her sister as though her life depended on it. "I shall be back before you know it."

Sara could not say a word for her tears.

At length, their respective husbands separated the two girls. The carriage doors slammed, and it was as if the sound of it signified the end of a chapter in their young lives.

The future looked very bleak and uncertain.

Chapter Eleven

Leon could not believe how easily everything was contrived. With a meekness that astounded him, Emily had allowed him to order their journey to suit himself. She seemed completely oblivious of the unusual number of outriders who accompanied their carriage, had never questioned him on their last stop when he had told her that they must switch coaches since the axle on their own coach had developed a crack. And when he had informed her of his change of plans, that they were not making for Falmouth but for Southampton where a ship of his brother-in-law's line was docked, she had accepted his explanations without demur. He had heard about the *Valclair* quite by chance in the taproom of the hostelry where they were dining, he had told her. The long ocean voyage would be much more comfortable aboard the *Valclair*. What he had not told her was that they were expected and that the *Valclair* was a merchant vessel carrying no passengers, a circumstance which suited his purposes admirably.

His methods were extreme, but he was prepared for the worst. If La Compagnie was on his trail, they would never have a better chance to ambush him. He was well aware of it and had taken every precaution. The coach in which they had started out was a decoy. Even now, it was taking the main road to Falmouth as originally planned, while he spirited Emily away to Southampton by back roads. In a day or two, before they sailed, he would have his answer. A report would be made to him. If no ambush had taken place, he must accept that he had allowed his imagination to run away with him. He hoped that was the case, but he very much feared that his instincts were as unerring as they had ever been.

Yet, he sensed that all was not as it seemed to be. As Rolfe had pointed out, it was years since he had been a member of La Compagnie. He was no threat to the society's new leaders—not unless there was something he knew that he was not aware he knew. Was it possible, he wondered, that he could identify the mastermind behind the resurrected La Compagnie? He examined that thought from all angles, and decided it was highly improbable. He had never been an important cog in La Compagnie's wheel. He had known only the members of his own small cell. According to Rolfe, every one of them, barring himself, had perished. And all of that had happened years before, when he was a mere youth.

Impatient with himself, he forced his thoughts to the future. He was carrying his wife off to his own domain. In New York, they would be safe. There was very little that happened there without his coming to hear of it. At the first hint of trouble, he had already mapped out his course. That thought brought a smile flashing to his lips.

In silent contemplation, through half-lowered lids, he allowed his eyes to make a slow inspection of his wife. She was involved in reading the latest copy of *Ackermann's*, which she had brought with her to while away the long, tedious hours of the journey. From time to time, she glanced out the coach window. Occasionally, she gave a telling sigh.

They were completely alone in an enclosed carriage. The thought acted on him like a powerful aphrodisiac. Emily was his wife. He could take her if he wanted to. He had that right.

He reined in that line of logic before he got carried away with it. He wanted more than access to his wife's lovely body. He could be patient . . . for a little while longer.

Soon, he would destroy every last defense she had ever constructed against him. She'd had years in which to arm herself for this final battle. Her arsenal was formidable: her childish antipathy to him, his past indiscretions, Sara's *tendre* for him, and now William Addison. Emily could pull arrows for her quiver out of thin air and every one of those arrows would have his name on it. If he tried to storm the citadel, she would make him pay dearly for it. He couldn't help smiling. He was thinking that he aimed to take the citadel by stealth.

He had made a beginning. In the last week or two, he had tried to establish normalcy between them. He hoped Emily was getting the message. He was consumed with more than the thought to tumble her in bed and have his way with her. He was at some pains to demonstrate that they could be friends as well as lovers. They could have a good life together.

And Emily, it seemed, was meeting him halfway. He was glad to note that his wife was putting a good face on it. He knew that she was reluctant to leave England. All the same, she was striving to keep an open mind about a country which, by her lights, must seem almost uncivilized. He studied the faint frown on her brow and wondered what she was thinking.

The farther the coach carried them away from Rivard Abbey, the more Emily contemplated what lay in her future. She saw at once that Sara's marriage marked a turning point. For better or worse, Leon was now hers. She tested the thought gingerly and was surprised at the little leap in her pulse.

She did not love her husband. That conviction was so firmly planted in Emily's mind, was of such long duration, that she did not have to think about it. Leon had an effect on her, that much she was willing to allow. But that was not love. That was a trick of nature to ensure the survival of the species. She knew she did not love Leon because he had made sure she hated him since the time they were children.

Yet . . . there had been a remarkable change in Leon's manner. He was being nice to her. It had started on the night of Sara's elopement. Everyone was in shock, Uncle Rolfe especially. The man seemed to have aged ten years. Without warning, he had rounded on her.

"A fine pair you girls make! Your father must be turning in his grave to see how both his daughters have turned out. God, where do you get it from? That's what I should like to know! There was never a hint of scandal attaching to any Brockford female before you girls came into the family. Two discreditable matches, one after the other! I don't know how your aunt will hold up her head for the disgrace."

At this tirade, all the color had rushed out of Emily's face. Aunt Zoë turned furiously on her husband. But it was the ice in Leon's voice which stayed Rolfe's spate of words.

"I don't permit anyone to talk to my wife in those terms," he said. Somehow, his arm was around Emily's shoulders, pressing her into the shield of his body. Grateful for his support, she sagged against him. "Time is wasting." His manner was as abrupt as his voice. "Do we go after Sara, or do we stand here arguing all night long?"

As suddenly as it had come upon him, Rolfe's anger drained away. With a half contrite, half cozening grin, he had apologized profusely, ending with, "Forgive me, kitten. You know I didn't mean it. Your case is not the same as Sara's."

Emily managed a tremulous smile, but Leon's tones were no warmer. "No. It is not. Anyone who knows her must know that she was the innocent party when we were forced to wed."

For Leon to rush to her defense surprised Emily as much as it warmed her. In the week that followed, when they had all removed to Rivard Abbey for Sara's wedding, she had occasion to be grateful for Leon's unfailing support. It seemed to her that the old scandal was resurrected and fingers were pointing at her. It was always thus. Men could commit folly after folly with impunity. A woman's reputation was fragile and easily destroyed.

The attack, an oblique one, had come from one of Peter's female relations. Lady Hester, Peter's sister, looked as sweet and as pure as bleached sugar. Only those who felt the blade of her tongue would have known that it was coated with poison. Emily soon discovered it for herself.

Uncle Rolfe had no time for the woman. "Don't let Lady Hester overset you," he said to Emily. "She's one of those who considers herself a guardian of the nation's morals. She has an opinion on absolutely everything. What she needs is marriage to some man who will trounce her once in a while. That's not likely to happen, though. She is allowing all the curly-brimmed beavers to pass her by while she holds out for a coronet."

Emily took to avoiding Lady Hester and her venomous tongue. Sensing Emily's discomfort, Leon became her shadow. She would feel his hand at her elbow, his arm loosely clasped around her waist, and those small gestures of ownership conveyed a wealth of meaning. In Leon's presence, no one dared say a slighting word to his wife.

She glanced at him from the corner of her eye, then allowed her gaze to settle on him fully when she observed that he had drifted into sleep. It wasn't true to say that he acted the part of the doting husband. On the other hand, he didn't act like the old Leon, either. He was like a stranger, though a charming one. It was as if he were trying to establish a new model in their verbal intercourse. In the space of a week, they had not exchanged one cross word. Incredible!

Nor had he made the slightest move to exercise his conjugal rights. Emily chewed on her bottom lip, wondering what it might all mean. Naturally, she was grateful, she told herself. Sara's presence at the Abbey was inhibiting, to say the least. Sara and Leon. For years, it had been impossible for her not to think of them as belonging together. Sara's marriage to Peter had made all the difference in the world.

Her thoughts had come full circle. She was married to Leon for better for worse. The future was what she would make of it.

From the opposite banquette, Leon angled his head back and studied his wife through lowered lids. Tears stood on her lashes. She brushed them away with impatient fingers. Leon was not quite sure whether he wanted to shake some sense into her or gather her in his arms and kiss those tears away. If she was pining for the loss of her girlhood home and her family, that was one thing. If she was pining for her lost lover, that was something else.

"What are you thinking?" he asked softly. Yawning, stretching his cramped muscles, he made a show of coming to himself.

Emily moistened her upper lip. "I have been thinking

198

about the future."

"Have you?" he murmured.

His tone was not very encouraging. She hesitated, then said in an earnest tone, "You once told me that you were ready to settle down, set up your own establishment, begin . . . that is . . . raise a family."

"I believe I did. Pray, continue."

He sat at his ease, his back propped against a corner of the coach, his eyes registering little interest in what she was saying. For all that, she sensed that he was as alert as a panther whose lair had been invaded by a hapless kitten.

She breathed deeply and gazed at him with eyes as clear as crystal. "What's done is done. There is no going back now, no point in repining for what might have been. I have come to accept that our marriage is indissoluble. I am willing to be a true wife to you, Leon." Her voice faded as she gave one last lingering regret to the dreams and fancies of a young girl. She wasn't thinking particularly of William Addison. She was thinking of that intense yearning for love and fulfillment which seemed to be bred into her very bones.

She did not know that her eyes mirrored her every thought. Leon absorbed the wistful expression, the tremulous curve to her lips, and he swore in a soft undertone. In a voice like velvet, he said, "So . . . you've persuaded yourself to make the supreme sacrifice?"

"No. I don't think of it like that."

"Then how would you describe it?" When she was searching in her mind for the right words, he said with sudden violence, "Answer me!"

Baldly, she stated, "I shall be a dutiful wife, I promise you. I won't make things difficult for you. I won't complain and make a fuss if you neglect me." She was getting into difficulties and did not know how to extricate herself. "All I want is a home of my own and . . . and children," she concluded helplessly.

"What does that mean, precisely—you won't make things difficult for me?"

"You know." Her eyes dropped to her clasped hands. "You explained it to me once before, don't you remember?" Her mind drifted back in time to the interview she'd had with Leon prior to their marriage. "You said that the rules are different for men and women. You said that a wife should be forgiving of a husband's follies." Sensing that she might have given him the wrong impression, she hastened to add, "Oh, I'm not asking for the same liberties for myself. Did you think that I was?" She leaned forward slightly as though to add weight to her words. "No, no! Affairs and that sort of thing are repugnant to me."

The deadly quiet that followed her reasonable assurances almost frightened her. She could not think what she had said to annoy him. But he was annoyed. Though his face was inscrutable, she was never in any doubt about that.

A muscle clenched in his cheek. "Our marriage has been consummated," he said carelessly. "For the present, my purposes have been served. I'm not in my dotage, Emily. I have years ahead of me in which to establish my dynasty. When that day arrives, you may be sure you will be the first to know."

Without meaning to, she had said something terribly wrong. She could not bring herself to say more, though she might have told him that she was only trying to do the generous thing. It's what she had thought he wanted. Well, if he wanted none of her, she wanted none of him. Affecting an interest in the passing scenery, she left him to stew in silence.

* * *

Some days were to pass before the axe fell. In that time, Sara went riding around the estate, sometimes in the company of her young cousins, sometimes with Peter. She would have preferred to be alone. Every tree, every dale, every nook and cranny in the place seemed to whisper to her of a time when she had not a care in the world and she was too young to know it. In those days the future had seemed full of promise. She was not yet one-and-twenty and she felt as old as Methuselah.

Peter came upon her when she was lost in reverie, gazing blindly into the waters of the old mill pond. It was where she and Emily had learned to swim. There had been an incident here involving Leon. Sara could not quite recall all the details. But one thing she remembered. It was she who had walked off with Leon and Emily who had been left to her own devices.

She jumped when her husband's hand touched her shoulder. "Peter!" she gasped. "You startled me!"

He brushed one warm finger across her cheek, removing a solitary teardrop. "Why so dismal?" he asked gently.

The answer to that question was too involved for Sara to attempt. She said simply, "Emily and I used to come here as children. It's where we learned to swim."

"You were very close?"

"Very." It wasn't quite the truth, but it wasn't a lie, either. They were sisters. In Sara's mind, all the complexities of their relationship were summed up in those few words.

"Take heart. You may see Emily sooner than you think."

"Oh?" she said, allowing him to direct her steps to where their mounts were tethered.

He assisted her into the saddle, then quickly mounted. His horse was restive. It reared up, and Sara watched interestedly as her husband imposed his will on the big bay.

201

Behind her stare she was thinking that appearances could be deceptive. Her husband had a drowsy-eyed look about him. He was good-natured, and inclined to give way to those of a more forceful temperament. That hadn't happened with the bay. The horse had quieted, as though conceding that the man on his back could not be moved by ill-tempered tricks or maneuvers.

Sara's brows drew together. She was thinking about the income from her fortune. She was remembering her wedding night and her initiation into the intimacies of the marriage bed. Her startled glance flew to her husband's face.

In the sunlight, his fair hair was touched with gold. One lock fell across his forehead, giving him a boyish appearance. His eyes were soft as they rested on her. Gradually, her unease melted away.

"I have decided," he said in his pleasantly modulated accents, "that you shall accompany me to Canada. I shall be on the move for much of the time, but you won't be alone. I have persuaded Hester to come with us. She'll be good company for you, Sara, and she knows how to run a house. And Leon has promised to consider sending Emily to us for an extended visit. Fort York isn't so very far away from New York, you know." His voice dwindled. "Sara? What is it? What have I said?"

She was gaping at him in openmouthed horror. Fort York was at the end of the world, or near enough to make no difference. As for his sister, Lady Hester Benson was something of a dragon. She was a paragon of propriety and very much in demand as a chaperone when young girls made their come-out. In short, Lady Hester was a killjoy who stood for no nonsense.

When he began to repeat himself, more slowly this time, as if she were a half-witted child, she interrupted angrily. "I heard what you said the first time, and the answer is no! Nothing will prevail upon me to leave England."

She would have dug in her heels if he had not reached for the reins and held her hands steady. The sleepy look was gone from his eyes, but there was a pleading note in his voice. "Sara, you are my wife. A wife's place is with her husband. It may be years before I return to England. That is no way for us to begin married life."

An odd mixture of fear and fury made her words more brutal than she meant them to be. "It was never in my mind to marry you. You know that! I made a mistake. I've paid for it. What you are suggesting is . . . is . . . a punishment, yes, that's what it is. It's a punishment. I don't deserve to be sent away from everything that is dear to me. I refuse to leave my family. I won't go, and you can't make me."

She squinted up at him as he straightened in the saddle. Before her eyes, the boyish good looks hardened into something quite different. Though his face and voice were expressionless, his words seemed to hammer into her brain.

"I'm sorry you feel that way. If it were up to me, I would leave you here. My wishes, however, don't come into it. I gave a solemn promise to your uncle that you would accompany me to Canada."

The words were torn from her. "But why would Uncle Rolfe wish to send me away?"

He hesitated, as if debating with himself, then said bluntly, "You know why, Sara. My dear, you have gone your length. England is too small for you. Your uncle has decided, and I concur with him, that you are due for a change of scene."

* * *

The attack came on the other side of the New Forest, near Wimborne. The decoy coach was set upon by three armed highwaymen. They got more than they bargained for. Two of them were wounded. The third got clean away.

Leon heard out the groom in silence before putting a few terse questions to him. "Were there any distinguishing marks on any of them, some way of recognizing them if you were ever to encounter them again?"

The groom, Ben Sharpe, was Rolfe's man and not unused to such escapades. He had a trained ear and eye. "They were young gents," he said, "no more than fifteen or sixteen, I should say. This was a lark. They were shocked senseless when we opened fire on 'em."

Leon digested the groom's words, then said, "What makes you think it was a lark?"

Surprise crossed Ben's face. "Them being young'uns hardly out o' swaddlin' clothes. That's why. The young quality don't care who gets hurt so long as they has their bit o' sport."

There was very little more to go on. Leon quickly penned a letter to Rolfe, amplifying the groom's report. Rolfe must take a very dim view of this latest development. Young boys of fifteen and sixteen were just the right age for enlisting in the cause. It seemed as though history was repeating itself. He wondered if he would ever be free of La Compagnie.

When he stood at the deck rail with Emily, he was not sorry to see the English coastline receding into the distance. If he was sorry about anything, it was that he had acted prematurely in coming to England to fetch his wife. If indeed he was a target of La Compagnie, it would have been better to put as much distance as possible between them.

He dismissed that thought almost as soon as it occurred

to him. America wasn't England. None of the attacks had occurred in America and he knew how to protect his own in his own domain.

"God, I can't wait to get home," he said.

At his side, Emily inhaled sharply and let out a long sigh.

Chapter Twelve

Emily could never forget that Leon had reproached her for an unbecoming reserve in her manner. She was too formal, he said, giving the appearance that she had a high opinion of herself. From the moment she set foot on American soil, Emily was determined to make a favorable impression. Everything about America was going to please her. She had made up her mind to it.

Leon's sister's house was as grand as any to be found in London and was situated on Broadway, with extensive gardens in back which swept down toward the river. The citizens of New York, she noted, were not above keeping chickens or cows in the pasture behind their stables. Domestic animals, including pigs, freely roamed the streets. Emily observed it all but was careful not to make a comment that might be construed as derogatory. Leon was watching her like a hawk.

It came as something of a shock when she divined that Leon's sister did not like her, and this before she had opened her mouth to say more than a few polite words of greeting. Claire Dillon was faintly hostile, and Emily could not understand it.

It was all the more perplexing and all the more obvious

because the rest of Claire's family welcomed Emily as if she had been the prodigal returning from a far country. Adam and Claire Dillon had five offspring, the eldest a daughter of fifteen summers, the youngest an infant daughter, and three boys somewhere in between.

"We have been waiting for this day to arrive for a long time, Emily," said Adam Dillon, embracing Emily warmly. She judged him to be a little older than her guardian and very distinguished looking with silver wings at his temples, a dramatic contrast to his raven black hair. She liked him on sight.

"Yes, a very long time," echoed Claire vaguely, then not so vaguely, "We were sure you would be here three years ago, when Leon went to England to fetch you."

Before Emily could respond, the awkwardness was smoothed over as Leon brought his nieces and nephews forward to be introduced in turn. Without exception, they were all the image of their father. Only Sarah, the eldest, had something of her mother's look about her—eyes as blue as the Mediterranean. Though the girl was arresting in her own way, she did not hold a candle to her mother. Claire Dillon, with her flaming Titian locks and fine-boned features put all females in the shade, to Emily's way of thinking. She had never seen a more beautiful woman in her life.

Emily's chamber was at the back of the house, overlooking the river. She was gazing out one of the long windows when Leon came through the connecting door.

"What do you think?" he asked.

She wasn't going to find fault with his sister. She could be as vague as the next person. "They seem like a devoted family," she said, "and as for the house, it's simply splendid." Looking about her with interest, she observed, "I suppose your sister had these pieces imported from England?"

She was referring to the several polished mahogany commodes and dressers of Heppelwhite design which graced the room.

"Why should you think so? We are quite civilized here in America, Emily. We do have cabinet makers, you know, and masons and seamstresses and others of that ilk. What we don't have is an aristocracy. Even so, you will find that the manners and modes prevailing in New York are not so very different from those in London."

The rebuke was faint, but for all that it was a rebuke. Emily chose to ignore it. "I'm sure I shall find everything quite . . ."

"Yes, I know . . . *charming*," he said dryly.

She gave him one of her sunniest smiles, and in what she hoped was her most *charming* manner, indicated that he should seat himself on the striped satin sofa. "Well?" she said at length when he gazed at her wordlessly.

Behind his blank stare he was thinking that he must be a candidate for either sainthood or an insane asylum. He had wanted this woman for more years than he cared to remember. He was no novice. He knew when a woman was ripe for plucking. She was highly susceptible to him. More to the point, she had indicated that she was willing for the marriage to become a real one. He was the one who had held off. On that long and tedious ocean voyage, he was the one who had retreated behind a wall of glacial reserve.

He had been almost blind with rage. That she would be a submissive, dutiful wife! That she would turn a blind eye to his infidelities! He wanted to murder her for her indifference. He would rather have her hatred than her complacency. Better to burn with unsated desire than accept her on those terms.

Brave words! His anger was no longer riding him. He was coming to see how much his pride had cost him. For five long years he had held off from his wife, giving her time to mature. Those five years seemed like child's play compared to this. For the first time ever, his wife was completely in his power. There was no guardian for her to run to. And now he knew what he had only suspected then, that behind that cool-as-a-cucumber air, Emily concealed a nature as sensual and as passionate as his own. He could hardly wait to get at it.

Emily cocked her head as her gaze rested on her husband's whimsical expression. Their eyes met and held. She knew what he was thinking without being told. He was remembering those two days and nights aboard his yacht.

Smiling tenderly at her adorably guilty blushes, Leon said, "It's the manner and modes prevailing in New York about which I wish to speak to you."

"Yes?" said Emily, ordering herself to look as unaffected as he.

"In these parts, it's not *comme il faut* for husbands and wives to go their separate ways."

"Beg pardon?"

"We Americans are more affectionate, more demonstrative, than our English cousins. If you were to treat me with the same reserve, the same indifference, that is, as you did in England, speculation would be rife. Tongues would begin to wag. In no time at all, everyone would think the worst."

Emily smiled dulcetly. Completely forgetting her resolve not to make things difficult for her husband, she said, "No doubt they would think that *you* had taken a mistress and *I* had taken a lover."

Leon's black eyes danced. "No," he said.

"No?"

"They would never believe that you had taken a lover for the simple reason that they know I would not permit it.

American husbands are not so complacent as English husbands, Emily. They don't permit their wives to have suitors, and lovers, and so on."

Her charm began to fray a little at the edges. "Perhaps you would be so kind as to tell me what I may expect?"

Leon's smile intensified. "For a start, you must remember that America is a republic."

"I'm aware of that," she said carefully.

"We shall dispense with the titular 'Lady,' if you please. Here you will be known simply as 'Mrs. Devereux.' "

She might have told him that as the daughter of a marquess, she was born a lady and she would die a lady. "As you wish," she said, and pressed her lips together.

"In America, we are all equals. There is no protocol to be observed as there is in England. Nevertheless, there are certain forms which you would do well to follow. You may depend on me to keep you right."

It sounded boring. "If there is no protocol, then how can I go wrong?"

"Knowing you, you'll find a way."

He couldn't help baiting her. It was exhilarating. And Emily brought it on herself. Her manners were so polished, her composure so unshakable. And her eyes, as of this moment, were the color of amethysts. When he made love to her, they would darken even more. The thought was an arousing one. It slipped under his guard before he had time to take evasive action. His body went hard with need. Emily didn't notice.

"All I am saying, Emily, is that you should take your cue from me. As I said, my family will expect us to be more than civil to each other. They will expect us to be affectionate. They will expect you to defer to my wishes. I don't intend that they should be disappointed. Do you take my meaning?"

Evidently, she did. In the weeks that followed, she gave him "affection" with a vengeance. Every soft look, every warm smile, her lightest touch—and there were many of those—all had his temperature leaping to boiling point.

He stole kisses in the garden. "Claire is watching us," he said, without any foundation for his comment. In the carriage, when he fondled her, he was more inventive. "The coachmen will carry tales below stairs." But in the summerhouse, when he pounced on her, with no one there to see them, his imagination completely failed him.

They were both trembling when he brought the kiss to an end. "What was that for?" asked Emily when she finally got her breath back.

He slanted her a lazy grin. "That was for myself," he said, and slowly drawing her into his arms, he kissed her again.

He had almost made up his mind to swallow his pride and accept her on any terms he could get when matters came to a head. Emily was introduced to Belle Courtney at a ball in the City Tavern.

Emily had not known what to expect when she heard that they were to attend a ball at the City Tavern. The very name made her shudder in revulsion. Her husband had told her that modes and manners were freer in America. She prepared herself for the worst.

It came as a surprise when she alighted from the carriage before what seemed to be the grandest mansion on Broadway. It was a residence fit for a king. Her surprise must have registered, for her sister-in-law made a remark in passing to the effect that, contrary to popular opinion in England, Americans knew how to put on a good show.

"What do you know about England?" Adam Dillon

teased, slipping an arm around his wife's waist as he led her through the great front doors.

Claire's reply was lost on Emily. Leon bent his head to her. "You mustn't mind Claire," he said. "She doesn't mean anything by it. America has been good to her, to us both. She doesn't allow anyone to criticize her adopted country."

"But I wasn't going to say anything," protested Emily.

"Weren't you?"

"No."

Laughter glittered in his eyes. "Not even, 'How utterly *charming*'?"

He had mimicked her accent to perfection. She opened her mouth and quickly shut it. He wasn't going to make her lose her temper. In any event, she didn't feel angry. She felt hurt. It wasn't only that Leon was taking his sister's part. It seemed that she could not put a foot right with Claire Dillon.

As they deposited their wraps in the ladies' cloakroom, Emily idly surveyed her reflection in one of the long mirrors. At her husband's behest, she was wearing her blue silk net, another small evidence to her way of thinking that she aimed to please.

Claire Dillon did not like her. Why? She wracked her brains and came up empty. It was so unfair. She wasn't a critical girl. She wasn't above pleasing. Yet, without her saying a word, it was taken for granted that she would find fault with everything.

For the most part, New York pleased her very well. It was a young, vigorous city. She felt quite at home with its Georgian architecture. The inhabitants might easily have been taken for citizens of any town in England if it were not for the odd inflection in their accent and some quaint, archaic forms in the language which had survived in America.

Good grief! They *were* English, or near enough as made no difference. True, they had their Dutch and French contingents, but so did England. As far as she could tell, only an accident of history and a Fourth of July celebration distinguished Americans from their British counterparts. Not that you could tell an American that. They were extremely sensitive. She wasn't going to offend them. She had made a resolve and she aimed to keep it. She was going to be the most agreeable girl at the ball.

Leon was indispensable, introducing her to scores of people. She could not help noticing that her husband stood high in the esteem of his peers. This fact was brought home to her once the dancing got started.

She was inundated with partners, all of them gentlemen who had been introduced to her by Leon. It soon became clear to her that the name of Devereux was practically revered. Her husband was a financier, in the great tradition of the Devereuxs in prerevolutionary France. Emily had heard most of the story before from her guardian. She heard it now as if she were hearing it for the first time. Except in general terms, she really did not know what a financier was. Nor did she know very much about Leon's early years. She knew that his parents had perished during the Revolution and that he and his sisters had been scattered, but that was all she knew. Her ignorance shamed her. A wife ought to know something about her husband's background. Leon knew everything there was to know about her. Why did she know so little about him?

The thought did not stay with her long. A more disquieting thought took possession of her mind. More than once, the word "war" was said in her hearing, and the speaker was immediately silenced when her presence was observed. She knew, of course, of the present furor over American and British shipping. If it came to a war between England and America, she did not see how she could remain in New York.

"Enjoying yourself?" The question came from Adam Dillon. He had come to claim Emily for a country dance.

Adam had none of his wife's reserve, and Emily felt quite at ease with him. He was Irish. Perhaps that explained it. He had more than his fair share of Irish charm. "I feel quite at home," she said, unwittingly bestowing the highest praise she could attribute to anything that was not English. "I might as well be at Almack's."

"Almack's Assemblies? Yes, I've heard of them. But they are exclusive affairs, surely?"

"I'd say Almack's was on a par with the City Tavern." His look was skeptical and she said gaily, "It's where the bluebloods congregate. And before you remind me that America is a republic, let me tell you that I can smell a blueblood a mile off."

Adam Dillon was thinking that his little sister-in-law was quite a taking thing when she let her guard down. "Bluebloods?" he quizzed. "Here?"

With a sidelong glance, she indicated a white-haired, elderly lady who was holding court at the edge of the dance floor. As Adam watched, several fond mamas brought their daughters forward to make their curtsies.

"The dowager Duchess of New York," said Emily in a confiding air. "A tyrant in her own way, but a benevolent one. On all matters of taste and deportment, the dowager duchess's opinion holds sway. Am I right?"

Adam's green eyes gleamed brightly. "You have Mrs. Burke's portrait to a nicety." What he refrained from saying was that Mrs. Sarah Burke was as close to him as his own mother and the godmother and namesake of his elder

214

daughter. "What about the young man who has just entered?"

Adam had a particular reason for singling out Gilbert Livingston. Though she was only fifteen, his little Sarah could not hide her partiality for the boy. Young Livingston was too much the ladies' man for Adam's taste. He wanted something far steadier for his Sarah.

Emily's eyes shifted to take in a strikingly handsome young man close to her own age. Her glance was returned with a bold, interested stare. Before Mr. Livingston got the wrong idea, she quickly averted her head. "Viscount Lothario," she drawled. "Every girl's secret dream and the bane of her father's existence." Her eyes were sparkling. "Young Lothario reminds doting papas too much of themselves in their salad days, you see."

Adam laughed. "Minx! You know too much." Then he added slyly, "And what about the lady in conversation with the dowager duchess?"

Emily turned her head and her stare was caught and held by Claire Dillon. Claire's eyelashes swept down, as though to blot out the sight of her. Emily felt the hurt spread through her like poison from a snakebite. Suddenly, the game had lost its savor.

"Well?" prompted Adam, unaware of the silent exchange. "What have you to say about Claire?"

She had to say something. She nodded her head wisely. "*Lady* Claire," she said. "The daughter of a marquess or my name isn't Mrs. Devereux." She meant it to sound lighthearted, but the hurt came through.

The smile on Adam's lips died. His voice was very gentle when he said, "What has Claire been saying to you, Emily?"

"Nothing . . . nothing at all," she answered truthfully. That was the problem. She didn't know what she had done

215

wrong, so she didn't know how to put it right.

"You must understand, Claire is very close to her brother. They lost both their parents during the Revolution. Of course, you know this. What none of us will ever know is what Leon was made to endure in the thick of all that bloodletting. His sisters, at least, escaped to sanctuary. But Leon . . ." Shaking his head, he continued. "Claire wants Leon to be happy, 'tis all. Don't be too severe on her. Now that you are finally here, Claire will come round, you'll see." What he was thinking was that the first chance he got he was going to tear a strip of his beloved wife. He had warned her in no uncertain terms not to meddle in what did not concern her.

Attempting to distract Emily, he said, "What about the lady in the scarlet get-up, the one with the collar of emeralds at her throat?"

Emily reluctantly allowed herself to be distracted. Adam's confidences respecting Leon mystified her. She would ponder them later.

The lady in question was the only real challenger to Claire Dillon. But where Claire's beauty was pristine, this woman's beauty was wanton. The knowledge of Eve was in every look, every gesture. No husband worth his salt would permit his wife to conduct herself with so little regard for propriety.

"Mrs. Worldly Widow," essayed Emily. "She doesn't have any female friends, nor does she want any. But the list of gentlemen who beat a path to her door are only to be found in Burke's peerage or its American equivalent."

Adam was convulsed with laughter. "Good Lord!" he said finally. "You terrify me, Emily! No, you may not give me my character. I don't think my vanity could take it."

"Who is she?" asked Emily idly.

"That," said Adam, "is Mrs. Belle Courtney."

Ever afterward, Emily would blame the collar of emeralds for the contretemps which followed. She wasn't jealous of the woman, she told herself. Where there was jealousy, there must be love, and she knew she did not love Leon. But for certain her feathers were ruffled.

Ruffled feathers be damned! She was ready to spit fire. Belle Courtney had been hovering at the back of her mind since Lord Riddley had referred to her as "Devereux's mistress." Leon, so Riddley had intimated, had given the woman a set of gems worth a king's ransom. Emily believed him. The emeralds at Belle Courtney's throat would have bought and sold Carlton House ten times over.

She was exaggerating, but Emily wasn't in the mood to be reasonable. She was incensed. It was *her* money that had put those gems around Belle Courtney's throat. It was *her* fortune that had made Leon Devereux a financier, and the envy of all his peers. Before his marriage to her, he was nothing, a penniless fugitive from the French Revolution. He was to be congratulated on his meteoric rise. He had managed to attach himself to one of the richest heiresses in all of England.

There was no containing her anger. She wasn't forgetting that where she had offered to put their differences behind them and make the marriage a real one, Leon had coolly informed her that things were to go on as before. He was in no hurry to change their present arrangement. And now she could see why. His mistress was more beautiful than any woman had a right to be. And more vulgar. In all probability, her vulgarity was part of her charm. Men!

There were other feelings Emily was experiencing, but she pushed these to the back of her mind. She concentrated on her sense of outrage. No man of integrity would spend his wife's fortune in decking out his mistress in such style.

When she finally came face-to-face with Belle Courtney, she was a seething cauldron of hurt pride. Mrs. Courtney was all smiles, and that irked Emily more.

It was Claire who made the introductions over supper. Emily sensed her sister-in-law's reluctance, and no wonder. She should be ashamed to introduce her brother's wife to his mistress. Leon and Adam had wandered into the gardens to enjoy a quiet smoke with some of the other gentlemen.

"I've been admiring your necklace all evening," said Emily, showing a perfect set of white porcelain teeth. "I'll warrant it cost a king's ransom."

Mrs. Courtney bloomed with pleasure. Claire slanted Emily an uncertain look.

"I couldn't say," demurred Mrs. Courtney, fingering the necklace in question. "It was a gift, you see, from . . ." Her voice trailed to a halt as Emily started to her feet.

A gentleman, a stranger to Emily, coming up at that moment, said, "What is it, Belle? What's happening here?"

Mrs. Courtney's eyes were riveted on the imperious young woman who looked as though she wanted to murder her. Emily's bosom was heaving, her nostrils were quivering.

The gentleman's brows came down. "Look here," he said, addressing Emily, "if you have insulted this lady . . ."

"Lady!" scoffed Emily. "What lady? I have it on my husband's authority that there are no ladies in New York, and he should know."

Mrs. Courtney gasped. Claire made a choked sound of protest.

Bristling, the gentleman demanded, "Who the devil is this chit?"

It was Leon's voice that answered him. Emily stiffened as her husband's hand manacled her wrist. "Drew!" he exclaimed. "Congratulations. I've only just heard the good news. So you've finally persuaded Belle to take that long walk to the altar! Oh, have you met my wife? Emily, this is Mrs. Belle Courtney and her long-standing and long-suffering suitor, Drew Deveril. *Deveril,*" he repeated for emphasis. "On occasion, people have been known to confuse our names."

Deveril! It was all coming back to her. Lord Riddley had corrected himself. The name was Deveril, not Devereux and she had not believed him.

Blushing like a guilty schoolgirl, she turned her shamed eyes upon her sister-in-law. Incomprehensibly, the ice in Claire's eyes had melted. A moment later, laughing, she turned away.

Chapter Thirteen

Later that same night, when Leon walked through the connecting door, Emily stole one quick, comprehensive glance and knew that her husband was in a playful humor. He wasn't smiling. He didn't say a word. But those black eyes were dancing merrily. She knew that look of old. Leon Devereux was set on tormenting the life out of her.

She swiveled on her chair to face the mirror and indicated to the little maid Lucy who stood behind her that she should continue brushing out her hair. Lucy hesitated and looked a question at the gentleman who reclined at his ease against one of the bedposts as though he had every right to be there.

He had discarded his jacket and neckcloth. Two buttons on his fine lawn shirt were undone, showing the hard column of his throat. His black knit trousers clung to his muscular thighs and legs like a second skin, prompting Emily to wonder how her husband had come by his athletic physique. Financiers, she supposed, must be like bankers. The only bankers she knew spent their days sitting behind a desk.

"I'll do that," said Leon, coming forward. "Lucy, why don't you get off to bed?"

Lucy glanced from one to the other. With a telling smile, she handed him the brush, bobbed a curtsy, and scooted out the door.

In that moment, when neither of them said anything, Emily was suddenly conscious of a number of things. Though she was in her nightclothes, Leon was almost fully clothed. The flickering candles cast a golden, intimate glow. The atmosphere was oppressive. Her skin was too hot. Breathing was difficult. She jumped when he set the brush down on the flat of her dressing table.

His long fingers combed through her hair. "Your hair feels like satin," he said. "It always did. See how it clings to my fingers?"

She sniffed, but she did not look up.

"What?" he asked.

"When we were children, you used to pull my plaits till my scalp was sore."

He laughed softly. "You never knew me when I was a child. I was ten years your senior. In those days, it might as well have been a century." He grinned wickedly and his voice dropped. "At long last, you have caught up to me, Emily. Sometimes I wondered if you would ever grow up."

She let that provocation pass. Suddenly determined to get her humiliation over and done with, she raised her eyes to his in the looking glass. "If I made a fool of myself this evening, you must take your share of the blame," she said.

"*If* you made a fool of yourself? Oh I don't think there is any doubt about that. Do you?" Releasing her hair, laughing, he collapsed against the bed.

Emily flushed, remembering how Leon had extricated her from her embarrassing predicament. Though not in so many words, he had let it be known that his wife envied the necklace on Belle Courtney's throat and had been pestering him all evening for a promise to buy something similar

221

for herself. It had taken some doing, but with Leon's quick thinking and Emily practically prostrating herself, the irate couple were finally placated.

If anything, her most humiliating moments came on the return carriage drive. Claire Dillon sat in one corner, laughing herself silly behind her hand. From time to time, Leon chuckled. Emily's cheeks were as red as poppies. Adam looked from one to the other, demanding that they share the joke. This only set brother and sister to laughing harder. Emily felt wretched. She had started the evening with such high hopes, only to become a laughingstock.

Gritting her teeth, she said, "It could have been avoided. You might have told me that the name of Belle Courtney's lover was Deveril and not Devereux. You wanted me to believe the worst."

"The worst?" His brows rose drolly. "Now what might you mean by that?"

She rounded on him. "Stop playing games with me, Leon. You know you wanted me to think that Mrs. Courtney was your mistress!"

He smiled in that old baiting way that never failed to rile her. Leaning forward with his elbows on both knees, he murmured, "Where is the wife who promised that she would not make difficulties for me? Where is the wife who promised that she would be forgiving of my follies, who would turn a blind eye to my infidelities? Tell me Emily, why should you care who my mistress is?"

She did not know why she should care. Wide-eyed, she stared at him. Without knowing what she was saying, she whispered, "Leon . . . who is she?"

His eyes were as serious as hers when he answered, "I don't know if I dare answer that question."

"But why?"

"You can ask *that* after what happened with Belle

Courtney? My dear, I would be afraid you would scratch the lady's eyes out."

His words slipped into her heart like a sliver of broken glass. Her eyes glazed over. She did not know what was the matter with her. She only knew that she longed to retreat to the little turret room at the Abbey where she could lick her wounds in private.

In the same lazy drawl, Leon demanded, "Is it still in your mind, Emily, to become a dutiful wife?"

A dutiful wife. The picture that flashed into her brain was nauseating. Had she really spouted that piffle? Had she really supposed that she could be content with a home and children while her husband dangled after other women? She remembered how she had felt when she thought that Belle Courtney was Leon's mistress. "I would rather die first!" she exclaimed, more frank than she meant to be. Picking up her hairbrush, she viciously attacked her blond tresses.

"You may forget I ever suggested such a thing," she said. "I have more pride than I knew I had." She forced herself to be calm, and succeeded for all of three or four seconds. "I refuse to share my husband with another woman," she told her furious reflection.

"Jealous, Emily?"

His patent amusement was the last straw. She spun to face him. She did not know that she was going to throw her hairbrush. Leon dodged it and it went flying harmlessly over the bed.

She was far more shocked than he. She never lost her temper, never threw things at people, never so much as said an unkind word. In the space of a few hours, she had made a spectacle of herself at the City Tavern, and now she had resorted to violence. Leon, and only Leon, had this effect on her. With nervous fingers, she combed long strands of hair back from her face.

Leon's eyes were reckless and wild and brimming with triumph. His lashes swept down and when he raised them, the look was gone. He sank to his heels before her and cradled her hands.

"Emily," he said softly, "one of these days you are going to have to take me at my word. I don't tell lies. I have no mistress. I already told you that. When you wouldn't believe me, I was annoyed. I did not see why I should keep on repeating myself. How could I know that you would pounce on poor Belle and give her the mauling of her life?" He couldn't suppress the chuckle which followed. Emily tried to pull out of his hands, but his grasp only tightened.

"It was the necklace," she said weakly. "It was the necklace."

"The emeralds?"

"I thought you had bought them with my money."

He inhaled and exhaled slowly. "No. But I already told you this. I should like to know what I have done to give you such an opinion of me, why you never believe anything I say."

When she did not respond, his hand tightened around her wrists, and she said quickly, "I do believe you. That is . . . I don't know you. I only know that boy who was cruel to me when I was a child."

His smile was whimsical. "Was I truly cruel to you, Emily?"

"You know you were."

At the passionate avowal, his smile gradually faded. "I don't want to be cruel to you," he said. "In fact, I never did want to be cruel to you. But I dared not be kind to you when you were a child. Things are different now. Let me show you how kind I can be."

His voice was low and fluid. It seemed to seep into her blood like a dose of laudanum. As he continued in the same vein, her eyelids grew heavy, her breathing slowed. He was seducing her with words.

This time, she could have stopped him. She knew she could have stopped him. And just as surely she knew that she didn't want to. Her body recognized him, was thrilling to him, was starved for the completion of his body moving upon hers.

He went down on his knees and draped her arms around his neck. Her head drooped on his shoulder. "Look at me," he commanded. Slowly, her head lifted. She tried to focus on him. "Violet eyes," he said, smiling, and let out a long breath. "Are you saying yes to me, Emily?"

She didn't want to talk. She wanted to kiss him. Before she could bring her lips to his, he repeated his question, this time more forcefully.

"Yes," she whispered.

"Then you had better make up your mind to what this means, Emily. There will be no going back. You will become a true wife to me. We shall share the same bed. When I wish to make love to you, I shall, and nothing will stop me." He let out a shaky laugh. "You had better say yes, darling, for I don't think I can stop myself now."

There was a moment of indecision. His heart almost stopped beating when her brow pleated in a frown. And then she smiled and said, "Yes," and his whole body began to tremble.

She wasn't thinking things through in her usual calm manner. Either instinct or intuition had taken over. If she surrendered herself to this man, he would never hurt her, not in any way that counted. The thought was so strange, so novel, she pulled back to get a better look at him.

It struck her that she had never attempted to grasp the

character of Leon Devereux. Her dislike was based on nothing more or less than *his* dislike of *her.* She looked at him now and was aware of a change that had worked on her gradually. She saw intelligence, and strength of character. But there was something more, something private and hidden, that he did not wish her to know about.

Before her mind could fasten on that surprising thought, he released the tie of her robe and pushed it down over her shoulders. She went as taut as a bowstring.

"Don't be afraid," he soothed.

Afraid? Fear was the furthest thing from her mind, and she told him so.

His eyes held hers as he unfastened each tiny pearl button from throat to waist on the bodice of her nightgown. He drew back the edges of her gown, exposing her breasts.

Suddenly, she turned shy. This wasn't what she wanted. She was sitting at her dressing table. Leon was on his knees in front of her. She glanced with longing at the turned-down bed, but Leon didn't take the hint. Her breasts seemed to fascinate him. They fascinated her, too. Something strange was happening. She could feel them swelling, throbbing, becoming engorged. Blue veins stood out, marbling the delicate white of her skin. Her nipples were like bruised berries. She felt ugly.

"Lovely. God, Emily, you are so lovely."

With the tips of his fingers, he traced the veins from her throat to the hardened peak of one breast. Her nipple contracted, as did the secret core of her femininity. She felt the moisture begin to pool between her thighs as her body readied itself to accept him.

He knew it. She didn't know how he knew it, but she knew that he did. His lips fastened on hers. In the space of a single heartbeat, his kisses became frenzied, frantic, demanding. His fingers worked furiously to free her of her gown. He started on his own clothes, but didn't get very far.

"I've outpaced you," he groaned, and pulled her down to straddle his hips, there, on the floor, bracing his back against the side of a chair.

Without explanation, she knew exactly what he meant. He was out of control. She could not believe that she had this effect on him. Leon always kept himself on such a tight leash. She was far more interested in this strange power she seemed to have over him than she was in the completion she had longed for only moments before.

His breathing was loud and harsh. "So, you like what you do to me?"

Her eyes were glittering with feminine triumph. "Yes."

"You . . . you she-devil!" He laughed recklessly, and releasing himself from his trousers, he thrust powerfully, filling her body with his sex.

He climaxed almost immediately. The spectacle excited her. His lips were pulled back, his nostrils flared. His features might have been carved from flint. The violence of his possession was explosive, the force in those strong masculine hands locking her body to his could have been frightening. But Emily wasn't afraid. His masculinity, his virility, enthralled her.

Afterward, he rewarded her with tender words of apology and sweetly lingering caresses. Finally, he rested, catching his breath.

Some minutes were to pass before he roused himself and urged her to the bed. She watched as he shed the rest of his garments. When he slipped in beside her, he caught her to the warmth of his naked length.

"What brought that on?" she murmured, turning into him. "Was it something I did? What made you lose control?"

Between short, openmouthed kisses, he said, "That was brought on by a number of things: anticipation, enforced celibacy, and last but not least, the sweet womanly scent of you that told me you were ready to mate with me."

Mortified, she looked away. She was ashamed of that scent. It wasn't pretty like the scents in the crystal bottles on her dressing table. She squeezed her thighs together.

With one long finger, he brought her chin up, his eyes searching hers. "Idiot," he murmured lovingly. "In some ways, you are still an innocent. Don't you know that the scent of you, aroused, wanting me, drives me wild for you?"

He smiled at her look of astonishment, and nipped her bare shoulder. "You forget. I was born French. To a Frenchman there is no sweeter fragrance on earth than the scent of the woman he loves."

It was the first time, the very first time that the word "love" had been used between them. Leon's intent look gradually faded when Emily showed no evidence that she had understood his oblique reference.

He pressed a kiss behind her earlobe. "Gardenia," he said. "Now that is pretty." His lips moved lower, to the pulse at her throat. "More of the same," he murmured. "It's very pleasant." Before she knew what he was doing, he had pressed a kiss to the underside of one breast. "Now this is more like it. This is the essence of my woman, my mate. Emily, open your legs for me."

She did not know how it was done, but in very short order all the power had slipped away from her. It was *his* eyes that glittered with triumph and she was the one who was losing control. It was *her* breathing that was labored, her moans that disturbed the silence. When he finally came into her she climaxed almost immediately, and as convulsion after convulsion wreaked her whole body, she was aware that he was holding off, his eyes never leaving her face, absorbing every feature as the sweet, mindless rapture swept through her.

When she sighed and went lax beneath him, he laughed softly in that reckless way of his, then he loosed the bonds of his formidable control, giving himself up to his own pleasure, driving into her, pounding her until he was spent and gasping for air.

"Don't sulk, my darling. It doesn't become you." He bit into her earlobe, dragging on it gently, forcing her to turn her head on the pillow. "That's better." He tightened his hold at her back so that she could not evade him.

Stung, she protested, "I never sulk."

"No? What about the time I caught you kissing Lord Jeremy in the old millhouse? You would not speak to me for a week afterward."

Her indignation knew no bounds. "I did not kiss Jeremy! He kissed me! We were only children, for heaven's sake. And if I did refuse to speak to you for a week, that was because you let Jeremy get off scot-free while you dumped me in the millpond. My gown was ruined. Worse than that—either you or Sara carried tales! Aunt Zoë would not let me out of her sight for weeks afterward."

"You were fourteen years old," he pointed out. "You should have known better."

She raised on one elbow to get a better look at him. "Oh? And I suppose at fourteen years, you were as wise as Solomon?"

"At fourteen years, I was kissing every pretty girl who was foolish enough to permit it." He had done a lot more than kiss them, but he wasn't going to let Emily know it.

"Aunt Zoë said you did a lot more than kiss them," she

retorted. "I heard her tell Uncle Rolfe."

He was startled into laughter. "Zoë knows nothing about it. A boy does not confide in his sisters. And you should not have been eavesdropping on grown-up conversations."

He was wondering if it was too soon to take her again, if she would think him no better than an animal if he pressed his attentions upon her. She was reflecting on what Adam Dillon had told her, that no one knew what Leon had suffered as a boy during the Revolution. Something else came back to her. On the night of the Prince Regent's fête, William Addison had warned her that Leon was dangerous, that he had a checkered past.

Dragging herself to a sitting position, she hugged her knees and stared into space. Leon propped his back against the pillows, his eyes curious as he waited for her to unburden herself. With one hand, he idly caressed her bare arm. When the silence became prolonged, he cupped her shoulder and turned her to face him.

"What is it, Emily? What are you thinking?"

"I was thinking about the stories Aunt Zoë used to tell about your family, when you were all children together. You were the youngest. I think you must have been spoiled."

"If you think that, then you are mistaken. I was the only son. One day, I knew I would be the head of my family as well as have control of my father's financial empire. I was never allowed to forget it. My education and training began from the time I was in short coats. Sometimes, I used to envy my sisters their freedom."

"That's not how Aunt Zoë tells it. She says that your mother attributed every gray hair in her head to anxiety over the scrapes *you* used to fall into. You were reckless and wild, Leon. That's what Aunt Zoë says."

He laughed, and brushed his lips against her throat.

"You know too much. Besides, what do girls know anyhow? They are easily shocked." When he touched his tongue to the seam of her lips, she sighed and leaned into him.

"You can't deny that you were reckless. As I heard it, you ran away from school and thwarted Uncle Rolfe's first attempt to bring you out of France. You were only — how old? — fourteen or fifteen at the time? Why did you do it, Leon? Where were you? How did you survive in that year before Uncle Rolfe found you again? I've often wondered."

The answer was clipped. "My parents were in prison facing execution. I had some fool notion of rescuing them. That is why I ran away from school. It was hopeless. I fell in with . . . friends. They took care of me."

"What friends?"

"Why all the questions, Emily? You have never shown the slightest interest in anything I have ever done. Why now? What has brought this on?"

She adjusted herself so that their eyes were on the same level. His look was so shuttered that the intimacy they had just shared might never have taken place. "You were never really my husband before now," she said quietly. "It's only natural that I should be curious about you. If you don't wish me to know, I won't press you."

His breathing was audible, his chest rising and falling. "That part of my life is a closed book. I don't allow anyone to open it, not even you."

Far from annoying her, his words moved her. Though she could not conceive what Leon was hiding from her, she knew it must be something dreadful. Leon would not cavil at blazoning his youthful misdemeanors, not to her. He had always liked to shock her.

Whatever it was he had done, he had suffered for it, was still suffering for it if she knew how to read her husband.

He was only a youth during the Terror in France. She thought that a boy of fifteen might be forgiven anything. She did not know where men got this quaint and utterly erroneous idea that women were too delicate to face unpleasantness.

When she touched a hand to his bare chest, he inhaled sharply. "Aren't you the least bit curious about me?" she asked playfully, trying to ease the tension.

Slowly, he relaxed and forced a smile. "I've known you since you were a child. There's not much I *don't* know about you, Emily."

"You don't know me that well!" she exclaimed, piqued. "You were scarcely ever in England these last years. Lots of things happened to me that you know nothing about."

"What for instance?" He was sure that she was going to mention her erstwhile suitor. Unthinkingly, he tightened his hand on her arm.

"Well, for instance . . . Oh, I don't know. Nothing of any significance, I suppose." She did not look too pleased about the admission.

His expression was very tender. "I was the most significant thing that ever happened to you, my sweet. When will you admit it?"

She glowered at him. "You were the second biggest calamity that ever befell me, on a par with the world falling on my head."

"Oh?" His lips twitched. "What was the first?"

Suddenly serious, she replied, "When my father died. He was murdered. Did you know?"

Not a flicker of emotion showed on his lean face. "Rolfe told me something about it. But you were only an infant. Surely you don't remember your father?"

She settled herself more comfortably, her back pressed to his chest. His arms encircled her. Though she could not explain it to herself, she was happier and more at peace with herself than she had been in a long, long while.

"I remember it as though it was yesterday. I was always closer to my father than to my mother. Mama's health was delicate, you see. She had Sara to look after and my grandmother was very demanding. Mama did not seem to have much time for me, but Papa made up for it." She smiled at some reminiscence. "He had promised to take me to look over a pony he had selected for my very first mount. I was so excited. I waited and waited for him to fetch me. He never did. I never saw him again."

She sighed, and turned her head slightly to look into his face. "It was in all the newspapers, just before you arrived in England. Did you read about it? He was murdered by an assassin's bullet. It was the first Sara and I had ever heard of it."

"Yes." His fingertips brushed without ceasing over her arms. His expression was very grave, as was his voice. "I'm sorry. It must have been a terrible shock to you."

"I could hardly believe it. When we were children, we were told that Papa was thrown by a horse, you see. Uncle Rolfe only wanted to protect us, I suppose. Still, you can imagine how we felt when we opened the newspaper one morning and read that our papa was murdered all those years ago."

His arms tightened involuntarily about her. "I'm sorry that it was one of my own countrymen who was responsible. There is no defense for what happened. I don't know how to explain it except to say that in those days madness stalked France. No one who did not actually live through it will ever understand how it was."

Her voice held a trace of bitterness. "My father was an Englishman. What did he have to do with France? His only crime was that he was generous to a fault. He gave

233

money to good causes, causes to which a group of fanatics took exception."

There was a long silence before she went on. "You mustn't think that I am so prejudiced as to lay the blame for my father's death at the door of every Frenchman."

"No?"

"No. Don't you think I know that your own parents lost their lives during the Revolution? It's fanatics of whatever persuasion whom I hate."

"Careful," he said, and there was no teasing light in his eyes. "That attitude is the beginning of fanaticism."

"Is it wrong to hope that murderers come by their just desserts?"

"Is that what you wish?"

"Certainly. Don't you? Don't all decent people wish for it, too?"

He managed a convincing smile. "You never used to be so bloodthirsty."

"I am not bloodthirsty. I want justice, that's all."

The silence lengthened. Emily's eyelids began to droop. Leon nestled her more closely to him. Before long, she had drifted into sleep, her head pillowed on his shoulder.

He was thinking that those days seemed so far removed, it might have been another life. He had hoped never to hear of La Compagnie again. Sighing, he turned into his wife, and drew her more closely to him with an arm clasped around her waist.

Chapter Fourteen

One month slipped into the next. Suddenly Christmas was upon them and then they were into the New Year. Leon was even more content than he had hoped to be. He gave his wife her fair share of the credit for this happy state of affairs. If she ever thought of William Addison or pined for her old life in England, he would never have known it. She had adapted to her new role with surprising grace.

They were in their own home now, a rented house on Cherry Street, and Emily had been in her element furnishing the place and hiring and training servants. He entered the foyer and paused there for a moment, savoring the pleasant odors that wafted to him from the kitchens. Before he had done more than remove his hat, Emily came out to greet him.

She helped him out of his warm winter overcoat. "How did your meeting go with Mr. Roberts?" she asked.

"He's a good risk. I think I shall lend him the capital he needs to get started."

"Steamboats? I just can't imagine such a thing." As she spoke, she carefully folded his coat and set it over the back of a chair. "Come and warm yourself at the fire. You look half frozen. Dinner won't be long, now that you are here."

He caught her easily by the wrist as she moved to lead him into the parlor. "What's that I smell?" he asked, wanting to prolong the moment of intimacy.

She raised her pert little nose to sniff the air and he quickly kissed her. Laughing, she pulled away. "Leon, what's got into you?"

He knew that he was standing there with a foolish grin on his face. "Put it down to a case of déjà vu," he said, and without releasing her, escorted her into the parlor.

"What? Isn't my niece here? I was beginning to think that young Sarah had taken up residence with us."

"You don't mind that she spends so much time with us, do you, Leon?"

"No. Of course not. I think it's rather touching. Sarah has become your disciple, do you know? She copies you lavishly. Adam was telling me that his daughter's inflection is almost as English as your own, and her brothers tease the life out of her because of it."

"I don't have an accent," said Emily, then pointed out reasonably, "How should I? I'm English."

Leon made no verbal response to this, but proceeded, with eyes glinting with laughter, to a sideboard where a decanter of sherry and two glasses had been set out. Within moments, he was handing a glass to his wife.

As they sat on opposite sides of the fireplace, sipping at their sherries and conversing on the events of the day, he was struck with the thought that the small domestic rituals that made up their married life held a charm for him far surpassing any of the society dos which they were frequently obliged to attend. If he had his way, he would never go to another ball.

"I received a letter from my sister this morning," said Emily at one point.

"And?"

She made a grimace, conveying distress touched with impatience. "She says much the same as ever. Would you care to read it?"

"That won't be necessary."

His sister-in-law's letters were boringly predictable. Sara was not settling in to the life of a soldier's wife. Peter was absent for long stretches at a time and Sara was not happy with only Lady Hester to keep her company. Nor was she happy with the society to be found in Fort York. It was not what she was used to. She had few friends. She was lonely. She begged Emily to join her for an extended visit.

"Did you promise Peter that we would go to Canada at some point?" Emily asked. She had picked up a piece of embroidery and was clicking her tongue, unpicking her stitches.

"I may have said something, you know, for politeness' sake."

"Sara has taken it into her head that it's all arranged and only the date of our arrival is yet to be decided."

"It was nothing so definite as that!"

His vehemence brought her head up and he said more calmly, "What's to stop Sara coming here to us for an extended visit? When I think of it, she would be much more comfortable here. New York is more cosmopolitan. There are more entertainments and so on, and . . ." He paused and grinned wickedly. "And there is no Lady Hester to make her toe the line."

This brought an answering smile from Emily. "Poor Sara," she said. "Who would have believed that such a charming gentleman as Peter could be related to someone like Hester? And they are devoted to each other, you know, or so Sara says. I think that's a splendid idea. I shall write at once and invite her to come to us."

There was a long silence as Emily bent to her embroidery. Leon's eyes rested on her, but he was involved in his own thoughts. He was thinking of his annoyance of a few moments before, when Emily had raised the question of their going to Canada. He didn't want to go to Canada. In New York, there had been no accidents, no attacks, nothing that could be construed as a threat to either one of them. He wanted things to remain that way.

"Do you wish to go to Canada?" he asked carefully.

"No!"

She said the word so emphatically than Leon suddenly recognized that a small part of what he had been experiencing was pique. If Emily had wanted to go to Canada, it might mean that she was becoming bored with domesticity in general and him in particular. That small expletive convinced him otherwise and he smiled.

She giggled.

"What?" Leon asked.

"I was thinking that we ought to invite Hester, too."

"Over my dead body!" he exclaimed, and they both laughed.

In the space of a month, everything had changed. The letter which Emily put into her husband's hand was not from Sara but from Peter Benson.

Leon scanned it quickly, then read it at a more leisurely pace. Coming to the end, he murmured, "Poor devil! I truly feel for him."

Emily took exception to this. "Of course, we must

238

sympathize with Peter, but it is Sara who has taken to her bed. She is the one we must think of now."

"You surely don't pity Sara?"

"Don't you?"

He threw the letter aside. "That girl is spoiled beyond redemption. What does she think she is playing at?"

"She's not playing! She is genuinely ill. 'Going into a decline' is how Peter describes it. He is at his wit's end. She has fallen into a deep despondency, Leon. I must go to her. Don't you see that?"

"What that girl needs . . ." He stopped abruptly and shook his head.

She knew what he was thinking. Sara was a past master at getting her own way. Her "decline" might be nothing more than a ploy to lure them both up to Canada. Emily was half inclined to think that was all it was. But she could not be sure. Sara had not wanted to marry Peter Benson. Nor would it be the first time Sara had gone into a decline. She felt things deeply, more deeply than Leon realized.

She told him nothing of this. She said, "I know my sister, Leon. For whatever reason, she wants me with her. For my own peace of mind, I must go."

He looked at her as though he did not see her. She said nothing, knowing that he was undecided, debating with himself. After an interval, he gave a resigned sigh. "Of course you must go. We shall both go. Besides, I have many friends and colleagues in Canada. We could kill two birds with one stone. You shall see Sara, and I shall look up old friends."

"Old friends?"

"Old friends," he said, and left it at that.

Emily was to ponder that remark for some time. His words had alarmed her. She was keeping secrets from Leon and had thought for one awful moment that he had discovered it. Then they might never go to Canada and she would never forgive herself if Sara's illness was as serious as Peter had described.

This was the thought that was in her mind as she lay in Leon's arms that night waiting for sleep to overtake her.

Feeling the wretchedness of her situation, she sighed, and he asked softly, "What is it, Emily? What's troubling you? Is it Sara? I promised you we would go, and I always keep my promises," and, turning her into him, he wound long strands of her hair around his throat.

She hated to deceive him. For a moment she hovered on the brink of confessing everything, but he drew her more closely to him and the moment slipped away as the pleasuring began.

Almost invariably, she cried in the ebb of their passion, not copiously, but tears would brim over for no apparent reason. It was all the more perplexing, because afterward Leon never failed to lavish her with praise and sweetly affectionate kisses.

"Why do you always cry," he asked, and there was a tenderness in his eyes. "Do I make you sad? Does this make you sad?" and he pressed a kiss to the valley between her breasts, kneading her soft flesh with his hand.

"You know it's not that. It's only that I never thought to find this joy with . . ."

"With me? Is that what you were going to say?"

Strangely, he had not taken offense. "Aren't you surprised, too?" she asked.

"Husbands and wives are supposed to find joy in their marriage bed," he said, which was no answer at all really.

She was still restless long after Leon had fallen asleep, but her thoughts had taken a new direction. She was thinking that her marriage pleased her far more than she ever thought it would. She was discovering that she liked her husband very well. In some things, she had completely misjudged him. Leon was no wastrel. He was no womanizer. He was very much in the stamp of his brother-in-law, Adam Dillon — a respected pillar of the community. It seemed that her uncle was right. America had been the making of Leon Devereux.

In fairness to Leon, she had resolved not to pine away for the impossible. Her girlish dreams of love and the memory of William Addison were locked away deep in her heart. Having once determined to make the best of the present, the present had turned out to be surprisingly agreeable.

Her thoughts had come full circle and she groaned, wondering how long her happiness could continue.

At one time, Albany had been an important center for the fur trade. It was on the old Iroquois trail and conveniently placed between Montreal and New York.

Leon arrived by boat. His friend, who had made the journey from Montreal, was there ahead of him. They met by arrangement in one of the newer coaching houses, which was abuzz with activity, for though the fur trade in the area had declined, Albany was now the state capital.

The gentleman who greeted Leon had the look of a Spanish conquistador. His skin was the hue of bronze, his cheekbones high and prominent. His eyes, like his hair, were as black as pitchblende. He was of an age with Leon and wore his finely tailored garments with the same careless ease. His name was James Fraser and he had met Leon when they were youths at university in England. Their friendship spanned more than a dozen years.

There was no effusive salutation, merely a firm handclasp in the American manner and a few words of greeting. It was James Fraser who led the way up the narrow staircase to a private parlor on the second floor where covered dishes were already set out on a sideboard.

"I was just about to dine," he said. "You will join me?"

Leon murmured his assent, and stood aside as the servants were dismissed. When the door was closed, he moved to the sideboard, following his friend's example.

The comestibles were hardly tempting — a stew of indeterminate ingredients, floury dumplings, and oversalted potatoes boiled to a mush. Leon helped himself sparingly. James was not so fastidious.

Chuckling, he remarked, "Eat and be thankful, Leon. It could be worse. It could be pemmican." Like his name, James's accent was Scottish, but only faintly. He was of mixed blood. His mother was an Ojibway Indian princess and his father, before his death, a partner in the North West Company. James had inherited his father's business interests, and was a trustee for his younger brothers and sisters. The fur trade had made him a rich man.

Leon grinned, remembering his introduction to pemmican, that unsavory staple of dried buffalo meat without which fur traders on the trail would starve to death. "You forget *I* am French. My palate is more refined than most. I've never accustomed myself to this English swill."

James cocked an interested eyebrow. "And Lady Emily?" he quizzed. "Is her palate French or English?"

242

Laughing, groaning, Leon admitted ruefully, "English, but one day I hope to rectify that." He could not help smiling, though the joke was on himself. His little wife was taking her duties as chatelaine very seriously. She had hired an English cook and was spending hours in the kitchen in their house on Cherry Street perfecting the woman's skills in preparing an English cuisine. If he never saw another suet pudding it would be too soon for him. Not that he had complained. The sight of his wife in the kitchen with a towel tied around her middle and flour on her nose and her hair coming undone was something to behold. It fascinated him. It enchanted him. Incredibly, it also aroused him.

Shaking his head as if to clear the image from his mind, he said, "And we shall dispense with the 'Lady,' if you please. This is America. Emily is plain 'Mrs. Devereux' here."

"But I am not an American," responded James, faintly baiting. "On my father's side, I am British, a Scot to be exact, as you well know. Frankly, I considered declining your summons. The British are none too popular in your neck of the woods at present. I feared for my life. There's talk of war, you know."

Leon smiled a slow smile. "You have never been afraid in your life!"

James laughed, but merely said, "Eat your dinner, and we shall talk business later, like civilized people."

Leon obligingly complied. Though there was much he wished to say to his friend, for the next little while, he was content to let the conversation drift. Before long, they were reminiscing about their own days at Oxford.

A bond had been established between them for the simple reason that they had both felt like odd men out,

James because he was of mixed blood and Leon because he was a foreigner. To English ears, they had peculiar accents. Had they been children, the taunts from their peers would have been made to their faces. Young Englishman who aspired to be known as "gentlemen" eschewed these barbaric methods. They hid their contempt, but it was there.

To Leon and James, this ingrained sense of English superiority had spurred them to prove themselves. Whatever an Englishman could do, they could do better. They rode better, they dueled better, they gamed better, they drank better, they whored better. These were the accomplishments of a young English gentleman. The only thing university did not do for them was give them an education. Few Englishmen ever sent their sons to university for that purpose, but rather to give them a polish, a veneer. When it suited them, these two fast friends wore the veneer without chaffing. But with them, it was not ingrained, could never be ingrained. Their early years had shaped them, more perhaps than they would have wished.

This last thought was in Leon's mind as his companion went to fetch glasses and a decanter of brandy. He was reflecting that in many respects his friend's road had been more rocky than his own. He had found acceptance and his niche in American society. James had a foot in two cultures and felt at home in neither.

Leon accepted a glass from James's hand. "Whatever happened to Miss Prentice? When I was last in Montreal, you were debating whether or not you should offer for her. But that was before you went off with the fur brigades."

"Her parents married her off to her cousin before anything could come of it," James replied easily. "It seems that not all my wealth could tempt her avaricious father to give his daughter into the hands of a half-breed savage." Before Leon could do more than register the bite behind the lightly spoken words, James went on. "But I did not come here to discuss my matrimonial prospects. Now, may I make my report on Lady Sara?"

Leon shifted in his armchair, settling himself more comfortably. "How is my sister-in-law?" he asked, his voice singularly lacking in interest.

"You will be pleased to know she has made a remarkable recovery."

Leon snorted derisively and James's eyebrows rose, but he continued in the same conversational tone. "But that was to be expected once I put a stop to the daily ration of peyote someone was forcing down her throat."

"What?" Leon sat bolt upright.

"It seems that her maid was dosing her with narcotics. Oh, not enough to kill her, just enough to induce a trance or a deep melancholy."

"Good God! It seems I have done Sara an injustice. What happened to the maid? What has she told you?"

"Nothing. She can't be found. When I introduced my own agent into the household, the girl took flight. She hasn't been seen since. Don't worry. If she has gone back to her own people, I shall find her. She is of the Cree nation."

"And Sara? You say that she has made a recovery?"

"A miraculous recovery. The poor girl still does not know what happened to her. She thinks that she was going insane."

"Damn! I thought . . . I hoped . . ." Leon shook his head. "I should have been prepared for something like this."

His friend eyed him consideringly for a moment before saying, "You must have suspected something or you would not have involved me. I am anxious to hear what you have to say. Why all the secrecy, Leon? And why was someone trying to poison Lady Sara?"

Inhaling deeply, Leon said, "There are things I am going to say to you which I don't wish anyone else to know. You are right in this. I had a suspicion, a very faint one, that there might be more to Sara's illness than met the eye. If it had been possible, I would have gone directly to York to investigate, but I dared not leave my wife unprotected. We must go together, and that means we must wait for the rivers to become navigable." He smiled faintly. "Emily is not like us, James. When she travels, she travels in style. She has no conception of what the wilderness is like and I have not enlightened her. She presumes that the journey to York will be in the nature of the journey from London to Bath."

James laughed. "I can imagine," he said.

The amusement gradually died and Leon said, "I have reason to believe that someone — or some group — wants to see me dead. There have been two attempts on my life so far, possibly three. What concerns me most, however, and what puzzles me most, is that my wife and her sister may also be targets."

He paused to marshal his thoughts, and he could not help admiring his friend's patience. Anyone else would have instantly bombarded him with questions. James knew the value of silence.

"These attacks occurred in England. I had hoped that they would stop once we were safely in America. And they did, or so I thought, until a few moments ago when you told me about Sara. I don't know what to make of it." He broke off to consider the puzzle, then continued.

"This is the second misadventure to befall Sara. The first was in London. At that time, I thought I was the target. Now, I am not so sure.

"You must see my dilemma. If it could be arranged, I would like Sara to come to New York where I can keep an eye on her. I don't doubt that her husband won't permit it, not as things stand between our two countries. I don't know what's to be done except that I aim to keep both those girls well guarded until I get to the bottom of this."

He paused before saying, "York is practically on your doorstep, James. I know I could count on you to do whatever was necessary to keep Sara safe."

There was just enough inflection on the last statement to prompt James to respond, "You may rest easy on that score. The girl is well protected. No harm will come to her now, not if I can help it."

"Thank you. As I said, as soon as it may be arranged, I aim to escort my wife to York to visit her sister. Our vigilance must not be relaxed, not even for a moment."

"And if there is trouble?"

"Then I shall spirit them both away to a place of safety, even if it means abducting Sara against her wishes."

"Against her wishes? Why not simply tell her the truth, tell them both the truth?"

"I don't know what the truth is."

"Now you are prevaricating. If their lives are in jeopardy, they should know it."

"What would I say to them? That Sara's melancholy was induced by a powerful narcotic administered by a serving girl? That the misadventures which have befallen us are deliberate attempts to do us an injury or worse? That my instincts are to be trusted? They would think that I had taken leave of my senses or they would raise questions to which I have no answers."

"I see what it is. You don't wish them to know that *you* are a marked man. Who is after you, Leon? You must have some idea."

The hesitation was brief but noticeable. Shrugging carelessly, Leon answered, "It would seem that the sins of my youth are catching up with me. I always feared that something like this would happen. I suspect that an assassin — or assassins — have been paid to wipe me from the face of the earth. Having said that, it still does not explain these misadventures to Emily and Sara. So you see, I was not misleading you when I said that I don't know what the truth is."

For some few minutes, both gentlemen were silent. Then Leon said, "I mean to ferret them out, James, whoever they are, with your help."

"You have it. But you know that already. I can't believe, though, that all three of you are targets. There is something not quite right here."

"Isn't that what I have been saying?"

"Have you thought that perhaps you are not a target at all? Those girls are heiresses. Who stands to profit if anything happens to either of them?"

"I've considered that. For the most part, their fortunes go to the surviving sister unless they have issue. In that event, their children would be their heirs."

"What about Lady Sara's husband, what's-his-name — Major Benson?"

"He won't be a pauper, but he won't be a rich man, either. No, the moneys go to the surviving sister unless, as I said, we have children. You may believe that my brain has chased down every possible avenue to find answers. I'm no further ahead than I was. As I see it, the only way to find out who is the real target is by a process of trial and error. Only then may we begin to put two and two together. Now, tell me about the steps you have taken to protect Sara."

Chapter Fifteen

The memory of the journey to York in Upper Canada would linger with Emily for many a long day. She knew, of course, that distances between villages in the New World were not to be compared to those in England. But nothing could have prepared her for the emptiness of this vast continent.

For the most part, the journey was made by water. They traveled up the Hudson and Mohawk rivers. The silence of the forests unnerved her. The isolation frightened her. Her most pervasive feeling, however, was one of awe. So must the world have looked, she reflected, when Adam and Eve were given dominion over the whole created order.

The journey was not without its humorous moments. Though the gentlemen were dressed appropriately in buckskins, her own garb seemed comical. She was garbed in the height of fashion. With her little silk parasol to protect her from the sun's rays, she might have been stepping onto a barge for a jaunt on the Thames. Leon and his guides saw nothing incongruous in her attire. She was a white woman. It was taken as a matter of course that she would wish to maintain the niceties of civilization. Only the Indians who met them along the trail stopped to stare. Emily was as curious about them as they were about her. But when she learned from one of the guides that some of the braves were more than a little curious, that they wanted to barter for her, she was aghast.

"You're worth your weight in furs," Leon teased after one tense encounter, when it seemed that one of the bolder-eyed braves would not take no for an answer. "I am a fur trader. You may imagine the temptation that has been put in my way."

"I see nothing to laugh at," she snapped, fear making her angry. "There are so few of us and so many of them. What's to stop them taking what they want?"

"I would stop them," answered Leon, patting the butt of his firing piece. "No, really, I know them. They would not risk injury or death for a mere woman, even if she does have hair the color of ripe maize. Now a horse—that is a different matter." Observing that she was far from reassured, he added more gently, "Emily, trust me. I know what I am doing."

Strangely, Emily believed him. He was as much at home here, in the wilderness, as he was in the ballrooms of Mayfair. She had often wondered how a financier came by his muscular physique. Now she knew. As often as it could be managed, Leon told her, he liked to spend time in the wilderness, pitting himself against the elements, surviving off the land. The trip to York was nothing to him. It was his practice to travel at least once a year, to Montreal, the hub of the fur trade. He was an investor and liked to keep abreast of things.

"Are we going to Montreal this time around?" asked

Emily. The question was an innocent one. When Leon's lids drooped to half-mast, concealing his expression, Emily became alert.

"It's not necessary," he demurred. "I made the trip last year. Besides, I have an agent there who keeps me informed."

"All the same, I should like to see Montreal." This suggestion was not an innocent one. She was testing him.

"That would not be convenient," he answered at once, then in a more conversational tone, "I don't know if I can spare the time. I am not a gentleman of leisure, Emily. While you are visiting Sara, I shall be fully occupied. York is the capital of Upper Canada. As a financier, naturally I am interested in the opportunities for investment to be found there."

Emily sensed a mystery. He did not want her to go to Montreal. Why? When he adroitly turned the subject, she became more curious than ever.

Though York was the capital of Upper Canada and the seat of British government, in 1812, to one newly arrived from England, it was primitive beyond imagining. Its buildings ran the gamut from the crudest of log cabins to spacious, dignified Georgian mansions. The population had yet to reach the thousand mark, and of those, a small though significant proportion were government officials. It was these select persons and the officers from the garrison who set the tone of society.

Emily listened with half an ear as Leon tried to prepare her for the disappointing reality of York. They were at the rail of the small schooner which had taken

252

them on the last leg of their journey from Oswego on the American side of Lake Ontario. She nodded now and then as her eyes eagerly scanned the approaching shoreline. She was not disappointed. To her, it seemed incredible that civilization should have made such inroads. Even from that distance, she could see that the small settlement was ringed around by dense forest.

"Leon, look!" she exclaimed, breaking into his explanations as they neared the wharf. She pointed to the ensign fluttering in the breeze.

"The Union Jack," murmured Leon dryly. "I shall have to accustom myself to the return of British protocol."

"Poor Leon," said Emily, and laughed.

It seemed to take forever before the schooner had docked and they were allowed to descend the gangplank. The wharves were busy. Theirs was not the only boat to ply the waters of Lake Ontario. Emily's eyes absorbed the spectacle, noting the assortment of bystanders, ranging from well-heeled gentlemen to Indians disembarking from birch bark canoes.

Emily was not expecting to be met. A journey through the wilderness was unpredictable. They might have arrived a few days earlier or later. She was reminding herself of this, attempting to quash an incipient sense of disappointment, when a gentleman separated himself from the crowd and came to meet them.

She hung back a little as her husband and the stranger greeted each other warmly. There was no surprise in the meeting. That thought had barely occurred to her before Leon was bringing her forward to make the introductions.

"Emily, allow me to present James Fraser. James

and I were at university together. He is one of the partners in the North West Company. Furs, Emily — that is all this reprobate knows."

Emily was conscious of a very close scrutiny from a pair of eyes even darker than her husband's. Then those eyes crinkled at the corners, and Emily let out a small, relieved breath.

"Lady Emily," he said, bowing over her hand. "May I be the first to welcome you to Toronto?"

She expected an accent, but not the one her ears picked up. Somehow the Scottish burr softened that first intimidating impression of the man. "Toronto?" she responded, somewhat at a loss.

"It's the Indian name for York," interjected Leon.

As they conversed, James led the way up the boardwalk to a waiting carriage. From snatches in the conversation, Emily deduced that James Fraser had known beforehand that they would be arriving that morning.

"I sent a messenger ahead," Leon said in an aside, in answer to Emily's questioning look. "Sara is waiting for us at the house. Peter will be along later. His duties have delayed him at the garrison."

When they came up to the carriage, Emily was handed in and the gentlemen turned back to await the unloading of their baggage, leaving her with the vague impression that she had been deliberately excluded from a private tête à tête. Minutes later, the gentlemen rejoined her. The baggage and boxes were stowed and they were on their way.

The house on Frederick Street was a well-proportioned, two-story brick edifice. Emily did not wait for the gentlemen. As soon as her feet touched the ground, she made for the front doors.

254

They were opened by a manservant who was every inch an English butler. This took Emily by surprise, for she remembered that Sara had often complained of the scarcity of trained servants to be had in York.

"That will be all, Paterson."

The butler inclined his head, acknowledging the lady who was descending the stairs. Then he retreated to a door leading to the back of the house.

"Hester . . ." said Emily, and came forward with hand extended.

Lady Hester Benson was a handsome woman on the wrong side of thirty, but only just. Her figure was slender and straight-backed, giving the impression that it was a crown she wore on her head and not a lace cap. Her features were refined, as was everything about her. Emily had no difficulty in seeing why Sara had taken a dislike to her sister-in-law. Any young girl of some spirit must chafe at the restrictions such a chaperone would undoubtedly impose, and Sara had never wanted for spirit.

In a voice as formal and as elegant as her pale-mauve muslins, Lady Hester greeted them all in turn, inquiring politely about their journey, never waiting for answers, but keeping up a monologue as she led the way to the front parlor.

The coldness of this welcome was dispelled the moment they were ushered into Sara's presence. At their entrance, she started to her feet, then threw herself across the room into Emily's arms.

After the first emotional greeting, with everyone talking at once and exclaiming over the joy of their reunion, Sara turned aside. Only then did Emily become conscious of another presence in the room, a gentleman who was waiting patiently to be noticed.

Sara started to say something, but Hester got there before her. With a coy little smile, she said, "There is someone here who is anxious to renew your acquaintance."

It was William Addison.

Emily was prepared for it. This was the secret she had been keeping from her husband. She had hoped to have a little time in which to prepare Leon for this encounter. She could almost feel Leon's eyes boring into her back. The hand which William touched was trembling like a leaf in a gale.

Then suddenly, Leon's displeasure did not matter to her. She was not thinking of William as her lost lover. Her sentiments were far more complex. He was a dear friend. He was the best that England had to offer. Their minds, their thoughts, their opinions, ran on a parallel course. She was suddenly aware of having lived under a terrible strain in the last number of months. In America, she was a foreigner and something of an oddity. Her sister-in-law disliked her. She was now among her own kind.

When she finally chanced a look at Leon, she knew that he was putting two and two together. That thought helped her to find her balance. "Leon, you remember William Addison?" she asked, keeping her voice light and cool.

She could never remember afterward the first few minutes of that conversation. She knew that everyone was civil if not cordial. But beneath the polite chatter, she sensed her husband's anger. It was a relief when the tea things were brought in and she could involve herself in the ritual of handing round tea and cakes. Hester did the pouring, and it came to Emily that Peter's sister was the real mistress of the house and Sara,

256

perhaps because of her illness, made no objection to this reversal of roles.

It was James Fraser who broached the subject of William's presence in York. "Mr. Addison is here on a reconnoitering mission," he said. "He has been assessing our border garrisons. Everything is of interest to him, even the Indians."

"Indians?" Leon stirred his tea, and flicked William a look of polite inquiry.

William's color had heightened, as though he detected an edge of derision in the other man's tone. "I am not here in any official capacity, you understand. I am simply a private citizen. Like every visitor, naturally, I am interested in conditions here."

"I beg your pardon," said James. "I understood that you were a representative of your government?"

"Only informally. That is, when it was known that I was planning to come to York, I was asked to keep my eyes and ears open. That is all."

"And what brought you to York?" asked Leon baldly.

Lady Hester took it upon herself to answer. "William is our cousin. Didn't you know, Mr. Devereux?"

"Your cousin?"

"Our mothers were cousins," William corrected.

"They were as close as sisters," Hester chided. "And when you were boys, you and Peter were almost inseparable."

"Inseparable?" William laughed. "At school, he was an infernal nuisance, always following me around like an overgrown puppy. There was three years difference in our ages. You know how it is when you are young."

"I remember," said Hester, smiling at him in an indulgent way. "And you will never convince me, William, that you were anything but kind to Peter."

"Lord, no!" he exclaimed. "And you know why. If I had been unkind to the boy and it had got back to my father, I would have taken a beating. My parents were sticklers for discipline."

"As were mine," Hester intoned, her eyes alighting for a moment on Sara, before moving on to Emily.

For the next few minutes, the conversation turned on the deplorable lack of discipline to be found in the younger generation. As was to be expected, Emily and Sara contributed very little, and when the butler entered to remove the tea things, Emily seized on the momentary lull to turn the subject.

"I understood from your letters that servants in York were as scarce as fifty-pound notes?"

Though she addressed Sara, again it was Hester who answered. "Mr. Fraser was kind enough to secure the services of Paterson for us." She flashed James a grateful smile. "Since his arrival, I may tell you that the pilfering going on below stairs has ceased altogether."

"Pilfering?" Emily inquired politely. "Do you say that your servants were stealing from you?"

"No," Sara said decisively. "Hester, how can you imply such a thing? Only one girl was involved, and she stole very little. Lace caps, bric-à-brac, that sort of thing. She never took anything of real value."

"What happened to her?" asked Emily.

Hester's nostrils were quivering. "Nothing happened to her. She was an Indian girl. The authorities can do nothing with the Indians, it seems. They melt into the woods and no one can ever find them again."

This reference to the Indian maid gave the gentlemen the opening they were looking for to return the conversation to its original topic. Before long, a full-scale debate was in progress.

"It seems a strange way to make peace," Leon remarked at one point, "to supply the Iroquois and Shawnee with guns and ammunition."

Emily had heard this argument before. If Americans were not denouncing the British for their piracy on the high seas, they railed at them for arming Indians who were hostile to American settlers. She had never known how to answer these charges, and listened interestedly to what William might have to say.

"Historically, the Indians are our allies. We have treaties with them. We have been supplying them with guns and ammunition for years past. There is nothing new in that. Why should we stop now?"

"Oh, I — and every other American — is aware of what has been going on these many years. For the moment, it is American settlers who are being massacred. One day, it might well be British settlers. And you will have no one to blame but yourselves."

William laughed, but it was a forced sound. "Your settlers are trying to move onto Indian hunting grounds, and your government encourages it. That is why you have brought down the Indians' ire on your heads."

"James, what do you think?" The question came from Sara.

There was something in her sister's tone that made Emily turn her head to look at her. Then James was answering and she gave her attention to him.

"I am a fur trader," he said. "Settlers spell death to the fur trade. In this conflict, I endorse whatever promotes the interests of the Indians."

"In short, self-interest," Leon retorted.

"Of course," James answered at once, and everyone laughed.

Emily was acutely conscious that Leon was biding his time, waiting to pounce on her. She owed him an explanation for concealing from him the knowledge that William was in York. She was anxious to get it over and done with. She hated the hostility he veiled from others but which seemed to come at her in waves. She was used to something different from him now and was coming to see how much she might have forfeited by her little deception.

Throughout the rest of that day, however, Leon carefully and politely treated her like a stranger. There were moments when they were alone, moments when he might have broached the subject of William's presence in York. He chose not to do so, and Emily's unease increased tenfold. He wasn't going to treat her little deception as though it was innocent and well meant. In his eyes, she had committed an outrage.

Such were her thoughts as she took her place at the dinner table that evening. There were six of them. Peter had arrived earlier from the garrison, apologizing profusely for the delay. General Brock had ordered fortifications to be built and some problem had arisen with the surveyor which had necessitated Peter's presence. He spoke in such vague terms that no one doubted he was being evasive. Leon was an American, and though the fortifications were there for any eye to see, a certain circumspection must be observed in the presence of an outsider.

His words and manner were anything but offensive. There was no awkwardness. With a mocking laugh and a knowing wink in Leon's direction, he reduced the secrecy to an amusing folly. It was deftly done, and set the tone for the conversation which was to follow. There would be no debate such as the one that had taken place that morning.

James Fraser was there, though William Addison had absented himself. He was engaged to dine with friends at the officers' mess, where he was a paying guest. Emily was relieved at his absence. The strain of conversing with William under Leon's watchful eye was removed, and though she knew she was not going to get off scot-free, her spirits lifted.

The dinner was as elaborate as anything she was used to in England. There were two or three kinds of meat, as well as fish and game. The gentlemen had no quarrel with the choice of wines and brandies their host had to offer.

Throughout that long dinner, Emily became an observer. It did not take her long to divine that beneath the banter, Peter and Sara were estranged. On Sara's part, there was a thinly veiled contempt. Peter was less obvious. Nevertheless, Emily detected a kind of defiant gaiety — he might as well be hanged for a sheep as a lamb.

There were other things she noticed. Her first impression, that Hester was Peter's real hostess, was reinforced. Hester was very much the grande dame and in her element. All matters relating to the household were referred to her, and Sara gave no indication that she cared one way or another. When she made a contribution to the conversation, her eyes invariably sought out James Fraser's, not deliberately, but almost without volition. Emily was used to observing this trait in her sister, but formerly it was Leon who had been the object of Sara's attention.

This thought gave rise to all sorts of speculation. Sara, it seemed, had outgrown her girlish infatuation for Leon. She was more natural with him, like a sister. Surreptitiously, Emily began to study her husband. Their eyes brushed and held, and in those few seconds a silent communication passed between them. He had caught her out. He was amused at what she was doing, was aware that she was covertly weighing each look and word because he was doing it himself. Suppressing a smile, Emily averted her head and concentrated on what was being said.

Peter, the gracious host, had involved James Fraser in a description of the fur trade, thinking that it might be of some interest to Emily. It was. For the first time, she learned that James was of mixed blood. His mother and his younger siblings lived in a house which his father had built for them on the shores of Lake Huron. She thought she might like to visit it, and made the suggestion.

Laughing, James shook his head. "No white woman has ever set foot so far west. Only the *voyageurs* and agents. There are no roads and few trails. We travel by canoe."

Emily thought for a moment, then said, "But I was sure you made reference to neighbors and other families you visited when you were a boy." She was not quite sure of this, for during much of the conversation she had been thinking her own thoughts.

"Those are fur traders' families," answered James. "In every case, the wife is of Indian blood."

To Emily's ears, the silence which followed betrayed a certain awkwardness. It was soon glossed over by a reference to Montreal as the center of the fur trade.

Emily sat back in her chair and flicked a look in her husband's direction. Leon was topping up his wineglass. He had nothing to contribute to the discussion on Montreal. It was odd.

Montreal. She could not help wondering about it.

Peter was waiting for Sara when she came in from the kitchen. "I poured you a glass of wine," he said, keeping his voice light. "You deserve it. That was a splendid dinner, Sara. I was proud of you."

"Were you?" she murmured. "I don't know why. You should be thanking Hester."

She accepted the glass from his hand and followed him into a small parlor where logs were still burning in the grate. Some time had elapsed since James Fraser had departed and their guests had taken themselves off to bed.

"It went quite well, I think," she said, for something to say.

They went on in this vein until, it seemed, they had run out of small talk.

Taking a quick breath, Peter said, "You will want to introduce your sister to York society. We must give more dinner parties, Sara, accept invitations to dine out. It would not be fair to Emily to keep her to yourself."

She smiled faintly. "I think I know what I owe my sister."

"Then you agree that you must make the effort to introduce our guests to our friends and neighbors?"

She inclined her head. "For as long as Emily and Leon are with us, I shall become a social butterfly." He frowned at her levity, and she went on more naturally.

"If you had been here, Peter, you would have known that Hester and I have arranged a full calendar of events for our guests over the next few weeks." When he remained silent, her brows lifted. "I thought you would be pleased."

"I am. That goes without saying. But I was thinking . . ."

"Yes?"

"You would not do as much for me."

She stared into her wineglass and he paused, sensing her withdrawal. As his frustration increased, his tone hardened. "Sara, they can't remain in York indefinitely. When they go, what then? Will you continue to remain hidden away in this house like a recluse?"

"They have just arrived and already you are talking of their going away?"

"All I am trying to point out is that when they go, as they must, I shall still be here. Can't we put our differences behind us? Can't you at least try to make something of our life here, for your own sake if not for mine? It could be so much better than you have allowed it to be. If tonight showed me anything, it was that you are still the same girl I married. You always enjoyed parties, far more than I. It's not good for you to cut yourself off like this. People are wondering about you . . . talking. How do you think I feel when I have to make excuses for my wife's absences? If you would only try to be a bit more accommodating."

"Like Hester, for instance?"

"Yes, like Hester. Do you think my sister prefers York to England? I assure you, she does not! She puts a good face on things, she has too much . . . Well, what I mean is, Hester is too proud to let others see her disappointment."

"Oh, yes, too proud by half. I think we are all agreed on that!"

"What does that mean?"

Instead of answering him, she said, "You are very close to your sister, aren't you, Peter?"

"Very," he said, hesitating as he sensed a shift in ground. "In many ways, as we were growing up, Hester was a little mother to me."

"And now she would like to be your wife!"

"That's a vile thing to say!"

She knew that she was being unreasonable, but she could not seem to get command of herself. "Is it? To all intents and purposes, she is mistress of this house. She is your hostess. Everything must be deferred to Hester."

"Because you relinquished your position to her! Sara, for heaven's sake, you were deathly ill. If Hester had not been here to take care of things, I would never have had a moment's peace. She nursed you. Can't you give a little credit where it is due?"

As though he had not spoken, she went on relentlessly. "You have a sister for your house and a mistress for your bed. Why won't you let me go?"

Hot color flooded his face. There was a tense silence, then he burst out, "I wondered how soon it would be before we would get to that." He brought his glass to his lips and drained it. Setting it down sharply, he said, "If you were any sort of wife to me, I would have no need of a mistress."

Her amusement turned to mockery. "I'm sure that is what all errant husbands say."

"The woman means nothing to me."

"I'm not finding fault. As you say, if I were more of

a wife to you, you would not stray." She leaned forward slightly as if to emphasize her words. "Do you still want me, Peter?"

He stared at her wordlessly, jaw tensed, chest rising and falling as his breathing became harsher.

She cocked her head to one side. "Promise me that we can go home to England and I shall welcome you into my bed—tonight, if you like. It rests with you, Peter." She raised one hand in a gesture of supplication, but quickly withdrew it as she saw the fury building in his eyes.

"You are no better than a whore, do you know?"

She tossed her head. "Why? Because I refuse to bear children in this uncivilized country?" Her tongue began to trip over the words as her thoughts outpaced her speech. "For God's sake, Peter, why do you keep me here against my will? I don't fit in. I'm not happy. I want to be with my own kind. I have money enough for both of us. We could be living in style in Mayfair instead of in this pigsty."

His smile was bitter. "And what would I find to do in Mayfair?"

His question baffled her and she stared at him dumbly.

Sighing, he said, "Sara, try to see it from my point of view. For the first time in my life, I feel that I am accomplishing something. If you would only give it a try . . ." His voice died away when she made a small sound of derision.

After a moment she said, "I don't know if I can take much more of this." She looked into his eyes. "You say that I am fully recovered from my illness. How can I believe you? How do you know? You were not here when I was at my worst. You are away so much of the time. It was . . . well, I don't want to think about it. Peter, I am frightened. Sometimes I fear I shall end up in a madhouse if I stay here much longer. Sometimes I think I might as well be dead."

"Sara! For God's sake!" It was a moment before his voice steadied. "All right. I shall think about it."

"You mean . . . we can go home?" Her voice was eager.

"I must remain here. In any event, it's not possible at present, not as things stand, not with the threat of war hanging over our heads. Don't try to argue with me on this. I shall think about it. I won't promise more than that."

"Peter, do you really mean it?"

His head was bent, his hands loosely clasped in front of him. He nodded and looked up. Very softly, he said, "You never loved me, did you, Sara?"

For a moment she hesitated. "I was . . . am . . . very fond of you," she said, and looked away.

Slowly, he got to his feet. He looked older. Weary, resigned. "I shall see you in the morning," he said and quietly left the room.

When the door closed, Sara let out a short breath. She had not wanted to hurt him, but she wasn't going to tell him a blatant untruth, either. If she had said that she loved him, he would not have given up so easily.

Love. She would not wish that affliction on her worst enemy. She had suffered its effects and she should know. There was a time when she had thought she would love Leon Devereux to her dying day. It seemed she was fickle. Once she had accepted that there was no hope for her, her "undying" love had died a quick and natural death. Poor Peter. He loved her and it gave her the upper hand. She frowned, thinking that she did not have everything her own way.

She had thought once that she could mold him to her every whim. He allowed her to go so far and no farther. Sometimes she hardly recognized him. Major Benson. He had taken to Army life like a duck to water. Unhappily, she was not cut out to follow the drum.

Her eyes traveled the small room, taking in the fine English furniture which had been bought at auction, from the home of a family that had sold it and had gone back to England. Sara envied that family. This house and its contents was regarded as one of the finest in York. It was Georgian in design and built of brick. Compared to the fine houses she had known in England it was a doll's house.

Surprisingly, Emily admired it. But Emily was fascinated with every aspect of colonial life. Sara shook her head in wonderment. She would have thought her sister too refined, too urbane for the rawness that was part and parcel of life on the frontiers of the New World. There was no accounting for taste.

Self-pity crept up on her slowly. Blinking back tears, in a flurry of motion, she extinguished the candles and climbed the stairs to her bed.

Chapter Sixteen

Emily knew that the moment of reckoning for concealing William's presence in York from Leon was finally upon her. As the maid moved around the chamber, shaking and folding away clothes, she debated with herself what course she should follow. She knew that she must be scrupulously truthful. She balked, however, at perfect honesty, unless it became absolutely necessary. She was afraid that if Leon were to discover the extent of her stupidity, the new intimacy they shared would suffer a blow from which it might never recover.

Before Leon came through the door from the little dressing room, Emily's mind was delicately balanced. But when she heard the ice in his voice as he dismissed the maid, a voice that could charm the shades in the underworld if he had a mind to, the scales tipped.

Clearing her throat, she said, "Sara is a little paler and thinner, but for all that, she seems to have got over her illness. Peter could not thank me enough for making the effort to come and see her. He says it was the expectation of our arrival more than anything that made the difference."

He was pacing like a caged panther. She was wandering around the room, keeping her distance, feigning an interest in various objects, as though she were a collector intent on making a purchase. When it came to her what she was doing, that she was acting as if she were afraid of him, she edged her way to the bed and plumped herself down. If there was one person she did not fear, it was her own husband.

He swung to face her and his eyes blazed. "Why didn't you tell me Addison was here?"

"You know why. I was afraid you would forbid me to come."

"Now why should I do that?"

Enunciating each word slowly and carefully, she said, "I was worried about Sara. You were reluctant to let me go to her. You know you were. I wasn't about to give you a reason to put me off coming here."

There was another reason, a more cogent one, for her not to be traveling at this time. Emily was beginning to suspect that she was with child. She knew her husband well enough to be convinced, in that event, nothing would have persuaded him to let her make the journey.

His eyes narrowed on the betraying color in her cheeks. "Is that all it was?" He paused and those sharp eyes seemed to narrow to slits. "Emily, what are you concealing from me?"

She was very calm, very much in possession of herself. "If you had cared to read my sister's letters to us, you would have known that William was here. It was no secret. If I chose not to mention his name, it was only because I know how you feel about him."

There was a lot more to it than that, but Emily wasn't about to confess all until she was cornered, and if she had her way, that wasn't going to happen anytime soon.

"You still haven't told me your impressions of Sara," she began, leading him carefully away from all mention of William Addison.

His voice gentled appreciably. "You're not still worried about Sara? Don't be. There is no cause for alarm. She has fully recovered. Your own eyes must have told you so."

She allowed herself a small smile. "Yes. I'll say one thing for Hester. She did not stint herself on Sara's behalf. As a nurse, she has no equal. Peter says that if Hester had not been here to manage things, he would have been half out of his wits."

"Hester, like most women, can be very managing when she wants to be."

For a moment, she had the uncanny feeling that he was toying with her. She looked at him closely, and dismissed the thought from her mind. "I still can't seem to warm to the woman, though. Uncle Rolfe says that she has an opinion on everything and now I know what he means. She thinks the Indians are foreigners. Can you believe that? I didn't dare look James Fraser in the eye after she made that remark."

"Why?" He was standing right in front of her and she had to angle her head back to look up at him.

"Why? Because it's a derogatory, callous remark from the mind of someone who thinks herself superior."

His eyebrows rose. "I've heard you use that word to describe me time out of mind."

She forgot about trying to distract him. He was casting up the sins of her youth. If they both played that game, they would be here till doomsday. Stung by the injustice of the jibe and his deliberate attempt to bait her when she was doing her best to keep the peace between them, she stuttered, "You . . . you unconscionable . . ."

"Foreigner?" he supplied when she floundered. "Or were you going to say 'Frenchman' this time around?"

She bolted to her feet. With no clear idea of what she was doing, but with a burning determination to make him listen to her without interruption, she pounced on him. If he had not had the agility of a cat, they would both have gone crashing to the floor. With one adroit twist and a backward step, he managed things so that they went tumbling to the bed. Emily landed on top of him.

Seizing the advantage, she grabbed for his wrists, flinging his arms above his head, holding him down, subduing him with her weight.

Between labored breaths, she got out, "If there is one thing I cannot abide, it's people who finish other people's sentences for them. I had a governess who used to drive me to distraction with that trick. You are going to listen to me, Leon Devereux, if it's the last thing you do. I was not going to say 'foreigner.'"

"No?"

"No. Leon, is it fair to cast up old history? I don't think of you as a foreigner. It's years since I flung that taunt in your face. I'm not a child anymore."

He wasn't angry. His tone was very gentle, very reasonable. "Nevertheless, you were the one who raised the subject by referring to Hester's conversation at the

272

dinner table. Why did you do it?"

She had been thinking of a way to distract him and had hit on the worst possible thing. Unsure of how to make amends, conscious that her cheeks were very warm, she said, "I swear I was not going to say 'foreigner.' What I was going to say was more in the nature of 'monster.' "

When he laughed, she felt something inside her unravel and with a great gusty sigh, she went on. "You are too sensitive, Leon. You hate to be reminded that you are French. You were born in France, weren't you? Aunt Zoë is French and she doesn't care who knows it. You should be proud to be French."

"I have a crick in my neck. Might I sit up?"

"What? Oh, sorry." She tried to slip off him, but in one powerful movement, he had shifted so that his back was propped against the bed and she was astride his lap.

"You were saying. I should be proud to be French?"

Distracted by the feel of so much potent virility beneath her, fascinated by the sleepy-eyed sensuality in his lazy grin, she groped in her mind for what she had been on the point of saying. "Yes, well, if there was no France, the world would be so much the poorer. Think of French philosophy and literature and art and so on."

"My mind is not so lofty."

She couldn't concentrate on what he was saying, for his hands were on the backs of her bare calves, clever hands, drawing patterns on her skin, moving higher with an excruciating lack of haste.

"Naturally, I wish to preserve the best of my French heritage. But I am a carnal animal."

273

His head had dipped slightly, and she could feel his warm breath penetrating her lips. "Carnal?" she repeated, but the thought was impossible to hold. The breath she inhaled was redolent of brandy and wine and the ripe vineyards of the Mediterranean, intoxicating, beguiling.

She was caught in a web so finely spun that she had yet to become aware of it. He spun another silken thread. "May I introduce you to what I consider to be the best that France has to offer?" and he took her mouth in a startlingly probing hiss.

When he released her, she nodded and managed, "I would be honored."

He rewarded her with a devastating smile, then he kissed her again deeply, wetly, and his hands slid higher, plundering the silken petals between her thighs. *"Plaisirs d'amour,"* he whispered against her lips. "To a Frenchman, that's the only thing that counts."

She was clinging to him like limp seaweed cast up on a rock. He brought his lips to the graceful arch of her throat. "Say yes to me, Emily. Let me show you how it can be, shall I? The pleasures of love, in the French manner."

He had to shake her before she got the word out. Then, eyes holding hers, he laid her back on the bed and divested them both of their nightclothes.

Emily had always enjoyed her husband's lovemaking, not least because she sensed the checks he imposed on himself for her sake. Occasionally, those checks had slipped a little. Sometimes she toyed with the idea of putting his control to the test. The thought excited her. At the same time, the thought brought a return of caution. Leon Devereux without restraints was an alarming picture. There were no restraints now.

His passion stunned her. It had never been like this before. He showed her no deference. There was no implicit understanding that she would allow him to go so far and no further. In the act of love, he had always yielded the power to her. This time, he was in control, he was setting the pace.

He was experienced. If she never knew it before, she knew it now. He demanded things of her he had never demanded before. The man was a master of seduction. There wasn't a thing he didn't know about turning that involuntary feminine no into a yes. He charted the course and she followed him.

He was greedy, wanting everything from her. Even so, he would have stopped if she had betrayed the slightest revulsion to what he was doing. Her response stunned him, inflamed him, made him bolder. He was wishing he had trounced her like this when they were first married. He had been too forbearing for his own good. All the years he had held off, all the waiting, focused now into an explosion of need.

It was the first time, the very first time, she had yielded him the freedom of her body. It wasn't enough for him. It was too unequal. He wanted her to hunger for him as he hungered for her.

He dragged her to a sitting position. Half crouched over her, he told her what he wanted from her. She didn't seem to understand. She wasn't used to taking the initiative or pleasuring him the way he wanted to be pleasured. He showed her how easily it could be done.

For a moment their eyes held. She gave him such a

look and his confidence faltered. He was going too fast for her, asking too much of her. Then she pounced on him, pushing him back into the pillows.

She was freer, more uninhibited than he could have hoped. She was also an apt pupil, too apt, too caught up in practicing her newfound knowledge of the male animal. She cried out in alarm when he tumbled her on her back and swiftly entered her.

He was rougher than he meant to be, punishing her, nipping at her with bared teeth, taking her with a violence that in his saner moments she would not have believed himself capable of. And she responded, wantonly, not submitting, but taking as much as she gave. It was glorious.

Afterward, lying beside her, fighting to even his breathing, his conscience smote him. He was so much more powerful than she. Had he hurt her? Frightened her? Forced her against her will? In the blinding throes of passion, he might have mistaken the nature of those little sounds she made, those little bites and scratches she had inflicted on his neck and shoulders. Oh, God, surely she hadn't been fighting him off?

"Emily?" he said urgently.

Twisting her head on the pillow to get a better look at him, hovering between awe and shock at what had just taken place, she said, "Is *that* how married people in France behave?"

Relief bloomed in him and he almost laughed out loud before he remembered that his little wife was due a lesson that she must never forget.

"How would I know?" he threw out negligently, and rolling from the bed, he reached for his dressing gown and shrugged into it. Belting it tightly, he came back to sit beside her. "Here, put this on," he said, and handed her her nightdress.

Her eyes were still love-dazed, but bewilderment was beginning to make itself felt. He had a very clever look about him that brought a belated return of caution. She slipped into her nightdress and settled back against the pillows. "But you said . . ."

"I know what I said." With one finger he tipped up her chin and looked deeply into her eyes. "Now," and there was nothing loverlike about him, "having got *that* out of the way, may we return to the subject at hand? We were discussing William Addison and you were about to tell me whatever it is you have been concealing from me."

Her jaw went slack. "You can ask me about William at a time like this? After . . . after what happened between us, here, in this bed, not moments ago?"

His laughter held a disquieting thread of derision. "Emily, I know you too well. I've had years in which to study you. I'm on to all your little ploys. Those tricks may have worked very well with your guardian, but they won't work with me. You wanted to distract me and I was willing to allow it because it suited me. Now, if you please, I am waiting for an explanation."

She wasn't ready to give him an explanation. She was quivering with indignation. "I may have thought to distract you, but only for a moment or two. You cannot believe that I was so devious as to try to seduce you. It never entered my head."

His eyes held a wicked glint of amusement. "No," he agreed, "because, my dear, I made it my business to distract *you*. It's what is known as being hoisted by your own petard."

Amethyst fire kindled in her eyes. He found the phenomenon truly interesting, but the flames made no impression on him. Between short, quick breaths, she got out, *"Love, in the French manner.* That was so much fustian, I suppose?"

He gloated deliberately. "I wondered how far you would go. Convict me. I took advantage of you. My dear, a man has fantasies. Didn't you know it? Normally, I wouldn't have dared ask so much of you. I'll say this for you, Emily, you are generous to a fault. And, no," he went on, correctly interpreting the shock that widened her eyes, "I have never indulged my fantasies with any other woman. My sweet, who could I find to match you for passion?"

She felt deeply betrayed and was torn between the desire to cry her eyes out and an equal desire to knock his head off. "By all means, let us talk about William," she said, then slipped in snidely, "I daresay he would never take advantage of a poor defenseless female."

His lips twitched in that nasty way that never failed to rattle her. "True," he said. "I daresay Addison dons white cotton gloves before he takes a woman to bed. I daresay he would run the proverbial mile if he knew what you were really like. Now, Emily, my explanation, and no more evasions."

She sat there with her knees drawn up, glaring at him. He moved and she said quickly, "It was all so innocent. William wrote to me, once, twice, when we were in New York. There was nothing in those letters that I would be ashamed to show anyone."

"Yet you did not show those letters to me."

She had expected him to explode with temper when

278

he heard that she had corresponded with a former suitor. Most husbands would have raved. His reasonableness, his forbearance, shamed her far more than any diatribe. Swallowing her pride, she said, "It was wrong not to tell you. I knew it was wrong. I had hoped, you see, that you would never discover it. When I wrote to William after that first letter, I told him that he must never write to me again."

"But he did write to you again?"

"Yes, but this time, I did not reply." She looked at him uncertainly and her hands went automatically to her hair, pushing back long strands of gold that lay across her shoulders. "I'm sorry, Leon. It was a cowardly thing to do. I didn't want any unpleasantness between us, 'tis all. And then, when we knew of Sara's illness, I was afraid to tell you in case you would forbid me to visit her."

He watched her through narrowed eyes for a moment, taking in her earnest expression. Quickly dropping a kiss on her upturned lips, he said, "I should beat you, but after the pleasure you have given me tonight, it would be too ungallant, especially for a Frenchman."

At the mention of anything French, her meekness instantly evaporated. When he doused the candle, she made a great to-do of removing herself to the far side of the mattress, as far from him as possible, where she perched precariously at the edge.

His warm breath on her shoulder almost sent her tumbling to the floor. Catching her back against him, laughing, he said whimsically, "I have other fantasies I have yet to share with you. I don't suppose your generosity would stretch so far? No? I thought as much," and with a string of barely suppressed chortles of laughter, he dragged her back to the center of the bed, anchoring her with one hairy, masculine leg thrown over hers and a hand possessively cupping one breast.

She lay there like a stone, listening to his breathing even as he slowly drifted into sleep. She had the last word. Suddenly levering herself up, she slapped him on the shoulder. Hard.

"What the devil?" Blinking the sleep from his eyes, he started up. "Emily, what . . . ?"

"I've just remembered something else we owe to France."

"Oh? What's that?"

"Napoleon Bonaparte!" she snapped and, viciously thumping her pillows, she settled back beneath the covers and composed herself for sleep.

Chapter Seventeen

Peter Benson found his sister in her bedchamber. She was at a small kneehole desk, her head bent over a ledger.

"Am I disturbing you?" he said.

There was no artifice in the smile she gave him. "You could never disturb me, Peter. Do come in," and she set the ledger aside, giving him her complete attention.

"You should not be here alone, Hester, doing the household accounts. You should be out driving. Didn't I see William just go off in a carriage with Sara and Emily? Surely you were invited, too?"

"Of course I was invited. William's manners can never be faulted. But they are young people, Peter. They don't want an old maid like me to spoil their outing."

He accepted the chair she indicated and quelled the small surge of irritation. He knew that to Sara and Emily, his sister was an object of derision. Admittedly, some of it was merited. Hester was her own worst enemy. She was too censorious, too ready to point out faults. Nevertheless, it galled him to see how her company was shunned by the younger girls.

His voice was light and teasing. "What do you mean, 'old maid'? There is only a year's difference in our ages. You are a fine-looking woman. If you wanted to, Hester, you could attach any gentleman you set your cap at."

Hester's serene expression clouded over, and Peter remembered that some years before, his sister had formed an attachment to an ineligible gentleman. Their father would not countenance the match, and shortly after, the gentleman had snagged a wealthy wife. Peter knew only the sketchiest details, having been away at university at the time. This great misfortune had cast a blight on his sister's life. She had become the proverbial maiden aunt, flitting from one sibling's house to another, managing their households and a brood of nieces and nephews with very little thanks for the great sacrifices she had made. Even he had not been above making use of her for his own ends.

Impatient with both Hester and himself, but for different reasons, he said, "You have made quite a hit with some of the officers at the garrison. Isn't there a single one who has taken your fancy?"

She made a moue of distaste. "You know as well as I do, Peter, that most of your young colleagues are here because they are fleeing some scandal at home."

"That's hardly true! There are many fine, upstanding men among them."

"Even if that were so, no one has offered for me, so this conversation is pointless."

"No one has offered for you because you don't encourage it. Hester, you mustn't allow something from the past to cast a shadow on your life. You should have your eye on the future." Having once embarked on a subject which he knew he would not dare touch upon again, he decided to be completely frank. "This isn't much of a life for you, always a guest in someone else's home. I never knew a woman who was more fitted to preside over her own establishment. Your accomplishments are incomparable. You know how to manage a house. You can sketch, draw, sing, and sew with the best of them. If you would only unbend a little, you could have almost anyone you want."

Her smile was very tight. "You are forgetting something, Peter. My dowry is nothing to boast about. And the sort of gentleman who would be willing to accept an impoverished wife is not the sort of gentleman in whom I would be interested."

"Our sisters married well enough," he pointed out.

Hester merely elevated her brows, and after an interval, when he saw that nothing he could say would make an impression on her, he laughed in a deprecating way. "No, don't get your hackles up. I promise not to interfere."

He adjusted his position in the small chair. "Sara and I are deeply in your debt, and I am not only referring to the way you nursed her when she was so very ill. If it weren't for you, Hester, I don't know how we would manage. Sara doesn't know the first thing about housekeeping and so on. She is young and her interests are . . . Well, as I said, she is very young."

Hester's brows drew together in a slight frown. "Like most girls of her generation, she is frivolous. Their heads are filled with nothing more exalted than

283

parties and ballgowns. Sara has no sense of what is fitting for a lady in her position. Peter, I do think you should put your foot down. People are talking. She is too animated. She flirts outrageously. Since she has recovered from her illness, there is always some gentleman or other calling on her, taking her out in his carriage. I've tried remonstrating with her to no purpose. You are her husband. You must be the one to correct her."

As was his way, he laughed this off. "Surely any pretty young girl is entitled to think about parties and ballgowns? Didn't you at her age?"

"Certainly I did. But I was also raised to know my duty. It's common knowledge that Rivard's nieces had the ordering of their own lives from the time they were in the cradle. And it shows."

When she paused, he took the opportunity to say, "When I was Sara's age, I was a drone, a wastrel. I led a life of indolence. You know I did. Yet, *I* changed."

Hester smiled. "That is because you are a Benson, dear. It's in the blood. There never was a Benson who did not make something of himself eventually. But those Brockfords." She shook her head. "They were never really good ton for all that they were marquesses. They marry foreigners, they have strange ideas of deportment. Well, just think of the scandal of your own nuptials, and as for Emily . . ."

"Hester!" Peter rarely lost his patience. Even now, he softened the reproof in his tone with a strained smile, but Hester knew enough about her brother to be wary of the hard look in his eyes.

"I beg your pardon," she said meekly, and fingered the locket at her throat. "You did not seek me out to listen to the ramblings of a lonely old maid. How may I help you, Peter?"

He felt guilty twice over, first because his sister had confessed that she was lonely, and second because his only reason in seeking her out was not to relieve that loneliness but to ask a favor. With a flash of annoyance, he wondered if women were born knowing how to make a man feel guilty or if it was something they passed on from mother to daughter like a sacred trust in each succeeding generation.

Hoping to spare her feelings, he said carefully, "It appears to me that if Sara had a little more responsibility, that is, if you would show her what is involved in the running of a house and managing the servants, she would learn very quickly. There are other things I have noticed, trifles that don't mean much to a man, but which I know weigh with women."

She wasn't giving him the least encouragement, but stared at him with a cold little face. Floundering, he pushed on. "Such as pouring tea for our guests and signaling the servants when to serve the courses at dinner, and consulting with cook about menus."

"Has Sara been complaining?" Her voice, so warm with sisterly affection a few moments before, had iced over, matching the look on her face. Before he could think how to answer her, she rushed on heedlessly. "I assure you, Peter, my only wish is to be of service. If Sara wishes . . ."

"That's splendid!" He was on his feet, grinning down at her with that disarmingly boyish grin of his. "I knew I could count on you, Hester. That's settled then. You have no idea how you have relieved my mind." At the door, he turned back. "Shall we begin tonight when the tea things are brought in? Let's make this as natural as possible. You and I shall engage in a very involved conversation so that Sara has no option but to act as hostess. And we shall go on from there, shall we?"

When the door closed behind him, Hester gave vent to her rage by knocking the silk cushion he had been reclining against to the floor. She felt like screaming, but would never have disgraced herself by indulging in such an unladylike display.

Frustrated rage brought the hot, salty tears to her eyes. It was happening again. Her usefulness was coming to an end and soon she would have to make a home for herself with another set of relatives.

Palming her eyes, she forced the unpleasant reality from her mind and indulged in her favorite fantasy. The house over which she presided was as magnificent as Osterley. The children who played on the lawns were *her* children. The handsome man by her side was *her* husband. The very things other people derided in her — her devotion to duty, her sense of what was fitting, her decorum — he applauded because they shared the same values. But it was more than that. He loved her. She loved him. Would the dream ever become a reality?

After a moment or two, she felt more in command of herself. When she opened the ledger to continue with her accounts, her expression was serene.

On a small rise overlooking the harbor, the riders dismounted and gazed out over the bay. The waters of Lake Ontario glittered like diamonds and the haze out beyond the Peninsula was slowly dissipating as a westerly breeze got up.

James Fraser glanced at his mount's mired forelegs and made a small sound of annoyance. "There is something to be said for our long winters. This mud is an infernal nuisance. I'd forgotten that York turns into a quagmire as soon as the warm weather arrives. I shall be glad to get back to Montreal."

Leon acknowledged his companion's words with a vague nod, but his eyes were still on the lake, following the progress of a schooner with white sails which had just left the harbor.

For a moment or two, nothing was said, then James threw out in a bating way, "So, in the short time you have been here, you have managed to make yourself the most unpopular man in York. Is that wise, Leon?"

This sally brought Leon's head round. Smiling faintly, he returned, "When people express inflammatory opinions in my hearing, I see no reason not to correct them."

James laughed at this. "To British ears, *you* are the one who is expressing inflammatory opinions. No, I refuse to be drawn into a debate about American shipping or the rights of American settlers. All I will say is that it's no bad thing that you will be returning to New York before long. When do you go, by the by?"

"If I had my way, we would go tomorrow, but there is no hope of that with the Governor General hosting a ball on the occasion of Emily's birthday."

"It's a signal honor, you know," James pointed out, mildly irritated by his friend's lack of enthusiasm.

Leon's eyes held a wicked twinkle. "So I've been told by Lady Hester. When she thought I meant to decline

Sir George's 'magnanimous offer'—her words, you know—she practically read me the riot act."

"Lady Hester? You surprise me. I thought she was just the type of female to make you do the opposite of whatever she suggested."

"You know me too well! Yes, I admit I was tempted, but I could see that not to accept would have caused considerable embarrassment to my host, not to mention my wife. Let's walk aways, shall we?"

By tacit consent, the two friends edged their horses round to face the direction of the town. Their own boots were no less muddied than the prime mounts they had acquired from Peter Benson's private stock.

At length, Leon said, "What about you, James? Do you go with the fur brigades?"

"I may. I haven't made up my mind" was the cautious reply.

Leon's eyebrows rose but he said nothing, provoking James to demand, "Now just what the devil am I to make of that supercilious look?"

Unperturbed, Leon responded, "Since you ask, I shall tell you. Sara is not for you. Her marriage may not be a happy one, but she will not enter into an affair with any man."

"Did I say anything about an affair?"

"No, but I know you and I know Sara. She may seem reckless and heedless of decorum, but that is only superficial. Scratch the surface and you will find that she is as straight as a plumb line."

James's look was frankly speculative. "How do you know so much about it?"

Leon bit down on a smile. What he was thinking was that his sister Zoë had the raising of Ladies Emily

288

and Sara. They might get up to all sorts of mischief, but Zoë had schooled them too well. Flashing his companion a look of mock commiseration, he said, "Sara is like Emily. She would never betray her husband. You will just have to take my word for it, James."

There was a silence, then James said, "And if I should prove you wrong? What then?"

Shrugging indifferently, Leon answered, "Sara has a husband. It's nothing to do with me. Now tell me about the Indian maid, the one who drugged Sara. You mentioned that you had picked up her trail?"

James was more than happy to allow the subject of Lady Sara to be dropped and seized on the opening Leon had given him. "What we did not know at the time was that she was married. Her husband is a guide, a free trader and sometime buffalo hunter by the name of Ducette. After she left here, she went to Lachine to wait for him."

"Lachine? Are you saying that Ducette and the girl went west with one of the fur brigades?"

"That's exactly what I am saying. There's more. The girl is with child. In all probability, he is taking her to his place in Ste. Marie. He has a cabin there and a few acres of land. I shall know soon enough. If she is there, what do you want me to do about it?"

They plodded on for some few minutes. Finally, Leon said, "It hardly seems pressing now."

"I agree. If you have enemies, Leon, they are certainly not here. There have been no accidents, no attacks for how long is it now — the best part of a year?"

Leon nodded and James continued. "As for the girl, what I think happened is this: We know that she was stealing things. What better way to evade detection than by ensuring that her mistress was indisposed? Not only did she manage to get Sara out of the way, but Lady Hester, too. Lady Hester was a devoted nurse. By all accounts, she hardly left Sara's bedside."

"Why did the girl run away when she did?"

"My man Paterson arrived on the scene. The girl must have known the game was up. I expect it suited her purposes very well to go off with her husband into the wilderness."

At some unspoken signal, both men mounted up. "Ste. Marie," Leon murmured. "That's home for you, isn't it, James?"

"It is."

"The girl shouldn't get off scot-free."

"Don't worry, she won't. When I catch up with her, I intend to throw such a scare into her that it will be years before she shows her face in this neck of the woods."

Leon sat back in the saddle, holding the reins easily as he looked out over the bay. When he turned to his friend, he was grinning. "All things considered," he said, "I think things have worked out very well."

They had just turned into King Street when they came upon a carriage stuck fast in the deeply ploughed ruts of the muddy thoroughfare. William Addison was mired to his knees from assisting the coachmen to hold his team steady. The frightened beasts were plunging about, their flailing hooves throwing up mud in every direction. A passing group of officers of the garrison had procured jute sacking which they were attempting to get under the wheels.

"Leon! James!" Sara waved her lace handkerchief

out the window to attract the attention of the mounted riders.

Sara's cries brought Emily to her side of the coach. When she caught sight of her husband a smile lit up her face, and she, too, waved a handkerchief to attract his attention.

"What do you think?" asked James. "Shall we go to their rescue? We could each take one of the girls and ride pillion."

Leon's expression was very bland, but his lips were not quite steady. "I wouldn't wish to show Mr. Addison in a bad light. He got my wife in to this fix. I have every confidence that he can get her out of it." And so saying, affecting not to understand Sara's and Emily's shrill appeals, he tipped his hat in salute and urged his mount toward Frederick Street. After a startled silence, James Fraser followed suit.

When Emily and Sara arrived home from their outing, having had to walk all the way from their stuck carriage, both Peter and Leon were on hand in the foyer to greet them. The girls had little to say for themselves. There was no need. Their scowling faces and muddy garments told the tale better than any words. Both gentlemen, who were immaculately turned out, were very careful to keep a straight face.

Chapter Eighteen

It was Emily's birthday. In honor of the occasion,
Sir George Prevost, the Governor General, was hosting a ball at Government House. York had never
seen its like before. Over a hundred members of
York's select society had received invitations. Every
off-duty officer in the garrison was expected to attend as a matter of course. The local tradesmen
were all in a flutter. Butchers, bakers, tailors, dress-
makers, were inundated with demands for their services. The regimental band was engaged to provide
the music. In short, by York's standards, it was an
affair on a par with the celebrations for a king's cor-
onation.

As they waited in the receiving line for the doors
to open to admit the influx of guests, Emily made
some comment in passing about the appointments of
the ballroom. Sir George smiled expansively and allowed his eyes to travel the length of the spacious
chamber, noting with approval the crystal chandeliers and the banks of hothouse flowers.

Though he held Lady Emily in the highest esteem, his object in hosting the ball went beyond paying homage to his charming guest. York was the capital of Upper Canada. He aimed to show that York was no primitive outpost but a center of culture and taste. Moreover, Lady Emily was highly connected. Rivard was her uncle. Sir George knew the value of impressing the niece of such a great man. When he was next at court, Rivard would know of him. A career diplomat could never have enough friends in high places.

"A hundred guests," murmured Sara, idly arranging the skirts of her pomona-green ballgown and reflecting that one good thing had come of her marriage to Peter. As a married woman, she could now wear the vibrant colors she preferred. "At Carlton House two thousand guests sat down to supper. Good grief! That's more than twice the population of the whole of York."

In his easy, gracious manner, Peter Benson unobtrusively removed the sting from his wife's words. "Lord, yes," he said. "I remember the occasion well. As I recall, Sara, you decried the Prince Regent's fête as a vulgar circus, and could not wait to be shot of London and all its follies." Addressing Sir George over his wife's head, he winked and concluded, "At heart, Sara is really a country girl."

Sir George allowed himself to be mollified, but behind his bland smile he was thinking that of the three ladies in the receiving line, Lady Hester was by far the most stately. Her pale muslins, though fashionable, were less eye-catching than the younger girls' get-ups. In the best sense of the word, Lady Hester was more truly the lady. As wife to a soldier or a diplomat, she would be a decided asset. How unfortunate that she was so hard to please that few gentlemen could measure up to her standards.

His unwary stare was caught and held by Leon Devereux and Sir George's mellow mood suffered a setback. He wondered what mischief the American might be devising to put him out of countenance. Leon Devereux lost no opportunity in making game of his betters. Insufferable fellow! If it were not for Lady Emily, he would have sent the fellow about his business a long time ago. He was here on sufferance. It would take very little to incite public opinion against the man, and then there was no telling what might happen. If war was declared or . . .

Whatever Sir George might have thought next was forestalled as two liveried footmen pushed back the glass entrance doors and the majordomo stepped forward to announce the names of the first guests. For the next hour or so, Lady Emily and her party were fully occupied in making the acquaintance of York's finest.

The last to arrive was James Fraser. By this time, the receiving line had more or less disbanded. Only Emily and Leon remained at their posts. It was not James who held Emily's interest, however, but the lady who accompanied him.

"Mrs. Charles Royston," intoned the majordomo, "and Mr. James Fraser."

Mrs. Royston had the look of a prima donna. Drama oozed from her every pore. Her smiles and gestures were exaggerated, theatrical, as were her arresting good looks. The crimson sarcenet outfit with black-edged ruffles along the puff sleeves and hem gave her a decided Spanish air. The thought amused Emily and she flashed a quick look at Leon. She was sure he would be stifling a smile.

His eyes were deep and fathomless, his face devoid of all animation. He might have been carved out of wood. And then he came to life, as though on cue, when the prima donna fed him his lines.

"Leon," she said. "Charles and I have been wondering if you were dead! Shame on you for neglecting old friends!"

"Barbara," he murmured, "I understood that you were fixed in Montreal."

As Leon bowed over the lady's hand, James answered the question in Emily's eyes. "Barbara is the wife of a colleague. We met quite by chance."

"We are both putting up at the Jolly Roger," said Mrs. Royston, smiling into Leon's eyes.

Emily's welcoming smile froze on her lips. Mrs. Royston was deliberately ignoring her. Why? If she was interested in the lady before, by this time, she was avidly curious.

In a jocular fashion, James interjected, "When I heard that Barbara had wangled an invitation to tonight's do, I lost no time in offering my escort."

At the tactless remark, something murderous flashed in Barbara Royston's eyes. "James," she remonstrated, her voice low and musical, "that was not polite. I did not 'wangle' an invitation, as you put it. When Sir George heard that I was in York, he insisted that I attend."

"And what brings you to York, Mrs. Royston?" asked Emily, determined that her companions would acknowledge her presence. Since Mrs. Royston's arrival on the scene, everyone, it seemed, was avoiding her eyes.

"Your husband and I are old friends, Lady Emily. When word reached me that he had come into York, wild horses could not keep me away." She tapped Leon playfully on the shoulder with her black ostrich fan. "I must come for myself, you see, and meet your little bride." Her beautiful eyes artlessly turned on Emily. "You must understand, Lady Emily, we were almost sure that Leon was hoaxing us. No one in Montreal could believe that he had a wife waiting for him in England."

Though everyone was smiling, Emily was not deceived. For her benefit, they were putting on a show, conversing in innuendo. If she were to remove herself from their presence, she was perfectly sure that there would be some very plain speaking indeed.

"I recall how it was," said Leon. He was the picture of innocence, a gentleman pleasurably passing the time of day in convivial company. His eyes, half veiled by the sweep of his dark lashes, swiveled to Emily. His voice was rich with amusement. "I must confess, Emily, that there were those in Montreal who refused to accept that I was a married man — fond mamas for the most part. They set their sights on me, and this in spite of my assurances that I was already bespoken." His gaze moved to Barbara Royston, and Emily could almost feel the current that leaped between them. "People believe what they wish to believe," he said quietly. "It's a grave mistake."

Emily's composure never slipped. She had years of training on which she might draw. She was glad of that training now, for behind her serene expression, her mind was in a frenzy, making deductions, putting two and two together.

So this was why her husband wished to keep her away from Montreal. It was where he sowed his wild oats! In New York, where he was regarded as a pillar of society, he conducted himself in an exemplary fashion. When he left civilization behind — and on his own admission, he shook the dust of civilization from his feet every chance he got — he reverted to form. Leon Devereux was wild. He was fickle. She had learned that heart-wrenching lesson on her sixteenth birthday. It was foolish beyond permission to hope that the leopard had changed his spots.

A shiver ran over her as she saw with awful clarity that she was poised on the brink of a great precipice. It was as though a blindfold had been removed from her eyes and she suddenly saw her peril. She was in danger of falling in love with the man! One more step and she would lose her balance and be lost forever.

The thought flashed into her head that she had already taken that irrevocable step, but she quelled it with a ruthless will. He wanted her to fall in love with him. Her refusal to do so was a challenge to everything that was masculine in his nature. Once she yielded to him, he would soon tire of her. If she did not watch her step, she forcefully reminded herself, one day she might turn into another Barbara Royston, a pitiful creature without pride, begging for the crumbs on his table.

It was all so subtle. Leon carried it off flawlessly, as did James Fraser — the small talk, the reference to common acquaintances and absent friends. Only

Mrs. Royston showed signs of strain. After Leon's barely concealed set-down, she had become subdued, and Emily sensed that the lady was beginning to realize that she had made a blunder. She pitied her.

"Charles remains in Montreal?" Leon queried at one point.

Rallying, with false brightness, Mrs. Royston replied, "He does not. You know Charles. He must go with the fur brigades. I don't expect I shall see him till September."

Laughing, Leon elaborated for Emily's benefit, "You must understand, Emily, fur traders are an adventurous lot. After a time, society becomes wearisome. The call of the Northwest is in their blood. Every spring, they begin to hanker for the great forests and plains, the rushing rivers and the thrill of pitting themselves against nature."

"Not to mention the fortunes to be made from a modest investment of capital," James murmured dryly.

Emily had a fair understanding of all that "fur trader" signified. It was a comprehensive term and might denote anyone from the rough *voyageurs* who manned the canoes to the wealthy entrepreneurs who financed and directed the whole enterprise from their offices in Montreal. Some of the wealthiest men in Canada had made their fortunes in the fur trade.

"Were you and Mr. Royston colleagues at one time, Leon?" she asked.

"Rivals," he corrected, then, as though he sensed the unfortunate choice of word, he went on with only a fraction of a pause. "I was an independent.

298

These days, there are few independents. Hudson's Bay and the Nor'westers between them hold a virtual monopoly. The fur trade is not what it used to be."

James and Mrs. Royston soon wandered off, and Sir George came to claim Emily for the opening dance. During the course of the evening, she saw very little of Mrs. Royston though she was constantly in her thoughts.

The lady loved Leon, and loving him, she had no shame. She was prepared to set aside her pride, her marriage vows, her integrity, to pursue him. It was a pathetic picture, a chilling picture, and one that Emily took to her heart.

Leon Devereux had a way with women. She had known this unpalatable truth when she was supposed to be too young to understand such things. She used to giggle about it. Leon was forever getting himself into amorous scrapes, and Uncle Rolfe was forever bailing him out. Not that Uncle Rolfe had minded. As a young girl, Emily had overheard enough set-tos between her uncle and Aunt Zoë to know that men and women held widely different views on what was appropriate conduct for the male of the species, especially a young, unattached male.

Without volition, her eyes moved over the crush of people, unerringly finding the sleek dark head and the broad sweep of shoulders, elegantly set off in snug-fitting blue superfine. He was laughing as though he had not a care in the world.

When William Addison came to claim her for his dance, her temples were throbbing. It was she who suggested that they forgo the dancing and escape to the gardens for a breath of fresh air.

It was a chilly evening and she went to fetch her wrap before joining him. When she returned, William was in conversation with Lady Hester.

The smile Hester turned on both of them was as wintry as the Arctic air.

"What was that all about?" asked Emily as she and William passed the sentry on duty.

William chuckled. "Lady Hester," he said, mimicking Hester's tones exactly, "has given me to understand that we have her permission to take a turn in the garden."

"What?"

"It seems she is your self-appointed chaperone."

Emily shook her head in exasperation. "I don't require a chaperone."

"I don't think that is how Hester sees it." He was still chuckling. "If it were not for the fact that she considers me good ton, I think she would have withheld her permission."

"Good ton? What does that mean?"

William's look was quizzical. Evidently he was still enjoying the joke. "On our mother's side, we are descended from dukes, whereas you, my pet, can go no higher than a marquess. And that's not all. The Morleyes — that's our mother's family by the way — are known far and wide as pattern cards of rectitude."

"Why, that sanctimonious, frozen-faced prude!" The vehemence of Emily's attack had almost nothing to do with Hester. She wanted to lash out at someone, and William's disclosures had simply provided her with a handy scapegoat. "I beg your pardon," she said. "That was unkind. I wish you would forget

300

I had ever said it."

"You mustn't mind Hester. She means well. Perhaps she is a little old-fashioned in her notions, but . . ."

"William, please. I don't wish to talk about Hester."

They had come to a bench, but it was too chilly to sit down. Turning aside, they lingered at a stone sundial.

His gaze was intent and searching. "What is it, Emily?" he asked softly. "What's wrong?"

William really cared for her. He was a nice man, a kind, goodhearted man. She would never reach the heights of ecstasy with him but neither would she sink into a morass of pain and humiliation.

Shaking her head, blinking back an unexpected rush of tears, she said, "I wish I had met you years ago, William, on my sixteenth birthday."

It was the leaping excitement in his eyes which brought her to her senses. "You must excuse me," she went on quickly. "I am not myself. I have a blinding headache."

Her words did not divert him. "If I had met you on your sixteenth birthday, Emily, what then?" She shook her head and his voice became more urgent. "Would I be your husband now? Is that what you were going to say?"

She denied it forcefully, but the damage had already been done. There was no way she could retract her incautious remarks.

"You deserve to be happy," she told him. "You should find yourself a nice girl and marry her."

"I did find myself a nice girl, and see what happened to me." He slanted her a whimsical grin. "I came to Canada to try and forget her."

"William . . ." she protested, and looked away.

He shrugged philosophically. "I shall never stop loving you," he said. "I never want to."

Now was the time to be brutal, as Leon had once been brutal with Sara. She should tell William the truth, that she had never loved him, could never love him. Leon had seen to that. William's touch did not thrill her. There was no ache for his possession, as she ached for her husband's possession. She was fond of him, but that was a far cry from love, and far less than he deserved.

She sighed, knowing that she did not have it in her to cause him such pain. Trying to let him down lightly, she said, "I am a married woman, William. I have no wish to indulge in an affair. I made vows which I intend to keep."

"And what of your husband? No, don't try to gammon me! There isn't a person here tonight who does not know that he is flaunting his mistress under your very nose! Emily, you can't love such a man!"

Very gently, so that there could be no misunderstanding, she said, "I made vows, William. Love has nothing to do with it."

"I knew it!"

She opened her mouth, then quickly shut it. The idea of discussing her marriage with anyone, least of all William, was unthinkable. Besides, William's mind was made up. Leon was right when he said that people believed what they wished to believe.

Before she could collect her thoughts, she found herself in William's arms. She curbed that first instinctive rush of resistance. In some sort, she felt that she had wronged this man and had no wish to humiliate him further. His ardor left her breathless but unmoved. Gently extricating herself from his embrace, without haste, she stepped back, certain that her lack of response must have told him what she could not put into words. She almost wept tears of frustration when she caught the flash of triumph in his eyes.

At half-past one in the morning, everyone sat down to supper. Sara had managed it so that she was seated next to James Fraser. The fur trader was like no other man she had ever known. On the surface, he was one of her own kind, a man of culture and refinement. He was also of mixed blood. It was the savage in him that both fascinated and repelled Sara. Her woman's intuition told her that he was equally fascinated with her. That thought curled around her brain, teasing her imagination into forbidden channels. He would be an exciting, virile lover, demanding things of his woman that she could not even guess at.

"You should be married, James," she said, her eyes flirting with him over the rim of her wineglass.

"Why?" He posed the question seriously.

"Why not?" Her reply was flippant.

His dark eyes, bright with mockery, flashed to her husband. Peter was seated with a group of young officers from the garrison. From time to time, his glance strayed to his wife.

James dismissed Peter Benson with a flick of his

lashes and calmly surveyed his companion. Everything about the girl irritated him. She was a spoiled beauty, a useless ornament who had no thought beyond pursuing her empty pleasures. She was also headstrong. It was common knowledge that she ran rings around her husband. In York, Peter Benson was an object of pity. James did not pity a man who could not manage his own wife. He scorned him, but beneath the scorn, a more powerful emotion was at work. Envy. He wanted this woman as he had never wanted any woman in his life.

"What I observe of married men, I don't like," he remarked finally. There was a curl to his lip which Sara found offensive.

She tossed her head, sending her blond ringlets to dancing. "Don't waste your sympathies on Peter. He has everything he wants."

"Except you."

She lowered her eyelashes, then quickly raised them. Dimples flashed in her cheeks. "Except me," she agreed demurely.

"If I were your husband . . ." he began threateningly.

Though she knew she was playing with fire, the risk of getting her fingers burned only heightened her exhilaration. "Yes?" she goaded, and fluttered her lashes.

Black eyes locked on gray and for Sara the sights and sounds of the assembly faded. Her breath fluttered, then caught in her throat. His next words hit her like a douse of cold water. "If I were your husband, I'd beat you senseless. And that would be only the beginning, my girl. If I had the taming of you,

you'd run a far different course from the one you have set for yourself."

"You think to tame me?" Her eyes were spitting fire. "I'd like to see you try," she scorned. "Don't confuse me with women of your own race, James."

He went as still as a statue. Deliberately setting down his cutlery, he said softly, "My race? What is my race, Lady Sara?"

Her bosom was heaving. "Indian women is what I meant. Those modes may serve very well among your own kind, but let me remind you, English women are gently bred. I am happy to say our husbands treat us with deference."

Though his smile seemed genuine, inwardly he was seething. Her inadvertent slur had betrayed her true sentiments. He was not one of her kind. He never doubted for a moment that she was attracted to him, and just as surely, he knew that in her heart of hearts she considered him beneath her, a dangerous specimen who titillated her curiosity.

He wanted to reach out and grab her and do whatever was necessary to disabuse her of the notion that she could toy with him as she had toyed with the gentlemen who formed her court that evening. One day, she would go too far and he would unleash that savage she believed lurked just beneath the surface of him.

Nothing of what he was thinking was evident in his voice when he said, "So I have observed, and a more wretched lot of milksops I have yet to encounter, not to mention their wretched wives." His eyes glittered with derision. "Tell me, Sara, are you happy?"

"Ecstatically," she snapped, "and you may call me *Lady* Sara." His laugh incensed her, all the more because they both knew she was lying. She was wishing she had never confided in him, had never told him that she was homesick for England. He was the most perverse creature, offering her a sympathetic ear one moment and in the next cutting her down to size with his acid tongue. She tolerated him for only one reason. In James's company, she was never bored.

From the corner of her eye, she caught a glimpse of her brother-in-law. Leon was stationed at the glass doors which gave onto the foyer. Thankful for any excuse to change the subject, she said, "Who is that lady with Leon?"

James followed the path of her eyes. Leon was in earnest conversation with Barbara Royston. As James watched, she caught hold of his sleeve.

"Well?" prompted Sara.

As to himself, James murmured, "That is a lady who does not give up easily."

James and Sara were not the only ones whose glances kept straying to Leon. Lady Hester clicked her tongue.

"I can almost feel sorry for him," she said.

Peter Benson made a noncommittal sound. He was thinking that after Hester had joined his little group, most of the gentlemen had wandered away within short order.

"He doesn't look very happy to see her."

Peter's bewilderment showed. "Who are we talking about?"

Hester leaned forward in a confiding manner.

"Leon Devereux and his mistress, Mrs. Royston. Everybody is talking about her. Last year, in Montreal, they had an affair."

With the appearance of stretching his legs, Peter half turned to glance toward the glass doors.

Hester giggled. "Did you see that? He removed her hand from his sleeve as though he were brushing away something unmentionable."

Frowning, Peter gave the couple his back. "It's not like you, Hester, to lower yourself to talk of such things."

The look she bestowed on him was very superior, very knowing, "Men have mistresses. We ladies know we must tolerate it. What is *in*tolerable is the little scene that is being played out before our eyes. Devereux is going to have to do something drastic to get rid of the woman. If a man must have a mistress, he should choose someone with a modicum of discretion."

Peter muttered something unintelligible under his breath and twisted himself in his chair. When his eyes next found the couple by the glass doors, there was a very thoughtful look to them.

"You allowed Addison to kiss you. I saw it with my own eyes."

Emily stared at her reflection in the looking glass, involved in removing her pearl drop earrings, wondering how she was going to disrobe when Leon had already dismissed her maid.

"It was a kiss between old friends, signifying nothing. And if we are apportioning blame for tonight's debacle, let's not forget Mrs. Royston. She is the reason you refused to take me to Montreal, isn't she, Leon?"

He came to stand behind her, his eyes capturing hers in the mirror. "Yes," he said quietly.

She was braced for his answer, and still it shocked her. Suddenly, she felt young and gauche, and no match for a man of Leon's experience.

Inching away from him, breathing deeply, she said, "And that is all the explanation I deserve?"

His powerful hands cupped her shoulders, drawing her back against his hard length. "Barbara Royston is not important," he said. "She never was. And don't change the subject. We were talking of you and Addison."

For the first time since entering her bedchamber, Emily became aware that her husband was seething with anger. "You can't be jealous of William Addison!" she exclaimed with so much incredulity, so much vehemence, that there could be no doubt she found the notion absurd.

For a long interval, Leon's eyes searched her face. Gradually, his rigid posture relaxed, and he smiled whimsically. "Forgive me, Emily. I misunderstood. I thought, you see, that you were paying me back in kind. I should have remembered that there isn't a vindictive bone in your body."

His head dipped and as his lips brushed the sensitive curve at the base of her throat, the fingers of one hand deftly released the buttons at the back of her gown.

"What . . . what are you doing?" she demanded, edging away from him, making a feeble attempt to pull out of his grasp.

He laughed softly and Emily wanted to slap him. He knew that William Addison was of no consequence because he knew her character. Her own uncertainties respecting Barbara Royston were not so easily laid to rest. A man of any sensitivity would have understood that. A man who really cared for her would have tried to reassure her, realizing that she had never been more aware of her own inadequacies as a woman.

Barbara Royston was a *femme du monde,* a woman who would be a match for any man. During that interminable evening, Emily had been tortured with lurid pictures of Leon teaching his mistress about male fantasies. Though she knew it was farfetched, she could not rid herself of the feeling that he was coming to her straight from the arms of another woman, and she could not endure it.

"It's late," she said, struggling to free herself. "I'm fatigued. Please, Leon. Let me be."

"I can't let you be. You know I can't." His lips were tasting the fragrance of gardenia on her shoulder. "Barbara Royston is not here by my invitation. She was never my mistress. Since my marriage to you, I have never had a woman in my keeping. I've had affairs, Emily. I have never denied it, but damn fewer than you would imagine." Kisses whispered over her face, and her lips opened to the gentle persuasion of his. "Only you, Emily, only you since our marriage became a real one."

"I want to believe you, but . . ."

"Believe me!" he said before he crushed her mouth under his.

309

She felt the familiar rush of helplessness, and the slow throb that began deep in her body, an involuntary yielding to a will that was greater than her own. As the pleasure rose in her, she forgot about Barbara Royston, forgot about William Addison. There was nothing in the world but Leon and the fierce pressure of his lips on hers.

When he pulled back, they were both breathing hard. "If I ever find you in Addison's arms again," he said, his eyes flashing with purpose, "I swear I shall kill him."

He was jealous. The thought leaped out at her, elating her, drawing the poison from every wound she had caused herself since she had first set eyes on Barbara Royston. Leon was jealous and he was bound and determined to erase every vestige of the other man's embrace.

With newfound confidence, she attacked him, pressing her lips to his throat, his hands, his hair, whatever part of his anatomy got in her way. Between fevered kisses, she issued him an ultimatum. "If you ever dare share your fantasies with any other female, I swear it will be the last thing you do, Leon Devereux."

His clothes were no barrier to her experienced fingers. He was laughing when she tumbled him into bed. For a moment their eyes held, and the laughter gradually faded.

Then his head lifted from the pillow, and he took her lips in a hungry demand, his body moving sinuously beneath hers, urging her to finish what she had begun. Heady with power, she exploited his profoundest secrets. His body delighted her, his response fanned the flames of her own ardor. She demanded more—everything he had to give, resisting him when he would have brought things to completion.

"More," she said. "I want more."

His laughter was strained. Hoarsely, he got out, "If you're not careful, you'll get a damn sight more than you bargained for. Now, Emily, now!"

Heedless of her protests, he slid his hands under her hips, lifting her, positioning her, burying himself deep inside her body. For a moment, gasping, they both stilled. Emily's lips sought his, and in a fury of passion, rolling, writhing, they came together, insensible to everything but the present moment and the relentless drive for completion.

As ever, at the last, came Emily's tears. Leon kissed them away, grinning with male satisfaction, immensely pleased with himself. There was a time when those tears had worried him. Now he accepted them for what they were—irrefutable proof that his wife's emotions were involved in this most intimate of all acts between a man and his mate.

Drifting into sleep, her head pillowed against his shoulder, she murmured, "I think I may have fallen over the edge of that precipice."

"What?" He saw that she was asleep. With infinite tenderness, he brushed back the long strands of hair from her face. He had exhausted her, and that made him smile even more.

Some time later, he pushed back the covers and reached for his garments. The night was not yet

311

over. He had a rendezvous with Barbara Royston, and one that he intended to keep. He would do whatever was necessary to protect his wife from the machinations of a jealous woman.

In a small private parlor overlooking the courtyard of the Jolly Roger, a man and a woman were in quiet conversation. The lady was in her nightclothes, the gentleman had yet to remove his cloak.

"I suppose you think that you have won our wager," said Barbara Royston. "To all appearances, it would seem that I hold no interest for Leon Devereux."

Accepting a glass of sherry from her hand, the gentleman shrugged negligently. "I don't wonder that you thought you could attach him. As I told you, the marriage was forced on Lady Emily. She has no desire to be wed to Devereux. Where you went wrong, Barbara, was in arranging to meet Devereux in a public place. Evidently, the man was afraid that his wife would take umbrage if he openly pursued you. I think I told you that she holds the purse strings."

She sighed and studied the amber liquid in her glass. "You may be right, but . . ." She shook her head.

"But?" he prompted.

"He was reluctant to meet with me privately. Damn the man!" Her smile was rueful. "You may believe that I tried every feminine wile to bend him to my will. I hate losing a bet."

He laughed. "But he did say he would come to

you later?"

"Yes, but only when it appeared that I might make a scene. Even so, I am not finished with him yet. I do not give up so easily."

He smiled. "I was thinking that you might still win our wager if you really put your mind to it. But I should not be encouraging you like this. I should be demanding my forfeit."

She threw her head back and pouted prettily. "You really are determined to have me, aren't you?"

"From the moment I first saw you in a crowded ballroom in Montreal," he admitted readily.

Her eyes narrowed speculatively. Challenging him, she said, "Yet, there is something here which I think I have not quite grasped."

"Nonsense! I was determined to have you. You would not come to me. So . . . I used your predilection to gaming against you. I mean to have you, Barbara. Better make your mind up to it."

Triumph glittered in her eyes. "You haven't won yet. Twenty-four hours is what you promised me."

He rose to his feet, and she rose with him. Roughly grabbing her wrists, he said harshly, "You are a Circe, and you know it."

Laughing, she allowed him to capture her in his powerful arms. As he kissed her, his hands moved over her, slipping inside her wrapper, sliding it down over her shoulders till her arms were imprisoned at her sides. She moaned and his hands moved to her throat, his thumbs coming to rest on a wildly beating pulse. When she opened her mouth to protest his rough handling, the pressure of his thumbs increased drastically. Too late, she struggled, but her strength was no match for his. In a matter of minutes, it was all over. She slipped soundlessly to the floor.

The last thing he did before quitting the chamber was to curl her inert fingers around a jeweled pin.

watchen was no match for his. In a matter of minutes, it was all over. She slipped soundlessly to the floor.

They were all the more guiltless the more that

Chapter Nineteen

Emily awakened to the sound of her name. A slow smile of repletion curved her lips. Before she could do more than register the sensation of well-being that seemed to permeate every particle of her body, the voice changed timbre, became rougher, more insistent.

"Emily!"

Blinking the sleep from her eyes, disoriented, she pulled herself up and reached for her wrapper. The voice came again from the other side of the door. Not Leon's voice, but Peter's. She had expected to awaken in her husband's arms. Frowning, she went to answer the peremptory summons.

"It's Leon," said Peter. "No, don't distress yourself. He is all right. That is . . . get dressed and come downstairs. Sir George would like a word with you. We shall be in my book room."

There was something far wrong here. As Peter turned on his heel, Emily cried out, "But where is Leon?"

His hesitation was slight and almost imperceptible. "That's just it, you see. We don't know."

"But . . . but he was here, with me, last night. After the ball, he came home here with me, in the carriage."

"Then it seems he went out again."

Emily was given no opportunity to voice the spate of questions that trembled on her lips. Already, Peter was striding along the corridor. She dressed quickly and was soon descending the stairs. Though she managed to maintain a composed facade, inwardly she was churning. That Leon should steal from her bed in the middle of the night after what they had shared! She did not know whether she was alarmed or insulted.

Carousing or gaming, thought Emily irritably. It must be one or the other. All the gentlemen seemed to indulge in such vices, even her brother-in-law, and always in the small hours of the morning when decent people were snug in their beds.

Other thoughts, more alarming thoughts, began to intrude. Gentlemen fought duels at the drop of a hat, and Leon was not the most popular man in York, not by a long shot. It was not unlikely that he had said something to which his neighbor had taken exception.

"Don't say he has been involved in a duel!" were the first words she said as Peter opened the book room door to her.

"It's not a duel."

Emily's fears subsided only to return in full force when two grave-faced gentlemen rose at her entrance, Sir George and William Addison. She was hardly aware when her brother-in-law pushed her into a chair.

Sir George cleared his throat. "Dear, dear . . . this is a bad business. That a gentleman should have to speak of such things to a lady."

His nervousness began to transmit itself to Emily. She found herself wringing her hands. "What is it?" she said, looking at each somber face in turn.

"Dear, dear! There is no way to break it gently. Lady Emily, it grieves me to tell you . . ." Sir George broke off and shook his head.

Emily was beside herself. "I want to know the worst," she cried out. "Tell me what has happened to Leon."

Sir George straightened in his chair. "Last night, your husband was surprised in the very act of committing a murder."

"Murder?" she got out hoarsely. "Who . . . ?"

"Mrs. Barbara Royston."

It was a full minute before she could find her voice. "And Leon admits to this?" she asked incredulously.

"No . . . that is, he resisted arrest and got clean away."

The next half hour was one of the worst in Emily's life. She could scarcely take it all in. Only one thing mitigated her sense of hopelessness. Leon was safe.

She pressed a hand to her temples trying to make sense of it all. Leon had stolen from her bed in the middle of the night to go straight to another woman—Barbara Royston, his former mistress. If it were only that! But Mrs. Royston was murdered, strangled, and witnesses swore that they practically caught Leon in the act. A few moments sooner and

317

Barbara Royston might still be alive.

Emily had to fight back the wave of nausea that rose to choke her. Clutched in Mrs. Royston's fist was a ruby pin with Leon's initials engraved upon it.

"We think he lost it in the struggle," observed Sir George.

Emily knew the pin. She had given it to Leon for Christmas. "He must have lost it," she said. "Or someone could have stolen it."

No one heeded her anguished protests, for Leon's subsequent conduct condemned him.

"What does it mean, that he resisted arrest?" Emily demanded.

It was William Addison who answered her. "He drew a pistol and held us off while he made his escape. It was only then that we discovered Barbara Royston on the floor of her private parlor."

Into Emily's mind flashed a picture of Barbara Royston as she had been the night before. It was beyond belief that so much beauty could be snuffed out in the blink of an eye. She could not begin to understand how and why it had happened. There was one thing, however, which she never doubted for an instant.

"My husband is many things," she said, appealing to each gentleman in turn, "but he is not a murderer. Who are these witnesses who surprised him coming from Mrs. Royston's rooms? Perhaps they are lying. Leon has made many enemies here in York. Until he is found and tells us exactly what happened, who is to say what the truth is?"

"Emily," said Addison gently, "you are clutching at straws and you know it. Does an innocent man run

318

away? And as for witnesses," he breathed deeply, "I was almost first on the scene, right on the heels of Major Benson."

"Peter?" If Peter was a witness against Leon, the evidence was irrefutable. Her brother-in-law was one of the few people in York whom Leon had not completely alienated. She trusted Peter as she trusted no other.

"It was Leon, all right. I'm sorry, Emily."

"But what were you doing there? And you, too, William? Were you following Leon? I don't understand."

There was an interval of silence, then Sir George coughed. "They were playing cards. The deepest play in town is always to be found at the Jolly Roger. Every gentlemen from here to Montreal knows it."

Emily was trying very hard to stave off the panic that beat inside her head. Marshaling her thoughts by sheer force of will, she finally said, "It doesn't make sense. Why would Leon murder Mrs. Royston?"

"Who is to say?" Sir George's eyes were soft with compassion. "Perhaps Mrs. Royston was a scorned mistress. Perhaps she threatened to tell you or her husband of the affair between them."

Emily shook her head. "That's not it," she said. "You all hate Leon because he is an American. You were waiting for something like this to happen so that you could have him in your clutches. Well, it won't do." The fight suddenly went out of her and she said imploringly, "I know Leon. He is not a murderer. Why won't you believe me?"

319

Sir George spoke very softly. "You tell her lady-ship, Addison."

"I had hoped it would not come to this," he said.

"William, please, I am not a child. Tell me!"

He exhaled on a long breath. "I warned you once to keep away from Devereux—and how right I was! At the war office, I came across a file . . . the source is unimportant. What it amounts to is this, Emily. I am almost sure that your husband was once known as Le Cache-Cache, Hide-and-Seek. Does that mean anything to you?"

"No," she whispered painfully. But it did mean something to her. Le Cache-Cache was the most notorious assassin of La Compagnie. She had read about the person in the newspaper accounts, when it seemed that the sect was once again on the rise.

Sir George cut in quietly. "Lady Emily, we suspect that your husband was once a member of a secret society originating in France. I see from your expression that you have heard of it. Yes, well . . . it was in all the papers. So you see, there is no point in protesting that Devereux is incapable of murder. The man is a trained assassin."

Her thoughts were leaping around, trying to absorb what she was hearing. Shaking her head, on a strangled sob, she whispered, "I don't believe you! There must be some mistake. I don't know how you came by your knowledge, William, but . . ." She turned tortured eyes upon her brother-in-law. "Peter, tell me it isn't true."

"It seems more than likely, Emily," he answered gravely. "But you may rest assured that Leon stands in no danger of prosecution from his involvement in that sect. At the time, he was only a boy. We are well aware that during the Terror in France, men did things which, in their saner moments, they would abhor. In normal circumstances . . . that is, we would not have divulged Leon's secret unless it was necessary. I'm still not certain that it has any bearing on the present."

Sir George snorted, throwing Peter off stride for a moment, and Addison took over. "We are not taking any chances — that is what Major Benson is trying to tell you. For Sara's sake if not for your own, Emily, you must be on your guard against Devereux."

At first, Emily did not realize that the conversation had moved on. Her mind was still grappling with the awful blows she had taken to herself. Leon, once an assassin of La Compagnie! Barbara Royston murdered and Leon a hunted man and the prime suspect! Gradually, it was borne in upon her that her companions had introduced a new element.

"Accidents? What accidents?" she repeated as if in a daze, and her brother-in-law embarked on a recitation which made her blood run cold. Step by step, he forced her mind back to a series of accidents that had occurred in England the year before.

"Your uncle was alarmed to say the least," he told her. "At the time, he was half convinced that the attacks on you and Sara were in the nature of a vendetta against himself."

"They were accidents," she protested. "They could have happened to anyone."

Peter shook his head. "No, not accidents, Emily," and he went on to describe the attack on Sara, when she had been narrowly missed by an assassin's bullet while she was out driving with Leon.

"It was a prank," said Emily. "A firework thrown by some street urchin."

"It was a deliberate attempt at murder," Peter stated baldly. "And not the first attempt on Sara, either. You took a fall riding Sara's mare, did you not, Emily?"

She swallowed convulsively and his tone gentled. "I could not believe it either when your uncle took me into his confidence."

"My uncle told you all this?"

"He wanted me to be on my guard," said Peter simply, then as an afterthought, "though I know that Devereux did not remotely enter his calculations."

For a long while, she sat there in stunned silence, half-formed thoughts chasing themselves inside her head. One thought finally took precedence. "But Leon was not in England when the accidents first began. If what you say is true, he can't be held responsible."

She could read in their faces that her words could not persuade them. "Emily," said William, "a man may send his agents to act for him."

"I shall never believe it!" she cried out.

"My dear Lady Emily." Sir George's tone was placating. "All we are saying is that the evidence against Devereux is staggering to say the least. Consider, if you will . . . It's possible the man is a trained assassin; he was surprised coming from his mistress's rooms *after* the woman was murdered. Let us say for the sake of argument that there is some sinister purpose behind the attacks on you and Lady Sara. Isn't it reasonable to suppose that Devereux is

322

behind those, too?"

"Oh, very reasonable," she shot back, almost beside herself in the face of so much dispassionate logic. "You are fitting all the pieces together like a puzzle. I understand all that. Only one thing is missing."

"Which is?"

She gazed at each gentleman in turn, appealing to them with anguished, tear-bright eyes. "What possible reason could Leon have for making away with either myself or my sister?"

Addison and Peter both looked away, and Sir George cleared his throat before replying, "We don't say that you are in any real jeopardy. In point of fact, we believe, that is, we *hope* that you may be the one person who is safe from the man's designs."

"What are you saying?" she asked harshly, painfully, and even as she voiced the question, she knew the answer that would be given.

Addison leaned forward in his chair and Emily's head jerked at the slight movement. "Emily," he said, "the man married you for your fortune. You told me so yourself. 'Devereux will never give up my fortune,' were your words to me. If anything happened to Sara, as things stand, her fortune would come to you. Need I say more?"

She knew what he was getting at. In the event of either her death or Sara's, the surviving sister inherited almost everything. In the unlikely event that they both died without issue, either Leon or Peter would fall heir to their combined fortunes.

"But Leon is a rich man," she protested. "Sara's fortune can mean nothing to him."

"You can't know that," refuted Addison. "Besides, wealth is relative. A greedy man is like a glutton. He can never have too much."

To every argument that she put forward in Leon's defense, her companions countered with an unwavering obstinacy, even when logic was on her side.

"I don't think that is very significant," reasoned Sir George, referring to Emily's claim that there had been no "accidents" for a year. "Who is to say how the mind of such a man works? All that may be said with any certainty is that Devereux is a dangerous person. I would be failing in my duty if I did not warn you in the strongest terms to put as much distance between yourself and Devereux as is humanly possible."

Her eyes went wide in her white face and she took a quick breath. "I don't understand."

William explained it to her. "If Devereux has any sense, he should be well on his way to the border by now. He knows very well that if he is caught, he will stand trial for murder. But in the event that he is hiding out, waiting his chance to complete unfinished business, we propose to get you and Sara safely away."

"Away? Away—where?"

"To England, of course," he replied.

When Emily returned to her chamber she was shaking like a leaf. To Peter's anxious offer to fetch Sara to her, she returned a curt refusal. She wished to be alone. Besides, Sara was still in her bed, and had yet to be apprised of the night's doings. Emily did not think she could bear a repetition of the scene in Peter's book room.

She paced the floor like a caged animal, her thoughts racing first in one direction then in another, settling on nothing for more than a second or two at a time. By degrees, she got herself in hand and made a deliberate attempt to sort everything through in a rational manner.

Leon a member of La Compagnie! She believed it. A host of half-remembered conversations and impressions convinced her of it. She had always known that there was something in her husband's past, something that happened during the Terror, which Leon wished to keep from her. She had known that his parents had perished during the Revolution. In her ignorance, she had assumed that it was this tragedy and all the events surrounding it that were too painful, too awful, to be broached. Never, in a hundred years, would she have imagined this.

Leon was once an assassin of La Compagnie, the group which was responsible for her father's murder. Incomprehensibly, the knowledge did not horrify her so much as move her to pity. Leon should have told her, and that he could not bring himself to the point was very much to her discredit, not to his.

Did he think that she would despise him? Was she really so unfeeling a person that her husband feared to reveal the truth about his past? She caught back a moan, remembering the annihilating words that had spilled from her lips whenever La Compagnie had become the subject of conversation. She had made no bones about the fact that she considered La Compagnie and all its proponents agents of the

Devil. But that was before she knew her own husband was once one of their number. She could not imagine what straits must have forced a young boy to follow such a course, but she knew that his circumstances must have been desperate. And he had not told her for the best reason in the world. He knew her too well. She was always so quick to think the worst of him.

It took all her willpower to move from that unpalatable truth to the events of that night. Barbara Royston was murdered and the evidence against Leon was overwhelming. Not only had he been discovered coming from her rooms, but he had resisted arrest. An innocent man did not run away, William had told her.

She refused to believe that Leon was a murderer . . . yet there was no getting round the fact that he had stolen from her bed to go to another woman. That image slipped inside her heart like a sliver of broken glass. Fiercely suppressing the surge of pain, she concentrated on the woman who had been murdered.

She had pitied Barbara Royston, but that was because she was so evidently a cast-off mistress. Emily was beginning to wonder if she had been deliberately misled. If the affair was over, why had Leon visited his mistress in the dead of night? It seemed more than likely that William was right when he said that Mrs. Royston posed some kind of threat to Leon. Perhaps they had quarreled. Perhaps Barbara Royston's death was an accident. But even as the thought occurred to her, she knew that she was clutching at straws. If there was a quarrel, then

Mrs. Royston had been murdered in the heat of passion.

Without volition, her mind jumped to William's words, "The man married you for your fortune." On the admission of her own guardian, Leon had used her fortune to make himself a wealthy man. It was never *her* he had wanted. From the time they were children, Leon had favored Sara. Their marriage was not of his choosing. Nor could she forget how callously he had turned from Sara once the marriage was accomplished. Could it be true? Was it only the Brockford fortune Leon coveted? In that event, he would not have cared which sister he married.

She tried to be fair. Leon wasn't the first man nor would he be the last to wish to marry where there was a fortune. As for keeping a mistress—it was a sordid business, true, but there was nothing unusual in that. It was the way of their world. That did not make Leon a murderer. There would be a reasonable explanation for every damning piece of evidence against him, if only she could think of it. There *must* be.

In spite of her protests, however, her mind was beginning to waver, was beginning to accept the awful reality of it all. Were the "accidents" exactly as Peter avowed—deliberate attacks on Sara? And if Leon had married Sara, would the attacks have been made against herself?

"No!" She moaned the word into her clenched fist. But a small voice inside her head refused to be silenced. *What if it were all true?* it whispered.

Once she allowed that possibility into her mind, once she forced herself to face the worst, a curious calm descended upon her. If Leon was guilty, then the last thing she wanted was for him to be found. He would be tried for murder and . . . Oh, God, that must never happen! For his own sake, Leon must leave Canada and never return.

How glad she was now that she had not told him that she carried his child. Leon would never let her go if he suspected the truth. And he must let her go if only for the present. She did not doubt that Sir George would take extraordinary measures to protect Sara and herself, measures which could prove disastrous to Leon. The rights and wrongs of it made no impression on her. She only knew that she would want to die if anything happened to Leon.

If it were all true. The words pulsed inside her head, over and over, forcing her to consider the unthinkable. If it were all true, if Leon was guilty of all the charges against him, he would not give up easily. Sir George might think that Leon was long gone. She knew her husband better than that. Leon was tenacious. He had waited five years before coming to claim her as his wife. A man who waited five years to secure a fortune was not about to let it slip through his fingers without a fight.

She did not know exactly how her moneys had been settled on the occasion of her marriage. What she did know was that from the very first, Leon was responsible for the ordering of her affairs. She understood only vaguely the intricacies of English law, but there was never any question in her mind that if it came to a legal separation, her fortune must return to her.

Suddenly conscious of where her thoughts were

leading her, she caught back a horrified sob. It wasn't true! She knew it wasn't true. It wasn't just her fortune. Leon really cared for her.

That thought was impossible to sustain for more than a minute or two. Her mind came full circle. Leon had never spared her a thought until they were forced to wed and even then he had hardly been an eager lover.

For some few minutes, she moved aimlessly around her chamber, opening and shutting drawers, touching objects without being aware of what she was doing. It was a long time before she could concentrate on the only course that was open to her.

Sir George proposed that she and Sara should return to England. It was childish, she knew, but it seemed to her in that moment that all the wisdom of the world resided in Uncle Rolfe. He had never failed her. He would know what was to be done to put things to rights, just as he had always done when she and Sara were children.

"Oh, Uncle Rolfe!" She covered her face with both hands as the tears forced their way through her tightly clenched lids. Before long, it was her husband's name that she was sobbing into her cupped hands.

"It's a damnable business!" Sir George imbibed slowly, scarcely aware that the Madeira his host had provided was his own particular favorite. "I trust it will never come to a trial." He shuddered violently, then gave his two companions a very straight look. "It is one thing to palm Lady Emily off with that tis-

329

sue of lies about a card game at the Jolly Roger, but let me tell you, gentlemen, a jury is a different matter."

Peter's brows rose. "I would rather have allowed the truth to stand," he said.

Sir George's annoyance showed. "What? That you, an officer and a gentleman, deserted your post to go dangling after tavern wenches?"

"I beg your pardon, Sir George, but I was not on duty."

"Yes! Yes! But you know what I am getting at."

William Addison took it upon himself to smooth things over. "Come, come, Sir George. Surely we are all men of the world here? Major Benson is not the only officer who amuses himself with women of that class."

"No," answered Sir George testily, "but he is the only officer who happens to be married to Rivard's niece. God, that's all I need! Rivard breathing down my neck! And now, of all times, when the Americans are on the point of declaring war!"

"I shouldn't think Rivard will raise an eyebrow," responded William, then hastened to add when he observed Sir George's heightened color, "In any event, I shall vouch for Major Benson. No one need ever know the truth."

Peter set down his glass sharply. His voice was very low, very controlled. "I want no one to commit perjury to save my skin."

"Brave words!" expostulated Sir George. "But have you considered the awkwardness of your position—and I am not referring to the embarrassment to Lady Sara? No, by your own admission, you were at the inn a good half hour before Mr. Addison. Good God, man, think what this might mean. You yourself might come under suspicion."

"Which is precisely why I wanted the truth to stand" was the terse reply. "Molly will vouch for me."

It looked as though Sir George might dispute his companion's avowal. After an interval, however, he said in a milder tone, "Well, well, tell me again exactly how it happened."

The decanter was passed round before Peter took up the conversation. "I was coming from Molly's room in the attics. I had just reached the turn in the stairs when the door to Mrs. Royston's parlor opened."

Sir George grunted. He could imagine the scene. Benson would not wish to be caught in a compromising position. He would have pulled back into the shadows.

"And as I told you," interjected William, "I was coming up the stairs."

"You, at least, were invited to the notorious card game?"

"I was."

"Go on."

"It was lucky for me that I saw Major Benson's shadow against the wall, else I might not be alive to tell the tale. I didn't know who he was, you see, so I reached in my pocket for my pistol."

"And that's when Devereux appeared?"

"It was," answered Peter. "Then everything happened so quickly. William hailed him, and the next thing I knew, he had a pistol in his hand and had whipped back inside Mrs. Royston's room and had

331

secured the bolt."

"If we had been quicker, we might have had him," said William. "For a moment or two, we were too shocked to move."

"And by the time we had burst through the door, Leon had gone out the window."

"What I don't understand," said Sir George, "is what prompted you to go after the man? What roused your suspicions?"

It was Major Benson who answered the question. "He had a pistol in his hand."

"But so did Mr. Addison," retorted Sir George. "Perhaps Devereux was simply exercising caution. What made you think otherwise?"

"I think I can answer that, sir," interposed William. "You must remember that I was ascending the stairs. When the door to Mrs. Royston's rooms opened, I had a clear view of the interior, a worm's-eye view, you might say. I saw her on the floor."

"Ah, now we are getting somewhere." Sir George brought his glass to his lips and took a small slip. "Go on."

"By the time we had burst through the door, Devereux had gone out the window. I got one shot off at him, but I don't think I hit him."

"What do you think, Major Benson?" asked Sir George. "Did Mr. Addison hit the fellow?"

"I didn't see, sir. I was on the floor, hoping to revive Mrs. Royston."

The silence was prolonged as the younger gentlemen waited for Sir George to voice his thoughts. Finally, he said, "I don't suppose there is any hope that we can keep Devereux out of it?"

"Keep him out of it?" asked William incredulously. "I hardly see how, sir. My shot roused the whole inn. Major Benson and I did not think to keep silent about the name of Mrs. Royston's attacker."

"Quite." Sir George let out a long sigh. He was thinking of the fine figure he had hoped to cut at court when he made himself known to Rivard. "I don't think I shall ever understand great men," he said as though to himself.

"Beg pardon?"

"Rivard. How could he permit his niece to marry such a man? You are quite sure, Addison, that he knows what Devereux once was?"

"I don't think there is any doubt about that. For some inconceivable reason, Rivard trusts him implicitly. As I told you, it was Rivard's action in removing the file that first roused my suspicions. You may believe, however, that I would never have betrayed Devereux's secret if he had not murdered Barbara Royston."

Another sigh fell from Sir George's lips. At length, he said, "Our first concern must be to see to the safety of Rivard's nieces. I won't have a moment's peace until they are once more under the protection of their uncle."

"And Devereux?" asked Peter softly. "Do we track him, sir, and bring him in for questioning?"

"Good God, no! That is . . . for appearances' sake, naturally we must put on a good show, but the last thing we want is a scandal on the magnitude that a trial would produce. Just think of all the dirty linen that must be aired in public! Besides, if Devereux knows what is good for him, he will be long

333

gone by now."

"And if he is not?" persisted William. "If he comes back to fetch his wife?"

Sir George blinked slowly, his thoughts racing ahead to trials and executions and worse: some fatal mishap to either Lady Emily or Lady Sara. Swallowing, he said, "The man is as dangerous as a wild animal. We would be fools to try to capture him alive." He looked at his companions and saw that there was no necessity for him to elaborate.

Chapter Twenty

It was decided that the sooner Emily and Sara left York the better it would be for all. The gossip, the speculation and finger pointing was so unpleasant that even Hester was persuaded to go with them. Since the ladies could not travel without a male escort, William Addison had very kindly offered them his protection until he had turned them over to their uncle's care. Peter accepted this offer with alacrity. As he explained it, there was no question of his obtaining leave to accompany them. He was a soldier and must remain at his post.

To avoid the curious stares of their neighbors, for the most part, the ladies kept to the house. This was a great trial to Emily, for Hester lost no opportunity in blackening Leon's character. After the first few attempts, she gave up trying to defend her husband, not because she believed him to be guilty, but because she saw that to defend him was futile.

With Sara, she was forced to take a different approach and one which was equally distasteful to her. The thought that she might be a target for murder preyed on Sara's mind. She was on edge and jumped at every stray sound.

"All the time," she said to Emily, her eyes huge in her white face, "I truly believed Leon was fond of me. I don't think I shall ever be sure of anything again."

Emily hardly knew how to answer her. Clasping Sara's hands to stop their trembling, she said, "Nothing will ever convince me that Leon is a murderer. However, Peter is right in warning you to be on your guard. It is only a precaution, Sara, until we can get at the truth. We must protect you — that is our first duty."

"I can't believe Leon wishes to harm me."

"That is not the point. As I said, our first duty is to protect you."

"Then . . . you are warning me against Leon, too?"

She had to force the words out, and they erupted from her lips in a broken sob. "I must, oh, God, I must."

James Fraser was a frequent visitor to the house. If Emily hoped to find a show of support for Leon from this quarter, she was to be disappointed. When the subject of Leon came up, as it frequently did, James had very little to say. She formed the impression that he was absorbing everything, calculating odds, forming judgments. It made her very uncomfortable in his presence and wary of saying anything.

Before the week was out, they had embarked on the journey which would take them home to England. The lakes and rivers were the main arteries of transportation. They were to be conveyed by schooner as far as Lachine, eight miles upstream from the port of Montreal, whence they were to take sail for Quebec. Their escort was small since Sir George was persuaded that Devereux was no longer a threat. In the foregoing week, Indian scouts had picked up his trail. It was exactly as Sir George surmised. Devereux had fled south to Oswego on the American side of the border.

Apart from a small detachment of enlisted men, their party comprised only seven people, the three ladies and their maid, Major Benson, William Addison, and James Fraser, who had delayed his departure from York for the express purpose of forming one of their group. The escort of another gentleman was always welcome, and James had generously invited them all to stay at his house in Montreal until such time as they had made their arrangements. It was necessary for Peter to return to York with his men as soon as he had delivered the ladies to their destination.

"The rapids at Lachine are spectacular," James informed them at one point, "though the bane of a fur trader's existence. One of these days, we shall build a canal to make the St. Lawrence navigable all the way to Montreal. As it is, everything must be hauled overland the last few miles or so. I fear we may have difficulty in hiring as much as a dogcart at this time of year. As I may have mentioned, the fur brigades will be there in force."

James was not exaggerating. The little town was bursting at the seams with raucous French *voyageurs,* those adventurers of *les pays d'en haut,* the interior, who manned the canoes for the agents of the North West Company.

"The *voyageurs* may be a little on the boisterous side," said James, addressing the ladies, "but don't let that prejudice you. To a man, they revere womankind and would make short shrift of any gentleman who offered insult to a lady."

And boisterous the *voyageurs* certainly were, thought Emily as she watched those undersize swarthy young

337

men in their feather caps and deerskin leggings load their long birch-bark canoes.

"What are in those parcels?" asked Sara, indicating formidable canvas packs bound with leather straps.

"Trade goods," answered James. "And supplies for the voyage."

"Where are they off to?" Sara had to shout above the clamor, for as they watched, three of the great birch-bark canoes, each with a crew of a dozen or more men, shot into the current. At the same time, the oarsmen, as one man, broke into song, and their fellows on the wharves cheered them on.

"They are making for the summer rendezvous at Fort William." James's voice rose above the din. "That's a journey of almost a thousand miles."

Everyone was suitably impressed and looked more closely at the frail birch-bark canoes and the men who manned them. "A thousand miles," murmured Emily, shaking her head in wonderment.

James read her mind. "The canoes are safer than they appear to be," he assured her, and smiled broadly.

"I'm sure," she replied, but thought inwardly that she would as soon swim the thousand miles as set foot in one of those contraptions.

They had no difficulty in finding accommodation for the night. James was one of the partners in the North West Company and seemed to be known to everyone. When in Lachine, he was used to putting up at the house of a certain Mrs. Deare, a widow whose husband had at one time served as one of the company's agents.

"I'm impressed," Addison murmured to Emily as their

landlady cheerfully vacated her own parlor for the convenience of Mr. Fraser and his guests. They had just sat down to dinner.

"I hope we are not turning some poor *voyageur* out of his bed," responded Emily in an aside.

James caught the remark, "*Voyageurs* are men of the wilderness, Lady Emily. They wouldn't thank you for a soft bed, nor would they waste their hard-earned money on the luxuries we consider necessities. Tonight and for the next five months or so, they will camp out under the stars. It's the life they know, the life they love."

There was something in James's voice, something in his expression, which brought to mind an incident at her birthday ball when Leon had described the life of a fur trader. She sensed now what she had sensed then, not only the admiration, but also the shade of envy.

Leon. She could not stop thinking about him, wondering where he was and what he was doing. Most of the time, she was in a daze, not knowing what to make of it all. That he had managed to give his pursuers the slip gave her hope. Above all, she wanted him to be safe. All the same, she had half expected to receive some message from him. There was no message. Leon either had not the inclination or the means of communicating with her. She knew it was unreasonable, but she could not shake herself of the feeling that he had abandoned her as a man discards a wrinkled neckcloth.

Leon had followed the only course open to him, she remonstrated with herself. In America, he was safe. She did not wish him within a hundred miles of herself or Sara. Especially Sara. In that event, if she came face-to-face with him now, she did not know what she would think, how she should act. It was better this way.

"Tell me you are hoaxing me, James," exclaimed Sara, interrupting Emily's train of thought.

"I assure you, I am not."

"A massacre? Here? In Lachine?"

In his calm way, Peter interposed, "It happened over a hundred years ago, Sara. There is not the least possibility of such a thing happening today. Besides, the Iroquois were ever friends to the British."

"Then who was massacred?"

"French colonists," answered James. "In those days, the French and British were enemies."

"But two hundred!" responded Sara. "And a hundred taken prisoner. What happened to them?"

"No one knows," answered James. "No trace of them was ever found. I daresay they made slaves or wives of the women. As for the men . . ." He shrugged eloquently and picked up his wineglass.

Hester's look was stricken, and William stretched out a hand to pat her comfortingly. When he turned back to James, his expression was thunderous, not that James noticed. His attention was on the bread pudding Mrs. Deare had set down at his place.

"That was before there was much in the way of law and order," said William, addressing Hester. "There were few settlers. Today, if one white woman were to be carried off into the wilderness, His Majesty's government would not rest till her abductors were captured and punished. You may take my word for it."

"Even so—"

"Gentlemen," cut in Peter brusquely, "you are forgetting that there are ladies present."

"I beg your pardon," said James without a pretense of regret. "My aim was merely to give you a little back-

340

ground on the area. I see now that it was thoughtlessness on my part. As Major Benson said, the massacre happened more than a hundred years ago."

The silence was awkward and eddied with unspoken undercurrents. Emily puzzled over it and soon came to the conclusion that James had not told the story from mere thoughtlessness. It was deliberate. She sensed his contempt for everyone present, herself included. He thought all of them too complacent and wished to throw them into confusion. Why?

Late at night, in the privacy of her own chamber, she remembered that conversation and shivered. On just such a night as this, the inhabitants of Lachine were surprised in their beds and brutally massacred. The less fortunate ones were captured and carried off as prisoners. On the American frontier, such things were still commonplace.

James came to her in her dreams. His hatred was palpable and it was no wonder. One moment he was a French colonist, the next, he was an American settler, and finally, he was an Indian brave with painted face and bloodied tomahawk. There was no mercy in his black eyes as he began to stalk her.

Sara was on the point of dousing the candle when Peter entered her bedchamber.

"What are you doing here?" she demanded, pointedly fastening her robe.

"Don't get your hackles up," he returned calmly, and proceeded to remove the feather coverlet from her bed. "I'm only keeping up appearances. The others expect us to share a room. I shall bed down here on the floor."

Though she tried, she failed to keep the venom from her voice. "Don't pretend you care about appearances!"

Peter removed his boots and placed them beside the empty grate. "I don't," he agreed, "but I thought you might."

"It's a bit late in the day for that."

"What?"

Suddenly aware of the hostility that flamed from every tense line of his wife's body, Peter slowly straightened. "I think you had better explain that remark," he said, instinct making him cautious.

"Molly St. Laurent," she said, not without a certain satisfaction. "Need I elaborate?"

"Ah."

" 'Ah?' Is that all you have to say?"

He shrugged. "What more *should* I say? It was inevitable that you would discover who my mistress is sooner or later."

Tight-lipped, she glared at him. Unperturbed, he proceeded to remove first his coat, then his neckcloth. His reasonableness in the face of her outrage incensed her all the more. There was something ugly in the laugh she forced.

"Good God, Peter, I never thought to see you take up with the town whore!"

The words were hardly out of her mouth before he had crossed to her, his usually bland expression a mask of fury. "Call me any vile name you like," he said, "but blacken Molly's name with your poisonous tongue, and I shall make you regret it. Do you understand?"

She was too angry to be afraid. "Molly!" she scoffed. "You dare to defend that . . . that woman . . . to me, your wife?"

342

"Now who is pretending? You don't want me. Molly does. She is a good-hearted, sweet-natured girl, and more than that I refuse to say."

Her lip curled. "Don't say you are in love with the woman!"

"What if I am?" he asked moodily. "Don't say you care," and as though losing interest in the conversation, he turned away to arrange a makeshift bed from the coverlet and one of the spare bolsters.

His words stunned her. Peter had loved her almost at first sight. There was nothing she could do, it had seemed, no cruelty she could inflict that could make the slightest impression on the deep well of his love for her. His devotion would have amused her if it were not so pathetic.

For no good reason, she felt bereft, just as she had when she had first caught sight of Peter with his inamorata. Though she was supposed to stay close to the house because of the threat Leon posed, James had persuaded her to take a turn in his carriage, saying that it would do her the world of good.

And it *had* done her the world of good. Her spirits had lifted and she felt more like her old self.

"Why so happy?" he had wanted to know.

There was no particular reason, and she said the first thing that came into her head.

"I am going home to England. Who wouldn't be happy to leave this godforsaken wilderness?"

"In the face of such joy," he had returned ironically, "would it be poor taste on my part to remind you that a woman lies murdered in her grave and an innocent man may hang for it?"

His words had brought a rush of guilty color to her

343

cheeks. "Do you say that Leon is innocent?" she asked, deliberately ignoring his taunt.

His brow furrowed. "What do you think? Or more to the point, what does Lady Emily think?"

"Emily . . . why . . ?"

"She has not confided in you?" he prompted. Then after an interval, "Now why does that not surprise me?"

Stung, Sara had made haste to correct him. Though she knew herself to be on shaky ground, she said convincingly, "Emily is not sure what to think."

"But you think he is guilty?"

"He ran away."

"Very true. What else could you think? And you, of all people, should know. As I understand, you have been acquainted with Leon since you were an infant in leading strings?"

"Leon was always secretive," she answered defensively.

"There is no question of that."

"And you? Do you say that Leon is innocent?"

"Oh, no, I don't say anything of the sort."

As they passed the Jolly Roger, her eyes had been drawn to one of the upstairs windows. Her husband's fair hair was unmistakable. A woman was in his arms. The embrace was not passionate, but rather comforting, and somehow all the more treacherous, all the more wounding because of it.

If Molly St. Laurent had been in the mold of a bold hussy, Sara would have dismissed her from her mind without a qualm. But Molly wasn't particularly beautiful or voluptuous or vulgar in the way that a gentleman's mistress was supposed to be. She was young and vulnerable and terribly in love with Peter. Sara knew all this because she had made it her business to find out.

Molly St. Laurent, according to Sara's dressmaker, was a decent woman who had fallen on hard times. She was a widow, and earned her bread by hiring herself out as a maid at the Jolly Roger. Mrs. Pendergast, the dressmaker, had winked and had hinted coyly at Molly's rich benefactor. And she, Sara, had nodded her head, and had smiled till she thought her face would crack, drawing the woman out until she had the whole sordid story. Not that Mrs. Pendergast knew the whole story. It was inconceivable to her that Molly's benefactor could be the husband of a member of the British aristocracy.

It was inconceivable to Sara, too. Burning with indignation, she slipped out of her robe and made a great show of getting into bed. For beauty, Molly didn't hold a candle to her. She paused, giving Peter a moment to drink in the sight of her in her filmy nightrail.

Without batting an eyelash, he said, "Shall I douse the candle or will you?"

Through set teeth, she replied, "You may believe that I don't give a straw what you do, or who you do it with. But just think on this, Peter. Once I am restored to decent society, once I am in London, I may very well pay you back in your own coin."

"Take a lover by all means." He sounded bored. "I wish you would. But permit me to give you a piece of advice. Try if you will to be a little less of the egoist. You are in love with yourself and it shows. My dear, it's a grave flaw which repels even those who are determined to love you." Then in an altered tone, he said, "I should know," and so saying, he doused the candle.

Sara was fit to be tied. Frozen with wounded pride, she lay in her cold bed like a block of ice. How dare he say that she was in love with herself! A fine opinion he

345

had of her character! An egoist! It wasn't true! Oh, it wasn't true! She didn't think only of herself. She was as good-hearted and as sweet-natured a girl as Molly St. Laurent, and if Peter didn't see it, he must be blind.

She didn't know how long she lay there, grinding her teeth together, fuming in silence as she listened to her husband's soft snores. After a while, the hard edge of her anger began to soften a little. She wouldn't allow that she was an egoist, but she was coming to see that she was not entirely blameless for the sorry state she was in. She wasn't really cold and unfeeling. She was unhappy and therein lay the source of all her troubles.

This truth seemed so self-evident and, at the same time, so novel, that she mulled it over in her mind for several minutes. The moment before sleep claimed her, she knew that she was on the threshold of a great and momentous discovery. England wasn't the answer. If only . . .

The following morning, when the ladies sat down to breakfast, their landlady offered the information that the gentlemen had left earlier to accompany Mr. Fraser on a tour of the warehouses and that they would return presently.

"What warehouses?" Sara's question was an idle one. Her thoughts were miles away.

"The North West Company's warehouses," replied Mrs. Deare. "It's where the trade goods are stored."

None of the ladies evinced a spark of interest, and after setting down the laden tray she was carrying, Mrs. Deare made an unobtrusive exit.

Conversation was desultory and soon faded into long,

thoughtful silences. Emily was subdued, having spent a restless night. Hester was preoccupied and Sara was seething.

It seemed that she was in everyone's black book and she did not give a brass button, she told herself forcefully. She had been judged and found wanting by them all: Hester, James, Peter, especially Peter. Only William remained unfailingly kind. And Emily, of course.

"Did you say something?" asked Emily.

"I was clearing my throat."

"Oh."

Sara regarded her sister from beneath the sweep of her lashes. How long had it been, she wondered, since she had really looked at Emily? That wan little face, those dark circles under her eyes—words could not speak more clearly of her sister's distress. She had an urge to say something comforting, but she did not know where to begin. What could she say? She had left it too long. The time to comfort Emily was when the crisis had burst upon them. As it was, they were almost like strangers— they, who as children had never been out of each other's pockets.

Without thinking, she stretched one hand across the table and patted Emily awkwardly. The surprise on Emily's face was enough to bring hot color rushing to Sara's cheeks. "I'm sorry, Emily," she said. "I'm so sorry," and she did not know what else to say.

The door opened to admit James Fraser, and Sara's hand dropped away. He gave them a long quizzical look and said, "I've been sent to fetch you. Our companions fancy themselves as *voyageurs*. You must come and see. They are trying their hands at managing one of the great Montreal canoes and doing not too badly, I might

347

say."

The ladies exchanged a quick look and resignedly rose to their feet. James's words did not surprise them. There was something in the air at Lachine, a sense of adventure, an undercurrent of excitement that was irresistible to gentlemen. The glamour of the fur trade made little boys of them all.

Outside the door of their lodgings, a coach was being loaded with their baggage. There was nary a sign of their escort, though their maid was already inside the coach. They took no coats, for the temperature on that May morning was warm. At James's suggestion, however, they fetched their parasols, for even a watery sun could inflict that horrid bane of a lady's complexion: freckles.

"This won't take long," said James, steering the ladies toward the wharves. "And we are only eight miles from Montreal, so there is no necessity for haste."

At the wharves, there was the customary pandemonium that had an odd order to it. The shrill calls of the agents who were overseeing the loading of the great canoes blended with the snatches of song which came from the crews who did all the labor. Several canoes were already manned and waiting for the signal to get under way. It was from one of these that a young *voyageur*, with a huge grin on his face, detached himself to meet them. His French was unintelligible to the ladies, though James Fraser had no difficulty in conversing with him. Their laughter rang out richly and James turned back, shaking his head, smiling.

"Major Benson and Addison, along with our escort, have embroiled themselves in a race," he said. "There is no cause for alarm. We are to catch up with them at St.

348

Anne's. You'll enjoy the little outing."

Before the ladies could grasp the full import of his words, they were swept up by three laughing *voyageurs* and deposited in the very center of one of the long boats. In vain, they cried out their alarm. The signal was given and a cheer went up, and as the great craft swung smoothly into the current, a dozen paddles sliced as one into the water.

Emily twisted her head and almost collapsed with relief. James was in the canoe with them, standing in the stern, steering the great boat with his paddle. His eyes glittered with excitement and his lips curved in a smile. Her relief soon gave way to indignation. Before she could take him to task, Hester got there before her. She had said only a few choice words, however, when one of the *voyageurs,* the *chanteur,* sang out the opening bars of "En roulent ma boule," and her voice was drowned out as the refrain was taken up by the whole crew.

Smiling wanly, shrugging philosophically, and casting a meaningful look at Sara, Emily forced herself to relax. There was no real cause for alarm. The *voyageurs* would set them down at St. Anne's and Peter and William would convey them back to Lachine. As soon as her feet touched terra firma, however, she was going to have the satisfaction of telling James Fraser exactly what she thought of his "little outing."

The "outing" was not the little jaunt they had supposed. An hour passed and there was no slackening of their swift pace through the choppy waters. Lachine was left far behind, as was the flotilla of Montreal canoes. Emily was itching to blister James Fraser's ears, but the *voyageurs* were indefatigable in their singing, so much so that she could hardly hear herself think, let alone talk.

349

Stewing in outrage, she adjusted her silk parasol to the sun's rays and feigned a serenity she was far from feeling.

After a while, she became aware that their canoe was flanked by two other vessels, one of which was smaller than their own Montreal canoe. She surveyed it for some few minutes, wondering idly why one of the *voyageurs* seemed out of place. It was impossible to get a clear view of him, but there was nothing untoward in his dress. He wore a red kerchief on his head, and his shirt was open at the throat, typical *voyageur* attire. He looked to be a powerful man, and Emily decided that he sat a little taller in the canoe than his companions.

Before she could think too deeply about it, the guide in the bow of the boat made a signal with his hand. Abruptly, the singing stopped and the oarsmen pulled hard on their paddles, guiding the craft toward shore. The smaller of the canoes, Emily noted, was following in their wake.

As they drew closer to the shore, the fine hairs on the back of Emily's neck began to rise. Whatever this place was, she knew it wasn't St. Anne's. This place was isolated. At St. Anne's, there was a church and a convent, that much she remembered. There was a dock here, however, so the place wasn't completely without habitation. Frowning, she scanned the shore for a sign of Peter or William and their canoe. There was nothing.

Her eyes flew to James Fraser, but he was occupied in steadying the craft with the aid of his paddle. She glanced over her shoulder, her eyes searching for the *voyageur* who seemed so out of place. Her eyes found him and then she knew!

"Sara!" she said tightly, and her senses were alive to

every sight and sound. "Sara, when we dock, you go first and don't wait for anybody, do you understand? There will be a path, oh, God, there must be a path! The path will lead to a house. This is a matter of life and death! Get help, Sara, or hide yourself until help arrives. Don't talk. Don't argue. Just do as I say. And don't look back. Hester, you stay exactly where you are."

Sara's eyes were huge in her face. For the first time, she, too, became aware of a number of incongruities. There flashed into her mind every dire warning her husband had made concerning her safety. Leon Devereux had tried to make away with her, might still try to make away with her if only he could get to her. It was for this reason that she was to return to England. But Leon was not here. Even so, something was very far amiss.

"Now!" shrieked Emily.

The shrill tone galvanized Sara into action. She was off like a shot. Emily made good use of her companions' momentary surprise. Before they knew what she intended, she lowered her little parasol and charged, sending two men flying overboard at one go. In the next instant, she dived for the dock and had dragged herself up. Brandishing her parasol in front of her like a rapier, she prepared to hold them at bay until they overpowered her.

No one made a move, except to haul their two hapless companions on board. Hester sat there with her mouth open as though Emily had taken leave of her senses. By degrees, men began to shake their heads and smile. Soon, they were laughing. Baffled, Emily stared at them.

"Emily!"

Emily's heart leaped to her mouth. The canoe with

351

Leon in it had almost touched the dock. A quick glance assured her that Sara was nowhere in sight. "Run, Hester!" she shouted, then picking up her skirts, she went haring off along the shoreline. She did not get very far before powerful masculine hands closed over her shoulders.

"Emily! Don't you know me?" There was a smile in his voice as he turned her to face him. "Emily, my love!" His dark eyes moved over her, then he pulled her into a crushing embrace. "Oh, God, this has been the longest week of my life!"

She was frozen in shock, her lips cold and unresponsive beneath the fierce pressure of his. When he pulled back, he was frowning.

"What is it, Emily? Are you sulking because I did not come for you sooner? I could not take that chance. And I dared not let James carry a message for me in case you inadvertently gave the game away. Emily, what is it? What's wrong?"

Coming up at that moment, James Fraser enlightened him. "Prepare yourself for a shock, dear boy," he said, taking no pains to disguise his amusement. "If I am not mistaken, the sweet wife of your bosom is quite convinced that you are a murderer."

The frown on Leon's brow intensified, then he laughed. "No, truly! Tell me what's wrong."

Emily opened her mouth, but no words came, only a hoarse sound that, in her own mind, was the beginning of an apology.

James clapped Leon on the shoulder. "Believe it!" he said, and there was not a shade of humor now in voice or visage. Contempt blazed out at her. "It grieves me to tell you, Leon, that your fine friends, to a man, are convinced of your guilt. Didn't I tell you how it would be? If they catch up to us, you're are a dead man."

Leon's arms dropped to his sides and he took a step back. His voice was without expression, as were his eyes. "I should have expected this," he said.

Emily stood woodenly, cringing from that cold look, knowing that she had made the worst mistake of her life and that she would never be given the chance to correct it.

Chapter Twenty-one

"Murderers! Rogues! I'll see you hang for this outrage!"

No one paid particular heed to Hester's harangue. The *voyageurs* smiled and shrugged off their incomprehension. Leon and James were rummaging in one of the packs.

The ladies had been rounded up like lost little lambs and herded, with every mark of respect, to a small abandoned cabin at the end of the path which led from the dock. They were subdued but no longer terrified out of their wits.

Leon found what he was looking for and tossed a bundle of deerskin garments upon the rickety table. "For the place where we are going," he said, "you will be more comfortable in these. You have five minutes to change and not a moment longer." He smiled insolently before continuing. "You may keep your drawers on, if it pleases you, but your stays and petticoats remain here."

At the mention of the unmentionable, Hester's thin lips stretched taut across her teeth. "You, sir, are no better than a . . ." She floundered as she groped for the foulest word she could think of.

In other circumstances, Emily might have admired Hester's courage. As it was, her mind was teeming with questions. She addressed the first one to James Fraser. "Where are William and Peter? What have you done with them?"

"They are safe and sound, locked up, along with their escort, in my warehouse in Lachine. No, really, no harm has come to them." His next words were terse and for Leon. "I'll wait outside. Time is wasting. We'd best be off."

Sara stirred and glared at him accusingly. "You told me that your *voyageurs* would never permit any man to insult a lady."

James answered negligently. "I lied," he said, and beckoned to his men to follow him out, leaving Leon alone with the ladies.

"Where . . . where are you taking us?" asked Emily.

"Into the wilderness."

At the blunt answer, Sara and Hester let out a startled cry. Emily stood a little straighter.

"Why?" she wanted to know.

"Why do you think?" His lips were pulled back in a parody of a smile.

"You'll never get away with it." Hester's brave words were belied by the tremor in her voice. "William and Peter will come after us. Nothing is surer. And if they find that you have harmed one hair of our heads . . ."

Leon slammed out of the cabin. After a moment of stunned surprise, Emily went after him. He had taken only a few strides before she caught up to him. Grabbing for his shirt-sleeve, she dragged him round to face her.

355

"Why did you run away?" she cried out. "Why didn't you stay and explain what you were doing in Mrs. Royston's rooms?"

By slow degrees, his posture relaxed. He no longer looked as though he were a rampaging panther on the prowl. Even his smile was more natural. Touching one finger to her cheek, he purred, "Barbara Royston was my mistress. Isn't that so, Emily? You're not that naive. You know why a man visits his mistress in the dead of night."

Once, when Emily was a child, she had fallen out of one of the pear trees in Rivard's orchards. All the breath had been knocked out of her body. She felt the same sensation now.

When he jerked his sleeve from her hand, she came to herself. "That doesn't explain why you ran away."

"Barbara Royston was dead when I got there. Murdered. When I stepped out of her door, two gentlemen were waiting for me. One of them was armed. What would you have had me do?"

"Are you saying that William and Peter . . . ?"

She was shaking her head, and the gesture brought his simmering temper to a boil. "Think what you like. You always do. But understand this. You will do as I say. And I say that if you are not changed in five minutes, I will forcibly strip the clothes from your back and dress you myself."

He moved toward the jetty where the crews were already in place, waiting patiently for the signal to get under way. James Fraser had stationed himself beneath the shade of a willow tree. Coming forward, he flashed Leon a quizzical look. Emily wasn't ready to give up yet.

She yelled at the top of her lungs. "I'm not going anywhere till I know where you are taking me."

Leon straightened and turned to face her, hands on hips. It was as though the panther had finally condescended to notice the kitten who was stalking him.

"Home!" he yelled back.

"England?" From that distance, he could not have heard the whisper of sound that died in her throat. Even so, his face darkened.

"To New York," he retorted, and gave her his back.

In the cabin, Hester and Sara had already donned the deerskin garments Leon had set out for them. Sara was white-faced and silent. Hester did enough talking for the three of them. She was gnashing her teeth together in helpless fury.

"How dare he ask decent women to wear the garments of savages! From the very first, I knew what he was. He is a foreigner. Didn't I say so? He wants to drag us down to the gutter where he belongs. This is an abomination. My brother . . ."

Emily brought the diatribe to a close. She pinned Hester with a steely look; her voice was tipped with ice. "We are going to New York. I don't know what route we are taking, but obviously we are going into the wilderness. Leon is right. These garments will be more comfortable. We wouldn't last a day in our tight stays and petticoats."

"New York?" Hester's eyes darted about before focusing on Emily. "And you believe him?"

"I believe him. Sara, help me get out of this gown." As Sara's trembling fingers undid each tiny button, Emily continued in the same controlled tone. "I don't believe Leon murdered Mrs. Royston, and even if he did, we are in no danger. If he had wanted to mur—make away with us, he has had ample opportunity."

Hester snorted. "You are a fool, Emily Brockford, if you believe that. Just mark my words! One by one, we shall all meet with a fatal accident and . . ."

The woman was on the verge of hysteria. Emily didn't think about what she was doing. She slapped her. Hard. Sara's gasp was as shocked as Hester's.

"Nothing is going to happen to us! Do you understand? We are going to New York. I've made the journey before. It isn't so very far away." She told the lie with commendable composure. She knew she did not understand half of what was going on, but she kept her misgivings to herself. One of them had to keep a cool head, and Hester and Sara were both near breaking point.

"But why, Emily? Why is Leon determined to take us to New York?" Sara was wringing her hands.

Emily voiced the answer without conscious thought. "Why? Because he believes that we are in danger and that we will be safer there with him."

"What did you tell them?"

Leon's face betrayed no emotion as he answered his friend's question. "Nothing."

"You told them nothing?"

"What would you have had me say?"

"Didn't you tell them you are innocent? Didn't you tell them that you were caught in a trap?"

"What? Tell them that we suspect either Addison or Benson or both of them together simply because they were armed and waiting for me outside Barbara

Royston's door?"

"Yes."

"No, I did not tell them, for the simple reason that I was caught inside the room with the murdered woman at my feet. And where were you, James?"

James's nostrils flared. "You know where I was. I told you. I was in my room drinking myself into a stupor. When I heard the shot, I came running out."

"So, on that fateful night, four of us—Addison, Benson, you and I—were all at the scene of the murder. Now which of us do you think the girls will believe?"

James glared, then laughed. "I see what you mean."

Removing the kerchief from his head, Leon wiped a bead of sweat from his upper lip, all the while his eyes scanning the river.

"They won't be on our trail for some time," said James. "Tomorrow at the earliest. That gives us a day's advantage. But, Leon, don't you think you are carrying this too far? I can understand your anger. I was angry, too. But it's another thing to let those girls go on believing that we are villains. They are half terrified out of their wits as it is."

"When I want your opinion, James, I shall ask for it."

"Fine."

A full minute was to pass before James unbent a little. "It would be the easiest thing in the world to set up an ambush," he said. "If I were you, I would take no chances. I would rid myself of Addison and Benson permanently."

"One of them is innocent. Perhaps they both are."

"You don't believe that and neither do I."

Leon's lips curved in a genuine smile. "James, you are a bloodthirsty . . ."

"Savage?"

"Scoundrel. But 'savage' will do just as well."

"You never used to be so squeamish."

"I've never killed a man in cold blood."

"Oh? What about France?"

Leon's lids drooped, concealing his expression. "Who told you about France?"

"Paterson. He is in my employ, remember?" James's smile was devilish. "He listened in at keyholes. Not that he understood the significance of what he heard. But I did. Le Cache-Cache! Now, who is the savage?"

"Who else knows?"

"Are you asking me if your wife knows?" Leon's tension communicated itself to his friend, and James's amusement evaporated. "Yes, she knows. Addison came across some file and put two and two together. Good grief, if that kind of slip is what we may expect from our War Office, Napoleon must be rubbing his hands in glee, not to mention you Americans. Oh, yes, and Benson and Sir George know. They were trying to convince Emily that you are a dangerous fellow and not to be trifled with. Evidently, they succeeded. I don't think anyone else was admitted to their confidence, but I could not swear it."

The profanity which burst from Leon was low and savage.

"Ah!" James would have said more, but Leon moved off quickly toward the cabin, shouting names as he went. Three of the *voyageurs* sprang from the smaller of the two canoes and went after him.

James could not contain his roar of laughter.

They weren't going to New York. They were traveling west on the Ottawa River. Emily was a tenderfoot, but she wasn't a complete ignoramus. They were moving farther and farther away from civilization. She kept her knowledge to herself, knowing that if she confided in either Sara or Hester, they would jump to the direst conclusion possible.

She had made up her mind that at an opportune moment, she was going to have it out with Leon. That moment never presented itself. The three ladies were in the center of the longest canoe. Leon was at the back of the craft, acting as steersman. James Fraser was in the other boat. He had offered to take one of the ladies with him, but at the very mention of separating them, Hester almost had been overcome with another fit of hysterics.

The deerskin garments were satin-soft and as comfortable as Leon had promised, allowing for far more freedom of movement than the fashionable gowns they had left behind. Still, Emily wasn't sure that to expose so much bare leg was quite decent. On the other hand, in the drawing rooms of polite society, she had bared a fair expanse of bosom without a ripple of conscience. The absurdity of ladies' fashions tickled her.

She lifted her hands to secure the kerchief on her head and her breasts wobbled alarmingly. The impulse to fold her arms protectively across her quivering flesh was hard to resist. knowing that she would only draw attention to herself, she forced herself to relax. She was almost three months along and, without stays, showing it. Her belly was still tight, but her breasts were ripe and heavy. Soon, very soon, she must tell Leon. She tried to imagine that moment and shuddered. He would force her to return to York where she could be properly looked after. She wasn't going to allow that to happen. She was going to stay with him where she belonged come hell or high water.

They were making another stop. Emily judged it to be eight or nine in the evening. The sun was fairly low on the horizon, but the light was still good. There had been many stops on the way. Every hour or so, the *voyageurs* needed to smoke their pipes. Occasionally, they went on shore. The ladies made no objection since it gave them the opportunity to stretch their aching muscles or take care of other needs which were too delicate to make known to the gentlemen.

Those occasional stops had brought about one major change in Emily. Getting on and off the canoe was no longer a thing to be dreaded. As they neared the shore, the *voyageurs* leapt out of the boats to prevent the rocks scraping a hole in the fragile underside. Emily leapt down with them and waded ashore. Leon was waiting for her.

"We are making camp for the night."

Leon's tone was no warmer than his expression. Emily didn't let that deter her. "Leon, we must talk," she said.

"About what?"

"About . . . everything."

"Fine. I'm listening. Talk."

He was making things very difficult for her. She chewed on her bottom lip. "If only you would explain . . ."

"I don't justify myself to anyone, especially not to

you. Now, if you will excuse me, I have work to do."

Defeated, Emily joined her companions, who had seated themselves on a fallen log well out of the way of the *voyageurs*. No one gave them a second stare.

"I say that we hide ourselves in the forest," said Hester. "William and Peter are bound to come looking for us."

Emily never took her eyes from the men who had been set to unload the canoes. "How long do you think it will be before they come to rescue us?"

"I don't know. A few days. A week. What difference does it make? We know that they will come."

"*How* do we know? I do know my husband, and Leon is expert in setting a false trail. Look how he had us all believing that he had fled across the American border."

"Then what are we going to do, Emily? It's all right for you. I'm the one who stands in danger."

Emily's eyes probed Sara's. "Do you really believe that Leon wishes to harm you?" she asked softly. "Don't you remember how it used to be when we were children? When Leon came to Rivard, I hardly saw you. There was something special between you both, some kind of affinity."

"That's what I used to tell myself, but don't you see, Emily, it's only what I wanted to believe? I was jealous of you. You were the elder. Everything always came first to you. When you and Leon took an instant dislike to each other, I was glad. For the first time in my life, I came before you."

"But later, long after Leon and I were wed, you loved him. You begged me to seek an annulment."

Sara looked away, then raised her head to meet Emily's intent stare. She shrugged helplessly. "I thought I loved him. I was wrong. You know, he wasn't in the usual way of the young men of our acquaintance. All the girls were mad for Leon. I am certain of one thing. He never gave me the slightest encouragement."

Hester had been listening to the conversation with diminishing patience. When there was a pause, she burst out, "This is all very interesting, but it is to no purpose. We still haven't decided what's best to be done."

Two sets of eyes were trained on Emily as though all the wisdom of the world resided in her. Almost by rote, she repeated what she had said before, that if Leon and James had wished to harm them, there had been ample opportunity.

Her words seemed to relieve Sara of her worst fears. They made no impression on Hester.

Referring to Leon and James, she said, "They are not our kind. Who knows what goes on inside their heads? Devereux is an outlaw. Fraser is a savage. It wouldn't surprise me if they intend to sell us to the Indians. In that case, we may never be found."

"Why should they do that?"

Hester's tone was vicious. "Because we are aristocrats and they are the dregs of society. This is a vendetta, don't you see? Look at us! They've dressed us like savages. They take a perverse delight in humbling us."

Emily shook her head. "You're letting your imagination run away with you."

"Then why am I here?" wailed Hester. "I am not involved in any of this. They could have returned me to Lachine if they had wanted to. I am an aristocrat.

364

That's what they've got against me."

"Emily?" Sara's eyes were dilated with fear.

Slowly, Emily rose to her feet. Her voice was hard with resolve. "Until I speak with Leon, we do nothing, do you understand?"

For the next little while, Leon was unapproachable. Setting up camp was quite an undertaking, and Leon seemed to be everywhere at once. The canoes had to be unloaded and set on their sides on the shore. A fire had to be started so that the one hot meal of the day could be prepared. By the time Emily was ravenously devouring bannock and pea soup, the darkness was almost complete.

She bided her time. The meal over, the *voyageurs* lost no time in lighting their pipes and passing round the obligatory keg of rum. Each man was allowed only one long swallow before the keg was reverently stowed in one of the packs.

It was James Fraser who came to escort the ladies to the solitary canvas tent which had been set up for their exclusive use. Leon threw one brooding look in their direction before moving off toward the smaller of the upturned crafts. Ignoring Hester's whining complaints about their sleeping arrangements, Emily darted after him.

When she called out his name, he spun to face her. Firelight played across the hard planes of his face, but she could not tell what he was thinking until he spoke. "What do you want?" he asked harshly.

"We have to talk."

"I'm in no mood for talking, but rather for bed." He

indicated the upturned canoe with the canvas sail which had been stretched across it.

"Let me come with you."

At her words, the air between them seemed to become charged with passion. Her body began to throb in anticipation. She could have drowned in the heated stare that held her so easily, so inexorably.

"Please?"

He hissed a yes into the silence. Dropping to his knees, he slid beneath the sail and extended one lean hand to her. When she complied with his command, as one man, the *voyageurs* let out an almighty roar. A moment later, they burst into song.

Beneath the canvas, it was almost as dark as pitch. Though Leon was little more than a shadow, Emily would have recognized him blindfolded. He had the curious effect of heightening all her senses. She knew the smell, touch, and taste of him. The moment he laid his hands on her, her very flesh leapt.

His lips were only a hairbreadth away when she cried out, "Leon, I mean it. We must talk."

"When did talking ever solve anything between us?" His hands were moving over her, taking intimate possession. "You feel good. You've been driving me crazy all day, you and this get-up."

He wasn't exaggerating. The loose deerskin robe had freed more than her rounded, womanly curves. Her movements were as graceful and as unaffected as those of a fawn. It was as though all the years of her vigorous training, the drawing-room lessons in ladylike posture and deportment, which he knew his sister had inculcated, were left behind with her stays in Jacques Lagimodiere's log cabin. There was nothing lewd

366

in the change in Emily. It was his imagination that was indecent. Even her breasts were more generous than he remembered. And her nipples, pouting, begging a man to kiss them and fondle them were almost more than he could resist. Whenever they had stopped on the trail, in spite of his justifiable anger, he had wanted to pounce on her and drag her behind one of the rocks and lose himself in the sweet womanliness between her thighs.

He took her chin between his cupped hands, forcing her lips open beneath his kiss. Wet. Warm. And the delectable taste that was only Emily's. He fought her power, This time, he was the one who was going to cast the spells.

Her fingers dug into his shoulders and he pulled back slightly, then rolled till she was under him, her back cushioned against the pile of blankets that served for his bed. It took a moment before it registered that his wife was resisting his embrace.

"We can't," she panted. "Everyone will know what we are doing beneath this canvas."

"They already know."

"But . . . they will hear us."

Though she could not make out his features, she knew that he was smiling. "I'm not making a noise," he said.

"Not now, but . . ." She groped for a polite way of expressing herself. "Later" was all she could come up with.

He chuckled. "When . . . *later?* When you make those little choked-off cries that drive me wild for you? When you come? When I come? Or at the *very* end when you bawl your eyes out?"

She punched him on the shoulder with enough force to make him wince. "I don't think this is funny. How could I possibly face your men in the morning, knowing that I know that they know that we know . . . What are you laughing at?"

His warm hands were making forays beneath the hem of her robe. "What the deuce is this?"

"Drawers," she said, "and don't think you are going to charm me into changing my mind."

Laughing softly, he whispered something in her ear that earned him another sharp slap on the shoulder. Nothing daunted, he disposed of the drawers. His hand slid between her thighs, nudging her knees apart, finding the creaminess which contradicted everything she had been saying. His finger probed deeper and Emily gave one of the choked-off cries he had referred to. Leon's breathing became labored.

His chuckle came out more of a groan. "Charm? Is that what you call this?" he asked, and flexed one finger deep inside her body. Her hips arched clear off the blankets and her head fell back. By this time she was whimpering. He buried his face in her hair. "And is this charm?" He raised his hips and ground the hard shaft of his sex against her belly. "Emily, help me. My 'charm' is killing me."

"Leon," she sobbed. "They'll hear us."

"They won't hear a thing. They are singing and won't stop until I give them the signal."

Her hands went to his waistband, freeing him from the constrictions of his breeches. When she cupped his swollen sex and stroked him the way he had taught her to, Leon thought that the end had come sooner than he had anticipated. One more touch and it would be over. He removed her hand and peeled out of his breeches.

"You are losing control," she purred, the lazy smile in her voice revealing a feline satisfaction.

"It's almost two weeks. What did you expect? I can't hold off any longer."

Later, much later, she turned her head into his shoulder. "They stopped singing a long time ago," she mumbled and nipped at him in playful punishment. "You lied to me!"

"The poor fellows were going hoarse. This is only an intermission. Once they get their wind back, they'll start up again."

He rose above her and pinned her hands above her head. "My affair with Barbara Royston was over long before I went to England to claim you. But I already told you that. I went to see her to buy her off because I was sure that she was out to make trouble between us. When I entered her rooms, she was already dead.

"There is something else you should know. She and her husband had an understanding. They went their separate ways. For appearances' sake, they would spend a few weeks together every winter, but beyond that, they rarely saw each other. Barbara had many lovers. I swear I was only one among many."

The sound of his breathing filled the silence. Emily waited, knowing that there was more to come.

"I never wanted you to know that I was involved with La Compagnie. If I ever catch up with Addison I think I shall *kill* him for betraying my secret to you. I permit no one to question me about a time in my life

369

I wish to forget." He paused momentarily. "And that is the only explanation you are going to get."

He kissed her as though he were testing the waters. When Emily angled her head back, opening her mouth wide to his invasion, he groaned and settled himself more firmly against her softness. A sliver of paper could not have slipped between them.

"This time," he whispered, tonguing her ear, "I'm really going to give you something to cry about."

Sara threw off her blanket and padded to the door of the tent. "This is absurd," she said. "How can we be expected to get to sleep with all that caterwauling?" She pulled back the flap and peered out. "Don't those *voyageurs* ever stop singing for more than five minutes at a time?"

Hester sniffed. "Perhaps *that man* should tell them what he told us." She was referring to James. "We start early in the morning. Where is Emily?"

"She wanted to have a word with Leon."

That man suddenly appeared in person in front of Sara, and she let out an infuriated yelp. "Must you always creep up on me?" Fear made her angry.

Unabashed, James responded, "Don't wait up for your sister."

"What? Where is Emily?"

"Her husband has consented to bed her."

Wanting to rile her, he took no pleasure in his success. She raised her hand and would have struck him if his reflexes had not been so finely honed. One yank, and she tumbled into his arms. Before she could get her bearings, she was on the far side of the tent where

370

no eyes could penetrate.

"You've always wondered. Just once, wouldn't you like to find out? I know I would." His tone was low and softly persuasive.

"What . . . what are you saying?"

"I want to make love to you. Tell me you want it, too."

She was tempted, not only because James truly attracted her, but because she was a scorned wife. No one betrayed Lady Sara Brockford with impunity. She hesitated on the brink and in that split second of indecision, she knew that her answer had been bred into her.

In an anguished undertone, she cried out, "James, I want to, but I can't."

His nostrils flared. "It's because I'm part Indian, isn't it?"

"No. You must believe me. I don't really care about that. If I ever said anything to make you think otherwise, it was only to deflate your colossal conceit. If you knew my uncle, you would know that we Brockfords don't set much store by a man's beginnings. It's what he makes of himself that counts."

He believed her and believing her, smiled. "Then what is it?" he asked softly.

"You wouldn't understand."

She wished that he would stop her mouth with hard kisses, or seduce her with his touch. Then the decision would be taken away from her. He did none of those things, and though her respect for him rose by several notches, perversely she damned him for a fool.

His hands dug into her shoulders and she got out, "It's Aunt Zoë, don't you see? It's the way she has

371

raised us." She managed a shaky laugh. "You wouldn't know it to look at me, but I swear to you, James, I'm a very conventional girl at heart. I could not betray my husband if he were a monster with two heads."

He stared at her as though she were a stranger to him, which, indeed, she appeared to be.

"It's the truth! Aunt Zoë . . . How can I explain it to you? She filled our heads with stories of honor and all that nonsense. If I were to go against the tenets by which she raised Emily and me, it would be like . . . well, like destroying the best part of myself. I know I am not half the girl that Emily is, I am not even half the girl that Aunt Zoë thinks I am. But I want to be. Can you understand that?"

His voice was harsher than he meant it to be. "Your husband may turn out to be worse than a monster with two heads. He may very well be a murderer. Have you considered *that?*"

"No. It's not true."

"Forget about Barbara Royston. Think about yourself. Would Benson profit by your death?" He had to shake her before she answered him.

"I don't know. I'm not sure how my moneys were settled. But even if what you say is true, it could never make a difference to us. Peter is my husband, don't you see? I must stand by him."

He had never admired a woman more than he admired Sara at that moment, had never wanted a woman more. For the first time in his life, the masculine instinct to protect a female not of his tribe welled up from some spring inside himself that he had not known existed. And wanting to protect her, he became ruthless in pursuit of his goal.

372

"He has a mistress, for God's sake. Molly St. Laurent. You know that. He doesn't love you. If he did, he would keep you on a tighter rein. He is indifferent, Sara. That's why he permits you the liberties you enjoy." He made a derisory sound. "God, if you were my wife, I would wring your neck if you tried to play your games with me."

She was trembling so hard her teeth were chattering. "Don't lay my transgressions to Peter's account. He never had a chance. I wouldn't listen to him."

"Because he is weak and you are strong. He is a cipher, Sara. Admit it."

"No," she sobbed out. "No. It's all my fault."

Scathingly, he burst out, "Your loyalty is misplaced. He's had a string of mistresses. Have you no pride?"

Her slap rocked his head back on his shoulders. He saw the blow coming but did nothing to prevent it, knowing that he had provoked her to retaliate. When she ran into the tent, he stood motionless for a long time, one hand nursing his scalding cheek.

By degrees, he became conscious that the *voyageurs* had embarked on yet another song. Smiling satirically, he moved to join them at the fire.

Chapter Twenty-two

On the second night out, there was no question in the minds of the *voyageurs* where Emily would be sleeping. With great guffaws of laughter and good-natured jibes, they set down the smaller canoe some ways from camp. No language was necessary to understand their comical gestures. They could not sing a note if their lives depended on it. Emily was thankful that the fading light concealed her blushes. She bent her head and made a great to-do of crumbling her bannock, but all the while she burned from the heat in her husband's glances as they bored into her from across the campfire.

When he set aside his utensils and came for her, she thought her heart would beat its way clear out of her chest.

"Emily?"

At the sound of his voice, Emily rose to her feet.

Hester rose with her. "Leave the girl alone." She had the look of a tigress defending her cub.

Emily was aware of every eye trained on them. Even the wilderness seemed to be holding its breath. Leon took a step back as if relinquishing all claim to her, and she found her voice. "Give me your arm, Leon, in case I stumble."

When Emily pushed past her, Hester's expression registered first shock, then outrage. At their retreating backs, she stormed, "If you force her, you will be no better than a beast of the field."

Leon spun round. "My wife may suit herself," he said, and strode off with quick, impatient steps. Emily had to run to keep up with him.

"Well!" Hester sank back on the upturned log which served as her seat. "Doesn't she realize that the man is a murderer?"

Sara didn't bother to answer. Instead, she calmly went on spooning soup into her mouth.

Once they were under the canvas, Leon hooked one arm around Emily's shoulders, pillowing her head against his chest. "Go to sleep," he murmured. "Morning will be here before you know it. You have done well today, but we have a long way to go yet. I don't want you overtaxing your strength."

Raising herself slightly, she said, "I know we are traveling west on the fur trade route. Surely, Leon, this it taking us far out of our way?"

He chuckled. "Very far," he agreed, "but very necessary nonetheless. The woods are crawling with redcoats. Where we are going, they won't show their faces."

"Where *are* we going, exactly?"

"To Ste. Marie. It's a trading post and settlement on a narrow strait of water separating Lake Huron from Lake Superior. It's ideally situated for my purposes. Across the strait is an American post."

She considered his words carefully. "How long before we reach this Ste. Marie?"

"Two weeks."

Her jaw dropped. "Two weeks?"

"I know." Patting her on the shoulder, he went on. "But don't upset yourself. I know what I am doing. I've made this journey more times than I can remember."

"That's not it! There is something at Ste. Marie, some particular reason for us going there. There must be."

"Why do you say that?"

"I . . . I don't know. Womanly intuition, I suppose."

It was a long while before he answered, and when he did, he spoke with reluctance. "You are right. There is another reason, though I am half inclined to believe that no good will come of it. There is this girl, an Indian girl, who was once in Sara's employ. She disappeared. We discovered that she was married to a guide, Doucette, and went along with him on one of the fur brigades to his place in Ste. Marie. I want to question her." He shifted his position slightly. "You remember that when we were in New York, Sara became deathly ill?"

"Of course. And we came to York to be with her."

His breathing made a soft, rasping sound in the silence. Finally, he said, "I was more concerned than I let on. You know now about the attacks in London?"

"Yes, Peter told me."

"Then you may imagine my thoughts when Sara became ill. I sent word to James and asked him to investigate. The short of it is, we discovered that Sara was being drugged and we believe the maid was responsible."

There was a pause before she said, "You don't trust either Peter or William, do you, Leon?"

"I don't trust anyone, especially when I don't know what is going on. All of us—you, Sara and myself—have been targets at one time or another. I aim to remove us from danger."

It was a fantastic story, and one that Emily was not sure she believed. Careful to keep the skepticism from her voice, she asked, "How can finding this girl help you, Leon? That's what I don't understand."

He shifted her until they were facing each other. "She may know nothing at all. On the other hand, someone may have put her up to it. If you are not tired, there are other things I can suggest to occupy your beautiful mouth."

Her hand clutched at his shoulder, wedging a space between them. "You think the maid will be able to identify the perpetrator of all these crimes?"

He stopped kissing her throat and moved to her mouth. "Yes."

"And you think you know who it is?"

His sigh betrayed the merest trace of exasperation. "Yes."

"Who?"

"Peter Benson, or possibly William Addison."

Before her brain had time to sift everything through, her tongue found speech. "But what possible motive could either Peter or William have for murdering Mrs. Royston?"

At the speed of lightning, he shot back, "What possible motive could *I* have for murdering Barbara Royston? Don't wrack your brain for a way out of it.

Why don't you admit that you are still not convinced of my innocence?"

"It's not that," she denied fiercely. "It's just that Peter and William don't seem . . ." This was the moment to stop, when she was aware that she had stepped from terra firma onto quicksand. Without thinking, she pushed on, trying to justify herself.

"What I mean is this. They both come from old and distinguished families. I know I am not saying this well, but don't you see, there has never been anything in their backgrounds to suggest such a thing?"

"Whereas I was once an assassin?"

"I didn't say that!"

"No, but it's what you were thinking."

Her hand curled into a fist, poised to strike him. Realizing that she was allowing her frustration to carry her away, she inhaled a calming breath, then another. "Leon," she pleaded, "if I believed that, would I be here with you now? Last night, would I have allowed you to make love to me? Would I have made love to *you?*"

Long fingers tightened around her throat and she caught back a startled cry. His voice was lazy with sensuality. His words were frightening. "Dear Emily, do you suppose that you are the first woman who has used her sex to barter with me for her life? I'll say this for an assassin's life. It has its compensations."

She shook her head. "It isn't true. I don't believe it," and on the very next breath, "Who was she, Leon?"

He left her so quickly, so silently, that she was apologizing to thin air before she knew it.

"Lève! Lève! Lève!"

Like a big bird of prey, the *voyageur* swooped among them, bellowing at the top of his lungs, desecrating the silence by beating a wooden spoon rhythmically against a tin plate. The din was earsplitting. *"Lève! Lève! Lève!"*

Emily's hand groped for Leon and found only his empty blanket. It was still warm from the heat of his body. At the next raucous cry, she got her bearings. Groaning, aware of every taut muscle, she slipped from beneath the upturned canoe, pulling the bedding with her. It took only a moment to fold the blankets and tie them with a leather thong.

Two days on the trail, she was thinking, and already she knew the routine well. It was as dark as Hades, and only three o'clock in the morning, but within a very short while, camp would be struck and they would be on their way. There would be nothing to break their fast but a drink of cold water. The *voyageurs* were a hardy lot and didn't believe in mollycoddling themselves. Three hours would pass before they stopped to consume the predictable meal of pea soup and cold bannock. Emily would have sold her soul for a cup of freshly brewed coffee.

It was only a step or two to the water's edge. She cupped her hands and buried her face in the cooling stream. Her movements were quick and efficient. There was little time for primping and preening. The *voyageurs* were impatient to be off.

When the signal was given, she picked up her bundle and made for the canoe, her eyes scanning the shadows for a glimpse of Leon. When she saw him, she was off like a shot.

"Leon, I know you slept with me last night."

He was crouched down, examining and adjusting packs as men picked them up to load them into the canoes. "This isn't the time to conduct a discussion."

"There never is a right time. From dawn to dusk, you are always busy." She wasn't finding fault with him. This was no pleasure jaunt. Sometimes it seemed that there were more tasks to do than men to do them. Time was the enemy. Even a tenderfoot like Emily had grasped that truth. In the woods around them, game was plentiful and they would have welcomed a change from their monotonous diet. They stopped for nothing except to eat and sleep.

He scowled up at her. "Look, you can suit yourself where you sleep. I already told you that. If you are afraid of me, I suggest you bed down with Sara and Hester or whomsoever you choose."

Someone called to him then, and he moved away. Emily wanted to pull out her hair by the roots, or his. Before she could vent her frustration at Leon, at herself, at a world that seemed wholly unjust, one of the *voyageurs* pounced on her. Though he was no taller than she herself, he picked her up as easily as if she were a feather and dumped her in the center of the boat. Hester and Sara were already in their places.

Beyond a stiffly returned greeting, Hester preserved a stony silence. Fine. Emily was in no mood for small talk, either. But when Sara made the effort to smooth over the awkwardness, Emily unbent a little.

"We are going to Ste. Marie," said Sara.

"Did Leon speak to you?"

"No, James did. Last night, after you and Leon had retired." Sara could hardly keep a straight face. Her eyes kept sliding to her sister-in-law's stiff-as-starch figure.

Emily wasn't amused. "What else did James tell you?"

"Oh, that he and the *voyageurs* will part company with us there. They are pushing on to Fort William."

This was news to Emily. It occurred to her that James might be laying a false trail to throw their pursuers off Leon's scent. One glance at Hester's unbending profile convinced her to keep this thought to herself. "Did he mention a girl, the wife of a guide?"

"Not to me. Perhaps he said something to you, Hester?"

For a moment it looked as though Hester was pretending to be deaf. Gradually, her expression altered and Emily deduced that either she knew something or curiosity was getting the better of her. Finally, she asked, "Which guide?"

Emily had to wrack her brain before the name came to her. "Doucette," she said. "The girl was once your maid, Sara. The Indian girl who ran away."

"What do they want with her?"

By this time, both Hester and Sara were avidly curious. Emily hesitated for a moment, wondering belatedly if she was betraying Leon's confidence by bringing the matter of the girl into the open. "Leon seems to think she may be able to help him clear his name," she said vaguely.

"My *maid?*" Sara looked at Emily as though she had taken leave of her senses. "What could *she*

381

possibly know?"

"Your *former* maid."

"I can't recall a single thing about her, except that she was exceedingly shy."

"I remember her," said Hester. "She was the one with light fingers. Nothing was safe from her. Plates, spoons, ribbons, notepaper—the girl was a veritable magpie. Unfortunately, I did not discover it till it was too late. If she had not left our employ voluntarily, I would have dismissed her. And this is the woman whom Devereux hopes will clear his name?" She made a sound that left her hearers in no doubt of her opinion. "He knows as well as I do that the girl would be laughed out of court. He is guilty, Emily, and the sooner you make your mind up to it, the sooner we can make plans to escape."

"I'm not leaving my husband," said Emily.

"Sara?"

Sara shrank under Hester's penetrating stare. "I . . . I'm not leaving Emily," she said.

On the first stop of the day, the girls took the opportunity to stretch their legs. Hester was sulking, and waved them away.

At length, Sara said, "This is like a nightmare. I keep hoping that soon I shall wake up. I don't know what to think, who to trust."

They had come to a thicket of wild raspberries, and Emily picked at them, not even aware of what she was doing. A mosquito whined close to her ear. Nearby, perched on the branches of a stand of birch tree, a small flock of grackles were inquisitively watching the proceedings.

Sara walked on and spoke as though to herself.

382

"Hester is not plagued with doubts. Leon is not English, ergo, Leon *must* be guilty. And the evidence against him is pretty strong."

Emily bit down on her lip and her eyelashes blinked rapidly. She could not find her voice.

"It's no use telling Hester that I've known Leon since I was a babe in arms." Sara's eyes lifted to Emily's and there was the hint of a smile in them. "You hated him then."

"I . . . I pretended to."

"Then I was right all along? You love Leon?"

"Is it so obvious?"

"Good God, no! Hester thinks you are secretly in love with William Addison. For a time I thought so, too. We debated the point last night. I don't think I persuaded her."

"But that's absurd! William is a friend, nothing more." Even as Emily said the words, her conscience pricked her. She knew perfectly well that William himself believed that she was partial to him.

"Do you know what I think?" Sara's thoughts had returned to the awful possibility that someone wanted to murder her. She breathed deeply. "I think that this is all a misunderstanding. Yes, that's what it is, a colossal misunderstanding, or someone's idea of a practical joke. Otherwise . . ."

She was on the point of bursting into tears when the crack of a pistol shot froze her like a statue. The grackles rose from their perches as one, croaking their displeasure. Emily let out a cry and took off in the direction of camp. Sara was right behind her. When they came within sight of it, the spectacle that met their eyes brought them to a standstill.

Hester stood in the center of a group of wild-eyed, shouting *voyageurs*. With her arms folded and head held high, she gave the impression of serene indifference. James Fraser wielded a pistol. He was yelling out orders. By degrees, the *voyageurs'* tempers calmed and they moved off muttering among themselves. Leon and a few of the men were examining the canoes.

"No harm done!" he called out.

"James? Hester? What is it?"

It was Sara who voiced the questions. Emily was limp with relief. When she had heard the report of the pistol, she half expected to find the camp overcome by soldiers.

James was practically spitting fire. "Try anything like that again, *your ladyship,*" he yelled down at Hester, "and you will find yourself trussed like a chicken for the remainder of the voyage—that's if my men don't take it into their heads to drown you first."

Hester was not intimidated. "My good man," she told him reasonably, "you cannot fault a prisoner for trying to escape."

"You weren't trying to *escape,*" he roared. "You were trying to disable our canoes. Do you know what happens in the wilderness when you deprive a man of his means of transportation? We could all have perished, and no one might ever have found our remains."

When he had moved away to join Leon at the canoes, Hester rounded on her two companions. "If you had only been here to help me, I might have succeeded."

Sara took offense at Hester's imperious tone. "And what good would that have done, pray tell?"

384

"It would have delayed us, then would have afforded Peter and William the chance to catch up with us. Sara, anyone would think that you didn't wish to be rescued!" and she, too, stalked off, leaving each girl to her own widely disparate thoughts.

That evening, when it was time to retire, Emily found herself in a quandary. She wasn't sure whether or not she would be welcome in her husband's bed. She hoped that Leon would come to fetch her. He never appeared.

With as much confidence as she could manage, she said her good-nights and picked her way to where the small canoe was lying on its side, conscious with every faltering step of Hester's gaze searing into her back.

"Leon?"

There was no answer. In the morning, when she awakened, she might have believed that she had slept alone, if Leon's blanket had not been warm to her touch. She buried her face in it and the scent of it, Leon's scent, twisted something deep inside her. She wasn't afraid of him, oh, God, she wasn't afraid of him! If only she could make him believe it.

They were one day out from Ste. Marie when the smaller craft developed a leak.

"The men will remain behind to repair it," Leon told the ladies. "They will catch up to us before long. These small canoes can travel twice as fast as the big Montrealers, especially when they carry no load."

Not thirty minutes after the Montreal canoe had taken to the waters of Lake Huron under full sail, the small canoe was launched without benefit of repair. Franchot was in charge and feeling all the weight of his responsibility. His orders were explicit. The canoe was to be concealed in one of the small inlets which fed into the lake. There, he and his men would wait it out. If their pursuers were hot on their trail, and he prayed to the Blessed Virgin that they were not, they must be delayed until Mr. Fraser was alerted of their presence.

Franchot was no coward. He was an experienced *voyageur* and not unused to the fierce competition in his trade. Disputes among rivals were frequently settled at knife point and more often than not with firing pieces. This was different. They were pitting themselves against redcoats. Redcoats! He could be hanged for treason! The British believed themselves to be masters of the Canadas. They regarded the French as ignorant peasants who should bow down and kiss their boots for the benefits that had come to them under British dominion.

He spat into the water. He wasn't thinking, as he so often did, that the British were foreigners whose language was barbaric. He wasn't thinking that he owed the company his loyalty for putting bread on his table. He was thinking that it was too long since he had been in the thick of a good fight, and he would back his *voyageurs* any day against all comers.

The house in the wilderness seemed to Emily something out of a picture book. At first sight, as

they approached from Lake Huron, she was half persuaded that it was a mirage. They had been traveling
for nigh on two weeks at a grueling pace. In that
time, they had not come across a single habitation.
The only evidence that others had made the journey
before them were the rows of crude wooden crosses
on the shores of the various waterways they traversed,
crosses which marked the graves of fur traders who
had succumbed to the perils of the voyage. Rapids,
portages, accidents and sickness—all had taken their
toll. That their own little brigade had come through
unscathed was taken by the superstitious *voyageurs* as
a mark of divine favor. The presence of the ladies,
notwithstanding Hester, was now regarded as a lucky
charm.

As they drew closer to shore, Emily observed what
she had not seen before. The stone mansion over-
looked a cluster of crude log dwellings. They had arrived at Ste. Marie.

"This is incredible!" breathed Emily. The sight of
fenced gardens, cultivated fields, and horses in paddocks in the virgin wilderness only added to her
sense of unreality.

Sara scarcely heard her. "How did such a house
come to be here?"

Recalling something Leon had once told her, Emily replied, "This must be James's home. I know a
little about it. His father built the house for his
mother on the occasion of their marriage."

Hester's tone was dry. "It's a nice little house, but
it's scarcely Osterley or Syon, or even Rivard Abbey."

Sara could not help turning her head to peek up at
James. Seeing that look, James let out a long sigh.

He was home. Very soon, Sara would meet the members of his family, and though he would have denied it with his dying breath, he wanted to make a good impression on her. He caught Leon's eye and knew that he had betrayed himself. It was Leon who looked away.

Before the canoe had touched the dock, a bell was heralding their arrival. People set down their tools and hastened to the water's edge. The inhabitants of the small settlement greeted them with an exuberance which was almost excessive. The *voyageurs,* who had taken the time that morning to shave and deck themselves out in their gayest apparel, cheered as much as anyone. Later, Emily would discover that they had good reason to cheer. The arrival of a fur brigade was traditionally marked by an impromptu celebration. There would be music and dancing and not least a respite from the predictable pea soup and bannock.

Sara clutched Emily's sleeve. "Look!" she breathed.

Emily obediently allowed her gaze to wander over the spectators on the dock. And then she understood Sara's astonishment. Ladies Emily, Sara, and Hester were the only white women present.

It was like no dance the ladies had ever attended. For one thing, it was held in a barn, and for another, the dances, if they could be called dances, were wild and unruly. For all that, they enjoyed themselves immensely. Even Hester had mellowed, and Emily knew why. They were no longer decked out in their deerskin robes, but in the borrowed finery of James's mother and two of his sisters. The gowns were a trifle old-fashioned but they would pass muster at a pinch. Surprisingly, at least to Emily's way of thinking, many of the Indian women present wore gowns which were almost indistinguishable from her own. It was Leon who explained it to her.

"Those are the wives and daughters of men of some substance, retired company men or agents. Out here, when an Indian woman marries a white man, she adopts his ways."

It was all very interesting, and at some other time, Emily might have wished to pursue the subject. For the present, she had other things on her mind.

"That Indian girl," she said, "the one who was once Sara's maid? Have you spoken to her?"

"Tomorrow is soon enough. She doesn't live right here in Ste. Marie. Doucette has a cabin a half-day's distance from the settlement."

Breathing deeply, Emily touched one finger to the back of his hand. "With all my heart, I pray that she can help you prove your innocence," she said.

A muscle clenched in his cheek and his eyes burned into hers. "If she were to swear that it was Benson or Addison, would you believe her . . . an Indian girl?" Her answer was too slow in coming for his liking. Excusing himself, he went in search of the restorative which he knew the *voyageurs* had concealed behind the outside privy.

Sara contrived things so that she could have a few words in private with James. The heat in the barn was too much for her, she told him. The screech of the fiddles and the foot-stomping were beginning to make her head spin Trying to contain his smile, he led her outside. It was still light, though the sun was fast disappearing behind the tops of the pine trees. He directed her steps to one of the paddocks where a mare was grazing with her foal.

"Do you know," she said, swatting at her bare arm, "I had never met with mosquitoes until I came into Canada?" She was nervous, and babbling to cover it.

"I know. Nor bears, nor wolves, nor porcupines, nor beaver."

He had taken the words right out of her mouth, putting a stop to her babbling, but he had done it with a smile. The constraint between them gradually relaxed.

In a more natural tone, she said, "Your house is charming, James, as is your family."

"Charming" was not exactly what she was thinking. "Astonishing" would not have been too strong a word. James's mother was retiring. Mrs. Fraser was not fluent in English and said very little. Her children were protective of her, and Sara had found that touching. Their warmth, their family affection, had completely won her over. In some ways, they were almost as English as she. The house they lived in, their garments, their manners and modes, right down to the ritual dispensing of tea, was as English as anything to be found in the whole of Canada.

She was coming to see that James had deliberately misled her. The error might have been hers originally, but he had done nothing to correct it, and much to fan her imagination. He wasn't a savage. He was as cultured and as educated as anyone of her acquaintance, as were his brothers and sisters. She wasn't angry with him. She was ashamed of herself. She had deserved to be taken down a peg or two.

"Tell me about your family, James," she said. "I think you mentioned other brothers, other sisters."

"There's not much to tell. All the men in my family, as you may understand, are involved in the fur trade. And the girls," he shrugged negligently, "they marry into it. For our kind, there isn't much else."

"Your kind?"

"You know what I mean. I am a half-breed, Sara. Your people view us with suspicion. It doesn't matter that we went to school in England. We may be as rich as Croesus. We are still not accepted, not unless we are willing to pass ourselves off as whites. I could do it if I had reason to." He let that last remark sink in before continuing. "But you met my sisters, Charlotte and Margaret. There is too much of the Indian in their features. In white society, they would meet with nothing but contempt—or worse."

Sara thought of the young girls whose manners and deportment far surpassed hers at the same age. Shaking her head, she said, "But in York you were accepted. There wasn't a door closed to you."

"True—up to a point. But it's a fine point. Parents of eligible daughters are careful to keep me at a distance."

She was afraid to answer him in the same serious vein, not because she did not feel for him, but because she felt too much. "Pooh!" she said. "When have you ever cared for eligible girls? James, you are a flirt! You would run a mile if some eligible girl set her sights on you."

He wasn't teasing her when he said, very softly, "Not if that girl were you."

Heat raced along her skin. She could hardly breathe for the lump in her throat. Her eyes grew very bright and her lower lip trembled. "James . . ." she got out hoarsely. "I brought you out here so that we could say our farewells, not so that you could make love to me. Tomorrow or the next day, you go to Fort William and we go across the border to America.

"I want you to know, that . . . that I will never forget you. I should like us to part as friends."

He clasped the proffered hand and debated with himself whether or not he should draw her into his arms and kiss her the way he wanted to, and in debating it, the moment was lost. "Sara," he said, "tell me the truth! If you were free, would you come to me? Damnation! What do I care whether or not you are free? This doesn't have to be farewell. Not if we don't want it to be."

Before she could give him her answer, they were hailed by two of James's brothers. Knowing that she had lost command of herself, with head down, Sara picked up her skirts and made for the barn.

"What do you want?" asked James without a pretense of civility when his brothers came up to him.

At twenty, Matthew was head of the house in James's absence. "Ma sent us out to keep an eye on you," he drawled in a baiting way. "We are chaperones, James. How does that strike your fancy?"

James's chin jutted out. "Peeping Toms, more like."

Matthew's chin bore a remarkable resemblance to his older brother's. "That ain't polite, James." He poked him on the chest, none too gently. "In point of fact, I would have to say that your manners are deplorable, just like you."

James straightened. "Try and improve them. I dare you."

Nathan, a youth of fifteen summers and the baby of the family, never knew when his brothers were serious or funning. He was taking no chances. To distract then, he asked quickly, "Why was the lady crying, James?"

"Sara was crying?" James didn't look as chastened as Nathan thought he should.

Conversation came to an abrupt end when Matthew's head went down and he charged, taking James by surprise, tumbling him to the grass. "You are getting to be an old man," he grunted, trying to dislodge his brother's stranglehold. "Give it up before I hurt you."

"Ma! Come quick! They are at it again!" bellowed Nathan.

James was laughing. A shadow fell across the wrestlers and both men stilled.

James blinked. "Who is it?" he asked.

Leon answered him in a laconic way. "Word arrived not five minutes ago from Franchot. Benson and company will be here by morning."

"Good," said James. "I'm spoiling for a fight."

Chapter Twenty-three

"How long will it take to repair?"

Under the major's watchful eye, the guide ran his hands over the beam of the upturned canoe. The damage was severe but not beyond fixing. Gaboury judged it the merest ill luck that the canoe had foundered on a submerged rock just as they were launching it. Not that Gaboury would say as much to the major. He knew Benson to be a hard man. With the major, failure was never an act of God. Someone must be held culpable. Gaboury respected the major, but he did not like him.

Peter tried not to let his impatience show. Gaboury wasn't an enlisted man. He wasn't used to jumping when his superiors barked out an order. "Mr. Gaboury," he said, "how long will the repair take? One hour? Two hours?"

The guide spat on the ground. "Be ready to leave when the sun is high," he said, and pointed overhead.

With these few words, Gaboury turned to two of his own men, young *voyageurs* but experienced men in spite of their paucity of years, and in a manner that the major could only admire, he barked out his own orders. They jumped to it. Before long, a fire was got going and pitch was simmering in a black pot. Linen rags were carefully laid out and strips of bark culled from a nearby stand of birch.

"Check your powder. Check your firing pieces." The major went from soldier to soldier, issuing instructions which were, by and large, redundant. These were not raw recruits. A few of the men were soaked through, having tumbled into the water when the canoe foundered. To a man, however, they knew that the first order of business for a soldier was to see to his weapons.

William Addison lolled against the side of a great granite boulder. His pistol was tucked inside the waistband of his breeches. When Peter came up to him, he said, "I hope this isn't some sort of trick. I don't trust Gaboury and his *voyageurs.*"

"There are seven of us and seven of them, but don't forget, my men are armed with muskets."

William made a face and Peter laughed. Referring to the muskets, he said, "Brown Bess may not be much to look at, but when she is warm and dry, and in the hands of the right man, there are few women who can match her performance."

"Meaning?"

One brow arched. "A trained soldier can load and fire her three times a minute. If you know of any woman who can match that, my men would like to meet her."

"Devil take them — if there is such a woman, *I* would like to meet her!"

The laughter soon faded and William said, "Getting back to Gaboury — you are sure he is not leading us on a wild-goose chase?"

"Quite sure. At every camp, there are signs that the women are still with them."

"Thank God for that."

"Let us rather thank God for James Fraser."

They had had this conversation before. When Devereux had abducted the girls, they had feared the worst. That nothing as yet had happened to any of the women, they put down to Fraser's presence. Once Fraser and Devereux parted company, there was no saying *what* would happen. The possibility that Leon was innocent, and therefore no threat to the girls, had never been raised.

A sudden cry of alarm had the major fumbling for his pistol. Before he could cock it, a volley of warning shots buzzed around his head. Both he and William dived for cover.

When the smoke cleared, the major saw at once that the situation was hopeless. Not only was the camp ringed around by three times their number, but half his own weapons were still useless. Three of his men, however, were in position, muskets braced against their shoulders. He gave a passing thought to the sentries he had posted.

He should not be surprised that their attackers had crept up on them with the stealth of Indians, he thought. Most of them *were* Indians or close enough to pass for them. What did surprise him, however, was that Devereux could command such loyalty. Fraser must know that by aiding him, he was putting himself outside the law.

"Throw down your arms!" came the call.

Not one of the soldiers moved from position, though they faced certain death. It wasn't that they were particularly brave, but they were well drilled. Major Benson was their commanding officer. His word was the only word that they would obey.

The moment was a tense one. Peter gave the order and the silent collective sigh of relief was almost palpable. James Fraser and his men moved through the camp, gathering the weapons into a pile. It was Leon who approached Peter and William.

"I'll take that," he said, indicating the pistol in William's breeches.

The man's complexion was almost purple. He was trembling, but not from fear—rather from rage. "You'll both hang for this," he said. "There are others who will come after us. You will never get away with it."

What followed happened so suddenly that it was over before anyone could get their bearings. In the act of throwing down his pistol, William inadvertently set it off, the shot narrowly missing Leon. Almost instantaneously, he was hit by returning fire.

The silence in that small clearing was suddenly electrified.

"Hold your fire!" bellowed Leon, and not a moment too soon. Men were taking aim, selecting their quarry.

While Leon went down on his knees to attend to the injured man, James spun around, his eyes searching for the culprit. It was his youngest brother, Nathan.

Trembling in his boots, Nathan croaked, "He fired first."

"You might have started a massacre!" Nathan's eyes fell away and James brushed past the major to join Leon beside the injured man.

"How is he?"

"Not good. The bullet is lodged in his hip."

"He's not dead?"

"No. He has fainted. We can do nothing for him here but staunch the flow of blood. We'd best get him to Ste. Marie."

In a tense undertone, Leon said, "Why didn't you give the order to hold fire?"

James shrugged helplessly, but before he could come up with an answer, Major Benson said, "This man requires the services of a physician."

The nearest physician was four hundred miles away in Fort William.

It was James who took the bullet out of William's hip, and Leon who assisted at the operation. James had hoped that Leon would be the one to do it, but that idea was scotched by Leon himself.

"But why?" James wanted to know. "You have a steadier hand than I. I've said it before. You missed your calling. You should have been a surgeon."

"Stow it, James. I'm immune to your flattery, And even if that were true, I still wouldn't do it."

The argument took place in the back parlor of the Fraser home, an unpretentious room which was occasionally used for food preparation and more frequently for family dining. The injured man had been set down on a table in the middle of the room. He had come to himself and was making quite a racket from the excruciating pain he was in. It took the combined efforts of Leon and Matthew to strip him of his boots and breeches. As instructed, Nathan had fetched a bottle of laudanum and was carefully counting drops into a half-glass of water.

"You never used to be so squeamish."

"It's not that. Look, James, would you remove the bullet if it were Benson lying here and not Addison?" Leon answered his own question. "Of course you wouldn't, because if anything happened to Benson, Sara would never forget that it had happened by your hand."

Leon looked James straight in the eye, and there was complete knowledge in that look.

Faltering, James said, "I take your point. I'll do it. Nathan, have you got that laudanum ready yet?"

Nathan, having become interested in the conversation, had stopped counting. "Coming," he said, and studiously started counting again.

Almost an hour was to pass before Leon went in search of the ladies. He found them in the dining room, standing around aimlessly. He was the first to speak, and it was to his wife that he addressed his remarks. "Addison's injury is severe, but it is not lethal. If it does not become infected, he has every chance of recovering from it."

Ignoring the ensuing babble of questions, he approached Charlotte Fraser. "Charlotte," he said gently, "we shall need a room on the ground floor where Mr. Addison can convalesce. He is going to be laid up for some time and will require constant attention."

Charlotte conferred with her mother. Of all the

ladies present, Mrs. Fraser was the most composed. It was as if she had been holding herself in readiness for this moment. The men had done their part. The rest was women's work. Calling to the younger girl, she immediately left the room, leaving Charlotte to explain.

In her quiet way, the girl said, "There is a room just off the back parlor, a maid's room. My mother believes that it will be convenient for all Mr. Addison's needs."

Leon was only too happy that Mrs. Fraser had taken his meaning without elaboration. Evidently, she understood about invalids and stairs and the necessity of chamber pots and proximity to the outside privy. To mention such subjects in the hearing of English ladies was considered indelicate. He looked at Hester and almost gave in to the temptation.

She had raised one hand, assuming control of the conversation. Leon propped a hip against the table and folded his arms across his chest. "What is it, Hester?" he asked, and managed to sound pleasant.

She looked down the length of her patrician nose. "Are we to understand that Mrs. Fraser and her daughters have the care of Mr. Addison?"

"You are."

"But . . ."

"Listen carefully to what I have to say . . ." and he spoke in that fluid, softly menacing tone that unfailingly secured the attention of his hearers. Deliberately, for effect, he paused, then began again. "At this moment, Major Benson and his men are held in the Common Gaol." He ignored Sara's quick rasp of breath and went on evenly. "James and some other men are with them now, taking the first watch. If you try to see them you will be turned away.

"Furthermore, if Addison had not sustained an injury, he would be there also. He is not a guest in this house. He is our prisoner and as such he is to remain incommunicable except to certain persons designated by myself or James."

If he saw Hester's raised hand, he gave no indication of it. "At any rate, he is in no fit state for visitors, for he is heavily sedated.

"There is one other thing I wish to say to you," and here he allowed himself a small smile. "I should warn you that the men who have been sent to guard Major Benson and Addison are armed."

Emily recovered first from the shock of his words. "Are you expecting an attack of some sort, Leon?"

Hester rounded on her. "Widgeon! He thinks that *we* are the ones who may try to rescue William and Peter!"

"That is not the only reason," said Leon, "but it did occur to me. And now, ladies, I beg leave to be excused. I have an appointment for which I am already late."

Emily was still smarting from Hester's barb. Perhaps she *was* a widgeon, but it was unkind of Hester to say so. It took a moment for Leon's abrupt change of subject to penetrate. "Appointment? What appointment?"

Hester was shrewder, more quick to put two and two together. "You are going to see that girl, aren't you? The one who was once our maid."

Leon acknowledged Hester's words with a slight

inclination of his head.

"Devereux, you are a fool," she scoffed. "The girl is an Indian. She stole things. She may swear your innocence on a stack of Bibles, and no one will ever believe her."

He straightened and came away from the table. "*I* shall believe her," he said simply, and then in a crisper tone, "I should be back by noon tomorrow. Be ready to leave with me then."

As he turned to go, Sara cried out, "But . . . but what is going to happen to Peter and the others?"

Over his shoulder, he replied, "They will be released in a day or two, once we are safely away."

After his departure, a pall fell over the little group. Conversation was sporadic and interspersed with long silences broken only by the sounds of coming and going in the back parlor. Before long, the ladies decided that the excitement of the day's events had taken its toll. They were ready for bed.

At the top of the stairs, before they turned away to their respective chambers, Hester spoke what she had been thinking. "My mind is made up," she said. "I am going no farther. Devereux can't make me, and there's an end of it."

She was terrified when her husband told her that he was bringing a fur trader, one of the English, to their little cabin. She had wanted to take her babe and hide in the woods till they were gone. Doucette would not allow it. They knew about her, knew that she was his wife. If they wanted to, they could make bad trouble for him. They could refuse to hire him on as a guide next year. They could turn him away at the posts when he brought in his buffalo meat and hides for barter. They might even stop him hunting the buffalo out west this summer. Then where would they be? Is that what she wanted?

It wasn't what she wanted. If her husband fell foul of the whites, they and their babe might starve to death, or she would be forced to return to her people and she would lose face.

No. That must not happen. She had her pride. She was the wife of a buffalo hunter. She went with him everywhere. No woman could skin a buffalo or dress the hides and dry the meat as well as she. As Doucette's wife, she had status. The other women envied her good fortune. And so they should.

Doucette was far above their husbands. He made more money than a common *voyageur*. He was a good provider. He had a temper, but he had never done more than slap her with his open hand. Some husbands beat their wives—men like her first husband. It was how she had met Doucette. The buffalo hunter had pounced on her husband when he was beating her. Doucette had knocked him to the ground and had threatened that he would cut off his ears if he ever came near her again. Her husband had slunk away and she had become Doucette's woman.

Doucette was strong. He would protect her. Other men feared him. He had promised that the fur trader would talk with her and then he would go away. She had nothing to fear. She had not done anything that was so very wrong. Still, she was wishing that she had gone back to her own people to have her babe. Or they should have gone on to the buffalo lands, far beyond Fort William and the long reach of the whites.

She heard their steps long before the door opened. Catching her blanket more tightly to her shoulders, she gave suckle to the babe in her arms.

Leon entered at Doucette's back and took a moment to examine the small interior. There was a scorched table with a lantern upon it. The woman sat on a cot against one wall. The single chair was beside a stone fireplace. In the empty grate there were fish bones and feathers. The stench of fish and stale tobacco smoke would have gagged a man of less sterner sensibilities. The one-room cabin was primitive beyond imagining.

He should not have been surprised. Doucette and men like him did not put down roots. Permanency was a concept that was unknown to them. They were adventurers. In a month's time, the urge would strike him, or he would hear of greener pastures and he would be off, taking his little family with him.

The woman could not be more than sixteen. God knew what she saw in Doucette. The man was ferocious-looking, like the villain of a child's fantasy. His hair was long and unruly and topped by a slouch hat with an ostrich feather sticking in its crown. A blanket coat covered his wiry frame. According to James, Doucette's services as a guide were unsurpassable, and to be had only when the buffalo season was over.

Leon's hopes, which had never stood very high, completely deserted him. He had come on a fool's errand and the sooner he reconciled himself to his fate, the sooner he would put his life in order. He was thinking of Emily, knowing that he would never permit her to live under the cloud which would follow him for the rest of his days.

He was here. If for no other reason than that, he might as well get on with it.

Speaking first in French, then in English, he said, "I am not English. I am an American, and when I leave here I shall be going across the water to my own country. I won't return. No one else wishes to question you. Only me."

The woman spoke neither language fluently and finally her husband translated in her own tongue. From her expression, Leon saw that she was still far from reassured. He decided he might as well be direct.

"You were once a maid to Lady Sara," he said, and waited till the woman had arranged her babe to nurse at her other breast. The action set up a train of thought that put Leon off course for some few seconds. He heard the woman's reply and gave her his undivided attention.

Her hair was dressed in elaborate knots and plaits. Her features were regular, her complexion dark, but no darker than her husband's, and Doucette was a white man. Leon made note of many small details and he came to the conclusion that she was a woman of the Cree. Among fur traders, it was generally acknowledged that there were no more comely Indians than the Cree. Again he wondered what the girl could possibly see in Doucette when she could have done so much better for herself.

Abruptly, he asked, "Did you try to poison your mistress?"

Her husband translated. For a moment or two, shock held her speechless, then she let fly with a torrent of words. The answer was an unequivocal *no*. What else had he expected the girl to say?

"Do you know who *did* try to poison her?"

By this time, she wasn't waiting for her husband to translate. Almost as soon as the words were out of Leon's mouth, she was shaking her head. He wasn't getting anywhere. He tried another tack.

"Lady Hester says that you stole things."

This was greeted by a cry of alarm and a spate of words directed at her husband.

Doucette answered for her. "She didn't steal things. She broke plates or scorched linens when they were drying by the fire and she hid them so that the older one would not find them."

Leon had no trouble in deducing that "the older one" referred to Hester. "Where did you hide them?"

Another conference, then, "When she went to the privy out back, she concealed them in her skirts and threw them into the latrine."

It was a trick employed by children and servants the world over to escape the wrath of their betters. Nobody was going to poke about in a latrine for evidence, unless perhaps a body was buried there.

Leon stared at the girl, catching the betraying dilation of her pupils before she quickly lowered her lashes. She was terrified now, where before she had only been wary of him. Why?

The words he said next were not the ones he planned to say. "But you didn't throw everything away. You kept something. And I am not leaving here until you give it into my hand."

Both husband and wife looked at him as though he had suddenly sprouted another head. Their jaws went slack. Doucette recovered first, and began to bluster. In an instant, Leon had him by the throat. When he saw that he had made his point, he let him go.

"Give it to me!" he hissed.

Doucette looked into those fathomless black eyes and his Adam's apple began to wobble. Though he did not know that he was staring into the eyes of a man who was once an assassin, instinct mixed oddly with superstition was painting lurid, fanciful pictures inside his head. The American was as sinister as Satan. Before taking him on, a man would need the protection of the Virgin Mary and all the saints. In that moment, Doucette truly regretted he had not led a blameless life.

Turning on his wife, he barked out an order. When she made to argue with him, he lifted his hand as though to strike her. She did his bidding, but sullenly. Keeping her child close held to the warmth of her body, she moved to the fireplace. One hand slipped inside the chimney, fumbling for something. A moment later, she withdrew a leather satchel. She kept her eyes down as she handed it to her husband. Without a word, Doucette put the satchel into Leon's outstretched hands.

Inside, there was a handsome leather-bound volume. Leon quickly leafed through it. Mostly ink drawings and sketches, he thought. The book had a propensity to fall open at one particular place. He examined the girl's face, then the page before him. It was a sketch of the girl. He had heard that Indians were superstitious to a degree about having their likenesses taken, but he could not recall the reason for it.

"Why did she take it?" he asked Doucette, holding up the book.

"She was afraid that her soul would leave her if she did not take her picture with her."

Leon returned to the book in his hand. After a few minutes' perusal, he lifted his head and stared blindly at Doucette. "My God!" he said. "What have I done?"

Hester awakened in the morning and lay for some few minutes unmoving beneath the covers, her eyes closed, savoring the sense of peace, the sense of certainty that enfolded her like a silken cocoon. Having come to the decision the night before, she had never slept better. Everything had fallen into place. It was all so simple.

She dressed herself in a leisurely fashion, wanting to look her best. Though she had slept late, there was no sense of urgency. She was not going anywhere. Besides, it was some hours before Devereux was due to return.

When she quit her bedchamber, she was humming under her breath. She was in a very good humor and was willing to acknowledge that Mr. Fraser's house was more splendid than she had at first allowed. It wasn't Osterley, by any means. There were only two stories. The rooms were small and the ceilings and plasterwork had little in the way of gilt or decoration. Nevertheless, it was a very fine house, a very English house, and would have proudly graced any small parish in any county in England.

At the foot of the stairs, facing the front door, a gentleman she didn't know was seated on a plain wooden armchair, nursing a pistol in his lap. Hester suppressed a gurgle of laughter and sang out a friendly greeting. The poor man seemed taken aback. Smiling, she went on her way.

When she entered the back parlor, her eyes lit on a number of young gentlemen who sat around the room employed in various occupations. Two were at the table and absorbed in a game of cards. One was slouched in a chair and appeared to be sleeping. Another was blacking his boots. Devereux had made no exaggeration. The gentlemen were all armed.

At Hester's entrance, conversation abruptly died. Matthew Fraser scraped back his chair and came to her at once.

"How is the patient?" Hester inquired, and her eyes strayed to a door on the right, a maid's room as she remembered.

Matthew was a little in awe of his brother's guests, but he tried not to show it. He told her exactly what his mother had told him earlier. "He is holding his own."

"That's something," said Hester. "Where are the ladies?"

"Out back, in the kitchen."

Hester didn't ask for permission. She thanked him and wove a path to the door which gave on to the back entrance. Matthew scratched his head. After a moment, shrugging the whole thing off, he returned to his game of cards.

When Hester opened the door to the kitchen, a

blast of heat almost overcame her. Emily and Sara, cheeks flushed, their borrowed gowns protected by voluminous pinafores, were at the ovens, removing fresh-baked loaves of bread with long-handled paddles.

"Why are you here?" asked Hester.

With the back of her hand, Emily wiped the sweat from her brow. "We sent Mrs. Fraser and the girls to bed. Would you believe that though they nursed poor William half the night, they had to bake the day's batch of bread before they could take their rest? For a household of this magnitude, the tasks are endless."

Ignoring the hint, Hester said, "I had no idea you were so . . . accomplished," and she moved around the room, lifting lids, opening drawers, poking into everything.

Emily's eyes narrowed on Hester. She was thinking that Peter's sister really was a fine-looking woman when she allowed her face to relax into a genuine smile. "Look here, Hester," she said, "we could do with an extra pair of hands. We're not finished yet. The men have to be fed, and they have appetites like horses."

Hester's eyebrows almost disappeared beneath the tiny curls on her forehead. "My dears," she said, "I wouldn't dream of interfering. Frankly, Sara, I didn't know you knew how to boil an egg," and smiling to herself, she slipped away.

"Well!" Emily and Sara glared at the closed door.

Slanting a half-hopeful, half-mournful look at her sister, Sara said, "In point of fact, Emily, I *don't* know how to boil an egg."

Emily scowled. "I know you don't. But what we

410

are having is well within your repertoire."

"What's that?" asked Sara.

"Pea soup and bannock," flashed Emily, and carefully slapped a large wooden mixing bowl on the flat of the table.

She waited until the fire had really got going before she left the barn and barred the door. She was sorry about the mare and her foal. Though she was really quite fond of animals, she could not let that deter her. This was a matter of life and death. Her little joke brought a smile flashing to her lips.

She had noted beforehand that the alarm bell was located under an old weathered table in the herb garden, close to one side of the house. It was heavier than she anticipated. Holding it out in front of her with both hands, she made the motions to set it to pealing. Good. Smoke was billowing out of the barn and the animals were becoming restive. Soon they would be howling.

The sound of the bell carried to the Common Gaol. Within its small confines, men heard it, but only faintly. They were engrossed in the little drama that was being played out between Leon Devereux and Peter Benson.

Not five minutes before, Leon had stormed into their midst, looking like a deranged man, shouting out questions, demanding that the major answer them.

Finally, he had thrown down a leather-bound volume. "Read it!" he said, trying to get control of himself. "Tell me whose hand it is in."

Peter read the page that Leon indicated. As if in

a daze, he lifted his head and his eyes moved from one intent face to the other.

"I asked you a question." Leon looked close to murdering someone. His control was at breaking point. He had not slept a wink in twenty-four hours, and the lines of fatigue and strain were etched deeply in his face.

Peter licked his lips. His expression was a combination of horror and disbelief. "I can't believe that Hester wrote this," he said. "If she kept a diary, I never knew of it. This is a forgery. Don't you see, it must be!"

Leon's eyes closed momentarily. "So, it is Hester," he said.

At his words, an uneasy silence fell, and in that silence the sound of the bell finally began to penetrate the men's thoughts.

Young Nathan was stationed beside one of the small barred windows. Frowning, but without alarm, he stooped down and looked out. He saw the smoke and instantly made the connection to the bell.

"Our barn is on fire!" he yelled.

James started up and rushed to the window. "My prize colt!" he cried out and groaned.

"Damn your colt, man!" Leon was at the door and had flung it wide. "Hester is in there with the girls."

Inside the house, Franchot, who was guarding the front entrance, was first to hear the bell. He ran outside and took everything in at a glance.

"The barn is on fire!" called out Hester, and

412

calmly continued to ring the bell.

With one quick prayer to the Virgin Mary for the lady who had the good sense to ring the alarm, Franchot dashed back into the house to get help. Matthew came running up at the double. Close on his heels came his motley crew of men.

Hester watched them go with a little half-smile. Then, setting down the bell, she turned back to the house.

In the kitchen Emily looked up from the batter she was beating. "What was that?" she asked.

"What?" asked Sara. "I didn't hear anything." She was flushed, as well she might be. Watching someone cook the bannock and doing it oneself were two entirely different things, she was coming to see. The *voyageurs* made it look so easy.

Emily cocked her head and listened. "It's the silence. Can't you hear it?"

"We never hear anything out here. The kitchen isn't part of the main building." With a wooden spatula, Sara made a stab at the bannock on the griddle. "How does one know when this is ready?" she asked.

Emily's head was still cocked to one side, her eyes staring at nothing in particular, listening intently. Not moments before, she thought she'd heard the sound of a bell, and voices, and other things she couldn't put a name to but which she knew were familiar. She tried to shrug off her vague uneasiness. Sara was right. Sounds rarely penetrated to the kitchen. Fires were all too common. In the interests of safety, house and kitchen were separated by a flagstone corridor.

Having convinced herself that she was letting her

413

imagination run away with her, she perversely set aside her mixing bowl and moved quickly to the door. "I'd better go and investigate. Keep an eye on those bannocks, Sara. They burn easily. Oh, and don't forget to stir the soup once in a while."

"What? Emily! Wait! I don't know . . ."

"Just stay at your post, all right?"

On the other side of the kitchen door, Emily took a few moments to remove her pinafore and smooth her hair. Satisfied that her appearance was presentable, she quickly crossed to the little back parlor.

The room was deserted. Her eyes made a quick inventory, noting the cards thrown down on the table in utter confusion. One chair was overturned. A pair of boots lay askew on the floor. Someone's coat with a pistol sticking out of its pocket was discarded in a heap on the sideboard. It was obvious that the men had decamped in a hurry.

Her pang of unease increased tenfold when the door swung on its hinges. Instinctively, Emily retreated a step.

Chapter Twenty-four

"The barn is on fire," said Hester.

The words acted on Emily like a salutary slap on the face, shocking her from her inertia. "Good God! Why didn't you say so at once?"

Heedless of Hester's answer, she darted through the door and made for the front entrance. As she came up to it she heard the braying of animals and the shouts of the men as they frantically led the creatures out of the burning building. Flames were shooting into the air.

"I've got the mare and her foal!" someone shouted, but the pall of smoke was so dense that Emily could not make out who it was. All she could see were darker shadows moving in and out of it. It was inconceivable to her that all this had occurred while she and Sara were involved in their mundane kitchen tasks.

Turning on her heel, she raced back the way she had come, calling for Hester and Sara. She hadn't the vaguest idea of what they could do to help, but she was sure there must be *something* they could put a hand to.

She had almost crossed the length of the parlor when she heard the murmur of voices. Her eyes were instantly drawn to the door to the room which had been turned over to William Addison. It was open. Emily faltered in midstride and moved toward it. Hester was speaking.

Emily's first thought was for the injured man. She was livid at Hester for taking advantage of the situation, going against Leon's express orders. She meant to get her out with as little fuss as possible so as not to disturb the patient.

Hester was sitting on the edge of the bed. William's right hand was clasped to her breast. Her tone was low and soothing, almost motherly. Addison's eyes were open, but he seemed groggy, not quite sure of his surroundings.

"Hester? Is it really you?"

"Yes, my love. I came to you as soon as I could. Did you think that I had forgotten you?"

Her words only seemed to agitate him. "You shouldn't be here. What if they find us together?"

She chided him gently. "Nobody is here. I have taken care of everything. Haven't I always, even when we were children?"

He coughed, and Hester raised his head to ease the spasm. Emily was rooted to the spot, afraid to give her presence away. She felt as though she were poised on the brink of solving everything.

Groaning, William fell back against the pillows. "I don't want to go on with this. I *can't* go on with this. Hester . . . all I ever wanted was you."

One hand smoothed his brow. "There, there! Don't fret, my darling. It will be just as you always wanted. We'll never be apart again."

"Do you really mean it?"

"I really mean it. It would never have worked anyway. Emily really loves Devereux, so you see there is no point in going on with it. I know that now."

He sighed and his eyes closed. "You'll have me? Just as I am?"

"You are all I ever wanted. Now go to sleep, William. When you wake up, I shall be with you."

For a moment, it seemed as if he were on the edge of sleep, then he started up feverishly. "I almost had him! Devereux! I almost had him!"

"I know. But none of that matters now. Kiss me, my love. One last time."

Emily was slumped against the doorjamb, her fist pressed against her mouth, her eyes tightly closed. When she heard the rustle of skirts, her eyes blinked open.

Hester was bent over William's prone figure. She had turned his head away, and her fingers caressed his head from crown to nape, stroking his dark hair as if to memorize the feel of it. William was evidently asleep.

"I love you, William," she whispered. "I love you."

It was only when she raised her arm that Emily saw the flash of a blade. She sucked in her breath to scream out a warning but before she had made a sound, Hester's arm came down, plunging the blade into William's neck. He jerked, but made no outcry, not even a whimper. It was Emily who sobbed out a strangled, "No! Oh, God, Hester, no!"

"Hello, Emily," said Hester, quite calmly, quite naturally, as though they had just met over the breakfast table.

Without haste, she moved gracefully to a low, unvarnished dresser. Emily could not see what she was doing, though she knew that she was lifting something, something heavy that required the strength of two hands. And then Hester turned and Emily found herself looking down the barrel of a monstrous, ferocious pistol.

Somehow, she hadn't anticipated that Hester would turn on her. She had sensed that with William's death, the last act of the drama had been played out. It seemed she had made a fatal mistake. She should have taken to her heels while she had the chance.

Licking her lips, stalling for time, she said, "You and William were lovers."

"Lovers? Yes, William and I were lovers, but not in the way you mean. From the time we were children, our souls were mated. I don't expect you to understand." Hester's tone was placid, and all the more unnerving because of it. No one would have believed she had just murdered a man in cold blood. "He never loved you. It was me. It was always me."

"But . . . he wanted me to get an annulment. He was going to marry me."

"And would just as swiftly have disposed of you as soon as you were securely tied to him. It really wasn't well done of you, Emily, to lead us on like that. If you had only made your feelings for Devereux known at the outset, we would have chosen another girl."

"One with a fortune," said Emily.

"Naturally. William and I didn't have two pennies to rub together."

418

Hester advanced a step and then another. Emily swayed in terror, but she found her voice. "William murdered Barbara Royston, didn't he, so that . . . so that Leon could take the blame for it?"

"You must see that Devereux had to be got rid of, especially once your marriage was consummated." Hester sighed in exasperation. "As I said, you really should have made your feelings known, Emily. You lied to William."

"I didn't lie to him!" Emily cried out. "I swear I didn't lie to him! I didn't want to hurt his feelings, 'tis all."

"Emily, I don't have time for all this chitchat. I must act quickly. You do understand that, don't you, dear?"

Emily wasn't sure if her mind was playing tricks on her, but she thought she heard Leon's voice far off in the distance. On one level of her mind, she was praying for deliverance. On another level, she was thinking up ways to delay Hester from pulling the trigger.

"What about Sara?" she asked quickly. "How does she fit into this?"

"On her death, her fortune would pass to you. Need I say more?"

"Then . . . that fall I took from the horse? That was meant for Sara?"

"Of course. Poor William! When he saw you take the tumble, he thought that all our hopes had come to ruin. He was sure you had broken your neck."

For a moment, a very fleeting moment, Emily was too flabbergasted to be afraid. "Are you saying that we were all targets: Sara, Leon, and myself?"

"My dear, I explained it to you. You were never

in any real danger."

"No, but I would have been if I had married William." Though she sounded quite indignant, it was her nerves that were making her babble so. "Well, that would never have happened, do you hear me, Hester? If you had made me a widow, a widow I would have remained for the rest of my days. Nobody could ever take Leon's place."

"I understand. I believe you."

Emily's eyes opened wide, then narrowed as Hester approached her. Sheer terror forced the words out of her mouth. "Why did you kill William?"

"It was the only way. If he had not been injured . . . Well, there is no point in going into that now. I was neither going to let him suffer nor be taken back to stand trial for murder."

Emily was running out of questions. In sheer desperation she said, "Where did you get that pistol, Hester?"

Hester smiled a knowing little smile, as though she understood perfectly what Emily was up to, but had decided to indulge her. "One of the men left it behind," she said. "I hardly hoped for such good fortune. I would have managed with the knife, but a pistol is so much better."

Her words provoked a new train of thought in Emily's mind. "Did you set the barn on fire, too?"

"No more questions," said Hester gently. "Time has run out."

Her mind screamed that she should do something, anything, rather than stand there motionless. It was horror and shock that held her captive. She didn't know that she had stopped breathing until Hester brought the pistol up with both hands,

420

pointing the muzzle straight at her heart. Then her lungs suddenly gasped for air, filling the small space with a sound that resembled the wheeze of a rusty bellows. Senses she had not known she possessed became acute. A confusion of images, scents, and sounds bombarded her. Her mind refused to grapple with the unacceptable and she became lost in the minutiae of her surroundings.

Hester's scent was sweet and cloying, and mingled faintly with the odor of stale perspiration. There was a small chip in the porcelain water jug on the washstand. The carpet was homemade, a kaleidoscope of colors on the freshly sanded floor. A small spider was foolishly spinning its web at the open window. If someone were to shut the window or open it wider, the web would be destroyed.

And then she stopped thinking altogether as she waited for the report of the pistol shot. She closed her eyes. "Leon, oh, Leon!" she whispered.

The gun went off, or so she thought until she opened her eyes. She wasn't dead. She didn't have a scratch on her. Hester had slammed the door in her face.

Her sense of relief lasted only a second or two. She had not even begun to think through all the implications of that shut door when the deafening sound of the explosion assaulted her ears and she staggered back, falling against the table.

Leon found her in that pose when he stormed into the little parlor. She raised her arm and pointed a shaking finger at the closed door.

"Hester and William," she quavered. "She killed him, then she shot herself."

Men were milling about, trying to get into Addison's room. The door was locked and too sturdy to break down easily.

"Go in through the window," Leon told Matthew. "Take someone with you. And be careful." He put his arms around Emily. "Are you all right?"

She was far from all right, but she nodded just the same. "It was horrible," she said, and collapsed against him.

Peter Benson's white face swam into focus. "Sara," he said hoarsely. "Where is Sara?"

Sara. She had forgotten all about Sara. She began to giggle, but the giggles suddenly turned into great gulping sobs. "She's in the kitchen. She's . . ."

Peter didn't wait for her to continue. As he shouldered his way past the group of men, James Fraser made to go after him. Leon's hand shot out, manacling James's arm.

James's expression was murderous. Leon weathered it and returned stare for stare. No words were spoken and men wondered what was afoot.

The door to William's room was thrown wide and Matthew filled the doorway. "They're both dead," he said.

Sara spun round as Peter Benson entered the kitchen. Tears were streaming down her cheeks. If she was surprised to see her husband standing there, he would never have known it.

"The bannock is ruined," she told him.

His eyes flitted to the griddle hanging above the live coals in the grate. "So I see," he said, and took a cautious step forward.

"The pea soup is burned."

"Yes, I can smell it."

"But I didn't know soup *could* burn."

"It's no great tragedy."

With both hands, she scrubbed at her face. "I suppose you are going to tell me that you broke out of gaol and have made Leon your prisoner. Is that what all the commotion was about?"

"I didn't break out of gaol. I was released. They know I am harmless." He was creeping up on her by inches.

"Yes, well, you must know by now that Emily and I are quite safe with Leon."

"I do know it."

She breathed deeply. "I daresay you'll be glad to see the back of me. We leave today for America, you know, as soon as we have breakfasted." She sniffed. "Whenever that may be," she added, and gave him her back.

"I won't be glad to see the back of you."

"It's very kind of you to say so, but I know you must be anxious to get back to your Molly. You love her. You told me so." She blew her nose into an embroidered handkerchief which she had found in her pocket.

He had her within arm's reach. "If I ever said such a thing, it was a damn lie. I never loved but one woman in my life, Sara!" His voice broke. "I thought I had lost you!"

She pivoted to face him, breathing his name, and he pounced on her, bearing her back against the wall. Emotions he could not contain were ripping his control to shreds: relief that she was safe, horror at his sister's part in all of this, the realization that life was fragile and transitory at best, a vague though fierce anger against he knew not what, and above all an unshakable determination to be master of the woman he loved. If he could not win her with kindness, he would hold her with sheer brute strength.

He kissed her until her head was swimming, and then he kissed her again. "Things are going to be different between us," he told her. "Where I go, you go. My bed is your bed. You'll never turn me away again." And because this masterful role did not sit too well with him, he pulled back slightly and said in a different tone, "Sara, say something!"

She flung her arms around his neck. "Yes, Peter. I say yes."

At dinner that evening, Peter Benson asked the principals in the matter if they would remain in their places, intimating that he had something of a very serious and particular nature he wished to discuss with them. When the others withdrew, five people sat around the table: Peter, Emily, Leon, Sara, and James. No one so much as cracked a smile. They were still overcome with the horror of the events that had occurred that very morning.

When they looked at him expectantly, Peter moved to shut the door, then he took his place at the head of the table. He held the leather-bound volume that had turned out to be Hester's diary. His expression was very grave when he set it down in front of him.

"We have a problem," he said, "which I am sure has occurred to us all."

At these opening remarks, Leon eased back a

little in his chair and stared intently into Peter's face.

Peter continued. "I have searched my sister's room from top to bottom, hoping to find . . . I don't know what — a last will and testament? A letter? She left nothing."

He paused. "The diary only goes so far. Don't misunderstand me. Though Hester's name is never mentioned, and others are referred to only obliquely, I am sure I could convince a court of law that it was written in my sister's hand and refers to events with which we are only too familiar. But as I say, it goes only so far, for the simple reason, of course, that it was stolen long before Barbara Royston was murdered."

He smiled, then, acknowledging Leon. "This leaves you in somewhat of a predicament. You have no way of proving that you are innocent of Barbara Royston's murder."

"But surely," interrupted Emily, "I can prove it. Hester told me, not moments before she . . . she slammed the door in my face. I told you all this."

"Possibly," said Peter. "But have you considered the fact you would have to return with me to York?"

"That is out of the question," said Leon at once.

"Quite. Then I have a suggestion to make."

"I'm listening."

Both men had locked glances and it was as if they were the only two people in the room.

Peter cleared his throat. "I intend to forge a letter in Hester's hand completely exonerating you in the murder of Barbara Royston. Furthermore, I shall make it quite clear that you were never at any time a member of La Compagnie or involved in any plot against Sara or Emily."

Peter's expression was very stern, very intimidating, when his eyes roamed slowly from one person to another. Emily found herself swallowing. And then he relaxed and gave that little half-smile of his, and he was the old Peter again.

"That is," he said, "with your permission?"

"It's a splendid idea," interjected James, speaking for all of them.

Leon's face and voice gave nothing away when he said, "Peter, have you considered what this will mean to you? I'm thinking of the scandal."

"I *have* considered it. And Sara agrees with me." Here he clasped his wife's hand. The eyes she turned up to him shone with emotion and pride. "What I am going to do is against the law. I know that. But it is *just*. I would never be easy in my conscience if I did not try to right a great wrong that was perpetrated by a member of my family.

"I had considered simply forging the letter and passing it off as the genuine article even to all of you."

"Why didn't you?" asked James.

There had been a visible relaxation of tension around that small gathering from the moment it had become clear that they were all of the same mind. When James handed round glasses and a decanter of sherry, they relaxed even more.

"There are some things that are not clear to me," said Peter. "I propose to give you a summary of what I know. This will be very informal. Please feel free to interrupt at any time. And I have questions also that I may put to you.

426

"In simple terms, what it amounts to is this. From the time they were children, my sister and William Addison loved each other. They had no money, or at least not enough for their purposes. They devised the scheme that William should marry a girl with a fortune. The girl they chose was Emily. Therefore, since Emily already had a husband, their first order of business must be to get rid of Leon."

Emily nodded and flashed a look at Sara. Their eyes met and held. What they were both thinking was that William was once Sara's suitor until Sara had proved fickle. Then William had set his sights on Emily. Another thought occurred to Emily. William's first wife was reputed to have died in an accident. For Peter's sake, she wasn't even going to mention it. For her own peace of mind she didn't even want to think of it.

"The plan was that, after a suitable interval, Emily would meet with an accident. Her fortune would thereupon pass to Addison, and he and Hester would marry."

There was a pause, and Emily said, "Hester admitted as much, just before . . . she ended her life. And when I asked about Sara, she said that in the event of Sara's death, her fortune would pass to me."

Under his breath, James muttered, "Greedy little bastards! Thank God they got their just desserts."

"I understand all that," said Peter gently. "I understand also that Leon was an obstacle that had to be removed. What I don't understand is why Hester and Addison thought for one minute that if you were free of Leon, you would accept Addison as your husband. There is no clue in Hester's diary, not a hint to guide me, at least, not after you came with Leon to America."

"I . . ." Emily shrank from the awful pit that had opened at her feet. She was remembering that she had once hoped to marry William when her marriage to Leon was annulled. And after, when that became impossible, she had blackened Leon's character in no uncertain terms. It was no wonder that William thought he could have her once her husband was out of the picture.

The ladies had not been permitted to read Hester's diary. Emily wondered just how much Peter knew. With his next words, she had her answer.

"I am not referring to anything that might have happened in London. That is well documented. But later, when you were here, and in New York."

Leon's comforting clasp on her shoulder steadied her. "It was all very innocent," he said. "Emily has done nothing for which to reproach herself. Addison simply became obsessed with the idea that he could have her. It was all in his mind."

"Yes," said Peter. "That seems reasonable."

"No!" Emily said the word before she could change her mind. This was not the time to be fainthearted. Leon must be her first consideration. It wasn't fair that things should be made easy for her when Leon's good name was at stake. What was she thinking? Leon's *life* was at stake.

She moistened her lips and clutched at her husband's hand, drawing strength from it. "In New York . . . that is . . . William and I kept up a correspondence, not regular, you understand. He wrote to me once . . . twice . . . and I replied." And then she burst out, "I didn't want to hurt his feelings, 'tis all. He was talking of coming to see me. I didn't want that. I wrote to tell him that it was not convenient. I was letting him down lightly. What else should I say? 'Don't come because I don't want you to?'"

"That's when Hester got the idea of dosing Sara with a narcotic. Not enough to kill her, just enough to make her ill." Peter's smile was grim. "She knew, or she hoped, that that would bring you into William's orbit once again. And, of course, it worked."

"Is that what happened?" asked Emily.

"According to her diary."

"I blame myself for not seeing it," James cut in. "But your maid had just run off. The inference seemed so clear at the time. No one knew anything about a diary."

After a pause, Emily went on doggedly with her story, more determined than ever to help Leon clear his name. "When I came to York, William was as ardent as ever. I tried to tell him he had no hope. He wouldn't believe me. But . . . and . . . he kissed me . . . and . . ." She was getting into a hopeless muddle and stopped in mid-sentence.

Again Leon rescued her. "As I said, it was all very innocent. Addison was obsessed with the idea that he could have Emily. No, the question that is going through my mind, Peter, is this. Why did Hester decide to take her life?"

Peter allowed himself to be diverted. "I think that is self-evident. Hester knew that you were on your way to see the girl, Doucette's wife. She must have known the girl had the diary. William was in no condition to go anywhere. The game was up . . .

and . . ." For the first time, Peter betrayed the strain under which he was laboring. His voice cracked, and he jumped to his feet, striding to one of the long windows to stare out at the lake. There wasn't a person in that room who did not feel his pain, and it was brought home to them that murderess or no, Hester had always been an affectionate sister.

In an attempt to give Peter a moment to come to himself, Emily said, "And on the journey from Lachine to Ste. Marie, Hester came to know that I cared nothing for William, that it was Leon I loved. So there was no point in going on with it."

"That's true," added Sara, her eyes straying anxiously to her husband's broad back. "Hester and I quarreled about it, but in the end she accepted it."

"Accepted what?" asked Leon.

"That I love you," said Emily.

"I have a question," said James, doing his part to cover the awkwardness. "It has to do with Barbara Royston. I am not clear in my mind how the whole thing came about. How are we to explain it? I understand about Leon's ruby pin. It must have been very easy for Hester to get hold of. But how could they have arranged for Barbara to be at Sir George's ball?"

By this time, Peter had himself in hand. He returned to his place. "We shall never really know. I intend to explain it simply as an opportunity which presented itself. They saw a way of getting rid of Leon and seized it. If it had not been Mrs. Royston, it would have been someone else. Quite frankly, I think that is exactly how it happened."

Sara put a tentative question. "Why not simply

make away with Leon? William tried it once, didn't he, that day in the park, when Leon and I were out driving?"

"He dared not be too obvious," reasoned Leon. "At that time, we thought La Compagnie was responsible for the attack. I'm sure Addison hoped that was what we would believe. I played right into his hands, for if I had known for a fact that the society was not involved, then I might have been on to his game all the sooner."

It was another half hour before the discussion wound down. Some questions would never be truly answered, but nothing that was of major significance. The candles were lit, and they sat around talking until James Fraser indicated that he was ready for bed.

"I must start early tomorrow," he said. "I am off to Fort William. I shall be gone long before any of you are awake."

His words acted as a signal to the others, reminding them that on the morrow, they would all be going their separate ways.

"Then this is goodbye," said Sara. She had walked with James to the door, a little apart from the others.

He gave her a wry grin. "I take back everything I said about your husband," he said. "He is a very fine man. There are not many like him."

"There are a few," said Sara. Her eyes were moist. "And I would have to say that you are one of them, James Fraser."

She watched him until he had taken the turn in

431

the stairs, then she turned back into the room. Peter and Leon were deep in conversation. Emily had a woebegone look on her face which she made a determined effort to banish when Sara approached her.

"You were always too softhearted," chided Sara, and held out her arms.

They hugged as they had not done since they were children.

"You have given me a memory I shall take with me to my grave," said Sara, setting Emily away from her.

"Oh?" Emily was thinking of their efforts in the kitchen and smiled.

"My elder sister," said Sara, "with a parasol in her dainty little hand, using it like a claymore to fend off a score of ferocious *voyageurs* whom she thought were out to harm her baby sister."

"You weren't supposed to look back!"

"I'm glad I did. That picture jogged my memory. When we were children, we were very close. I was always first with you, wasn't I, Emily? I just didn't know it till now."

"We were orphans. Who else should come first with me but my own sister?" Fighting to stave off tears, Emily got out, "What happens now? Have you persuaded Peter to resign his commission and go with you to England?"

"Certainly not!" said Sara, adopting a scandalized air. "In my marriage, my husband makes the decisions."

"That will be the day," retorted Emily, and laughing together, they hugged each other one last time.

Emily waited until she and Leon were in the privacy of their own room before she asked him what he and Peter had found to talk about while she and Sara were saying goodbye.

"You seemed so serious," she said.

Eventually, he responded. "I was thanking Peter for scotching the report of my involvement with La Compagnie. In the letter, he is going to make it appear as though Addison invented the whole thing to discredit me."

"I'm glad," said Emily. She knew how sensitive her husband was about La Compagnie.

He shook his head. "I can hardly believe that Peter and Hester come from the same family. He is as straight as a die and she was completely warped."

"That's how I feel about William. There was a time when I thought we had so much in common. To be perfectly honest, it used to chafe me a bit that he was so straitlaced. How could I have made such a mistake?" After a moment, she went on. "Leon, you read Hester's diary. How could this have happened? They were both so proud. I know that they were truly scandalized by some of the things my family did in the past. Hester, in particular, had such high standards. Sara and I could never live up to them."

He gave her such an intent look that she felt as though he were trying to read her soul. "What they wanted," he said, "was the appearance of things. They were never like you and Sara. Integrity played no part in their scheme of things. They were proud. You are right in that. They wanted people to admire them, to look up to them. It was all a sham, only they could not see it."

"I shall never understand it."

"No. You wouldn't."

He removed his neckcloth, then his coat, and tossed them over the back of a chair. He was shaking his head, laughing softly to himself.

Emily's lips curved in an involuntary response until he spoke to her in that softly fluid tone that never failed to either melt her bones or make the fine hairs on the back of her neck stand on end.

"You have some explaining to do," he said. "You love me. You said so in front of a roomful of witnesses not an hour ago. You love me. And don't try to wriggle out of it."

Chapter Twenty-five

The silence was absolute. Emily was a girl who prized honesty if no one was hurt by it. But there was such a thing as a woman's pride. He was laughing at her and that got her dander up.

Marching across the room, she flung open the door to the wardrobe. "We must get an early start tomorrow," she told the inside of the wardrobe. "We should pack our bags."

He was grinning. "Your eyes sizzle when you are in a temper, do you know? They are glowing like amethysts."

She ground her teeth together. Time seemed to slip away, and she was a girl again, and Leon Devereux was the horrid boy who was the bane of her existence. "I haven't the time for this," she mumbled. "I'm going to pack."

"My love, we have nothing to pack. You are forgetting, we arrived with little more than the clothes on our backs."

She rounded on him furiously. "I see nothing to laugh at."

"Ah, but that is because you are not standing in

my shoes. Revenge is sweet, they say, and they are so right," and he collapsed against the bedpost, hooting with laughter.

She made up her mind then, that if she were to be hanged, drawn, and quartered, she still would not confess her love for him. Love? What love? No woman could love a man who amused himself at her expense.

Drawing on her rapidly depleting reservoir of dignity, she said, "I have had enough of your jests. I am going to bed."

He pounced on her so fast that her head swam. "I am not finished with you yet." He wasn't laughing at her now. His dark eyes were smoldering. "We should have had this out a long time ago."

His fingers were digging into her shoulders. She wriggled and he released her at once, retreating a step, giving her room to breathe.

There was faint mockery in his voice. "Hester's diary made interesting reading in other respects," he said.

"Oh?" Once again, the awful pit had opened up at her feet. She skirted it gingerly. "Hester and I were not particular friends. I never told her anything about . . . anything."

He folded his arms and propped one shoulder against the bedpost. "Perhaps not, but Addison did. He quoted you quite freely."

She was afraid of that, and stared at him mutely with great, wary eyes.

"Correct me if I am wrong. You told him that I was," and he counted each item off on the fingers of one hand, ". . . a womanizer, a gamester, and a veritable hellion."

She tried laughing the accusation off. "I may have exaggerated a little. On the other hand, you always had a reputation for wildness, Leon. And on my sixteenth birthday you did your best to live up to it."

He smiled wryly. "It always comes back to that, doesn't it? The night you surprised me with Judith Riddley?"

Her heart contracted as the memory came back to her, but she wasn't lying when she said, "I scarcely ever give it a thought."

He gave the oddest smile, then suddenly asked her, "Why do you think I married you, Emily?"

She looked at him blankly and groped for a bit before responding. "You know why. We were forced to wed after we were found together in the little turret room."

"That's not why. Try again."

Her eyebrows rushed together. "I'm not in the mood for playing games, Leon." He was leading her into a trap. She could sense it, just as she had always sensed it when they were children. She would fall on her face, and he would walk away laughing.

"Indulge me," he said. The tone he employed set her teeth on edge.

She forced a smile. "You married me for my fortune."

"If it was a fortune I had wanted, I would have married Sara."

"Why didn't you? When we were children, you always favored Sara. You couldn't stand the sight of me."

"That was because you made things so difficult for me. But we are getting off track. You haven't hit on the right answer yet. Emily, don't you know why I married you? No? I'll give you a clue, shall I?"

He held her head steady with both hands and his mouth brushed over her lips, again and again, then sank into them, taking his fill of her. Hunger. Heat. Longing. When he pulled back, she was shaking; her heart was pounding, but no more than his.

"Well?" he got out hoarsely.

Her eyes searched his, and her hands came up to clutch at his shoulders. "You want me," she said. "Is that it, Leon? Is that why you married me?"

He gave her the sort of look a schoolmaster might give a pupil who was eager to learn but as thick as a door. "You are getting warmer. I won't deny that when we are in the same room, the air between us crackles, but it is so much more than that. Emily, don't you know yet that I have . . ."

He was giving her the victory. This time, he wasn't going to be the one to walk away laughing. If she wanted to, she could have him groveling at her feet.

It wasn't what she wanted. It wasn't what she had *ever* wanted. She didn't want to humble him. She wanted him to . . .

Before he could get out another word, she sealed his lips with her fingers. Behind her eyes, her mind exploded with impressions, images, fragments, and a comprehension that rocked her back on her heels. "We have loved each other since we were children,"

438

she breathed out, and her mouth gaped open.

He laughed shakily. "Yes. Though I was never a child. You were the child, and that's what made it so damnable for me."

"And that's why you were so horrid to me?"

"It was a case of protecting myself. I had to make you hate me, but I wasn't going to let it last forever."

"When? When did you know?"

His look was sheepish. "It would only shock you if I told you."

"I want to know."

He laid her gently on the bed and came down beside her. "Shall we say that I finally decided there was no good fighting it when I came upon you kissing that boy? I was crazy with jealousy."

"And you ducked me in the pond?"

"Yes."

Her eyes went round. "Leon, I was no more than thirteen or fourteen."

"I told you it would shock you."

Laughing, she flung her arms wide. "I loved you even then. If you hadn't made yourself so hateful, I would have known it."

"Yes. And think how impossible our situation would have become. I had no money to call my own. You were too young. Your uncle guessed how things stood, and . . ."

"Uncle Rolfe knew?" she asked incredulously.

"Who do you think suggested that I go to America? It was for the best. It gave me a chance to prove myself. Claire's husband loaned me the capital I needed to get my start in the fur trade. I was determined that I wasn't going to come back empty-handed. You were, after all, Lady Emily Brockford, and a great heiress. I knew I wasn't fit to kiss the hem of your gown . . ."

She punched him on the shoulder, but she wasn't laughing. "Don't say that! Don't *ever* say that!"

He gave a lopsided half-smile and went on as though she had not interrupted. "I wasn't the poor relation, either. Far from it. When I felt I had something to offer, I came back for you."

"On my sixteenth birthday?" she said.

He turned her into him and kissed her softly. "Yes. And I made a mull of everything. Emily, once and for all, we must exorcise the ghosts of the past."

Her eyes slid away from his, not because she was shy, but because she knew she could not conceal the pain the memory of that night evoked. "I remember that when you kissed me I was frightened."

"I'm not surprised. I was ravenous for the taste and feel of you. I was all reformed, you see. I had not had a woman in . . . I don't know how long. I didn't want any other woman. I wanted *you*. But Rolfe saw us together and after that he wouldn't hear of it. He said that you were too young to marry, that I should give you time to stretch your wings, that in another year or two . . ."

"You are going too fast for me!" She pulled herself up to her elbows. "You asked for my hand in marriage?"

"Yes."

"And were refused?"

"Yes."

She let out an infuriated yelp. "I think I shall throttle my uncle when next I see him." She chewed on her bottom lip, then looked down at him consideringly. "And you started drinking, and you were horrid to me."

"You know why," he answered moodily.

"So, your hopes were disappointed and you turned to Judith Riddley for solace."

There was a pause. "Yes." With one hand, he cupped her nape and drew her down till their eyes were on a level. "I'm not going to apologize for all the Judith Riddleys there were in my life while I was waiting for you to grow up, so don't even think it."

She lowered her head till they were nose to nose. "I'm not asking you to. But make a note of this. I don't share the man I love with any woman."

His lips turned up and he edged her closer, wrapping his arms around her. "There is a place in my heart with your name on it. No other woman can fill it. No woman ever could, not even when you were a child. Only you, Emily, only you."

He kissed her lingeringly, moving his lips from the curve of her throat to her eyelids. "I paid for that night a hundred times over. Before then, you were unaware of what was between us, but I knew I could have you whenever I wanted." Her lips tightened, and he laughed, rubbing at them until they softened beneath his. "You know it, too. Afterward, I had to deal with your hatred, and I was never sure of you again, not until tonight when you declared your love for me in a roomful of people."

She looked deeply into his eyes. "When I was sixteen, I was hurt. My dreams were crushed. I wanted love, and ours was a forced marriage."

"Not to me. Never to me. But it wasn't the marriage I wanted for us, either. And so I went away. But I couldn't stay away. And when I came back it was always the same story. You showed your contempt for me, and your uncle held me to my promise."

"Promise? What promise?"

He frowned in concentration. "I must have been mad to accept his terms. No, I was desperate. I would have promised anything to have him agree to our marriage. After that debacle with Judith Riddley, I thought I had lost you. Marriage, under any circumstances, was preferable to nothing."

She drew herself up to a sitting position and hugged her knees. "Leon, you have lost me again. Did you have an understanding with my uncle? Is that what you are saying?"

His head shifted on the pillow, and he gazed up at her with gleaming eyes. "I promised him that I would give you time to get over your fit of the sullens before I made our marriage a real one. Rolfe struck a hard bargain. He demanded up to five years if it was necessary, and like the overconfident fool that I was, I agreed to it. I knew I had to give you some time to come round, but even I could not have foreseen how tenacious you would be in your hatred. Five years is a very long time."

"*Fit of the sullens?* You and my uncle . . . !" Her bosom was quivering with outrage. "Devious! Unprincipled!"

He made a grab for her before she could strike

him. Laughing, rolling with her, he covered her body with his, subduing her struggles effortlessly. Between fierce kisses, he told her, "Time ran out for you when you reached your majority. No, don't be angry sweetheart. You should pity me. Those five years while I waited to claim you were the longest of my life."

She stopped struggling and lay panting for breath, looking up at him with questioning eyes.

"You once asked me why my sister Claire acted strangely with you. Do you remember?"

She nodded. "And you said . . ."

"It doesn't matter what I said. The truth is, Claire knew that I was desperately in love with you. It was obvious to her that you cared nothing for me, else you would have come to me sooner. In short, I was miserable and Claire blamed you for it."

"I . . . I thought she might have heard that I was pressing for an annulment and that William Addison was my suitor?"

He went very still, very quiet. Then all he said was, "No."

"Don't brood about it," she said softly, nuzzling his throat. "I never loved William. I was in love with the idea of love."

"How could I know that? You weren't a child anymore, and you hated me with a virulence. That's what gave me hope. If you had been indifferent to me, I might have been able to let you go. I don't know."

She adjusted her head on the pillow so that she could see his face more clearly. "Why didn't you tell me that you loved me? All this time . . . why didn't you tell me?"

He regarded her steadily with eyes that had turned several shades darker. "Would you have believed me? I don't think so. Besides, you were my wife. Our marriage was a real one. I wasn't unhappy with the way things had turned out."

She stared at him wordlessly, hardly able to believe that she had inspired so great a devotion. There was nothing special about her. She was just a very ordinary girl.

"Why me?" she asked wonderingly. "That's what I don't understand. What made you love me?"

He shifted to his side, relieving her of his weight, and he looped one arm around her waist. "You were . . . different, special. I saw in you all the things that had become lost to me during the Revolution. Honesty. Integrity. Virtue. You were like a bright new shining penny and I felt like something that had just crawled out of a sewer. Naturally, I was drawn to you, though I didn't want to be. And later, when my admiration turned into something quite different, I was in the middle of it before I knew it had begun. As I told you, I fought against it the only way I knew. Much good it did me!"

She pressed herself close to him. "I'm glad you don't give up easily. If you had not come back for me, I might have married William, and God knows what the end of that would have been."

His hands ran over her back, soothing away her fears. "I should have called him out in London at Carlton House when I found you together. I wanted to, but I was afraid that if I killed him,

444

you would hate me forever, and I would not take that chance. Had I done so, I might have saved us all a great deal of trouble."

They fell silent as their thoughts shifted to the events of the last few weeks. Emily shivered and burrowed closer to the warmth of her husband's body. She didn't want to dwell on the past. The future was all that mattered.

She pulled back so that she could watch his expression when she told him. Smiling shyly, she said, "Our child will be born on American soil." To add emphasis to her words, she curled her fingers around one of Leon's hands and planted it firmly against her stomach.

When comprehension dawned, he didn't look overjoyed, he looked stricken. Emily threw her arms around his neck. "Darling, what's wrong? Don't you want to be a father? It won't be so very bad, you'll see."

He took her mouth in long, wet, deep kisses and his hands moved over her ceaselessly, as if to reassure himself that she was real and unharmed. Eventually, he said, "Oh, God, I only hope . . ."

"What?"

He was about to say something about his sense of unworthiness. He looked into eyes that were radiant with love and trust and everything a man could wish to see in the eyes of the woman he loved, and he checked himself. "I only hope you want this child as much as I do."

Her eyes filled with tears of relief and joy. "And I hope . . ."

"Yes?"

"I hope that we have a son who is in the image of his father, in every way."

His lovemaking had always thrilled her. This time, it was infinitely sweeter, infinitely more precious.

He did not give her the words until he had brought himself fully into her body. "I love you. At last I can say it. I love you, Emily."

Her response was incoherent, a quick catch of breath and small sounds without form or substance deep in her throat.

"Tell me," he said fiercely.

Somehow, she managed to choke out the words.

Breast to breast, fingers laced above her head, they gazed without smiling into each other's eyes. They were in thrall to the mystery that had set them apart from all possible lovers. She was his. He was hers. It was meant to be.

Their eyes glazed over and the world contracted to the next sigh and moan and the caress of a lover's lips against bare skin. Desire quickened to a white-hot flame, consuming them in the relentless drive to be both possessor and possessed. At the height of the act, Leon muffled his cry of triumph against his wife's breast. Emily wept softly into her husband's neck.

A long while later, Leon eased himself from her body and gathered her close. with tongue and lips, he brushed over her face, absorbing each tender tear, savoring far more than the sensual pleasure of it.

"Holy water," he said, teasing her, "sanctifying our marriage."

446

Emily sniffed and sighed and snuggled closer. In another moment, she had drifted into sleep. It amused him to see that there was a smile on her lips.

Leon lay awake for a long while after. He was thinking that he would never forget his wife's words to him when she had told him that she was with child. She hoped for a son who was in the image of his father.

As he leaned over her, love tightened his throat. "I want a daughter in the image of her mother," he whispered.

Emily did not awaken, but she responded to something in her husband's voice. Reaching over, she felt for his hand and carried it to her softly swelling abdomen.

By degrees, Leon relaxed against her, his forehead resting against her nape. The wind rattled the windowpanes, and he heard the lonely call of a wolf far off in the distance and the answering cry of its mate.

A new day was dawning and the taste of it was sweet.